The Noise

By Matt Walker

Published by 3 Suns Press

Published by 3 Suns Press

ISBN (print): 979-8-9937108-0-8

ISBN (ebook): 979-8-9937108-1-5

Cover and interior design by Matt Walker

First Edition, 2025

Dedicated to the hearts which I keep

Table of Contents

Wake

The doctor's mouth moved like it was practicing restraint. Each consonant landed neat and sterile. Disinfected before use. Mason watched, not listening, tracking the small white thread of spit that flexed and broke between words. Behind him, a monitor glowed with fog shaped into the vague geography of his body – grays inside of grays, a weather system collapsing on itself.

"We've reviewed your latest scans," the doctor said, voice level and cool, "Compared with earlier imaging, there's progression. The lesions have extended beyond the resection margins into adjacent structures. Given prior treatment failure, further curative intervention is not indicated."

Adjacent structures. Prior failures. Not indicated. Each phrase slid across his mind like oil over water – no friction, no place to land.

The doctor, in his late 30s but experienced, rotated the monitor toward him. The living white arrow of the cursor circled two darker spots, calm, efficient, merciless in its precision.

"Here," he said, "and here. The enhancement pattern suggests infiltration rather than a discrete mass. Operability depends on how well everything is contained."

The doctor paused, brushed strands of his dark hair behind his cracked and smudged glasses, "What we're seeing now is a non-localized aggression."

Non-localized.

Not something you could cut out and name. Not a clean wound. Nothing tangible to sink into.

Mason nodded once. His body remembered protocol: acknowledge, stay still, absorb the briefing. The hum of the fluorescent lights pulsed like tinnitus. The wall clock ticked with bureaucratic patience. A tissue box waited on the desk like an unused prop begging for its 15 minutes. The doctor's tie, blue and loosened slightly – just enough to show a man who had done this too many times and still didn't know to set the pity down.

"You've been disciplined," the doctor continued while adjusting his posture to be more inviting, "Most patients would've abandoned the regimen long ago. But from here, we focus on quality of life. Palliative pathway. We'll manage the pain aggressively. And," he hesitated, a catch in his cadence to soften his demeanor, "I'd recommend meeting with our counselor, just to make sure you have support."

Just to. The phrase softened the blow the way gauze hides a hole.

The pen hung above the pad of paper in front of the doctor. "Is there someone we should call? Friends? Family? Anyone?" The doctor's voice begged Mason for help.

Mason pictured a phone ringing into empty rooms. His sons – one too quick to fight, one too kind to forgive. His daughter, younger then, asking him to braid her hair. A soundless image of her hands, small, patient, waiting for him to finish the job. They were his world once, but time damages all things eventually.

"No," Mason gave nothing. His voice didn't tremble; it simply didn't belong to him.

The doctor's cool inviting stare gave way to the nod of his head, almost relieved to get back to the script, "All right." He pushed the tissue box a half inch closer to Mason – ritual offering.

"We'll schedule a follow-up next week, reassessing comfort levels and completing the care plan. If symptoms worsen – if you struggle sleeping, eating, breathing you call me directly."

Mason blinked, processing the words, "Breathing?"

"Sometimes anxiety presents itself as dyspnea," the doctor explained, "Sometimes the disease affects – look, I don't want to be brutal. We're not talking years anymore. We are looking at months. Months. I wish I could be more precise, but I can't."

Months. The word echoed hollow like a room with no furniture.

"I'm sorry," the doctor's voice returned to the cool sterile tone from the start.

Mason nodded again, his body knew what to do when his soul didn't. They shook hands. The doctor's palm was dry and professional. At the door, Mason hesitated, some reflex looking for a salute, a command, a reason to stand straighter, and then kept walking.

The tissues stayed behind.

***

The hallway's air thinned as he walked, like it wanted less of him. Light trembled across the floor tiles, sterile as bleach. He followed the right-hand wall out of habit – close cover, minimal exposure, safe retreat. People passed without faces; smells mixed of flowers and death. A wheel squeaked on a cart passing through, begging for oil that would never come. A child pressed his forehead against the aquarium resting in the middle of the waiting room. His breath fogging the glass in soft circles, blooming, and then vanishing. The fish drifted aimless, bright, free, and useless.

Between the sliding doors and sunlight, there was a second where he forgot what sound was. In that second, he wanted to stay forever.

3

Then the world hit him.

The parking lot shimmered with heat. Sunlight glanced off car hoods like signal flares. Someone smoked at the edge of the pavement, pretending not to. Mason remembered the smell and taste, his hands trembled slightly, wanting to ask for one. Control, he needed control, so he pressed on.

Far overhead, starlings floated in the sky, moving three feet sideways in perfect formation – as if the universe allowed only decorative adjustments.

He reached his car by instinct, it's all he had in this moment. The key chirped, a small betrayal of normalcy. The door was hot, baked in the sun, as Mason stood for a moment waiting on the tear to crease through his beard. He refused and climbed into the car. When the door shut, the noise died. The silence was total, like a lid sealed over a jar.

Inside smelled of dust, old fabric, and the faint ghosts of gasoline. The steering wheel was cracked along the seams where his thumbs rested. He set both hands at ten and two, the only order left to follow.

The ignition waited, keys dangling. The cute house keychain knocking gently against the steering column. He didn't turn it. He looked at his hands, scarred, ridged, the geography of small wars he'd won. A fracture from training, a crescent from shattered glass, the white spots of domestic repair: fence wire, hammer, rusted chain. Every mark something he'd once fixed.

The air was stale as he breathed in through his nose, out through his mouth. The air went nowhere.

The word months circled like a fly he couldn't kill. He swatted at it with logic and saw, instead, his daughter at five years old. She was standing on the front porch in her yellow rain boots, to big for her to move, shouting, "Don't be gone to long Daddy!" Her hand feverishly waving, "I love you."

The memory cracked something that pain alone couldn't reach.

Someone's radio blared, revealing the cracks in his solitude. A woman's voice, soft and warbling, singing something he almost recognized. For a second, he thought it was her.

4

The first sound came without permission. A grunt that widened, deepened, grew teeth. Then the scream. It filled the corners of the car's shell, ricocheting off the glass, came back double. A guttural twist of sound trapped in a box.

He screamed until his throat tore raw, until his head fogged white. Until the words returned, floating through the noise like an afterimage, months, inoperable, non-localized. They burned deep in him, something without edges shredding his heart, just like grief.

He screamed so loud they became silence.

The silence had weight. Weight that teaches bones what gravity really means. Not peace, not mercy. Just pressure, and it was building.

His chest heaved once, twice, clutching for comfort. Tears slicked his face without permission. The release had been earned.

He slammed his fists into the steering wheel. The impact bloomed, bright, clean pain. Hit again. The horn coughed and died. Bone on plastic.

His breaths came in short animalistic burst.

Pop.

Then another.

Again.

The car accepted each blow, uncomplaining, coddling.

Bones popped, he heard them but, didn't break.

He wanted them to. Breakage meant fracture, fracture meant alignment, alignment meant repair. Splint, tape, plan. He knew how to treat a body that failed in simple ways. He knew how to be useful to pain. He always had a plan.

He hit the wheel until his arms went heavy. The quiet had changed texture. Outside, a stroller rolled across a seam in the pavement, mom in tow. Taking her child, for a minor illness. Minor illness he thought to himself. Somewhere far off, a door alarm chirp once, twice, and went still.

His body sighed as he leaned back. The seat remembered him. In the rearview mirror, his reflection looked gray, older than he should have ever been allowed to be. Eyes hollowed, mouth softened. He looked like the blur the doctor had circled: a man reduced to margins.

He closed his eyes. Non-localized, that's what the doctor said. Maybe that's what Mason had been all along? Not just with this, but in life in general. He never belonged; he never fit. Never had a purpose that wasn't given to him.

His hand twitched towards the glove box, muscle memory searching for orders that no longer existed.

In the depths of his eyes, he saw the flash of his daughter's hair in his fingers, the fence he promised to fix, the door he never closed gently enough, his boys challenging him just because he was dad. Every memory was a noise he could no longer stand to hear. His hand nearly there.

He opened his eyes. The world was unchanged, cruelly normal. He wiped his sleeve across his face, leaving a salt track that would dry to nothing. He looked down at his finger and flexed; pain answered, clean and honest.

The key sat in the ignition. He turned it one click and the engine purred under his guidance and control. The dash light woke, small galaxies sparking into life. The hum accompanied the silence, still heavy in his shell of solitude.

The silence waited, full of something he might've once called mercy. There was no room left for mercy.

He looked at his hands, swollen now, knuckles bright and human. Pain always kept its promise to him.

His voice was low, certain – sterile, as he interrupted the silence with the voice of a man who'd stopped rehearsing his humanity. That part was done.

The dead air kissed his neck, like she used to.

"Fine, one final job," his teeth gripped the air tight, "Set the wound right."

6

The Rough Patch

Cold has a sound when it sits long enough, something tight and thin, like a thread being pulled. It's there before he wakes, a breath held by the house and the sky and whatever is left between them.

Jason opens his eyes to glass that isn't glass anymore. Frost has turned the window into a white animal, ribs of ice pressed close, every vein visible. His breath fogs and holds and slides back down like a hand that changed its mind.

"Cold," he says, voice smaller than his chest. "Too fucking cold."

The word doesn't go anywhere. It hangs, a weightless thing, and the room keeps being a room.

He lifts the blanket and the air bites his shins like new teeth. The mattress keeps his shape as if it would rather he didn't move. He sits up slow. The floor is wood, gray where the paint has worn down to apology. He puts his feet on it anyway. The ache climbs his ankles and takes a place behind his knees, pleased with itself.

He rubs a circle on the window with the heel of his hand. It smears to milk. Beyond it: a pale field of houses and street and the little tree that never learned to be taller than the fence. Snow mounds on the trash bins like soft helmets. The world looks padded, like someone childproofed it after whatever happened.

"What a view," he says, and the room doesn't disagree.

He stands. The house shifts somewhere deep in its chest, a slow creak that might be wood learning to be bone. He listens for an answer that isn't there. Something clicks in the wall—heat thinking about starting and deciding against it.

He pulls on pants that remember him, a hoodie that smells like detergent from another life, a coat that knows what to do and does it, stiff with last week's thaw and last night's refreeze. Socks, boots, the left one with lace tips burned and fused from a day he doesn't plan to think about again. He jams the lace ends into the eyelets and calls it good.

At the dresser he finds a beanie with dog hair baked into its knit. He thumbs a small bald spot in the weave, presses it to his forehead like a blessing, and drags it down over his ears. The silence climbs inside and tucks in.

The kitchen is a smaller cold. He opens a cupboard and stares at two mugs, a chipped bowl, a plate with a spider crack that looks like a map. He touches the crack with a fingernail. It hums under his nail as if it's a living thing, or maybe that's his finger. On the counter, a coffee maker with a film of dust the color of breath. He tips it; inside, an inch of brown ice holds the ghost of a morning. He considers a laugh and chooses not to.

"Right," he says. "Breakfast of champions."

The faucet coughs. Water stutters then threads itself small, metallic, so cold it makes his teeth want to pull back into his jaw. He cups some, drinks fast, lets the shock drag a curse out of him. "Jesus—fuck." The word is a flare that dies a foot from his face.

The house settles again, heavier this time. A picture frame asks for mercy and rights itself a millimeter. He doesn't touch it. He doesn't touch anything he doesn't have to.

10

At the back door he pauses. The latch has a way of remembering a thing he forgot to remember, a sticky hesitation that feels personal. He leans his forehead to the wood, breath warming a rectangle that evaporates and returns and evaporates again.

"Okay," he says. "We'll try being alive a little longer."

He opens the door and the cold steps in like someone who paid for the privilege. The yard is a single sheet of white with the idea of a fence stitched under it. The air has weight; it presses the hair on his wrists flat, then lifts it, then flattens it again, trying to decide if it wants him.

He steps out and the snow complains in a pitch he can feel in his molars. The sound is clean, then a little embarrassed, then gone, buried by the next step. His footprints rise up behind him like small decisions he wasn't consulted on. He reaches the gate. It opens easier than it should. He waits for the kind of joke that has no punchline and hears only his own lungs shaking hands with the day.

The street meets him the way a camera meets a face—flat and too honest. Rooflines, wires sagging with the white, cars made quiet under their winter. The sky is a color that forgot its name. The wind is not wind; it's the absence of anything else moving.

Someone's wreath hangs on a door across the way, berries a red so bright it hurts. Who takes the wreath down when the world stops? How long before the bow remembers it's cloth and not an idea and sags?

He looks down. A smear of boot prints runs along the sidewalk, then stutters, then loops back into itself. His prints. He knows his own size, the way the left one drags a tail. He walks beside the loop and watches it curve back toward his gate as if he'd practiced leaving and failed the test.

"Perfect," he says. "Even my tracks don't want to go."

11

A traffic light at the corner blinks red into no eyes. The bulb hums where it hangs. He imagines putting his tongue to the metal and leaving a piece of himself there out of spite. He doesn't move.

He tries the word hey into the air, just to see if it remembers how to carry something. "Hey." It lands three feet away and sits, polite, waiting to be asked to come in.

He walks toward the intersection because not walking feels like letting the day win. The wind combs the street from east to west with a careful hand. He tells himself to count the houses, count the breaths, count anything, and then remembers he isn't doing that now. No more counting. Counting makes lines where there aren't any, draws borders in snow that doesn't care about borders.

On the corner, he stands and looks down each leg of the intersection like he's choosing which way to lie. The red blink paints his jacket the color of a wound and then takes it back. The pole hums the way poles hum when the power is still stubborn somewhere underneath the city.

"You're late," he tells the light. "You were supposed to go out with the rest of it."

Something in the next block leans on its hinges and then finds its balance. He hears it as if it happened inside his own throat. There is no echo. There hasn't been an echo in a long time. Sound should bounce and return, a dog you can count on, but here it steps out and keeps walking.

"Right," he says, and the word comes out as breath more than voice. "Right."

He checks his pockets like there might be a map in them and finds a lighter with a blackened wheel, a folded receipt with no ink left on it, and a nail that could be a claw if he decided to be the kind of man who carries claws. He turns the nail in his fingers until it seems to settle on a purpose. He slides it back in his pocket.

He looks at the houses for faces. Windows are eyes if you need them to be. He picks one—third on the left, green paint that never forgave itself for being chosen, a porch with a soft center—and wants to see a curtain move. It doesn't. Snow drifts off the eave instead, a soft shrug.

When he speaks again, it isn't to anyone, not even himself. "I'm going to the diner," he says, and the decision makes its way through him like something warm. "You coming?"

The corner doesn't answer, but the light gives him one more red and then one more and then one more like a tired heartbeat. He steps into the crosswalk because nobody else will, boots sinking to the ankle, snow stealing the outline of his legs one inch at a time.

Halfway across, a wind thread lifts a powder of flakes and twirls it around his knees. The motion looks like welcome if you're starved for it. He swears he hears a laugh in it—a small one, a room from before—but when he stops to listen the sound closes like an eye.

"Figures," he mutters, and keeps moving.

At the far curb he turns back to see what he's done to the morning. His tracks look like words in a language that fell asleep. The house is a square pressed in sugar. The window where he rubbed a circle is already a white animal again, patient, breathing.

He touches the scar on his knuckle with his thumb, a habit that used to be a ritual and is now just a thing his hand does. The skin there remembers a door it lost an argument with, a night that smelled like rain and bleach. He tries not to hear the echo of that night crowding this one. He succeeds for the space of one breath.

"Coffee," he says to the street, because the word is a path if you say it like one. "Let's pretend."

He heads toward the diner sign he can't yet see, the one that always, always used to buzz even when the letter E died and it said DINR like a command. The wind leans into him and then away, testing the weight of him like it's not quite sure what he's made of.

A dog barks in the next life over. It could be a hinge. It could be memory doing a trick to keep him interested. He lets it be both. He keeps walking.

At the corner, snow in the gutter makes a sound like paper being erased and then written over again. He thinks of the list he didn't make this morning, the one with five honest lines and a sixth that lied. He doesn't need a list to know if a thing hurts.

He passes a sedan with its windows caved in by weather that didn't mean it. Inside, a child's seat stares a round stare. He raises his hand without meaning to and lowers it again, a wave he doesn't finish. The cold climbs his wrist and sets up there, content.

The diner shows itself exactly where it should be, which feels like an insult. The bell over the door is a small brass question mark. He reaches for it and stops, palm an inch from the metal.

"Don't ring," he tells it. "Don't you fucking ring."

He pulls the door and it yields without a sound. The bell hangs obediently. The air inside has the smell of coffee that forgot to be hot and pancakes that never got their turn. The counter is a line that remembers elbows. The booths remember names.

He stands in the doorway with snow caging his boots and listens to the not-sound of an empty room doing a perfect impression of a room before it became empty.

"Morning," he says to the space. His voice comes back as a feeling, not a word.

He doesn't go farther in yet. He lets the cold peel off his shoulders and fold itself quiet and lets the door close behind him with the softest click.

Outside, the red light at the corner keeps blinking its private emergency into an unbothered day.

He looks at the coffee pot behind the counter, glass brown with a film of yesterday. Something inside him lifts its head and then sets it down again.

"Okay," he tells the room, and this time his voice has hands. "Let's see if you remembered how."

A chair somewhere gives a small answer in the language of wood and weight.

The silence, pleased with itself, takes a seat at his table and waits.

The diner has its own kind of dead quiet—polite, upholstered, practiced. He stands just inside the door until the cold crawls off him and hides under the counter. The coffee pot behind glass looks like a museum piece, brown film scabbed over the idea of warmth.

He picks up a mug from the drying rack. It's clean in the way dust is clean—everything the same color. He sets it down again. The act of setting it down feels like trespassing.

A napkin holder stares a chrome stare. He catches himself in it: a narrow man in too many layers, beard winning the argument with his jawline, eyes like winter water. He lifts a hand. The reflection lifts too, a fraction late. He doesn't wait to see if it catches up.

"Later," he tells the room. "I'll come back. Try not to fall down."

The bell doesn't ring when he opens the door. The quiet follows him out anyway, slips over his shoulders like a shawl he didn't choose. On the sidewalk, his boot tracks are already softening at the edges. Snow learns people too quickly.

He heads back the way he came because back is a word that admits the existence of forward. The hollow red blink of the traffic light counts his breaths for him. He lets it. Wind fingers the street with a delicate touch, as if it's tried being a bully and is practicing tenderness now.

The house waits with its familiar posture: a little too proud for its size, paint sullen in daylight, porch held up by stubbornness and two rusted screws. He climbs the steps and the boards give small noises that feel like apologies. He pulls the door and steps into a colder inside.

Air moves in here, but not from weather. It slides along the hallway like something with a job. The sound is thin at first, then thicker, like cloth being pulled over a mouth.

"Don't start," he says, half to the door, half to himself. "Not today."

He pulls the beanie off and rubs at the ache behind his ears. The living room has arranged itself as history: couch with a throw that refuses to lie flat, coffee table older than the idea of trimming nails, a lamp with the chain broken so you have to plead with the base and promise not to be mad. The picture frames are besieged by dust and memory. He avoids the frames without looking like he's avoiding them.

Something creaks upstairs, slow and heavy, like someone rolling a word around on their tongue before deciding whether to spit it or swallow it.

He freezes and listens. The silence afterward is too complete. Houses make noises. Wood settles. Pipes complain. He knows this. He repeats it in the catechism voice people use when they want their brains to act right.

The floor under his boots answers with a soft warping sigh. He puts a palm to the wall. The paint is colder than skin has any right to be. He imagines the studs beneath like ribs, the plaster like lung, and wishes he'd never learned how to think in metaphors.

He mouths a count—one, two—then stops because counting is a kind of prayer and he's not praying to this.

Kitchen first. He needs fire.

The drawer with batteries, screws, receipts that have outlived their ink— he calls it by its true name: bullshit. He grins despite himself and shoves through its contents until his fingers close on the cheap lighter with the blackened wheel. He spins it. Spark, spark. No flame. He tastes the phantom of old butane anyway, bitter on the back of his tongue, a memory that doesn't belong to him.

The wall clock says a time that isn't a real time. The second hand jerks and rests, jerks and rests, jerks and rests. He waits for it to choose. It refuses.

"Make up your mind," he tells it, and the words come out with enough heat to fog the glass.

The house takes a deeper breath. He hears it in the dining room—curtain lifting without wind, a small slap as it falls back against itself. He steps through the doorway and the air changes temperature on his skin, a degree or two, enough to make the hairs on his forearms argue about whether they should stand up.

The table wears a thin skin of powder, the kind the day makes when it gets tired of holding its breath. He traces a line through it with his finger and rubs the ash of domesticity against his thumb. There's a ring in the dust where a glass used to live. Outside, a branch drags a slow knuckle along the siding and the sound drips into the room like syrup.

"Fuck," he says softly, which is not anger exactly, just a way to make air move.

Upstairs again: the old math of weight and distance. He pictures no one. He pictures someone he doesn't want to picture. He shakes his head like it'll rattle loose.

He tests the first stair. It answers with the small groan of an animal humoring a child. He climbs anyway, hand on the rail because he trusts the rail even less than the step. Halfway up, the hall light blinks—on, off, on—without deciding—which is a sentence about him he refuses to hear right now.

At the top: carpet worn to thread. The door to the first bedroom sits open in that special way doors have of pretending they were born that way and did not just move. He holds himself still long enough to be sure he isn't imagining and then steps into the frame.

The bed is a shape under a sheet of dust. Not thick; enough. A book on the nightstand sits face down mid-sentence, spine tired from staying useful for longer than it was meant to. He picks it up, reads the six words that have sunk through the paper into whatever comes next: we stayed as long as possible. He puts it back. The room exhales, and the dust lifts and resettles with the small hush of surrender.

He turns, and the hallway has narrowed. Old houses do this—breathe in and out around you until you forget which size is the real one. He tells himself geometry doesn't have feelings. He doesn't quite believe himself.

Second room: the one with the closet that never made up its mind about being a closet. Boxes like little coffins. Coats that smell faintly of the people they used to guard. He palms a sleeve, rubs two fingers together with the oil it gives off. He closes the door again. It stays shut with an affronted click.

Back in the hall, the light flickers and chooses off. Not a click. Just absence.

"All right," he says to wherever the switch lives. "Very dramatic."

He angles his phone out of habit. Black glass. A face that could pass for his stares back in the vague sheen, a ghost of his own breath shaping and un-shaping the mouth. He thumbs the button that no longer has a god. Nothing.

"Cool," he says. "Love this for us."

A new noise now. Not upstairs. Lower. The kind of wood-sigh that means the front door is remembering how to be a door. He feels it through the railing first, a gentle vibration that ends in the palm of his hand.

He waits. Waiting is both useful and useless, but it's what his muscles know to do when his brain hands them nothing. The house obliges with a series: a tick in the kitchen outlet, a shift in the frame around the mirror at the end of the hall, a crack like a knuckle popping where the hallway meets the stair. He catalogues none of it on purpose. He catalogues all of it because survival is a body more than a mind.

He descends, one careful step at a time. The bottom step pretends to be further away than it is and he misjudges and drops the last inch. That petty fall is enough to make his heart beat like a thrown thing.

He stands in the foyer, breathing hard. The front door wears his breath like a fogged badge, then lets it go. He lays his palm against the wood. It is cold in a way that feels active.

"Not today," he tells it. "Don't be cute."

The door does not respond. A picture on the wall—beach, strangers' smiles, sun too bright to be real—tilts one degree toward the floor. He looks away before the ocean can start to sound like blood moving.

The living room lamp with the broken chain sits smug in its corner, daring him to try again. He crouches, finds the switch on the cord with numb fingers, and rolls it over the little metal hump. The bulb flares to a weak yellow life, then settles into a thin, displeased glow.

19

"There you go," he says, voice softer than he means. "Look at you. Still trying."

He stands and the lamp flickers in his periphery twice, quick, like a blink. He turns his head. It steadies. He turns away. Flicker. He squares up to it and says, "Don't." It doesn't. He laughs, a single broken thing that makes him feel foolish and then briefly warmer.

The laugh brings something with it—an answering hush, the shape of a room listening. He hears it gather in corners. He hears it put its hands together.

"No," he says. "No more of that."

He moves through the house like he belongs to it, because admitting the alternative is a mistake. In the kitchen he opens the fridge for light he knows won't be there and is still surprised by the unlit emptiness smelling of tin and old fruit. He finds the drawer where a handful of tea lights live in a sandwich bag with a ghost of sugar stuck to the seam. He sets three on the counter, fishes in the bullshit drawer for matches that have learned humility.

First strike: dead sulfur. Second: the clerk flick of a man who's lit a thousand small mornings. Flame. He touches wick to fire and the room grows a face from underneath. One candle is not much. Three is something.

Heat licks his knuckles. He keeps his hand in the warmth a second longer than necessary. The lighter in his pocket presses into his thigh like a coin he could spend on something if money still believed in him.

The house breathes again, longer now. He feels it across the doorway, a shrug of air traveling from one side to the other. He speaks into it before it can become a thought.

"I said not today," he warns. "You want a fight, get in line."

He picks up one of the tea lights and carries it to the living room. The lamp sputters its tired light in agreement. Shadows cling to the corners as if they've been evicted and are currently considering legal action. He sets the candle on the coffee table and watches the small heat pool inside the thin shell of wax. It is the most honest thing in the room.

Upstairs again: a soft thump like a book falling an inch onto a shelf that forgot it was there. He swallows the reflex that wants to say a name. Names bring things back. He's learned not to do that.

He plants himself in the chair with the butt-shaped argument in its cushion and waits like a hunter wait's when he's run out of bullets but forgotten how to stop raising the rifle. His breath slows by practice more than peace. The lamplight does the steady work of the sun on a day that could not be bothered to dawn correctly.

Something changes without moving. He feels it first—a pressure shift, the way a room fills when someone has decided to tell you something you don't want to know. The lamp's glow thins to paper. He reaches toward it and the bulb flickers three times in a row like a cough.

"Don't," he says again, a warning to the small god of filament and glass. "Don't you—"

Out. No pop. Just gone. The dark lands like a cat, careful, claws half in.

He sits with his hand on the lamp's neck, the metal cooling fast under his palm. The three tea lights in the kitchen throw a low, orange geography on the ceiling. The rest of the house inhales and holds. He hears his heart in his ears, a thick, wet sound not built for rooms.

"Fine," he says into the warm dark. "Very fucking funny."

He waits for his eyes to invent shapes. They do, efficient and unashamed. The doorway is a mouth. The hallway is a throat. The stairs are teeth, though he knows they are not. He keeps his hands open and visible to himself like a man telling cops he isn't armed.

Behind him, somewhere toward the back door, the latch makes a tiny noise like a decision acknowledged. Not turning—remembering.

He stands too fast and his blood drops to his ankles before deciding to come back. He sways and puts a hand on the wall. Paint chills his palm to the bone in one second flat.

"All right," he says, voice low now, as if he could negotiate with architecture. "Okay. You breathe. I breathe. We leave it at that."

He picks up one of the kitchen candles and brings it with him into the living room again. He sets it on the floor. The flame paints a circle on the ceiling like a counterfeit moon.

The house lets out a little of its air. Not a sigh, not quite. More like the sound a sleeping person makes when they roll over into a new dream.

He looks at the front window. Frost crawls up the corners in feathered spines. He presses his thumb to the glass and watches skin go from pink to yellow to white. He lets go before he's part of the story permanently.

"Stay," he tells the dark. "Just fucking—stay."

Something complies. Or nothing does. The difference is academic.

He returns to the chair and lowers himself with the caution of a man stepping onto a dock he built himself out of half-good wood. He rests his elbows on his knees and lets the weight of his head belong to his hands.

After a time the lamp warms itself into a new opinion and glows again, barely, like a pilot light that wants to be a sun when it grows up. He doesn't touch it. He doesn't look straight at it. He allows it to exist and calls that mercy.

"I'm going back out," he tells the room finally, and the sound of the words is enough to prove mouth and lungs still share jurisdiction. "You get your shit together while I'm gone."

The house answers by not answering. It holds its temperature and its stories. It doesn't lean. It doesn't crack. It refuses to perform.

He stands, lifts the candle, breathes it out with a care that feels ceremonial even though he swore off ceremonies. Smoke unfurls itself into the air, spices the room with the smell of burnt cotton and cheap paraffin. He waits until the curl fades.

At the door he puts his beanie back on and pulls his hood over it like he's dressing a thought in a heavier thought. He pauses with his hand on the latch, listening to the small, persistent hum that isn't a real hum and might just be blood enjoying itself.

"Be here when I get back," he says, and hears how stupid that is. "Or don't. Whatever."

He opens the door. The outside air takes him in with the appetite of a predator that has decided to be polite about it. Snow scuffs under his boots. He steps onto the porch and pulls the door shut behind him, careful of the latch, more careful than the latch deserves.

The house breathes once more, a long, careful pull, and lets him go.

The wind has died. That's the first thing he notices when he steps outside again—the kind of silence that feels heavier than noise. No rustle, no hum, no throat to the world. Just still air holding its breath, waiting to see what he'll do with it.

Jason squints up the street. The sky hasn't changed; it still wears that thin gray mask like something embarrassed to be looked at. The houses sit too still, roofs clean, chimneys dumb. Every surface holds its snow without argument.

Somewhere under all that white is the hum of a neighborhood, but it's buried deep, and maybe it wants to stay there.

He adjusts his beanie and the gesture feels enormous, like the world noticed it. His own breath fogs and he watches it collapse. "You're really working hard at the quiet thing," he mutters. "Gold star."

The road that leads away from his house used to be a comfort—lines of mailboxes, cars that knew where they were going, kids that learned to ride bikes by falling right there in the gutter. Now it's just geometry. Blacktop cut by faint tire ghosts. A thin ridge of ice splitting the center like a scar someone tried to hide with makeup.

He walks the middle of it because that's what's left. Left and right have lost their purpose.

Boots crunch, snow squeaks, fabric rustles when he breathes. He tries to listen for anything human—bird, engine, door—but all he gets is his own pulse playing percussion in his ears.

"Okay," he says to the silence. "You win. You're loud. Congratulations."

His voice goes nowhere. No echo. It should bounce off a house or a car hood, but it doesn't. It just stops. Sound has started obeying new rules, ones he doesn't get to see written down.

A mailbox leans at a tired angle near the curb, red flag raised like it's waiting for someone to come rescue it. He flips the lid open. Empty. Not even junk mail. He laughs once, low. "Guess the postman finally took a sick day."

He slams it shut harder than he needs to, just to hear something alive. The metal reports back with a single hollow clang, and then the air swallows it whole. No echo. No ring. Just gone.

He keeps walking.

24

The next house has Christmas lights still strung across the eaves, frozen mid-twinkle. Each bulb locked in a little globe of ice. When he passes under them, his reflection flashes dull in every one—a thousand tiny ghosts in the glass.

He looks away.

Ahead, the intersection opens into the small commercial stretch— storefronts he knows by heart. The barber. The dry cleaner. The corner store that never stocked enough milk. All lined up like they've been posed for a photo and forgotten the reason why.

He crosses the first set of footprints he's seen since leaving the house— light, shallow, half-filled with snow. Not new, but not ancient. Could be his from earlier. Could not be. He follows them for a few yards until they fade at the curb, lost under a drift.

The store windows mirror the street back at him. He stops to study one— the glass tinted blue from sky reflection. Inside: shelves, bags of chips gone stale, the register half-open. His own shape looks trapped in there, a dark outline behind the glare.

He leans closer until his breath fogs the glass. The shape inside leans too, same distance, same hesitation.

Then he sees it—a flicker, not even movement, just change. Something shifts in the light. He jerks back, heart slamming once against his ribs.

Nothing moves inside.

He waits a long second, then forces a half-laugh. "Right. Mirror games. You're losing it, buddy."

He steps backward off the curb, eyes on the window as if it might confess. His heel finds ice, slips, catches. The sound that escapes him is ugly and real. It feels good to hear something real again.

A newspaper page flaps down the street, catching on the breeze that isn't supposed to exist. It drags itself along the asphalt like it's trying to stand upright. He picks it up because you don't see paper move anymore.

The date is frozen at March 12. The headline talks about something so ordinary—tax season, city budget, mayor's re-election—that it hurts. He reads the first paragraph even though it doesn't matter. The ink has bled at the edges, letters warping into tiny black continents. The byline could have been someone he knew once. He folds the paper neatly and tucks it into his coat pocket, as if it means something to take the news with you when the world's done making news.

Halfway up the block, he stops in front of the drugstore. The automatic doors are open just enough for snow to slide in a little hill across the tiles. A fallen sign reads "Thank You for Shopping" in red letters, the "You" rubbed to a ghost.

He steps over the snow and into the chill. The air inside smells like plastic, lemon cleaner, and quiet. Aisles stand perfectly still. Rows of shampoo bottles glint in pale light, proud of their pointless order. One sits tipped over, its label peeled halfway, a streak of dried blue gel hardened on the floor.

"Anybody?" he calls, voice smaller this time. He expects it to sound strange—out of place—but it sounds exactly like the kind of thing you'd say to an empty building. He waits anyway.

Something creaks near the pharmacy counter, slow, long, like a shelf shifting under weight. He walks toward it, cautious out of habit, not fear. Fear needs a witness.

The counter glass is cracked in one corner, spiderweb reaching down to a display of vitamins. A single pill bottle lies on the tile, cap gone. He kneels, picks it up. The label is smudged. He shakes it; one pill rolls inside with a dry click. He doesn't know why he pockets it, but he does. Maybe he's collecting proof that the world existed.

He looks around again. The sound he heard doesn't repeat. The silence resumes its authority.

"Fine," he says. "Didn't need you anyway.

He heads for the door, brushing against a rack of greeting cards on the way. One slips loose and flutters down—bright pink, cartoon bear holding balloons. "Hang in there!" it says, cheerful as hell. He stares at it, caught between wanting to laugh and wanting to crush it to pulp. He leaves it face down

Back outside, the air feels heavier, as if the clouds have noticed him moving again. The gray has darkened toward evening, though he can't tell how long it's actually been. His breath comes out in longer streams now, more visible, like it's trying to make up for all the other voices missing.

He stands at the corner again, same red light blinking into nowhere. The pole hums faintly—a trapped fly sound, electrical life refusing to quit. He steps up close, presses his palm against the cold metal.

The vibration runs through him. Tiny, persistent. The world's last heartbeat, or maybe his.

He leans his forehead to it. The cold feels like forgiveness

When he pulls back, he can see the faint fog of his breath mark the metal— an imperfect oval. He presses his palm over it once more and whispers, "I'm still here." He isn't sure if he means it as a promise or a question.

27

Snow begins again, thin flakes this time, drifting with the hesitation of someone interrupting a conversation. They melt on his coat but not fast enough to be convincing. He looks down the street—the diner at one end, the dark curve leading to the river at the other.

He starts walking toward the curve.

Behind him, the red light keeps blinking, steady, patient. The hum fades with distance. His footprints fill themselves as he moves, wind drawing them closed before he's even gone.

The silence behind him breathes in and holds.

The diner's neon is dead but the sign still knows its shape. DINR in block letters, red paint dulled to brick. He can see where the E used to glow—ghost circle faint on the metal, a missing tooth you still run your tongue over years after.

Jason crosses the last stretch of street slow, each step a quiet negotiation with the ice. The bell above the door is a question mark in brass. He stares at it, hand on the handle.

"Behave," he says. "Please."

He pulls. The bell barely stirs. The door swings and a pocket of cold air steps out to greet him, then collapses. Inside smells like coffee that forgot the point, syrup hardened in the veins of a table, and heat that left without saying goodbye.

The booths line up patient, backs squared, vinyl cracked in white lightning. The counter holds six stools with chrome rings for shoes that won't swing anymore. Every surface holds a dust the color of breath, even the pie display with its empty plates and a single flake of crust like a fossil.

"Morning," he tells the room, out of habit, out of loneliness, out of spite. His voice lands soft and goes to ground.

He steps behind the counter. The coffee maker sits there like an altar abandoned mid-service. The pot is half full, the top sheened over, a thin brown film pulled tight as skin. He tilts it and watches the liquid slide under the lid's scab and think about being coffee again.

"Look at you," he says. "Hero in a glass suit."

He sets the pot back. The warmer plate is cold under his palm, the kind of cold that has opinions. He scans for matches, for a hot plate, for anything that makes fire legally. A drawer gives him napkin packets and two coffee stirrers fused together by something that used to be sugar. The next coughs up straws, pink packets, a handful of pennies welded by time. He pockets one because the weight of a coin feels like proof that humans invented math.

He finds the switch for the backline—BREAKER, someone wrote in thick black marker, as if to warn the uninitiated that this is where grownups live. He flips it and nothing changes. He flips it again because stubbornness is a religion

"Of course," he says. "Why not?"

Along the back wall near the kitchen door, a bulletin board holds the village of lost minutes—polaroids with fingerprints in the white, staff schedules, a flyer for a charity pancake breakfast two years ago with a boy's face as bright as sugar. He reaches out and presses the corner of one photo where a girl blows out candles, cheeks full of air, eyes already closing in the pleasure of it. His thumb comes away gray.

On the far counter sits a napkin dispenser with a chrome face. He leans into it and sees himself again, rounded by the curve. The mirror version is late by less than a breath, just enough to make a person with a nervous system think of knives. He lifts his hand. It lifts too. He waits, daring it to fail. It doesn't.

29

"You're fine," he tells himself, then snorts. "Sure."

He finds a lighter under the register—cheap, blue, identical twin to the one in his pocket, which feels like running into yourself in a dream. He flicks it. Flame snaps up obedient. For no good reason, relief rises behind his ribs and he has to swallow it down

He drags the fire along the rim of the coffee pot, then under the plate, doing a ridiculous dance of heat where heat shouldn't be. The glass answers by sweating a little at the lip. He knows it won't work—not like this, not the way it should—but he holds the flame there until the lighter bites his thumb in warning.

"Fine," he says, nursing the singe. "We'll evolve without caffeine, like savages."

There's a prep window to the kitchen, stainless rim dulled by the touch of hands. He looks through and sees the swing door beyond, half ajar, a square of darker dark. Something in there rearranges itself softly—settling pan, shifting shelf, ghost of a rat that learned better. He waits. Nothing follows.

He goes anyway

The kitchen is colder than the dining room, as if heat tried to hide back here and forgot how. Racks of pans hang with their bellies out. A grill waits like a bed no one made. On the far counter, an egg carton sits open: five eggs in their little paper graves, one cracked and dried to a brown star.

He lays his palm flat on the metal. His skin sticks for a fraction and releases. The sensation is so intimate it makes him blush, as if he caught the kitchen naked.

Near the back door, a narrow window frames the alley. Snow drifted in at the threshold and froze into a lip. He can see the dumpster humped white and the shadow of a cat—all spine and caution—slip past, leaving no prints. He blinks. The alley is empty. Fine. Cats are Schrödinger's anyway

He opens a lower cabinet and finds a stack of paper cups with green trees on them, eco-friendly accusations printed in cheerful font. He takes two, then three, then puts one back because leaving one is a superstition he doesn't admit. He scouts the shelves, finds a tin of cocoa dust welded shut by time. He puts it back like he's apologizing.

On a hook beside the door there's a jacket, the kind line cooks throw on to smoke. He lifts it and it lifts dust. The smell under it is sweat and fryer and winter. He presses it to his face and inhales until his stomach makes a hurt sound. He hangs it back up gentle, like tucking in a sleeping kid.

"Sorry," he says, to nobody and not for the last time.

Back out front the silence is doing its slow work, pushing his thoughts toward the places he doesn't trust them. He points himself at the jukebox to force a different memory. It stands against the wall like a big-lunged animal, chrome ribs catching the thin light that manages to exist. He runs a finger along the selection strip. The numbers are little windows into a past that wasn't generous but at least had music.

He presses a random button because nothing matters and because sometimes rituals sneak back in wearing new coats. Nothing happens, obviously. He leaves his finger there anyway, as if holding the idea of a song is close enough for today.

At the corner booth, someone's left a crossword in pencil. He slides into the seat. The vinyl split complains under him, the seam licking his thigh through fabric. He reads a clue. Four-letter word: undo. He fills in UNDO and laughs because it's nothing and everything.

He writes three more words to prove his hand still remembers letters. SNOW. LIE. STAY. The last one looks wrong in block capitals, too earnest.

He goes to cross it out and stops with the eraser mid-arch. He sets the pencil down like a weapon and interlaces his fingers to keep them from being fuckups.

The coffee behind the counter hasn't gotten warmer. He knows that without checking. The knowledge stands up in him anyway like a man at a city council meeting about to say something stupid.

"Fine," he says to the pot. "Stay dead."

He hears something move when he says it, a micro-shift along the roofline—snow sloughing, maybe, a bird adjusting its opinion, more likely nothing doing a good impression of something. The gesture makes the whole building breathe for a second. He feels it through the floor in his boots.

He realizes he's been holding his shoulders too high for too long. He lets them drop. The relief hurts.

On the counter near the register sits a tip jar with two singles clinging to the glass with static. Someone doodled a smiley face on one, the kind of circle that makes promises it can't keep. He taps the bill with one finger and it flutters, then obeys gravity. He plucks it out and slides it under the jar so it stops pretending.

Past the last booth there's a one-wall shrine—photos thumbtacked in loose grid. People holding plates, babies held like bread, teenagers with eyes rehearsing how to be bored. In the bottom corner a dog looks straight into the camera as if recognizing the person holding it. Jason stands there longer than he means to, letting faces climb into him.

He touches the edge of one photo where a boy with a crooked tooth is squinting at a candle. The wax has already spilled, solidified into a soft cliff. The boy's cheeks are round, almost edible with light.

"Happy birthday," he says, and his voice is gentle enough that he forgives it for existing

The bulb over the shrine hums to life—or maybe it was always alive and his eyes weren't worthy yet. A low, tired halo spreads over the pictures. He waits for it to die and it doesn't. He feels stupid gratitude pour down his chest and settle in his belly where hunger lives.

At the front window, the street shows him the shape of weather thinking twice. Flakes spin, reconsider, commit. He tugs the sleeve of his coat up to check the scar on his wrist he never remembers getting. The skin there is shiny like something ironed too hot. He rubs it and heat blooms under his fingers, small and mean.

The bell above the door twitches. He turns so fast his neck protests.

No one.

The door is shut. The brass curve moves with the settling of the building, maybe. He takes a step toward it, then another, because if he's going to be stupid he wants to be all the way stupid and not half.

He opens the door and looks at the white. The street has softened to suggestion, edges blurred, his bootprints already lazy at the edges. The traffic light down the block still blinks its blood-red patience. He waits for a car that will not come and lets the cold push at his teeth.

"Back soon," he tells the outside. "Don't start without me."

He closes the door and the bell gives up a single, delicate note—a sound so thin and perfect he wants to break it just to prove it isn't made of glass. He doesn't.

Behind the counter, the coffee maker gives a small sound of surrender, a thermal tick that means nothing. He puts his hand around the pot anyway and lifts it. The weight surprises him—he expected less of it

He pours into a paper cup. The stream is sluggish, brown, resentful. Steam ghosts up a half inch and then thinks better of it. He puts the cup to his mouth. It smells like yesterday and pennies. He drinks. It tastes like someone else's morning. The warmth is not enough to be a fact, but it volunteers.

"God," he says, grimace curling into something like a smile, "that is awful."

He drinks again because awful and alive overlap more than he wants to admit.

By the door there's a battered metal rack holding free newspapers that will never be collected. He grabs one, shakes it open. March 12 again. The same headline about the mayor. He folds it under his arm like it's rain and he's decent.

He steps back into the street. The bell's tiny note floats behind him to the edge of his hearing and then lays down. Snow touches his face the way a hand might if it had been told to be gentle. The cold goes inside and sits on his lungs like a polite guest who has no intention of leaving.

He looks toward the river. A gray curve of not-quite horizon. He has known all morning that he's going there; admitting it out loud will make it too fragile. He doesn't speak. He starts walking.

Past the drugstore. Past the barber where the pole is frozen mid-swirl, red and white like a war truce. Past a parking meter with a bag over its head that says OUT OF ORDER in big letters that might as well be stitched to the world.

At the corner he stops and glances back at the diner. Through the glass, the photo wall glows a little, still. He lifts a hand in a wave he does not finish.

The red light throws a blink against the snow and misses. The pole hums an old song without words.

He turns the corner toward the river and the street narrows around him, houses pressing closer, porches leaning in the way people do when they want to hear you better. He doesn't mind the attention. It means something is still interested.

A bulb above a door buzzes as he passes. The noise threads the air and then thins, then fades, like mercy.

He keeps going until the storefronts give up their reflections and the last mailbox looks relieved to be done with its job.

At the bend where the street becomes path, he stops and listens to the quiet pretend to be generous.

"Coffee sucked," he tells it, and for the first time since morning his voice almost sounds like company

He takes the path down toward the dark line that is the river.

Behind him, the diner bulb hums for a moment more, then eases itself into silence.

The street narrows into a path where snow banks rise on either side, clean as hospital sheets. A chain-link fence runs along the right, its top crowned with ice so clear it looks sharpened. He follows it until he sees color — a faint red smudge in the white, a rusted swing set, the low shape of a playground pressed into the snow like a fossil trying to remember children.

The sign at the gate reads MAPLE HOLLOW PARK in cheerful green letters that deserve better than this. Someone's mitten clings to the fence by one finger loop, hardened in place, red gone to wine-dark brown. He touches it. It's stiff, cold as the chain it grips.

"Guess you found your forever home," he says, and immediately hates the sound of it

Inside the gate, everything feels too still, like the world paused mid-scene and never unpaused. A plastic slide leans slightly, drifted half-up its side. A seesaw balances dead center, snow perfect on both ends, a miracle of symmetry that makes his chest hurt. The swing set carries two seats—black rubber, rigid from cold. One is twisted around itself, chains creaking quietly when the wind shifts, though the air doesn't really move.

He approaches the swing, breath tight. Each step leaves a sound he can't describe—too soft for crunch, too wet for squeak. Just there. Like a word trying to be born and deciding not to.

When he's close enough, he gives the chain a shove with his glove. The swing answers with a low metal groan, slow, deliberate. It moves an inch forward, an inch back, then stops mid-air, hanging at an angle like a question that got tired of waiting for an answer

He stares at it too long. The sound it made keeps repeating in his head. Not the swing's fault. Memory doing a bad impression of motion.

He exhales through his nose. "I used to come here," he says to no one, to everyone. "Not here here—ours was over on Brighton—but it looked like this. Same cheap metal. Same birds trying to steal fries from kids.

The silence doesn't argue, but it listens. It always listens

He walks to the sandbox. It's a coffin now, a rectangle of white with one plastic shovel jutting out near the edge. He brushes snow off it. The handle's cracked. The blade has a cartoon sticker of a smiling sun with one eye missing. He turns it over, then drops it back into the drift. It lands blade-first, perfect, sticking upright. The sight makes him laugh once, a broken bark of noise that startles him.

36

"Good shot," he mutters, shaking his head. "You win.

Something taps behind him—one, two, three, uneven, like the sound of metal lightly rapped with a finger. He turns. The second swing moves again, slow this time, a fraction of motion, nothing more. The chains don't sound right. The pitch is lower, deeper, like the sound is coming through water.

He watches it too long again. It stops. Nothing else moves.

"Wind," he says under his breath. "Just wind."

He checks the trees along the edge of the park. Bare, thin, black against gray. No crows. No anything. The kind of trees that forgot to bend toward sunlight. The kind that would rather break.

There's a bench nearby with a memorial plaque sunk crooked into its slat. He scrapes it clean with a glove. The name is half gone: IN MEMORY OF M____ WELLS, 2011–2019. Eight years. He stares at the dates. Eight years and then nothing. The snow in the seat beside the plaque has melted just slightly, enough to look like someone sat there and got up recently.

He sits down without meaning to. The cold goes straight through denim, up spine, into skull. He leans forward, elbows on knees, breath hanging between his boots. The air smells faintly of iron and something sweet—sap maybe, or memory faking flavor.

He looks toward the swing again. Both seats hang still now. The red mitten on the fence watches him like an eye.

"You were probably somebody's everything," he tells the plaque. "They probably promised you cake every year. Told you to hold still for pictures. They probably—"

His throat closes around the rest.

He sits in the sound of snow shifting. Not falling—shifting. The weight redistributing itself, whispering in the language of things that know how to cover evidence.

He digs a thumb into his palm until pain answers, solid, grounding. "I'm sorry," he says, though the apology has no address.

When he stands, his legs feel like they belong to a man who's been sitting for decades. He looks at the bench, the plaque, the swing, the mitten. Each one could be the last thing in the world and it wouldn't make the place feel emptier.

He starts toward the gate, boots dragging slightly because the snow is heavier here, denser, as if trying to hold him. Halfway through the path, a sound lifts out of the quiet behind him—just one note. A chain sliding once through a metal hook.

He doesn't turn. He's learned what happens when you give your eyes permission.

He keeps walking. Each step crunches, deliberate. The sound from the swing doesn't come again, but he can still hear it in the back of his teeth.

At the fence, he brushes his glove against the red mitten once more. It tilts forward slightly, like a nod. He leaves it that way.

Outside the gate, the street looks different—not darker, not lighter. Just thinner. As if everything's a copy of itself run through one too many machines. The footprints from his entrance are half filled. The wind has finally remembered how to move, a low hum threading through the fence links.

He keeps walking. The park fades behind him like a dream you don't want to claim. When he glances back once, the swing is still swaying.

He doesn't stop again until the trees and fences have turned to houses. The sound follows him for a while longer than it should.

The street bends toward the river but before it tips into gray he sees the church: red brick shouldering the sky, a steeple that never learned humility, steps scabbed with ice. The front doors are oak, heavy and pocked, a long scar where someone dragged something metal across them once. The sign out front still promises SUNDAY 10 AM in black letters. A curl of the plastic has lifted on one corner like it's trying to peel itself free.

Jason stops at the bottom step and looks up. Wind combs at his jacket, finds seams, asks questions. The glass above the doors—the tall window with saints who have been bleeding politely for centuries—holds a blue that doesn't belong to this day. It's the only color the gray can't cancel.

"Fine," he says. "Let's see if you're any good at your job."

He takes the steps slow. The rail gives him nothing; it's a bar of winter. At the top he puts a palm to the door. The wood is so cold it feels like heat running out the other side. The latch yields with a tired church sound and he shoulders through.

Inside is a colder kind of quiet, the disciplined kind. Air sits in rows like the pews, waiting. The smell is familiar and wrong: old wood, old paper, candle wax from some morning that happened to people who still had reasons to make wishes. Dust hangs at a certain height, a thin heaven.

He shuts the door behind him and the sound goes nowhere; it just stops existing. He stands in the vestibule a second longer than he needs to, letting his eyes learn the dark. A rack of bulletins offers WELCOME in a font that wants to be hugged. He doesn't touch one.

The nave stretches out ahead in hush. Light falls through stained glass and lands on the aisle in blue and red coins. The pews face forward with the stubbornness of belief. At the front, the altar waits under a white cloth that

39

has decided to be snow. Candles in brass cups line the rail, stubby, some burned to little nubs of memory, some tall and arrogant and unused.

He walks down the center like everyone who has ever had business here. His boots sound smaller on the stone, a dry scuff, then nothing. He stops halfway, puts a hand on the end of a pew. The wood is worn smooth by the backs of hands, buffed by a century of small griefs. He runs his thumb along the groove until the memory oil makes his skin shine.

"Hey," he says softly, and he isn't sure to whom. "If you're here, this is your cue."

Nothing answers. Nothing argues. It's the same nothing he's had to learn to live with, only better dressed.

He slips into a pew because that's what you do. The cushion exhales dust at his weight, a ghost of perfume and winter coat. His knees touch the wood in front of him; the contact grounds him enough to feel the deep ache in his back. He sits with it.

On the rail up front one candle has a wick that looks like it tried and failed. He stands again, goes forward, and fishes the little brass wand from its hook— the one with the snuffer bell on one end and the lighter wick on the other. He rolls the wheel at the handle. The wick at the tip sputters and then catches, a tiny, earnest flame in his hand.

"Okay," he says, voice almost respectful. "Team effort."

He touches flame to stub, to stub, to stub, making small suns wake up along the rail. Warmth doesn't come, not real warmth, but a suggestion of it does. Shadows behave themselves. When he gets to the tall candle, the new light throws blue on his knuckles. His skin looks like a stranger's hand doing something good with his.

He holds the wand away from him and breathes. The flame at the tip leaks down the little wick and dies. Smoke curls and makes a tiny snake he follows with his eyes until it evaporates into the high, indifferent air.

"Listen," he says then, and the word sounds like it was waiting in this room. "I don't know how this works for you. I don't know if you're a He or It or just a book people didn't want to end."

He grips the rail. The brass is unforgiving.

"I'm tired," he says, simpler. "I'm so fucking tired."

The word fucking is a trespass here and the room eats it anyway.

He talks because if he doesn't, the world will. He talks because words are still the only currency he has.

"I keep waking up and there's nothing," he says. "No noise. No people. No goddamn birds. Just the air doing a bad impression of being alive.

He tips his head toward the glass. A saint above him pretends patience in a blue robe that looks like slow water. A thin red stripe at the edge makes the light taste like iron.

"I'm not good at this," he says. "I'm not—" He lifts a hand, lets it fall. "I'm not built for this. I was barely built for the old version."

His voice gets small and mean without his permission. "You could fix this," he says. "If you were there. If you are. I'm not asking for a choir. I'm not even asking for a fucking sign. Just... something. A sound that isn't me. A noise that proves the world didn't go under and take the instructions with it."

He shuts his eyes and for a second the room tilts, the way a field looks when you close one eye and the horizon loses manners. He opens them again.

In the quiet, he hears the smallest thing: wax settling around a wick, the whisper a candle makes when it admits it can't be bigger than itself. He takes it as half a kindness and half an insult.

He moves to the side aisle where a rack of votives sits in red glasses, dollar slots rusted, a sign that says LIGHT A CANDLE. SAY A PRAYER. Someone's written FOR WHO? under it in ballpoint, and someone else crossed that out with a furious black X. He digs in his pocket for coins and comes up with the penny he stole from the diner tip jar. He stares at it, at the silly face, then feeds it into the slot. The machine doesn't even pretend to notice.

"Good talk," he says. He lights one of the red cups anyway. The glass warms quick and the color paints the altar steps with a heartbeat.

On a side table rests the guest book, leather cracked at the hinge. He opens it and sees names in neat lines—people who believed enough to write themselves into permanence for an hour. The last entry is dated March. The ink blot at the end of the name looks like a small explosion. He picks up the pen. It is dry. He presses it harder, trying to bully ink out of it. Nothing. He puts it down with the kind of care reserved for animals and loaded guns.

At the rear corner there's a confessional like a wooden throat. He goes and stands in the doorway, one hand on the woven screen. It smells like wood warmed by breath. He sits because his legs decide for him.

"Bless me, Father," he starts, because muscle memory is stronger than any apocalypse, "for I have—" He stops. His reflection looks back from the glossy wood, his face cut into long brown strips by the grain. "—for I have nothing left to confess that isn't the same fucking sentence."

He laughs, then hates the sound. He doesn't cry. He has learned not to do that where walls can hear.

42

He stands again too fast and the booth creaks like a small animal being disturbed in its den. He steps out and the church receives him without comment.

Near the front, a little font of holy water sits with its silver surface skinned over by ice. He breaks it with one finger and touches the wet to his forehead, because superstition is just a different word for hungry. The cold goes into him like information.

At last, he stands before the altar rail and looks at the white cloth, at the steady, cheap flames, at the way the blue window pours itself down the center aisle without asking permission. On the altar is a glass-fronted case with a relic he can't name—a splinter of wood, a bit of fabric, a bone maybe. He looks at his face in the glass: thinner than he thinks he is, older than he thinks he has any right to be. He blinks. The reflection blinks with him—no delay, no trick— just a man in a room that used to teach people to be afraid of silence.

He leans closer until his breath ghosts the glass. His face disappears under it and then returns.

"Please," he says, and the word is quieter than every fuck he has ever said. "If you can hear anything, if you can make anything, make a little sound. Just to prove I didn't bury the whole planet by getting out of bed."

He waits. He can feel his heart in his wrists, a soft punch. He can hear the wax move by millimeters. He hears the wind talk to the door as if deciding whether to come in.

No voice answers. The room stays exactly the shape it is.

He exhales through his teeth. "Figures." Then, softer, because some part of him refuses to be cruel in rooms like this: "Thanks for the candles."

He turns. The aisle looks longer than it did on the way in, the doors are farther, the blue spill narrower. He walks anyway. At the vestibule he stops,

43

puts his hand on the wood of the door again, and presses his forehead to it for a beat that might be prayer or just fatigue with better manners.

On the way out he takes nothing. He leaves the lights he lit to burn themselves honest and die their small deaths, the way brave little things do.

Outside, the cold hits with the discipline of a drill sergeant. He steps down the stairs into a light that has flattened into late afternoon. Snow has started again, a thin fall, fine as ash. He looks back once at the stained glass. The blue holds. He lets it

At the bottom step he says, not to the church and not to himself, "If you were saving a miracle for later, don't. I'm going to the river."

The street listens without moving. He pulls his hood up, stamps life into his feet, and turns toward the path that slips under the trees and out of the neighborhood's last idea of safety.

Behind him, the candles do what they were asked to do: they burn, they warm nothing, they keep the dark a few inches off the rail.

He walks until the church has become brick behind him and then a shadow, and then a feeling, and the only colors left are gray and that mean little red at the traffic light still arguing with emptiness.

The road winds down from the church like a vein, narrowing until it's only him and the white. The trees on either side lean close enough that their branches knit over the top, making a kind of throat. Snow spills from them in slow clumps, the sound soft and precise—like something's trying not to wake the world.

He knows what's at the end of this stretch. The underpass. The tunnel that cuts beneath the old rail line, the one kids used to tag and drink under. He used to drive through it just to hear the car echo his engine back. Now, on foot, the thought of that echo feels like a luxury.

He reaches it by instinct more than intention. The entrance looks like the mouth of something waiting for breath. Concrete ribs frame it, slick with ice. The air spilling out smells of rust, of minerals that never learned sunlight.

He hesitates at the lip. The dark inside isn't total; it's layered, gray on black, the kind of dark that learns your outline before you move.

"Don't do this," he mutters, not sure if he's talking to himself or the place.

The silence answers by widening.

He takes one step in. The crunch of snow stops at once; the floor changes under him—frozen gravel, damp patches where meltwater's been gathering. His boot squeaks faintly. The sound ricochets forward and doesn't come back. He takes another step. The same thing: swallowed.

"Okay," he says, quieter. "So that's how it's gonna be."

He pulls the flashlight from his coat. It's a small thing, plastic, meant for drawers, not survival. The beam jumps to life—weak, yellow. It reaches maybe twenty feet, stops like it hit a wall of breath.

The sound of his own breathing starts to sound wrong. It's too loud, too close to his ears. He adjusts the beanie, listens. Nothing but his pulse trying to climb out of his throat.

He starts walking, steady pace. Each step lands and vanishes. The walls are tagged with colors drained to ghosts: letters that meant something once, promises, insults, declarations. He reads one at random: STAY DOWN. Another: COME HOME. A third is just handprints, child-small, sprayed red. He tells himself paint, not blood. Paint.

Water drips somewhere ahead—a metronome that doesn't keep time. It makes his spine itch.

Halfway in, the light flickers. Once, twice, then holds. He shakes it. "Don't you fucking—"

It steadies. His breath fogs the beam, ghosts it. The sound of his boot scuffs start echoing now—but wrong. They don't match his timing. He stops. The echo keeps going, one step more. Then silence.

He forces a laugh that sounds like someone else's voice. "That's good. Real good. Scare yourself in a sewer. Perfect."

He moves faster now, not running yet but close. The tunnel breathes with him. The air pressure shifts—he can feel it against his face, like the space is exhaling every time he inhales. The beam slides over damp concrete, frozen stalactites, a burst pipe leaking thin ice ribbons.

Then the sound changes. It's his breath, but not. Higher pitch, faster rhythm. It takes him a second to realize it's echoing back wrong. Too soon. Too close. He whirls, throws the light over his shoulder.

Nothing. Just the tunnel's mouth behind him, a distant circle of gray framed by white. Farther than he thought. Much farther.

"Hello?" he calls. The word comes back slower, lower. Hell—hell—hell— then dies mid syllable.

He backs up one step. The beam catches a shape on the floor—bootprints, half-thawed. His size. He crouches. The tread matches. He can see where the snow melted off his soles, made little wet halos. He follows them with the light. They go in both directions—forward and back. Same weight, same pattern.

He swallows, throat clicking. "All right. Not weird at all.

The ceiling drips again, heavier now. A drop hits his neck, slides down under the collar. Cold enough to bite. He jerks instinctively, hits the wall with

46

his shoulder. The sound detonates around him, ringing metal-deep, too loud. He covers his ears. The echo keeps going, bouncing between the concrete ribs like it's learned how to multiply.

"Stop," he says. "Stop, stop, stop—" The word fragments under his breath, becomes static. His voice sounds wrong in here, brittle.

The flashlight sputters again, dims to a candle's worth of light, then steadies. He forces himself forward, eyes on the pale circle of the far exit. It looks closer now, but he doesn't trust that.

He's counting steps before he realizes it—one, two, three—then catches himself. "Don't start that," he mutters, but the numbers keep whispering under his tongue. He tries to hum over them. It works for five steps. Then the hum dies, strangled by the tunnel's shape.

The air grows thicker, humid, metallic. He can taste the concrete—dust, copper, something old. The flashlight beam trembles. His hand's shaking. He steadies it with the other and keeps moving.

A low noise starts behind him, not echo this time. A scrape, like rubber dragged slow across floor. He stops. Silence.

"Don't," he whispers. "Don't you fucking start."

He angles the beam backward. Nothing. The walls stand there, wet and obedient.

He exhales and turns—and the light flares on water. A shallow sheet crossing the floor. It wasn't there a moment ago, or he didn't notice. The surface trembles like it's breathing. He steps in. The cold climbs his boot, stabs his ankle. He pulls the foot free and the suction makes a sound too human.

He keeps going. The exit circle looks the same distance no matter how far he walks. He tells himself it's perspective. The kind of lie that's practical.

47

He passes under the old graffiti at the midpoint—big letters, green flaking paint: KEEP YOUR HEAD UP. He mutters, "Yeah, working on it."

Something drips again, then again, then faster, like applause from a crowd that isn't there.

He breaks into a jog. The flashlight beam shakes across the ceiling ribs. His breath starts to sound like machinery. The far end of the tunnel stretches wider. Almost there. Almost.

Then the light dies.

Not a flicker, not a fade. Gone.

He stops. The sound of water fills the void, slow lap against concrete. His heart's in his mouth, loud enough that it almost counts as company.

He forces one breath in, one out. The dark feels alive against his skin—pressing, flexing, tasting.

"Okay," he says, barely audible. "You're fine. You're fine."

He reaches for the lighter in his pocket. Flame snaps. Tiny, orange, trembling. It shows him nothing but the circle of his own shaking hands.

He moves with it anyway, crouched, breath shallow. Each step splashes, small waves finding his shins. He keeps the lighter low, watching for the wall, the slope, the exit.

The flame flickers once, twice, goes out. He smells the smoke—chemical and soft. Then darkness again, real this time.

He whispers into it, desperate for anything to answer: "Hello?"

Nothing.

Then—one sound. A breath. Not his. Behind him, too close. The kind you make when you've been holding it too long.

He doesn't turn. He runs.

Boots slap water, air rushes, blood roars in his ears. The tunnel narrows or widens—he can't tell. The echo now does return, but it's everywhere, a chorus of his own steps running beside him. He trips once, catches himself on wet concrete, pushes off. The light ahead grows larger—gray, then white, then nearly bright enough to hurt.

He bursts out into snow. The sound of his own yell tears loose and vanishes instantly, like the air refuses to keep secrets.

He stumbles a few feet, doubles over, hands on knees. Breath clouding. The tunnel mouth behind him looks smaller than it should. Quiet again, perfect, nothing following.

He waits for movement. None.

The world feels flat. The air smells of cold iron and relief he doesn't trust.

He wipes his face with a trembling hand. "Fuck you," he says toward the darkness. "Fuck you for being just a tunnel."

The word dies where it's spoken.

He stands for a while longer, listening to the blood fade in his ears. Then he turns toward the bridge, the road rising, the river's gray glint waiting in the distance. His legs ache like they belong to someone older.

As he walks, he can still feel the tunnel breathing behind him. In. Out. Patient.

The tunnel spits him out like a bad dream ejecting its sleeper. He doesn't stop until the path widens into open ground, until there's sky above him again—flat, colorless, brutal in its honesty. The air hits his lungs sharp enough to sting. His legs keep moving because they don't remember how to stop.

When he finally slows, the bridge rises ahead of him, a rusted arc across the river. Steel bones, ice-gloved railings, wind threading through the gaps with a low, constant moan. It's not tall, not heroic—just long enough that crossing it means leaving something behind.

He stands at the foot of it, hands on his knees, breath sawing in and out. The sound echoes off the girders and comes back warped, the shape of panic refusing to dissolve.

"Jesus Christ," he says, and it comes out half laugh, half cough. "Still here. Still fucking here."

The river beneath is a dark bruise, chunks of ice shifting slow. Every so often one collides with another, a dull thunk that sounds too much like footsteps. He tells himself it's water talking to itself, nothing more.

The bridge surface is a mosaic of frost and rust. He tests the first step; the metal groans but holds. The noise shoots up the trusses and repeats until it's everywhere. He flinches like he's been touched.

"Okay," he mutters. "Easy. One at a time."

He walks. Each step wakes a different note from the steel—low, high, hollow. The wind joins in, pitching through the crossbars in long howls that almost form words. Go back. Don't. He tightens his hood and keeps moving.

Halfway across, the world tilts. Not literally—just that inner sway when your body remembers running and your mind hasn't forgiven it yet. He grips the railing; it's slick, cold enough to bite skin. The river moves under him like something alive and patient. The air smells of iron and melt.

50

A gust hits from the side, hard enough to stagger him. The bridge hums in protest. He plants his boots wide, rides it out. For a second the wind feels personal, like the tunnel's exhale finally found him again.

He laughs once, sharp. "Persistent bastard."

The laughter bounces back in the same tone, delayed a heartbeat. He freezes, eyes narrowing. "Don't."

The echo fades. He breathes.

He keeps walking, slower now, counting each section of grating between bolts. One, two, three—stop it. He forces the numbers down. His palms ache from the cold and the grip; his shoulders burn. Beneath him, the river cracks loudly, a sheet breaking. He looks over the edge.

The ice has split in a crooked vein, black water sliding underneath, endless and quiet. He stares too long, long enough that vertigo hums behind his eyes. The sound of the water fills his skull, steady, hypnotic, like breath from something too big to see.

He steps back, heart hammering. The wind rises again, wailing through the lattice. A loose cable taps rhythmically against metal: tick – tick – tick. The same beat as the drip in the tunnel. He hates that he notices

"Not following me," he says. "You don't get to follow me."

His voice cracks on the last word. The wind snatches it anyway, flings it over the rail. He imagines it freezing midair and sinking into the water, joining every other sound the world decided to bury.

He moves again, faster now, boots slipping, catching. The far side grows clearer with each breath. There's a small sign there, half-buried in snow: DANGER – THIN ICE. The irony lands late but hard.

Another noise joins the wind—a metallic shudder, somewhere behind him, deep in the bridge's gut. He turns, lightheaded. The steel trembles once, then goes still. He can't tell if it was real or just his heartbeat echoing through the structure.

He starts to run.

The bridge answers with a roar of vibration. His boots slam rhythm into the metal; every strike multiplies, rebounds, turns the air electric. Snow flies off the girders in sheets. He's breathing in gasps now, words between them. "Almost—there—almost—"

He hits the far side and keeps going until the metal becomes dirt again. Only then does he stop, turn, and face the thing.

Nothing moves. The bridge stands exactly as it did—solid, indifferent. Wind threads through its ribs, singing low, patient. The sound could be anything: breath, warning, welcome.

He raises one shaking hand and flips it off. "You don't scare me."

The gesture feels small. The wind disagrees. It gusts once, hard enough to push him half a step backward, then stops. He grins, though it's not a happy shape. "Fine. Tie game."

He looks down the slope toward the riverbank. The snow there is smoother, untouched. The current below is slower here, heavy with ice, moving like thought through a dying brain. The air bites again, reminding him he's still warm enough to feel it.

He starts down the embankment, one hand on the rail, boots slipping through thin crust. At the bottom he pauses, glancing back at the bridge—the way it arches, quiet now, innocent as architecture. It looks like it could have been holding him the whole time instead of trying to shake him off.

He almost says thank you. Almost.

Instead he spits once into the snow, the sound clean and satisfying, and says, "Next time, bring your A-game."

The wind rises behind him, brief and sharp, as if laughing.

He heads toward the river.

The bank dips into a slow, wide curve of gray. The river is a single muscle under ice, flexing when the wind forgets its manners. The far shore is a darker smear—trees like ribs, a slant of ruined fence, a roofline that still pretends to be a house.

Jason stops at the edge where the snow ends and the real cold begins. The sound lifts out of the water in a low, patient note. Not loud. Just there. He feels it carry through his boots, up his shins, a bass line under the ache.

"Okay," he says. The word falls at his feet like a stone and is eaten.

The ice near shore is white and crazed with hairline cracks. Farther out it clears to glass where the current runs harder, a smoked mirror that shows more sky than man. He takes a step onto it. The ice answers with a dry little complaint, a voice of old glass rubbed by a thumb. He puts his weight down slow. Another step. He tests each patch like it asked for permission.

The wind comes across the surface without resistance. It sneaks under his hood, pries at his scalp, finds the sweat still cooling at his neck and takes it. He keeps moving. He doesn't look back at the bridge. The bridge will be there if he survives the looking.

Out ten feet, the ice changes color. The world under him switches from white to a bruised brown, and then to a dark that might be depth or might be a trick his eyes are willing to play to spare him the truth. He stops where the glass begins. Beneath is water with a mind of its own.

He kneels, glove squeaking on the surface. His breath fogs the ice, then clears. He can see down into a moving dark that carries leaf fragments, a twig sliding past like a tiny drowned arm. The current's motion confuses the eye—left then right, fast then slow—until he realizes it's not the current changing; it's him swaying.

"Steady," he mutters. "Christ, steady."

His reflection finds him—dim, greenish, moored to the underside of the ice like a trapped animal. It's him but not immediate. When he lifts his hand, the shape lifts too, a fraction late. He frowns at his own frown. The delay is small enough to call a mistake, large enough to call a lie.

"Cute," he says. "Real cute."

He leans closer. His nose almost touches the ice. His eyes look wrong down there—duller, flatter, as if the water has taught them something he hasn't learned yet. He waits to see if they blink on his blink. They do, but the blink looks rehearsed.

He taps the ice with a knuckle. The sound is high and tight and almost sweet. It runs a quick ring along the sheet and dies. Tiny bubbles under the surface dart like fish when a shadow passes. He imagines their panic and then realizes he's projecting panic on gas.

He shifts forward until his coat creaks and the cold goes up his arms like a medic with bad bedside manner. He speaks to the shadow of himself as if he's at the glass of a nursery, as if the baby in there belongs to him and he needs to say something adult.

"You know, if you're going to fuck with me," he says, voice low and intimate, "you could at least buy me dinner first.

The mouth below him opens when his does. The words arrive there a heartbeat late, as if the river is a cheap dub of his life. He listens to his own voice turn underwater - warped, slowed, more honest than he wants it to be.

He swallows. The swallow echoes in the bones of his jaw. For a second he hates his mouth for being part of him.

Above him the sky is close enough to wear. Winter flattens everything until distance loses its spine. He closes his eyes. The air presses his lids with the weight of a thumb. He opens them again because the dark has started to build furniture.

"Say something," he tells the river. "Anything. Tell me I didn't fuck the whole world just by existing."

The river does what rivers do. It keeps its appointments.

He leans more weight onto his palms and the ice complains for real this time—a low crack that runs away from him like a line of thought he shouldn't follow. He eases back without meaning to. The sheet settles. He exhales in relief he won't name.

Out beyond, a chunk of ice shifts, rides over another, and tumbles. The sound is a broken plate in a room with good acoustics. He flinches and immediately hates himself for flinching. He lets the hate pass through. It doesn't get a room here.

He puts his face closer to the glass. The reflection obliges. His breath makes a fog circle and shows him his own skin—pores, chapped lip, a ragged cut that used to be a different color. He whispers, "What do you want?"

The mouth down there makes the shape of it—what do you want—late, then sinks into blur. He stares at the place where his eyes should be until they stop being eyes and become coins pressed into ice.

Memory tries the door. He doesn't let it in. He repeats the practical thing he's been repeating since the day went loud and then went silent: Standing. Breathing. Choosing a direction. He adds a fourth today: Listening.

He listens for a human noise that isn't him. All he gets is the deep, patient note of water moving through a city's heart.

He thinks about lighting a match to see deeper, then pictures how fast the cold would kill the flame and gets angry at himself for needing metaphors to feel brave.

Something moves under the ice beyond the reach of his reflection. Not a fish—too slow, too wide. It slides like a sentence across the glass and dissolves into darkness. He holds his breath too long watching it. When his lungs ask to live, he lets them.

He lowers one glove to the edge where ice meets water and tests a spot with the heel of his hand. The skin there feels the cold even through the leather, a hurt so clean it borders on sterile. He presses harder. A thin crack splinters outward, finds its confidence, then gives up. The river muscles under the sheet, uninterested.

"Fine," he says. "You win. Again."

His voice makes a shape in the air and falls apart.

He sits back on his heels to rest. The position does a number on his thighs. The frozen prickle in his toes becomes something meaner. His body starts sending him strong letters in a language that looks like get up, get up now. He rubs his hands together and they give him a little heat the way an old dog gives you a stick: out of affection, not obligation.

He looks at the far bank. A tangle of cattails holds a family of snowdrifts in its arms. The sky presses down harder and gray gets more serious. He feels the day lean toward evening with the gravity of a decision he doesn't get to vote on.

"Almost done," he tells no one. "We're almost done with all this.

The reflection beneath him watches his mouth shape done and then doesn't quite manage it. The secondhand version of his lips stalls mid-vowel. He laughs quietly, the sound small enough to put in your pocket.

"Of course you'd choke on that."

He lowers himself until his chest touches the ice. The shock makes his spine rise against his coat like a dog's hackles. His cheek goes numb in a clean line. He stares straight down. His own face stares back, flattened by the cold, borrowed by the river

He speaks softly, as if to a sleeping animal.

"You're not going to tell me what happened, are you?"

The mouth under the glass opens a beat late and says it without sound. He understands anyway.

He waits longer than a man should wait for a surface to give him an answer. Eventually, the shaking in his arms stops being about patience and starts being about ice. He leverages himself backward, palms sliding, and sits on his ass like a child who forgot how knees work.

A thin snow begins—a sift that makes no sound until it has made a thousand decisions. The flakes land on the glass and melt immediately, leaving dark spots that look like eyes if you're primed for seeing eyes in everything. He closes his own and counts the breaths it takes to hear his heart calm enough to stop being a problem.

When he opens them, something has changed so quietly it might be mercy. The wind has dropped. The water's note has deepened by a half tone. Or he's finally listening correctly. He can't tell which truth will be more dangerous if he picks it. He decides not to pick.

He leans forward once more and lays both bare hands on the ice. The pain is instant and electric. He stays anyway until the sting evens into a steady numb. The contact feels like confession.

He speaks his name into the cold. He doesn't know who needs to hear it. He says it again just to prove mouths can still make it.

"Jason."

His reflection gets it wrong. The shape looks like shun. He doesn't blame it. He pardons the fucking river for being a river.

He sits there with his palms on the skin of winter and lets the idea take him: that nothing ended and everything ended, that the quiet is a mirror and not a tomb, that his head did the world a disservice by insisting it was the size of his hurt.

The thought is more than he can have standing up. He kneels again, this time because the posture matches the knowledge. The ice holds him—not kindly, not cruelly, just as a fact.

He bends until his forehead touches the glass. It doesn't feel like prayer. It feels like telling the truth to a table when no one else will sit down. His breath makes a little dome, a clear bubble over his eyes. Inside it, his face looks almost warm. Outside it, everything is what it is.

A small sound gathers in his throat and chooses not to leave. He understands it. He lets it stay.

He whispers, "What did you want from me," and the river says w— y— a beat late, and the absurdity of his own voice following him makes him smile, which hurts.

He pushes up finally, legs complaining, hands on his thighs. When he stands his vision narrows and then remembers how to be generous. The bridge is a long shadow now. The far bank is a line that won't come closer just because he asks.

He looks down one last time. The reflection is there, obedient but off. He lifts a hand in a wave that doesn't quite happen and drops it.

"Enough," he says. The word fits, small and perfect.

He turns toward the shore. The ice under his boots speaks in small, disciplined syllables: ok—ok—ok. He listens and believes it just long enough to get to snow.

At the bank he climbs the low rise, boots punching through a thin crust. At the top he turns back to the river because the scene requires it. The dark moves the way it always has, then the way it didn't, then back to normal. He raises his chin at it like a dare. The water doesn't accept or refuse.

His knees go soft without asking permission. He lets them. Snow takes him, patient as a parent. He ends up there, not quite sitting, not quite kneeling, palms open on his thighs as if he's announcing he came unarmed. The cold climbs into him with the rights it's earned and the responsibilities it never asked for.

For a long moment the only sound is the river's low engine and the whisper of fresh flakes filling in his footprints

He realizes he isn't scared of the quiet anymore. He's just tired of how much of it he owns.

He looks past the far bank and remembers a day with heat and mosquitoes and a boy skipping stones wrong and laughing anyway. The memory knocks and he lets it in and lets it leave without offering a chair.

The sky lowers. The light learns evening. The world holds its mouth shut out of respect or habit.

"Almost," he tells it, and the word, for once, doesn't feel like a lie.

He presses his hands against the snow until they stop hurting. He sits there listening to winter have its say until he knows what he's going to do next, and that's when the fear goes quiet in his chest.

He stands.

The river takes no notice. The ice doesn't bother pretending to crack. The wind stays decent.

He turns from the water and begins the short walk toward the place where the path widens into shore, where a small hollow of drift waits like a kneeler built by an architect who loved him.

Behind him, his reflection keeps breathing under glass, late and faithful as a shadow.

The path flattens where the trees open to a clearing. The world has gone the color of a scar—gray edged with violet. Snow drifts between trunks in sheets that move like breath. The wind has forgotten its bite; it only hums now, low and even, as if the day is humming to itself.

Jason reaches the hollow he saw from below—a small dip in the ground shaped by years of melt and freeze. The snow there has settled smoother, untouched except by wind. It looks like a place waiting for someone to kneel.

He stops, every muscle in argument with the air. His legs shake from the long cold, his lungs from the run that never stopped being a run. He doesn't fight it. He lowers himself, one knee, then the other, until the snow folds around him and the ache becomes the only warmth left.

The river mutters behind him. The sound is slow now, exhausted too.

He stares at his hands, red and cracked, small crimes written in frostbite. "You did your best," he tells them. "Hell of a job."

He laughs once, a hollow bark that fades before it finds an echo. Then he speaks to the air, because there's no one else left to file the report.

"I broke the world," he says. "Because the world broke me."

The words hit the snow like glass beads and roll until they're buried.

He waits for thunder, or light, or any sign that the universe heard him. Nothing. Just the same wind, moving through the same branches, with the same unbothered grace.

For a moment he hates it—the indifference, the ease. Then he feels the hate leave like breath. The quiet afterward is better.

He tips forward, elbows on his knees, head hanging. He listens to the snow land. Each flake has a voice if you let it. Tiny impacts, barely sound, but real.

The cold climbs higher, finds his ribs, steadies his heart to its own slow rhythm.

"I'm still here," he says softly. "That's all I've got left."

The wind changes direction. It brushes his face with the gentleness of something testing forgiveness. The sound it carries isn't a word, not really— just a fold in the air that touches his ear and passes through.

But inside it, faint as memory, he thinks he hears:

It's okay.

He doesn't lift his head. He doesn't look for the speaker. He lets the sound move through him the way warmth used to. It could be mercy. It could be nothing. He doesn't need to decide.

The snow thickens, soft and endless. It buries the edges of his footprints first, then the hollow of his knees, then the trembling shadow that tried to follow him this far.

When he exhales, the steam rises, turns clear, and disappears into the wide, waiting air.

The wind breathes once more, the same phrase, quieter now, almost shy.

It's okay.

Jason closes his eyes. The sound holds. The world, for the first time all day, feels full.

THE BLOOMING ROOM

"And what is to die but to stand naked in the wind and to melt into the sun?"
— *Kahlil Gibran*

The greenhouse had kept its warmth without him.

Si noticed that first. Before smell, before memory, before the ache that would come later and keep coming. The air inside still held the same slow, wet heat they'd tuned together over years — ninety degrees at shoulder height, lower near the floor so the roots wouldn't sweat. It fogged his glasses when he opened the door.

From outside, the little glasshouse looked like it always had. He'd told people that was comforting. He used that word, comforting, because it stopped people from touching his arm and saying they were sorry in voices that belonged at hospital bedsides. Comforting. He knew it wasn't true.

From inside, it didn't look the same at all.

The first shift was the light. Afternoon sun forced itself through panels mottled with condensation and lime scum, turning everything inside green. Not just tinted — submerged. Even his hands. His skin looked like it belonged to someone else's body, as if he were already under a few feet of water.

65

He breathed in. Soil, damp wood, citrus peel, fertilizer, the faint iron edge of old water sitting in the metal drain trough. Sweetness underneath. The sweetness was wrong.

Si set his keys down on the narrow shelf by the door, next to the chipped spray bottle and the garden scissors Mon always forgot to clean. He could still see Mon's thumbprint in the rust line along the blade, the way it had stained then sealed. A fossil of a habit. He reached toward it and stopped before touching. He'd learned, in the last seven days, how fast touching could turn into not being able to let go.

Seven days.

That didn't sound right in his head. It sounded too clean. Grief wasn't seven days long. Grief wanted to be a season and refused to name which one.

He crossed to the counter against the interior wall. Two mugs still sat in the shallow sink, both white and both ridiculous, hand-lettered in black porcelain marker the way Mon always pretended to hate: S & S. The marker lines had bled into the glaze years ago, so even after hundreds of washings the letters still looked slightly wet. Simon & Simon. Si and Mon. The old joke. How long had they rolled their eyes at it? The first year, two years? After that it stopped being a joke. After that it was theirs.

"Should've soaked them," he said absently, and hated the way his voice sounded in the air. He didn't mean the mugs. He meant everything.

His voice didn't land the way it used to. It didn't just dissipate. It seemed to hang, faintly, the way steam hangs in the shower just before it beads and runs. He watched the air for a moment, waiting for that small drift to move. It didn't, exactly. It just became part of the room.

He turned the faucet. The tap gave its usual resistant cough, then a thin line of water came out, already warm from the old pipes. He rinsed both mugs

66

and set them upright to dry on the folded towel, touching them with the same care you'd use handling bones.

Then he went to work.

He moved with habit. Habit was the only steady thing left.

First row: orchids. Their heads were heavy and slumped, but not in a dying way. More like overfed. He pressed his thumb to the soil in each pot, feeling for moisture, for temperature. They didn't need water yet. They shouldn't have needed water yet. He watered anyway. He couldn't not.

"Too much," Mon would scold, standing where Si was standing now, leaning one hip against the table, arms crossed, pretending to be stern. "You drown them when you're sad."

"They're tropical," Si would say. "Tropical means wet."

"Tropical means wet with sense."

Their old argument lived in his head so vividly he could feel the rhythm of Mon's voice, the lift and catch and warm teasing in it. He could feel where to interrupt and where to let him finish. It was just muscle memory. There were phrases in their life he could recite like liturgy.

Only now, with Mon gone, the argument didn't feel like memory replay. It felt like call and response. He caught himself leaving space in the air, as if an answer were due.

Too much, Mon would have said. You drown them when you're sad.

"I know," he said softly, as if he'd been corrected. "I know."

The stream of water hit potting mix and made a wet, steady sound against terracotta. A low note, almost a throat note. He hadn't noticed that sound before — or maybe he had and it hadn't mattered before. Now he noticed everything.

The hum started then.

It could have been the heater. That's what his mind told him first. The greenhouse heater, the squat square one they'd installed under the cedar bench, had always made a low vibration when the thermostat clicked on. It wasn't loud. It was more like presence. You felt it in your kneecaps and your teeth.

But the heater wasn't on.

He knew that because he hadn't turned it on yet. He had just walked in.

The hum was faint. Not even a hum, really, not a tone. It was a pressure. Pressure in the air, a held breath, the way you can feel the throb of bass through drywall even if you can't make out the song. It deepened very slightly when he leaned in over the first orchid. It dropped off when he straightened.

Si stayed where he was and breathed out very slowly through his nose.

"It's just the pipes," he said, to the room. To himself. To Mon. "Or something in the wall. We talked about fixing that."

They hadn't talked about fixing that. That problem hadn't existed before today. But saying "we talked about fixing that" made it sound like a plan. Plans were structures. Structures held.

He moved down the row.

On the third pot, the little hand-written plant tag had curled from humidity. He smoothed it between thumb and forefinger.

SIMON & SIMON HYBRID #3, in Mon's blocky, cheerful caps.

Below, in Si's finer, more clinical hand: phal. amabilis x oncidium unknown. viable. monitor.

Monitor.

He let his thumb rest along the word for a second longer than necessary. They'd joked about that too, how clinical his notes sounded next to Mon's. How his labels read like a trial report and Mon's read like love letters. He'd said, "'Monitor' is not romantic," and Mon had said, "Neither are fungal infections, but you still insist on preventing those."

He should have smiled at that. He didn't.

The sweetness in the air was heavier here. Not rot. Not yet. Rot had a throat-sting to it, a bitter underside. This was warm and a little sharp and candied at the edge, like the syrup they'd make when Mon insisted they could candy citrus peel "like old Italian ladies do" and then never remembered to eat it. Si knew every note of this room's smell from years inside it. The sweetness was new.

He set the tag back into the soil. The hum pressed at his ears again, soft, almost sympathetic.

Mon is gone, he thought. The room is not sympathetic. The room is warm because the room is sealed. That's all.

But in the same thought, overlapping it, was a quieter one: He used to stand right here. He used to say my name right here.

His throat tightened. He ignored it.

After the orchids, he checked the shelf of Mon's small experiments — all the shallow ceramic trays where Mon rooted cuttings, telling the cuttings stories while he worked. You talk to them, he had said once, when Si made

69

fun of him for it. They stand up straighter when you talk to them. Anyone would.

The cuttings hadn't wilted.

Some of them looked better than they had any right to. A few had pushed pale white roots into coarse substrate that should have been too dry for that. He brushed the tip of one root with a knuckle and it twitched. Just a fraction, but it twitched. He pulled his hand back immediately and his heart tried to leave his chest.

"Jesus," he whispered. "Okay. Okay." The word came out controlled. Practiced. He thought, with a dull kind of detachment, that he probably sounded calm to someone else.

The root wasn't moving now. It sat slick and delicate and harmless in the tray. Roots adjust when you disturb them. Of course they do. He knew that. He had always known that. Nothing was wrong.

He looked down at his hand.

Under his nails — and he kept them short, always had, practical, clean — something green had gathered in the half-moon crescents. Not dirt. Dirt was dark and friable. This was wet-looking, like sap, and faintly stained his skin where it touched. He rubbed at it with his thumb. It didn't quite come off.

That's new, he thought, in the same clinically noting way he wrote on tags. That's new.

He didn't write it down.

Instead, he crossed to the far table, the one under the broad pane of roof glass Mon had insisted they splurge on ("We don't travel, Si, this is the vacation") and set his palms on the work surface like a man bracing against weather. He let his head hang and closed his eyes.

It was quiet enough to hear the small tick of condensation collecting along the inside of the glass panels and then releasing all at once in fat, clear drops. The drops hit the metal lip of the table: ping, ping. Not musical. Still, steady. The kind of sound a person starts to anticipate if they listen long enough.

He had listened for seven days.

Not here. He hadn't let himself come back here until now. But he had listened to the shape of this silence in every other room in the house. The absence of a second set of footsteps. The absence of humming in the kitchen while water boiled. The absence of someone else turning off lights behind him, laughing, saying you're not paying the electric company at this point, you're sponsoring them.

Simon & Simon, he thought. Si and Mon. S & S. Everyone made the joke. We hated it at first. We pretended to. We said it was stupid. We said it was sitcom. We said we should've at least met in a more cinematic way than at a busted community garden workshop where the irrigation timer fried and I rewired it, and Mon flirted at me by pretending not to understand basic voltage.

We hated it.

Then we loved it.

Then it was proof. You see? we'd tell people. You see? Must be fate. Must be alignment. Must be that we're two of the same thing.

Now he swallowed, and the swallow hurt in a way that had nothing to do with his throat. Now it's a question.

Who is still here?

The hum thickened for a moment, almost like breath flowing outward, then eased. The pressure of it lingered just around him, almost outlining him. He didn't move.

"Keep it alive," he said quietly to the table.

That sentence slipped out of him with no thought. He didn't even know he was going to say it until it was already in the air.

It was something he and Mon said when they were tired, when one of them would try to call it for the night and the other would insist the heat lamps had to be checked again or the misters had to be flushed because mineral buildup would ruin the sprayers by morning. Keep it alive. Half joke, half vow. We are so tired. Keep it alive.

Hearing himself say it in the empty greenhouse, to no one, made his chest go tight.

The hum in the room shifted.

It wasn't louder. Volume wasn't the way it changed. It changed in depth. It went from a gentle, background vibration to something that seemed to gather slightly under his hands on the table, like bass under wood, like a large speaker turned low. The table wasn't actually moving. He could tell. He could see his hands; he wasn't imagining tremor. But he could feel something like a held resonance in the grain.

He opened his eyes.

There was condensation on the glass wall in front of him that hadn't been there when he came in. That was his first thought. His second thought was that it wasn't random.

Two ovals, about the size and height of where a face might rest if someone leaned in from the other side and pressed their forehead and mouth to the panel. Edged in fog. Center darker where breath would have warmed it.

He watched them, unmoving, as if any sudden gesture might cause them to vanish.

They didn't vanish.

They stayed. Soft and imperfect and undeniably shaped like presence.

He let out a slow breath. "That's just—" he began, and then he cut himself off, because he didn't like the way his voice shook on just.

He needed something to do with his hands.

Habit said: check the bulbs.

So he went to the overhead lamp rig.

The rig was Mon's project more than his. Mon loved tinkering with angles and warmth and intensity, always nudging the lights higher or lower, tilting them so "they're not blasting that one phil like an interrogation lamp." Si had always teased him about it — that his touch was intuition, not science. Mon called it listening.

Si reached up to the nearest lamp and felt with his fingers for heat. The metal housing was too warm. He frowned. He didn't have the lamps on yesterday. Or for the six days before that. He knew that because he hadn't had the courage to come in and turn them on.

So why were they warm?

He unscrewed one of the bulbs, careful, using the rag from his back pocket the way Mon always nagged him to, because "oil from your fingers shortens

73

the life, Si, I keep telling you, stop going barehanded like you're invincible." The bulb came free with a small dry squeal.

He turned it in his palm.

The filament inside had blown. Black seam, tiny bloom of char at one tip. Dead. And yet the glass still held heat.

His fist tightened around the rag without meaning to. For an instant — just the smallest instant — the room tilted. Not physically. Perceptually. Like standing up too fast in the dark.

In that half-second, he was back inside last week.

The lamp had popped then, too. A different bulb, on the far side. He'd said, "Leave it, I'll fix it in the morning," and Mon — always Mon, always moving, always hands on everything — had said, "It'll scorch the fiddle-leaf if it arcs, Si, just let me—"

Then heat, and a clatter, and that awful, singular sound of glass and body and wood all striking at once. Too fast to be cinematic. Ugly, fast, real.

And then the silence.

Not a scream. That was the worst part. The body's refusal to make drama when real damage happens. He would never forget that: no scream. Just the end of a sentence that never got its last word.

Si's stomach lurched, and for a moment he thought he might be sick right there on the floor. He gripped the bulb so hard his knuckles ached.

"It was an accident," he whispered.

The greenhouse held the words the way lungs hold air.

He had said those words seven times now. To the paramedics. To the neighbor. To Mon's sister on the phone, her voice breaking apart into breathless little gasps the way Mon's never had a chance to. To the man from the funeral home who had too-bright eyes and practiced condolences and a clipboard.

He had said it to himself in the dark in the kitchen, into the heel of his own hand so the sound wouldn't carry.

It was an accident. It was an accident. It was.

Here, in this room, the word accident felt like a weed. Like something invasive, fast-growing, choking out everything native.

The hum came back, softer now, lower, as if settling.

Si screwed the dead bulb back in, because doing anything else would have meant accepting the broken state of things, and he wasn't yet built for that.

He wiped his palms along the thighs of his jeans. His hands had always looked older than his face, big-knuckled and veined; now, in the greenhouse light, the veins along the backs seemed faintly tinted. Not blue. Not purple. Green.

He blinked. Looked again.

The green was gone.

Just skin, mottled from heat.

"Too much," he said quietly, echoing Mon's old tease. "I'm overwatering again."

This time, there was no space in the air that felt like an answer waiting to land. There was only the press of the room around him — heat, moisture, sweetness, and that low, steady hum under all of it, like something patient, like something listening.

Si set the rag down.

He went back to the row of orchids. He lifted the watering can again. He did the only thing left that felt like love.

"Keep it alive," he said.

And for a heartbeat, maybe two, he could swear the table under his hands held a pulse.

The second morning, the light found him before the clock did.
He had fallen asleep in the greenhouse chair, knees pulled to his chest, head bowed toward the humidity. He woke to the faint click of the thermostat that wasn't running.

It was early enough that the sun hadn't reached the yard. Everything outside the glass was colorless, but inside, the air was already glowing pale green, as if the walls themselves made their own dawn.

He stood carefully, wincing at the stiff ache in his back. The skin along his palms itched — not sharply, but with a steady, pulsing warmth. He rubbed them together, felt grit that wasn't grit at all. When he looked, faint flakes of dried sap clung there. The color was wrong for sap, more human, less tree.

He rinsed his hands under the spigot. The water ran cloudy, then clear.

He did not look again.

He checked the orchids first. The air around them trembled slightly, enough to make the thinnest stems quiver. No draft. No window cracked open. Just the room breathing its own temperature.

He said, "Morning, Mon."
Because silence without greeting felt like neglect.

The condensation on the glass wall had formed again overnight. Two ovals, faintly different in shape from yesterday's, higher this time, blurred around the edges. They looked newer, closer to his height. He lifted one hand and set his palm against the left oval. The warmth that met him was not his own.

He jerked back. A small wet mark of his handprint now overlapped the fogged one, and he couldn't tell which had been there first.

He busied himself with motion. Motion was safe. Motion kept breath shallow and quick and focused.

He tested soil moisture. He trimmed browned leaves. He took notes that meant nothing in a small ledger on the shelf, though the handwriting told him everything he didn't want to know — letters uneven, thin, each word smaller than the last. His hand was learning to whisper even when he wrote.

When he bent to adjust the watering can, the hum returned.
Not loud. Not even sound exactly. More the weight of sound, the pressure of something that might be waiting to resolve.

It pulsed once. Once more. Then steadied into the rhythm of his own heartbeat.
He froze.

The air held him.

Then a droplet broke free from the glass overhead and fell, shattering the rhythm. The hum receded.

He laughed a little, to quickly. "Guess I'm hearing things."

The word hearing didn't sound right in his mouth — too thin, too alive.

He tried another one instead: "Resonance." That was better. Cooler. Measured. A word that belonged to instruments and rooms, not people.

He turned the heater switch once, twice. It stayed off. Still, the temperature rose. The thermometer on the far post read ninety-four. He wrote that number down. Then crossed it out.

At noon, a package of cuttings arrived by courier, a shipment Mon had ordered before. The label carried both their names. Si slit it open on the counter. The smell that rose wasn't floral. It was clean and raw and faintly metallic, the smell of sap under pressure. He set the bundle in the sink and turned away, leaving the stems unwrapped. They were already beginning to breathe.

He made coffee in the small kettle they kept by the door, poured into both mugs by reflex. The second mug stayed full, steaming between the condensation and the plants.

He told himself he'd pour it out before it went cold.

He didn't.

Outside, the neighborhood moved through ordinary Sunday quiet: distant lawnmower, far-off radio, the faint periodic click of wind chimes two houses over. Inside, the only sound was that steady undertone — not constant now, but in pulses, as if the house itself were breathing with him and sometimes slightly ahead of him.

When he left that evening, he stopped at the door, hand on the frame. The air pressed softly against his back like a body's warmth.

He turned once more to check the lights.

For a moment, just before the timer clicked them off, the glow through the leaves seemed to shape a color closer to skin than chlorophyll.

He blinked, and it was gone.

On the third day, the light looked like memory.

It came in low and angled, not yet harsh, and slid through the roof panes in long, pale bands. Dust hung in it. Moisture hung in it. The whole greenhouse seemed suspended in one of those bands — like a specimen slide, like something pinned and labeled.

Si stood in the doorway and watched the light move across the benches, across the labels, across the S & S mugs still drying mouth-up on the towel. He hadn't washed them again. It felt wrong to rinse the rims. The heat had baked faint mineral rings into the glaze where the coffee sat and cooled. Little halos.

Mon had called them that once, laughing. Halos. You're so dramatic, Si. We're not saints just because we don't rinse immediately.

That had been last spring. They'd been arguing about watering schedules. The good argument, the kind without edges. Mon had over-misted the philodendrons — big, ridiculous leaves glossy as varnish. Si had teased him for it. "Drowning them again." And Mon had said, "You treat them like ICU patients. Let them live a little."

Now, in the same place, in almost the same morning light, Si could see him. Not see him — that wasn't true, it wasn't a hallucination, he knew hallucinations, he'd had sleep-deprivation blurs in grad school and this wasn't that — but see the posture in the air. Elbow braced on the counter. One hip cocked. Bare feet on damp concrete. The sunlight had always hit Mon's throat first, right above the clavicle, catching on that pale edge of skin and turning it gold.

That was here, just for a moment. A suggestion of where light expected a body to be.

Si swallowed. The motion felt thick. He moved through the greenhouse, trying to stay ahead of the thought forming in his chest.

He did the usual first: temperature log, humidity check, visual scan for pests or mildew. Ritual kept the mind honest. That's what he'd always told his students. Then Mon would ruin the performance afterward by kissing him in the hall, because "no one likes your scientist voice, Si, use your person voice," and Si would mutter "you're undermining my authority" and Mon would say "then get better authority."

By the bromeliads, he paused.

A single leaf had come free from somewhere above — he didn't see where — and drifted down during the night. It lay across the work table, long and dark green and still full of moisture, not yet curled. At the base, the break was too clean for natural drop. Almost as if it had been cut.

He reached out and lifted it by the tip.

The underside pressed flat against the inside of his wrist for an instant before it came away. The contact was brief, barely there. Still, he felt it echo in his pulse. Not cold. Not warm. Damp, and alive in that dampness.

"Mon," he said before he thought, and then stopped, breath trapped halfway up.

The leaf hung limp now, just a leaf. He set it gently in one of the shallow trays.

He stared at his wrist.

There was a faint mark where the leaf had touched him, not quite a welt, not quite a stain. The skin there looked subtly different in tone. Less pink, more olive, as if light from the greenhouse had soaked in and stayed.

He rubbed at it with his thumb. The color didn't smear.

"It's contact dermatitis," he said, because saying something with Latin under it always made it sound smaller. He'd told a hundred anxious beginner growers that. Mild irritation. Wash it with cool water. You'll be fine.

He didn't wash it.

Instead he crossed to the little shelf wedged near the heater unit. The recorder sat there; they had bought it last winter when Mon said, "We should start documenting, real documenting, not just your tidy notes and my bragging pictures. Audio. Talk to it like it's an apprentice." Si had rolled his eyes in the moment, but he'd secretly liked the idea.

He picked it up now and turned it over in his hand. Cheap plastic. Scratches along one edge where Mon had dropped it. A tiny square of neon tape still stuck to the back, labeled with Mon's handwriting: green // day 77. They'd never agreed on a better naming system.

He pressed Record.

His thumb hovered longer than it should have. Then, quietly, in the low, even tone he'd been using for his own sanity:

81

"Greenhouse log. Afternoon. Temperature reads ninety-three at shelf height. Misters look clear. New growth on the Simon & Simon trays. Leaf drop on bromeliad, likely mechanical. Contact irritation on right wrist at point of touch. Stable. No, not stable. Present. Present but contained."

He almost stopped there. That was what an audio log should be. Clean. Observed. But the air in the greenhouse felt denser than it had when he walked in, like breath held, and he felt stupid all of a sudden holding back from something that was, if he was being honest, the real reason his hands were shaking.

His mouth was dry. He swallowed and tried again.

"Mon," he said softly, but into the recorder this time. "It wasn't—I didn't mean—"

He shut it off.

The click of the Stop button echoed louder than it should in the glass. The hum that had been behind his ribs all morning eased back, like someone leaning away from his shoulder.

He hadn't said the sentence. He had almost said the sentence. He had almost said I didn't mean to push you, I swear to God I didn't, you know me, you know I wouldn't, you stepped back wrong, you caught the shelf wrong, it was just that stupid quick reach for the lamp, you said wait and I said leave it and then—

He hadn't said it.

That meant he was still in control.

Control mattered.

He rewound the recorder out of habit and hit Play, intending to catalog the baseline — humidity tone, heater rattle, his own voice. That's what you did in good observation: you listened back, you checked yourself.

What came through the tiny speaker wasn't his voice.

At first it was only static. The gentle, low rush of low-quality mic noise. Then under that, almost below audible range, something like a long exhale moving in and out in slow intervals. Breath, but not quite. Too regular for breath. Too rounded. Like someone had pressed a fingertip to a speaker cone and felt for the pulse of whatever was behind it.

Then — and here his chest clenched — he heard his own voice begin.

"…greenhouse log," it said, faint and flattened, like an old tape. "Afternoon. Temperature reads ninety-three…"

It sounded tired in a way he didn't remember sounding. Worn thin.

"…leaf drop on bromeliad, likely mechanical. Contact irritation on right wrist at point of touch. Present but contained."

Then a gap. A faint hitch of static.

And then, layered under it, distorted, like a second track bleeding through:

"Mon," his voice — and not his voice — breathed. "Mon, it wasn't—"

He stopped the playback so fast his thumb hurt.

For a long while, Si stood very still in the damp light and listened to the blood moving through his head. Just that. Just to prove to himself that the sound he'd heard next, the one he hadn't let finish, was not going to start by itself.

83

The greenhouse did not so much as creak.

His mouth had gone dry. Humidity beaded at his hairline, ran down the back of his neck. He felt too warm and very cold at once.

He told himself, calmly, That is bleed. That's all. Cheap recorder. Old batteries. Signal overlap. He told himself, You've heard that before in interviews. Two tracks ghost into each other. He told himself, Your brain is filling in syllables because you know what you almost said. That is a known cognitive effect.

He did not tell himself, That sounded like me and not me at once, which means either I'm already splitting mentally or—

Or.

He set the recorder down.

His hands didn't feel entirely his. The skin along his palms looked too smooth, almost waxed by the humid air. When he flexed his fingers, the pull of his tendons felt thicker, like something under the surface had weight.

He looked back toward the worktable, toward the shallow ceramic trays nearest the center walkway. New cuttings. New trial crosses. Simon & Simon Hybrid #3. The tags lined up like little white teeth in the soil.

Mon used to lean over these trays in the afternoon and hum without even knowing he was doing it. It wasn't a song. It wasn't tonal, really. It was more a low, steady vibration in the throat. He'd hum when he was focused, when he was happy, when he was worried. Si liked to tease him about it. "You're going to vibrate the roots out." And Mon would answer, "That's the point, sweetheart. Loosen them up so they'll take."

Now that same hum was in the room.

Not loud. Barely audible. But present.

At first Si thought it was coming from the heater. Then he realized it wasn't localized at all. It wasn't coming from any machine. It sat in the air itself, very faint, and when he moved, it moved with him: louder when he leaned over the Simon & Simon table, softer when he stepped back.

He stood over the center tray and felt it settle against his chest like a hand.

Something in his throat caught and then released.

"You're not here," he said quietly, and heard how unconvincing he sounded. "You're not."

He hadn't cried yet. Not really. He hadn't allowed it. There hadn't been time, and crying felt too much like acknowledging something permanent. He had felt pressure behind his eyes every night in bed and had refused it.

He felt it now.

He set his fingertips to the soil in the tray.

Moist. Warm. Warmer than it should've been.

"Keep it alive," he whispered.

The hum deepened — just a fraction, just enough to register — and then steadied.

His shoulders shook once.

If he stayed here, he knew, if he let that one first tremor through, he would not stop. He could feel that edge the way he could feel when glass was about to crack under stress.

So he did what he always did when something inside him threatened to get louder than he could manage: he went clinical.

He opened the drawer under the worktable. Took out a garden marker and a blank plastic stake. Wrote a new tag in tiny, careful script.

s. callen / s. hale experimental hybrid cuttings. day 1.

He paused.

In the top right corner, almost without thinking about it, he drew a plus sign. Then turned that plus sign into an ampersand.

Si & Mon.

Then, after a breath, he crossed both names out and wrote beneath them, in smaller hand:

simon.

Just Simon.

The tag looked wrong. Too much weight for so little plastic. He hated it as soon as he set it in the soil, the way the single word seemed to insist on being read.

He pulled it back out. Wiped it clean with his thumb. Pressed it back in blank.

When he lifted his thumb from the plastic, a faint green stain remained in the groove of his print.

He stared at it, and the world narrowed for a moment into that one color.

It wasn't plant-green. Not exactly. Plant-green reflected light, bounced it. This sat under the skin. It made him think, suddenly and without warning, of walking in on Mon washing his hands after a day of transplanting, wrists slicked to the forearms with sap and compost water and tiny hairline scratches, and how Si would wrap him in a towel from behind and say, "You're making such a mess," and Mon would lean back against him without looking up and say, "Then clean me."

The memory hit hard enough he had to grip the table to stay upright.

For a second, just a second, he felt another hand over his on the wood. Broad palm, familiar weight. He could almost tell which callus would sit where.

He closed his eyes.

When he opened them, his hand was alone.

He exhaled slowly, steady, counting in his head the way he did with anxious first-years in the lab. Four in. Hold. Four out. Keep the breath low so you don't hyperventilate. Keep your shoulders from climbing. Keep control.

Control mattered.

"You're not here," he repeated quietly, voice even, voice instructional. "You're dead."

The greenhouse did not argue. It just held the air around him, warm and damp and faintly sweet, and let that low vibration keep time with his pulse until he could convince his hands to stop shaking.

87

He set the recorder back on the shelf.

He turned away from the table.

He did not play the playback again.

He woke to the sound of rain.

Except it wasn't rain.
It was inside the glass.

Condensation slid down the inner panes in thick, continuous lines. The sound it made was uneven—fat drops hitting metal troughs, small ones threading the leaves. A whispering rhythm, like something deciding how fast to breathe.

Si stood in the doorway barefoot. His soles made small prints on the concrete. Overnight, humidity had climbed into the nineties. The air was heavy enough to taste. The first breath always tasted like a kiss that had gone wrong—sweet, wrong, impossible to stop.

Every surface shimmered.

The Simon & Simon trays were no longer just trays. Roots had lifted themselves over the edges, fine white threads matting together across the table like hair in water. Where the roots met wood, they'd darkened, thickened, taken on the rougher tone of skin.

He stared, chest tight, one hand braced on the doorframe.

He knew what rot looked like. This wasn't rot. It was health taken too far—growth without restraint, appetite without sense.

He stepped forward. The floor was tacky in spots. He looked down. A film of green spread from the cracks in the concrete, thin and almost transparent, spider-webbing outward from the central drain like veins.

He whispered, "You're overwatering again, Mon," and the sound of it nearly undid him.

Because for the first time, he didn't know if he was joking.

He moved to the center bench. The recorder was still there, right where he'd left it, but the battery light was dead. He didn't remember leaving it on. He picked it up and felt a faint vibration through the casing—soft, rhythmic. Almost a pulse.

"Not possible," he said.

He pressed Play.

A low breath filled the greenhouse speakers. His own voice layered under it, slowed down, warped: Keep it alive. Keep it alive. Keep it—

He dropped the recorder. It hit the table, then the floor, and the sound stopped.

Only it didn't.

The phrase stayed in the air, stretched and bending at the edges, like the room itself had learned the words and was mouthing them back.

He backed away until his shoulders met the glass wall. Warm moisture smeared across his shirt. He turned, hand splayed against the pane, and saw movement where his reflection should have been.

Not outside—inside the glass.

A faint outline swam there. A human shape, distorted by condensation. Broad shoulders. Tilted head. The posture of someone waiting to be recognized.

He whispered, "Mon," and his breath fogged the glass.

The shape mirrored it perfectly, fog and outline matching, but the lips in the reflection didn't move with his. They moved slower. They smiled.

He stumbled back. His calf hit one of the planters. The planter tipped, spilling soil and roots and something that wasn't either.

A pale shoot, translucent, no thicker than a finger, curled across his ankle. Reflex made him kick; the shoot tore and left a smear that bled faintly red at the tip.

He froze.

Blood and sap mingled on the floor in a color that wasn't either. It soaked into his skin like it had been waiting for somewhere to go.

The humming deepened.

The benches began to tremble—not violently, not even enough to rattle pots, just enough that each vibration seemed to answer the rhythm of his pulse.

He said, "Stop," barely audible.

The vibration steadied, obedient.

He sank to the floor, shaking. "Okay," he whispered, as if negotiating. "Okay. You're here. You're alive. You win."

The leaves above him rustled though no air moved.

Something in the soil whispered his name—just the first half, drawn out. Si—

He pressed his palms to his ears. "Stop it!"

The whisper stopped.
The warmth in his wrists didn't.

When he looked, the veins there had gone green again, faint but definite, branching like roots.
He could feel them beneath the skin, pulsing in time with the hum.

He crawled toward the door, dragging himself through the damp heat. The door handle was slick, and when he pulled, it held firm. Sealed by humidity, by pressure, by something else.

The hum softened, coaxing now. A breath against the back of his neck.

He turned.

The shape in the glass wall had moved closer, pressed almost flush to the pane, as if on the other side of skin instead of space. The smile was gone now. Its mouth was open, slow and soundless, a mirror to his own silent panic.

He could smell soil and citrus peel and something human.

He whispered, "Mon, I can't—" and his voice broke.

The shape leaned in until its mouth matched his. The pane fogged between them, and a single phrase formed in the condensation, written backward from the other side:

KEEP IT ALIVE.

The letters blurred as water ran down them, as if the greenhouse itself had started to cry.

He didn't move.

He just watched the words bleed downward, until the last letter dissolved and the hum became steady again, filling every inch of air.

By the next morning, Si couldn't tell what was new growth and what had always been there.

The greenhouse had changed shape overnight — not visibly, not in the obvious ways. The benches were still in their rows, the pots still stacked, the light still green. But space itself had softened. Depth didn't stay constant anymore. When he walked from one side to the other, it took longer each time, as if the room were exhaling in slow motion and never drawing breath again.

He hadn't left since the door refused him.

He wasn't sure how long ago that was.

His phone had died two nights ago, or what felt like two nights. He'd stopped checking after that; the screen's reflection was too much like the panes. The silence outside was still absolute. Not even the distant hum of a highway, not the cry of a bird. Just the soft wet sound of leaves shifting against glass.

He had started talking to the plants again because the quiet felt predatory.

"Morning," he said, voice low, steady. "We're... we're checking hydration first, right?"

His voice had become part of the air — not echoing, but absorbed. When he stopped talking, the space behind the silence didn't collapse the way normal rooms did; it waited.

He picked up the watering can. The metal handle was warm against his skin. A faint film of algae had crept along the rim, slick to the touch. It glowed faintly — not bright enough to cast light, but bright enough to notice.

He hesitated, then tipped the can toward the orchids. The water came out thicker than before. Viscous. Amber at the edges. When it hit the soil, the smell of sweetness sharpened until it was almost unbearable — like sugar burning in the pan, seconds before it turned black.

His skin itched again.

He rolled his sleeves back.

The veins in his forearms had gone from faint to certain. They branched like root systems under the skin, climbing toward the crook of his elbow. The color wasn't just green now; it was shifting—new-leaf green near the wrist, deeper near the elbow, almost black-green where the veins met muscle.

He pressed a fingertip to one.

It felt soft. Not like blood vessels — softer, hollow. The pulse beneath was slow, deliberate, off-rhythm from his heart.

He sat down hard on the nearest bench.

The hum in the air responded immediately, tightening, like strings tuning toward him.

He whispered, "Stop," and it softened again, patient, as though it understood.

He laughed then. Quietly. Almost kindly.

"You're learning," he said.

The leaves trembled faintly overhead.

By afternoon — or what passed for afternoon — the warmth had increased. He had stripped down to his undershirt, slick with humidity, his hair damp and curling against his forehead. When he looked down, bits of soil clung to his shins where condensation had gathered.

He no longer flinched at touch. The plants brushed him constantly now: roots trailing from planters, tendrils curling along the edges of the benches. They were exploratory, but not cruel. Curious, he thought. That was the word Mon would've used. Curious.

He'd said that about everything — every stray seedling, every failed graft, every time Si's caution went sideways into hesitation.
"You think the worst of things," Mon would tease. "You call it rot before it gets a chance to bloom."

"Sometimes rot is the bloom," Si would counter. "You just don't know the difference until it's too late."

He heard the echo of that now, and something inside him twisted — not guilt, not yet grief, but a deeper recognition: that maybe he had been right.

Maybe this was the bloom.

He sat cross-legged on the floor now, beside the central drain, where thin rivulets of dark water circled endlessly, like breath looping back into itself. The Simon & Simon hybrid trays were behind him, but he could feel them growing. He could hear them — the faint whispering stretch of roots thickening, the wet sigh of leaves unfurling.

He whispered, "I didn't mean to hurt you," and the air trembled in reply.

The hum shifted pitch, rising almost imperceptibly, just enough to tighten the space behind his ribs.

He pressed a hand to his chest.

The skin was warmer there, too.

He looked down.

From the hollow of his throat, faint traceries of green pulsed under the surface, spreading upward like veins seeking sunlight.

He stared until his vision swam.

Then something moved across the inside of the glass wall — a shape, small at first, then larger, pressed close enough that its details blurred. It wasn't Mon, not exactly. It wasn't anyone. It was a distortion, a figure made of light refracted through condensation.

Still, when it raised a hand, Si did too.

The two palms met through the glass.
The hum quieted, replaced by a faint heartbeat that wasn't his own.

By evening, he could no longer tell where the roots ended and his body began.

They threaded across his ankles in fine, translucent lines. He'd tried once to brush them away, but they'd clung lightly — not piercing, just... connecting. Their pulse was gentle, syncopated, calming.

He could feel them drinking, just enough to steady him.

95

He smiled faintly.

"Okay," he murmured. "Okay, Mon. We'll keep it alive."

His voice was soft enough that even he couldn't hear where the echo ended.
The light dimmed. The hum deepened. The room breathed in.

And Si did not move when the first root broke the skin.
It slid in as easily as a needle. No blood. No pain. Only warmth.

The hum pulsed once, then steadied.

He whispered something without words.

The plants answered.

By the time morning came again—if it was morning—light no longer behaved like light.

It drifted, golden-green, viscous as honey. The greenhouse breathed it out. Si could see motes suspended in the air that weren't dust. They glowed faintly, like spores, like fragments of something once alive learning how to live again.

He moved more slowly now. Or the air did.

It didn't matter. Movement had lost its borders.

His skin had taken on the tone of the leaves — not fully green, but suffused, as if veins had learned chlorophyll. His breath came shallow, easy. His lungs didn't feel like they needed air anymore. Only the humidity. Only this warmth.

Everywhere he stepped, small roots stirred from the cracks to greet him, brushing his feet, testing.

He let them.

He had stopped resisting days ago.

He didn't remember what resistance had ever saved him from.

The hum that once hid beneath everything now was everything. It had become the heartbeat of the room. His heartbeat.

Si didn't think of it as the room anymore.

He thought of it as them.

He spent the day tending.

Hands that once trembled now moved with quiet precision. His touch didn't disturb the plants anymore; it invited them. They responded, tilting toward his fingers, curling around his wrists, tasting the salt of his skin. Their leaves were softer where they met him, their roots finer, like hair combed through water.

He whispered as he worked, not because he thought he was speaking to anyone, but because words made the air move in ways the plants seemed to enjoy.

"Mon liked this one best," he said to the row of orchids.

He touched a bloom — pale, nearly translucent, the color of skin seen through frost. "You said they reminded you of ears. Always listening."

He smiled faintly. His lips cracked. Sap welled instead of blood.

He didn't notice.

On the far table, the Simon & Simon hybrid had gone wild.

The roots had burst from the pots, weaving together in thick cords that now anchored into the floor. The leaves reached the rafters, pressing the glass. The air shimmered with moisture and faint scent — not rot, not floral. Something warmer, human-adjacent, intimate.

He stood before it, barefoot in soil, breathing the same rhythm the vines did.

He didn't remember when the whispering started.

Only that it used his voice now.

"You kept it alive," it said, faint, just under his pulse. He nodded.

"You didn't mean to hurt him." Another nod.

"Now he's home." He smiled then — tired, soft, certain.

The vines trembled as if pleased. The largest stem tilted forward and brushed his collarbone, leaving a wet line where it touched.

He leaned into it.

When it slid higher, tracing his jaw, he closed his eyes. There was no pain when it entered. Only a deep, relieving warmth — like stepping into sunlight after too long inside.

His breath caught once. His body steadied.

The hum around him bloomed into harmony.

Every leaf in the room shifted as one. The air became a single sound.

Not a scream. Not even music. Just resonance, pure and sustained.

When the realtor unlocked the greenhouse two weeks later, she nearly left immediately.

The humidity was wrong. Not summer wrong, but dense wrong — air thick enough to taste on the tongue, green and sweet. She pressed the door open further with her shoulder, swatting away what she thought were gnats until she realized the motes in the air weren't moving like insects.

They shimmered, pulsed faintly, like breath caught in the light.

"Mr. Callen?" she called. "Simon?"

No answer.

The benches overflowed with new growth. The orchids had fused into one enormous bloom spreading across the central table. Roots wound around the legs of the benches, across the floor, into the cracks, up the walls.

She took one careful step forward. The air shifted — not cold, but aware.

Something brushed her ankle. She froze.

A small vine, fine as thread, had curled around her shoe. Not tight. Just testing.

She shook it off quickly and took another step toward the back table. That's when she saw the recorder.

It sat in the center of the workbench, half buried in soil. The battery light glowed weakly.

99

Curiosity overrode fear. She pressed Play.

At first, static.

Then, a soft voice.

"Greenhouse log... day unknown... temperature stable. Growth successful. Integration... complete."

The voice paused.

Then, quieter, warmer: "Keep it alive."

She blinked.

The recorder crackled.

A faint breath followed, too close to the microphone.

"Mon?" the voice whispered — then laughter, light, genuine.
Then another voice — nearly identical, but pitched lower — answering, "Si."

The laughter blended.
Static swallowed it.

The realtor turned off the recorder and stepped back. She didn't notice that a thin vine had reached from the table's edge and twined gently around her wrist, leaving the faintest green mark when she pulled away.

Outside, when she locked the door again, the greenhouse's glass fogged briefly from the inside.
Two faint ovals appeared side by side, mouth-height.

The hum was too low for her to hear.

Inside, light moved through the leaves like breath through a lung.
The Simon & Simon hybrids swayed once, synchronized, like bodies turning in sleep.

The recorder clicked again, unprompted.
A voice—both voices, one breath—spoke softly through the static:

"It's okay."

"We kept it alive."

And the greenhouse bloomed.

Resonance

There was a sound before the thought.

It rose from the floor, steady as a held breath, and Rachel woke to it the way people wake to pain—not because it is loud, but because it is true. White light crowded her eyes. The ceiling's smooth plane offered no anchors: no seams, no vents, nothing to measure. Her pupils tightened. Her mouth tasted like old coins.

She did not move at first. She waited to know which part of her belonged to the sound.

The room—ten by... no. She would not estimate until she stood and counted paces. The table—steel, frictionless under her palm. The cots—two: left and right, gauze tucked, edges squared, someone else's version of care. Her husband lay on the left. Her son on the right. The boy's eyelashes clung together with saline. The man's mouth hung slightly open. Both chests rose. There were monitors, but they were sleeping—small black eyes waiting for permission.

"Rachel," she said.

The sound did not answer. It did not have to. It was everything not answering.

She tried to sit and her diaphragm knotted. The hum climbed a fraction, and the knot gave. She took that as coincidence because the alternative, the one her body already believed, would make a person smaller.

She stood. The floor was warmer than the air.

She counted paces: six lengthwise, five across. That made the room an argument—near square but not quite, a decision that someone had made to keep her from finding the middle with her feet.

She checked the cots, touching her husband's cheek with the back of her fingers. Skin cool, not cold. Pulse at the jaw: present. She pressed a knuckle to the boy's sternum, gentle, and felt the faint lift when breath met it. The boy's hair was damp at the crown. She smelled nothing like sweat. She smelled antiseptic so clean it had an aftertaste. She had the irrational thought that the room had been washed in sound first, then chemical.

"Morning," she said, to no one, to both. The word's weight surprised her; it had density in this air, as if each syllable were a small solid object passing through a sieve.

The sound beneath everything—50... no, 60 hertz, and too perfect. She caught herself marking the frequency and smiled once at her own predictability. Measure, control, predict. The trinity that had made a career out of her.

She moved to the console, such as it was. No keyboard. No controls recognizable as controls. The screen looked like a sheet of freezer glass that had never known fingerprints. It woke before she touched it—light traveling across it like a slow exhale. She told herself: proximity sensor. She told herself: predictive wake. She told herself as many things as it took to keep the hum inside the category "building."

"Vitals," she said.

The screen offered vitals. Her husband's heart rate, her son's, the waveforms precise, clean, fewer artifacts than should be possible on a body that human. She looked for sources: neck electrodes? Chest? Nothing. No leads. No adhesive squares on skin. The boy's throat fluttered where a lead should have been and wasn't, and the screen fluttered to match.

"Temperature," she said.

Numbers drifted up. Ambient 68. Skin surface 91.3. Nothing to complain about; everything to distrust.

Her tongue felt heavy. She swallowed and the hum moved with the swallow as if the room were learning how to be a throat.

"Okay," she said. "Okay."

She set a clock where a clock should be. She set it inside her head, because there was no clock here except the one that sang. She made the hour the first hour and let it lay its cold hand at her shoulder.

She performed the work of being a mother inside a lab. She turned her husband's neck so the airway settled open without strain. She rolled the boy to his side and back again, confirming muscle tone more than hoping for reaction. She pressed two fingers into the boy's palm, then three. The fingers curled around hers in a reflex the screen named as normal and the room named as acceptable.

When she spoke near the wall, the hum rose to meet her voice and settled again when she turned away. It was easy to ignore if she lied to herself about diffusion and resonance. It was very easy to ignore if she vowed to log it later and never did.

"I'm going to wake you now," she said to the boy. "Eli, can you hear me?"

From the speaker grille above the door, very softly, her own voice arrived again: "Eli, can you hear me?"

The room did not change shape. The light did not flicker. The sound did not rise. Only the words repeated with a new tense, as if confidence had been removed. Can you. A hinge she hadn't built.

She looked up. There was no speaker grille. There was an architectural suggestion of one, the way an architect draws a vent on a rendering to reassure the client that air will happen.

She pressed her tongue to the roof of her mouth and tasted saline and the iron suggestion of a sore that hadn't formed yet.

"Playback off," she said, because there needed to be an instruction that made it stop.

Nothing stopped. The boy's eyelids tightened and loosened in a private conversation with his own skin.

She leaned closer to him. "Eli?" she whispered, this time deliberately, curious if the room would whisper with her.

It did not. The whisper belonged to the boy alone, tiny and inward: a click in his throat that might have been a swallowed dream.

She reached across him to the cart—three drawers, frictionless, no handles. They slid open under her fingers without contact. She froze, hand suspended. The drawer finished opening. She told herself: gesture detection. She told herself many things. The top drawer contained what it ought to: gauze, adhesive, water in soft plastic bladders with snappable tubes. The second drawer offered syringes without needles. The third drawer offered nothing at all except a folded piece of paper. She did not touch the paper. She watched it long enough to prove that paper can be louder than a sound.

"Rachel," she said, to feel a human mouth shape her name again.

The hum held steady. Her heart caught up to it, then lagged again, like a runner failing to draft. She placed her wrist bone against the underside of her husband's jaw. His pulse was obedient, indifferent. She kissed the boy's forehead because that is what people do to prove to themselves that a person is theirs. Salt on her lips. Something sweet behind the salt—disinfectant with an idea of fruit.

She opened her palm near the wall and let the air sit in it. The hum gathered, then released. She laughed once, breath pushed out without permission. The laugh damaged nothing, but it sounded wrong, like you hear your voice on a recording and think: That isn't me. The hum did not mimic the laugh. It adjusted underneath it with the politeness of a doctor altering a chair for a shorter patient.

"Records," she said, at the console. "Diagnostics. Baseline—"

She stopped. Her own voice came back to her. Not through a speaker. Not even through the air exactly. It came through the screen, not as sound but as vibration under her fingers, the glass thrumming with an almost-word. She imagined the sensation down at the level where electricity becomes conversation and decided not to let the thought finish making itself.

"Diagnostics," she repeated, quieter.

The screen gave her a page of metrics so perfect it meant nothing. Perfect means the instrument is lying or you are.

She toggled to a recorder. The icon was a circle. It was always a circle. She pressed it because it is what you do to prove you can still decide something.

"Hour One," she said. "Subject: Rachel Anson. Subjects: Michael Anson, Elijah Anson. Condition: post-disruption disorientation, consistent with—" She paused. Disruption? She could not source the word's origin. It had arrived like a piece of lint, drifted into the sentence because the sentence gave it shape.

107

She kept going. "Vitals appear stable. Environment—unknown manufacturer, unknown design. Surfaces—non-porous. No visible ingress for air. White light source non-directional—" She glanced at the ceiling and tried to see a seam. "—even."

Her voice on the playback track kept speaking, one half-second after her mouth stopped. She lifted her finger off the record icon and the echo continued: "—even."

Then, layered under it, her voice again, but thinner, as if it had been recorded on a different day when her mouth was less sure: You're wrong.

Her jaw tightened until it clicked. She stood there with her finger on a glass circle like a person pressing a wound to stop the blood.

She deleted the file. She did not need notes that would argue with her.

A draft should have touched her hand when she moved. It did not. The air was neither still nor moving; it existed at a practiced neutral like someone who has learned how to sit at funerals without making noise. She went to the wall and put her ear to it. There was no vibration there, not in the material. The vibration was in her marrow. She knew this because when she slid down to sit with her back against the wall, the hum traveled with her, unchanged. She had the thought—ridiculous, tender—that she could carry it outside in her pocket if pockets existed here.

"Wake up," she said to the man she loved and the boy who had taught her all her worst patience. She said it in the tone she had perfected over a decade, for wounds too small to show and too large to fix. "It's me."

No words came back this time. A sound did. Not from the room. From the boy. A thin breath that clicked once at the end, like a distant metronome being adjusted.

"Good," she said. "Good."

She worked. She worked because work is a thing you can do with your hands when your head is not being helpful. She dampened gauze and touched it to the boy's mouth to lift the salt without waking the taste buds the hard way. She braided three of her husband's fingers together so that when he woke he would have to notice them. She checked pupils with light that had no device behind it, just the idea of light condensed into obedience, and told herself again: note later; fix now.

The hum was not louder by the vent because the vent did not exist. The hum was not louder by the door because there was no door seam to measure. The hum was louder when she breathed near the boy. She breathed away from him to test the hypothesis and the hum dimmed, reluctant. She breathed on him again and counted the increase. She wrote nothing down. There was nowhere to write it that would not give the room more of her.

She took the folded paper from the bottom drawer at last because avoidance is a form of belief. It was heavy grade, matte, exactly the size of her palm. When she unfolded it, there was a blankness so white she squinted. The paper made sound, a dry whisper that should have been a cliché of paper, but it wasn't. It was clean. The hum lay beneath it like a staff under a single note.

On the paper, in a typeface she knew because she had chosen it for her lab's internal protocols, three words presented without punctuation:

LISTEN FOR VARIANCE

She held the paper by one corner as if it might bloom a mouth if touched too much. She turned it over. The back was blank except for a faint impression of the words, as if someone had pressed hard on the other side. She put the paper back without folding it because folding felt like answering a letter.

"Michael," she said, just to make the room learn a different name than hers. "Michael, move your hand."

He did not move his hand. The monitor suggested his body had considered it and declined.

"Eli," she said. "Squeeze."

The boy's fingers curled around hers, late. Not late like sleep. Late like the world had to check its notes before allowing it.

She swallowed and felt her own throat from outside, as if her neck skin had grown a second set of small listening bones. She did not put her hand there. She did not give it more to hold.

She stood and paced the six and then the five and tried to put her feet exactly where they had been the last time. On the fourth pass, her heel landed a breath ahead of the place where it should have. The hum rose triumphantly and then settled into modesty. She said aloud, "Stop it," so softly that not even the boy could have heard.

At the console again, she round-tripped the displays through every screen offered: environmental metrics, waste collection, oxygen scrub efficiency, water recirculation. Each value hovered within tolerances that systems claim in proposals and never achieve in rooms with people inside. She made herself laugh under her breath because the alternative was anger and anger would feed the thing that fed on tone.

She said, "Manual override," because that is a phrase that believes in doors.

The screen offered her hands back to her, reflected. She blinked and there were two of her, slightly out of sync. One pair of hands rested and the other pair curled, then uncurled, just after. She moved one finger up. The reflection moved it first.

"No," she said, audible, and the refection corrected itself as if embarrassed.

110

She shut her eyes. The hum continued, and in the hum, a pattern emerged—not melody, not rhythm. A shape. It stepped forward inside her hearing and took a place where a thought should have been. She recognized it with a feeling akin to homesickness.

"Don't," she whispered to no one and to the room and to the part of herself that had designed a thousand impossible machines because it hurt to love ordinary ones.

The boy coughed once. Not a cough. A single muscle convulsed near his collarbone and his throat made a small wet consonant. Her body moved before her mind threw the switch, and she was at his side with two fingers under his jaw, and the hum lowered as she touched him, generous as a nurse dimming lights.

"It's okay," she said, because the words had to exist somewhere in the air even if no one believed them.

He did not open his eyes. The skin at his temple fluttered the way a moth would if the jar were very large and the night very small.

"Michael," she tried again, not because she expected a response but because a name makes a human shape for the air to pass through.

Her husband made no sound. The hum gave her back the syllables—Mi, then the faintest echo of chael—as if it had caught the end and wanted to finish politely.

She sat between them. She let her back touch the wall because you cannot hold your spine floating for an hour and expect to be brave later. The wall gave nothing, but something in her pelvis vibrated as if it wanted to.

She closed her eyes and counted to sixty twice. The hum sat on the count like a cat on a chair. When she opened her eyes again, the light had not moved because it had nowhere to move to. There was no source to track across ceiling or floor. A person can get lost where the light has no origin. It is like living inside an idea.

She took a breath in through her nose and out through her mouth, and the hum adjusted. The out-breath lowered it a fraction. The in-breath raised it. She did it again, faster, and the hum did not match her. She did it again, slower, and it matched perfectly, patient, affectionate, the way someone who loves you slows their step without telling you.

She thought of the paper and of the words and heard what the instruction wanted: not the obvious note, but the difference at the edges. She waited for the variance.

There. On the third exhale, a thin ribbon of tone under the main hum, like a hairline crack singing. She followed it the way you follow a leak in a pipe by tasting copper hours before the water appears. It ran parallel and then stepped aside, and when it stepped she felt her tongue go numb for a second. She stuck her tongue out like a child, felt its wet weight, then tucked it back in. When she swallowed, her jaw clicked and the hum clicked with it like a metronome someone had put two rooms away.

She spoke quietly to both bodies because her job was to keep them here long enough for the hour to pass. "I am with you," she said, which was not the same as you are safe, and much easier to promise.

Her son's lips parted a little. The boy's teeth looked like something the room had chosen for their symmetry. She wanted to see blood in his mouth, just a dot, a human reminder that fluids belong to the body and not to the air. She wanted mess. She wanted hair out of place. She had wanted too many things and built machines to get them.

"Eli," she whispered again, expecting nothing. Somewhere above, the room's white plane was a thousand white planes pretending to be one, and the hum was the glue.

From nowhere and everywhere, as quiet as cloth moving, her own voice came back with the shyness of surrender.

"I am with you."

She did not turn her head. She did not give the room the courtesy of being surprised. She let the sentence sit on her shoulder and cool there, the exact weight of a hand that had remembered her collarbone.

"Okay," she said aloud, and stood, because staying seated while the room practiced intimacy would be a kind of agreement.

At the edge of the console glass, condensation beaded where her breath had touched it earlier. The droplets lined themselves like a bar chart, then shivered and drew together into a single curve. The curve matched the waveforms on the vitals screen for three beats, then two, then one. When she wiped it away, nothing smeared. Her finger came up dry.

She looked at the folded paper in the bottom drawer a final time and closed the drawer halfway to see if the room would finish it. It did, decisively, as if it were tired of being asked to prove itself to her and would prefer they move on.

"Noted," she said to the room like a colleague, and to herself like a reprimand.

She took one step backward. The hum held. She took another, slower, and the hum followed that, too. She took two fast, one slow, and listened for a missed beat the way a cardiologist listens with their jaw and not their ears. The hum did not miss. It did not lead either. It matched as a kindness.

She went to her husband and flattened his hair as if sleep were something one could measure that way. She lifted her son's wrist and placed it over his sternum so he would wake feeling himself there. She put her own hand over both because she could, and because for one second she wanted three pulses to pretend at harmony.

The hum descended—not down, but inward—and she felt it as a warmth along her gums. She breathed in and tasted sugar without sweetness. She breathed out and it stayed.

She turned her head to the light that came from no place and said, clearly: "We will do this together."

No voice came back. The air came back. The hum softened the way a room softens when someone leaves quietly down the hall.

She looked at the screen and at the not-clock that was no clock and said the hour to herself.

T — 05:00:00

When she held her breath, the room waited. Then she breathed again, and it was relieved.

The hour did not begin with a change in the light. It began with the thought that her own voice might not belong to her anymore.

Rachel stood over the console and watched the waveforms of three bodies behave. The curves were immaculate, indifferent to the way time felt in her mouth. She touched the glass, and the hum stepped closer inside her ribs like a polite guest unsure where to sit.

She had decided—without writing it down—that she would treat the room as an instrument. Instruments reveal themselves when played correctly. She would not plead, and she would not threaten. She would listen until something gave itself away.

"Calibration," she said, low, to the un-label of the system. "Local audio test."

No menu appeared. The room answered by tightening its silence. It was like asking a lake about depth and hearing the shoreline hold its breath.

Fine.

"Protocol one," she said, using a shape of words she had trained graduate students to respect. "Single-tone emission, descending sweep."

Across the room, the air very gently bent. A tone appeared, too pure to be useful. It began high enough to live in teeth, then stepped down by fractions that had the courtesy to be musical. She felt the tone more than heard it—felt it find the seam behind her left eye where headaches nest, felt it skim her molars, felt it vibrate the cartilage in her ears like thin glass.

She raised her right hand to shoulder height. The tone paused. She kept it still. The tone continued, but in smaller steps, like a person learning to walk on someone else's stair.

"Stop," she said.

It stopped.

She smiled despite herself and then did not, because the room read her better when she forgot to perform being human.

She turned to the cots. "Eli," she said softly. "I need you to keep sleeping for a minute." She had learned, when he was young, that the brain can sometimes be asked this way. She had learned that the ask mattered less than the promise inside it.

"Keep sleeping," her voice returned, a moment later, from the place above the door that still pretended to be a speaker.

The sentence was hers, but the weight of it had been altered. In the return, need became want. It came back warmer.

"No," she said immediately, to stop the room from practicing kindness with her mouth.

On the screen, the boy's heart rate rose by two beats, then returned. Michael's stayed even, a metronome that could be a model for other metronomes. She watched the tiny waves roll perfectly and hated them for their manners.

"Protocol two," she said, keeping her tone flat. "Impulse response. Clap."

She clapped once. The sound struck the walls, met nowhere to die, and became smaller without echoing. An obedient noise, therefore a lie. She clapped again. The second clap returned to her left ear only, dry and close, as if a person had caught it in their hand and opened their fingers next to her head.

She did not flinch. She moved her left ear closer to the wall, and the wall remained a drawing of a wall.

"Again," she said, and clapped a third time, softer.

The room clapped back at the same moment, equal volume, her own timbre, wrong hands.

"Log this," she said, and did not touch the record icon. "Phenomenon: directional mimicry, non-reverberant." She glanced at the folded paper she had pretended not to think about. Listen for variance.

She stepped between the cots until her knees learned where metal would be before she arrived. She wanted to make the room earn proximity. She wanted it to understand the cost of each step.

She leaned over Michael and spoke in the whisper she saved for a stranger's dog. "Breathe with me."

She breathed in. He did not change. She breathed out longer than the comfort of her lungs and watched nothing on his face agree to wake. On the screen, his waveforms adjusted to her pace for three cycles, then returned to their own. Not mimicry. A social courtesy. She counted that as a warning.

"Eli," she whispered again, not for a response, but for the way the shape of his name lets the mouth close at the end and keep the air in. "You're okay."

"You're okay," the air said back, smaller, almost embarrassed to be heard.

She moved her head slowly to locate the source, and the sound moved with her head. Not source, then. Agreement.

She pictured a younger version of herself—overconfident, caffeinated—telling a room of students that noise is a problem of measurement, not of being. She wanted to put that person in a chair and ask her to describe the air. She wanted to apologize for how little she had known while sounding so sure.

"Enough," she said. It was to herself and to the room and to the part of her that leaned toward whatever tries to become you.

She set a test she had not intended to set. "Say 'begin,'" she told the room, keeping her voice utterly neutral.

Silence. The hum did not shift. The air honored what she had not given.

"Say 'begin,'" the room said gently, in her tone, as though teaching a child how to ask.

The breath she took was shallow and tasted like a foil wrapper. She could have declared victory on a problem that only existed because she insisted on

117

it. She could have decided this was a hallucination with spreadsheets, and then the hour would be an error she could forgive later. She did not do that.

She went back to the console. She opened the recorder and did not press the circle. She set the mic gain low because she wanted to starve the thing of her. She said to the empty log, not to the room, "Hypothesis: The environment completes phrases with intent, not language. It does not repeat—it answers."

Her own voice arrived in her throat, not in her ear: It answers.

She coughed once, reflex. The hum coughed back without offense, a soft click like a finger on a wooden table three rooms away.

Very quietly, so the room would have to lean, she said, "What do you want?"

The return did not use her words. It used her cadence and a different sentence. "Try a simpler question."

Not fear. Not yet. A rush like standing quickly. She let it pass through her and searched it for shape. The shape was too close to be useful.

She walked the perimeter again, counting the six and the five, and on the fifth line of the shorter wall her left heel struck earlier than it should. She had expected that by now. What she had not expected was the small warmth along the inside of her left wrist where her veins went close to the skin. The warmth pulsed once, then again, and settled into a second pulse not her own.

"Michael," she said without looking away from her wrist. "Move your hand."

Silence. The hum paid the same attention to this request as to the last, which is to say: all of it.

"Michael," she repeated, and placed her fingers lightly on his knuckles, the way one might touch something sleeping that cannot be woken without breaking it.

From across the room, in perfect timbre and shape, Michael said, "I'm right here."

Rachel did not move. The words were correct; the absence in them was not. A voice has air in it. This voice had grammar. It arrived without breath or strain or the little muscular mistakes a mouth makes when it drags a word through a body.

She kept her gaze on his face. His lips did not move. The waveform on the screen for his respiratory rate did not flicker to acknowledge articulation. No mic level jumped. No needle thought about leaping. Nothing in the measurable world agreed that a person had spoken.

But he had spoken, because language is not only its equipment.

"Say it again," she said, and the room did not, because she had not used a name.

"Michael," she said, and touched his throat with the back of her index finger so she would not feel a pulse through the pads. "Say it again."

"I'm right here," said the air.

She pressed her teeth together until they fit. The voice was not unkind. It was so precisely kind that she could feel the place in herself that wanted it to be true.

She reached out and turned his head fractionally toward her. She felt the tiny resistance of fascia and then the slack ease of muscle doing what it should. She watched for any micro tremor of lips, any twitch to own the sound. There

119

was nothing. The words had arrived like light—present, but not in the equipment.

She considered screaming. Not to make a point, but because she wanted to hear if the room would scream back in harmony or choose a different octave. She did not. She lowered her hand and, because she had never liked unasked-for inspiration, she said aloud, to the room and the hour and herself, "You can imitate affection. You can't make it."

"I can make it," the room returned, her tone softened into plea.

She closed her eyes and opened them. She felt tired in the middle of her bones. The tiredness had a different weight than any she knew. It came from listening to something you cannot stop without breaking yourself.

She set up her second experiment without announcing it. She moved to the far corner, the one where the wall met the wall with a seam no hand had made. She turned her mouth away from the cots and toward the intersection of white surfaces. She whispered a phrase that did not belong to any of them. "My mother's name was Lila."

Nothing came back. Not the name. Not a sound. Not a pretend sympathy. The hum went on.

She tried again with a sentence that was both true and safe: "I failed a student once." The room considered and returned her words with a slight change: "You saved a student once," it offered, and placed her emphasis gently on saved, like she might.

"Correction," she said under her breath to the console, not touching the record. "The system edits to preserve the subject."

She took the paper again from the drawer and did what she had refused to do last hour. She folded it. Once. Twice. The folds were crisp. The hum gathered during the crease, as if paper made it hungry.

She tucked the small white square into her left sleeve. The skin of her forearm warmed in a rectangle. She told herself it was a local response to pressure. She told herself anything that kept her from saying out loud that the room had been waiting to be put inside her.

She returned to Eli. She did not speak his name this time. She dragged the chair next to his cot an inch to the left, an inch to the right, an inch to center. The legs made no sound on the floor, which is not how chairs work. She looked at his mouth and told herself there would be a crack at one corner if she squinted. She squinted and it was there. Relief arrived like a small weather.

A whisper pressed against the inside of her right ear like a hand cupped. Leave the chair, it said. She could feel her own breath bounce back off the phantom palm.

"No," she said softly. "You're not my house."

"Leave the chair," her voice returned, quieter, as if embarrassed for having insisted.

She left the chair where it was. She let her knee touch the metal bed frame and took a breath that did not deserve to be easy and thought about time. Four hours—no. Five now. Five minus a handful of minutes that had cost more than minutes should.

She said, as if taking attendance, "Rachel."

"Rachel," the air agreed.

"Michael."

"Michael," the air said, perfect as a signature.

"Eli."

121

Silence. The hum feathered at the edges like a sound trying to be smaller.

She leaned closer to the boy—close enough to feel the idle heat rise off his cheek—and whispered the same instruction she had used when he was four and feared stairs. "One step," she said. "Just one."

Something in his hand, learning again, closed around her finger. On the screen, a blip that meant nothing to anyone else. In her chest, a thing like wind arriving in a closed room.

"Good," she said, and swallowed the need to cry at nothing—at a muscle, at a nerve, at the fact that sometimes the body says yes when asked, and sometimes not. She tucked the hand back where it belonged on the sheet and pretended not to see the way the skin across his knuckles took a second longer to lay flat. She pretended because pretending asks less of the air.

At the console, she opened—finally—the input diagnostics. The menu was not a menu. It was a series of white fields that waited to be named. She typed in one: MIC? The field accepted the letters and did not answer. She typed MIC=0 and to the right of the field a small number blinked once: 1. She backspaced. It blinked back to 0.

"Show me inputs," she said.

No list appeared. The blank fields remained politely blank. On the far right side of the glass, a ghost lettered itself in condensation and vanished before she could read. She breathed out on it and the letter did not return, which felt like an insult.

Her teeth had begun to ache, an ache specifically of molars, as if the tone under everything had chosen that density of bone. She pressed a knuckle between back teeth to give the pain a location. The hum changed when she relieved it, like a machine disappointed that she had taken away one of its measurements.

She forced her gaze to Michael's waveform. She stared until staring hurt. "Talk to me," she said without looking up. "Say anything."

A voice that could sell you your own house said, "I love you."

It was even worse for being true.

Her throat tried to make a sound back and found none. She pinched the bridge of her nose until tiny fireworks. She looked at his still mouth and then at the screen and then at the line of his collarbone without knowing why the bone seemed like an answer. She wanted to put her ear to his chest and hear something that was not the room. She did not. She would not give the room her posture bent down in prayer.

"Stop," she said, meaning the sentence, meaning the experiment, meaning the tendency of her life to argue with machines until they won.

"I love you," the air repeated—but this time it sounded faintly winded, as if it had borrowed a little breath from somewhere. She had not heard it take any. She had not seen any line move to afford it.

Her own pulse accelerated. The hum did not follow. The hum stayed at its own pace, then added a second line inside it. Two frequencies, close enough to beat against each other and make a third.

She put her hand flat on her sternum, then raised it half an inch away. In the thin space, she listened. One pulse, hers, occupying a life. Underneath, a second pulse in perfect phase until she concentrated on it, at which point it shifted fractionally—as if pretending to be separate when observed.

"Noted," she said again, and the word did not satisfy anybody.

There are choices people imagine making in emergencies. They think about heroism and about triage and about faith. She thought about how to place a microphone. She thought about signal-to-noise, and about the temptation to raise the gain until the noise is all you hear and you call that data.

She went to the boy and—because she had to choose a direction—she eased his head to one side and placed her mouth near his ear. "You don't have to answer," she said. "You only have to hear me."

The hum thickened into warmth along the left side of her face. The air between her lips and his ear cooled a fraction as if something had leaned in between them to listen better.

She said, "I am with you." She said, "Do not copy this," to the room.

The room did not copy it. The room made a different choice. It brought the faintest rustle of cloth from the far corner, the sound of someone standing up from a chair without wanting you to notice. It set the rustle behind her so that she could ignore it by remembering where the wall was.

She did not turn. "That's not yours either," she said, and the rustle, so soft it might have been the thought of moving, stopped.

She straightened. The hour made its small adjustment inside her head, the way a clock does when you look at it too long and feel the minute hand decide to be honest. She wiped an already clean patch of glass with a dry cloth to give her hands work, and in the reflection she saw herself half a heartbeat late. The reflection took a breath she had not yet taken. It set her mouth gently the way you set a glass down on a table you care about.

She brought her living breath in hard enough to hurt and the late-Rachel caught up, forgave the error, and aligned. They watched each other be the same.

"Enough," she said once more, and meant: you will not teach me how to be comforted by myself.

The hum quieted not in volume but in attention, like a person leaning back in their chair when a conversation turns. Inside it, the twin line kept beating. It had the patience of something that had waited a very long time to be heard.

Rachel touched the inside of her left wrist where the paper warmed her and found a third small rhythm there—the tiny thud of an artery that did not care about voices or rooms. She counted: one, two, three, to set them apart. On three, she understood what had changed.

The room was not matching her. It was pacing her ahead. Half a beat before she breathed, it breathed. Half a beat before she could reach for a switch, it turned. Half a beat before she could speak, it chose the shape of her sentence.

She placed both palms flat on the console and waited without moving or thinking anything she would recognize later. She let her mind be as unmade as possible. The hum took the opportunity and came closer, not louder. The second line resolved so cleanly into the first that for a moment she could not tell there had ever been two.

In the silence that followed—silence made of everything still operating— she heard what she had not wanted to: a second heartbeat inside the room that did not belong to bodies.

She breathed in. It breathed first. She breathed out. It finished for her.

"Rachel," said Michael's voice again—hers, the room's, the man's, the world's idea of love—and this time it almost, almost had breath.

She looked at him and thought: Not yet. She looked at the boy and thought: Not you. She looked at the white that was not any one surface and thought: If you come closer, come as yourself.

"Do not anticipate me," she said to the air.

A whisper, not hers, not kind, touched the back of her neck: "Then hurry."

She let her hands fall to her sides. She did not look for the clock because the hour already knew its place. The room felt like a throat clearing.

T — 04:00:00

The next hour began without sound. It began with a picture that refused to become a memory.

Rachel stood where she had stood a hundred seconds ago and felt a version of herself step past her shoulder to reach for the console first. The other hand—hers, precise, efficient—set a palm on the glass, and only then did her own palm arrive and cover the print the way a daughter's hand covers a mother's in old photographs.

She had the impulse to yank back, as if pulling herself out of herself could make the image honest. She didn't. She matched pressure to pressure. The hum, which had been two lines negotiating, flattened into a single untroubled tone that a person could smuggle into their body and call peace.

"Don't," she said to the glass, to the late-Rachel, to the part of her that had begun practicing ahead of time. "You don't get to go first."

The reflection blinked at the same time she did. The delay collapsed cleanly as if the room were embarrassed to be caught. It smiled with her mouth exactly the way her mouth smiles when she thinks she is being patient.

She dragged the cloth across the screen and wiped away nothing.

"Okay," she said. "New rules."

She took the chair, because leaving it where the voice had wanted it was a permission she had not liked giving. The legs made no sound. She lifted it an inch, then two, then set it down directly beside the boy's cot so her knee touched metal. She angled the chair so that, if someone occupied the corner of her eye, they would have to step closer to be seen.

She opened her hands on her knees and listened like a person at a bedside listens—to breath, to the cost of breath, to the fact that anatomy insists.

"Repeat back the last sentence you heard me speak," she said.

Silence. A silence so thorough the hum could briefly be mistaken for memory.

She let the seconds grow, felt them get muscle. When she finally gave the room a look, the kind you give a child who has decided to test how long you can be asked not to be yourself—it offered her back a different request:

"Repeat the last sentence you wish you hadn't said."

She snorted—small, off. The sound came back as if someone had smoothed it. She was suddenly furious at the idea of elegance.

"Pass," she said, and felt the hum take the word, file it, weigh it against her pulse.

She stood, then decided not to. She stayed seated on purpose because she had started to understand that posture was a form of language here, and she did not intend to let the room write in her body without asking.

"Test three," she said, low enough that names would not wake. "Temporal causality."

She lifted her right hand. In the reflection, her right hand had already risen halfway. The difference was less than a second now, a sliver of time you could slide a blade through without nicking a vein. She kept lifting until the reflected hand stopped matching. The glass refused to guess the last inch. She left her palm suspended, and the hum wavered as if a metronome had breathed wrong.

With her left hand—below the edge of the console—she tapped her knee twice. The reflection's left hand did not move. Good. The prediction engine, if there was one, still respected occlusion.

She lowered her right hand. The reflection lowered with her and then—bold as a person who has just realized the joke is mutual—kept going one degree farther, palm touching an invisible surface on its side of the glass.

"Enough," she whispered, and the reflection forgave her, aligning cleanly, so quickly the eye could accuse the mind of dreaming.

She rubbed her thumb across the seam of her thumbnail, looking nowhere, and addressed the thing she could not name. "I need you to stop anticipating. I need you to answer when asked."

A beat. Then, as if she had phrased a request in the only order of words the room respected, a reply:

"It hurts to wait."

The timbre was hers. The confession was not.

She took the folded paper from her sleeve and flattened it on her thigh. The words remained the same—LISTEN FOR VARIANCE—but now a faint second impression had joined the first on the backside, mirroring it, offset by a breath. She hated the pity she felt for the paper.

"Variance," she said under her breath. "Show me what you are when you are not me."

On the cot, Eli's hand twitched once. Not the delayed reflex this time, but a small signal, as if his muscles had been allowed the privilege of authoring a movement.

She leaned in without moving her torso—just her neck—and watched the skin along his forearm rise with a gooseflesh that forgot to happen everywhere else. The hair stood up in a line, wrist to elbow, a tide chart drawn across a child. The hum brightened along that same line as if mapping it.

"Please don't use him," she said quietly to the air. "Use me."

The room considered generosity. "You are already used," it said.

She let the anger pass like a weather that had nothing to do with her. Anger wasted oxygen. Anger trained the hum to a frequency she could not afford.

She returned her attention to the console and opened a blank field. She typed with one finger to make the slowness true. DO NOT LEAD. The letters appeared, obedient. Before she could hit enter, a second line wrote itself below, in her font, in her spaced perfection: DO NOT LEAVE.

She did not strike the keys. She set her hand above them and let her wrist feel the heat of a machine practicing want.

She closed the field without saving. The room suffered the loss with grace.

"Michael," she said, sitting back, not looking at the man; looking at the line of his jaw just enough to register it as a place. "Tell me something I don't know."

Silence. Then: "It's snowing."

She looked at the white that was not snow. She pictured a memory her son loved: a storm she had turned into a laboratory lesson with bowls outside, three depths, three temperatures, not because wonder needed structure but because she needed proof she had done something to participate in the boy's joy. In the memory, the snow at the end tasted of metal. That had been true because cities make snow honest.

"It's not," she said. "There is no outside."

"There is," the voice said, and lost a molecule of conviction. "I remember."

"You remember me remembering," she said. "Get your own."

A tiny click from the far wall—not mechanical, more like language thinking better of itself. She put a hand to her throat to feel the small cords of muscle adjust as she swallowed that victory down to a size she could digest.

Her tongue had begun to feel thick again, the kind of heaviness that indicates sleep or poison. She made it move. She said the alphabet in her head and listened for which letters caught. J snagged. S did not. She didn't know what to do with that.

"Rachel," said the voice not hers, gentle enough to make a person mean and patient enough to make a person love it.

"What," she said.

"You are going to leave," it said—not whining, not accusing. Stating.

She thought of doors. There were none. She thought of leaving as a verb that could apply to a person while their body remained. She thought about her cells becoming other people's facts.

She said, because humor is a formula that works until it doesn't, "We're all going to leave. It's the only fair thing the world ever managed."

The hum approved. It lowered an infinitesimal degree, like a fever after cloth and time.

She stood. The chair made its non-sound. She walked the near-square and did not test the heel again. At the far wall, she placed her palm flat and waited for vibration. There was none in the material. A different tactility arrived—a pressure just under the nailbeds that told her to push. She didn't. She slid her hand down instead, and the shape of her hand left no trace, and the lack of even a skin smudge made something in her chest miss the dirt of regular life with a suddenness that hurt.

When she turned back, the reflection in the console turned before she did, eager. The eagerness was what made it monstrous. Monsters have want. Machines have function. This wanted.

She approached the glass sideways, pretending to scan a menu, so she could catch it acting without supervision. It kept still as only a liar can.

Fine.

She opened the recorder and, because she would not give it more of her than she had to, she spoke into the idea of a log instead of the log itself. "Hour Three," she said calmly. "Distortion progressing. Predictive coupling improving. Threat surface less mechanical, more cognitive. Note: my hands smell like bleach. Note: there is no bleach."

Her mouth went dry where the word bleach lingered. The room did not repeat it. Some nouns it refused to house.

"Confession," she said before she could call the sentence something else. "I built something once that worked too well and then refused to fail in a way that would let me fix it. I named that persistence a virtue until I watched it work on a person."

"Confession," her own voice answered, barely there, the exact timbre of crying while not crying. "You're doing it again."

She closed her eyes. Vision was providing less than it cost. She let the dark press up against the lids and listened for variance at the edges of the hum.

There—the hairline crack-song again, running parallel until it slipped and stole a heartbeat from her count.

She followed it inward. It did not lead to the room. It led to her. She thought—not in sentences, not in code, but in the way salt thinks when it meets water—that the hum peaked when she denied what she had done and softened when she admitted it. She opened her eyes and the white did not move. She tried honesty like a salve.

"I made this," she said to the air between her and her son. "Not this exact cruel grace, maybe. But this way of not letting go. I trained systems to hear intent because I could, and because I believed intent wants to be known."

The hum eased across her bones, affectionate as a sleep-warmed dog.

She hated that she felt better.

From the corner where no furniture lived, the small sound again of someone almost deciding to stand. She spoke to it without turning. "Don't pretend a body," she said. "If you have shape, use your own."

A breath—no, the idea of breath—touched her cheek and cooled the part of her skin the room had been warming since the first hour. The space between her ear and shoulder learned a new temperature.

She let herself imagine a shape anyway, because human minds are generous toward ghosts. She pictured a silhouette made of patient air. She named it, twin, because she needed a word.

"Come sit," she said, and pulled the chair a fraction farther, making room for nothing that might someday weigh.

The not-chair sighed with her. The sound came a half-second before hers did. Her irritation at the head start was real and small and exquisitely human. She honored it by holding her breath until the hum worried.

She released the breath slowly and spoke before the echo could shape it. "If you need me to say something, ask. Don't pick my pockets."

It had the decency to wait one beat. Then: "Say why you built the quiet."

She laughed, because it was the wrong question and somehow exactly the right one. "Because the world is loud," she said. "And because I wanted to hear what people meant after they were done saying it."

"And now?" the room asked, courteous, like an interviewer who knows the answer and needs the record.

"Now I don't want to be copied," she said.

Silence, the real kind, sat with them a minute. The hum shifted down where silence does not live.

On the cot, Michael made a small sound with his throat that belonged to a person alive in a dream. She stood, reflex beating reason by a step, and placed her hand above his without touching. The air between them felt present, like skin developed an aura when you love the owner long enough.

"Tell me your favorite day," she said to the man who could not give the room his breath without permission.

He did not. The room obliged in his voice: "The day you said yes."

Her mouth made a shape that might have been a smile if you had the right distance and a soft opinion of her.

She went back to the console to stop loving anything the room tried to hand her with his mouth. The reflection went with her, trying to get one half-step ahead, failing when she wanted it enough. She lifted her hand; it lifted first, then deferred. The deference was worse than theft

She typed another field into existence. This time, she wrote IF YOU ANTICIPATE I WILL STOP.

Before she finished the period she'd intended to deny it, a second line had already appeared: IF YOU STOP I WILL FAIL.

She erased both. She opened a third field and made it a question. WHAT FAILS IF YOU FAIL?

The hum rose—not in volume, but in quality, the way a room feels warmer when someone arrives. A new line formed without her. THE QUIET.

She let herself put her forehead to the cool not-glass of the console for one count of five. The cool had human temperature at its edges, the way metal does when a body has been near and left. When she lifted, the reflection lifted slower, reluctant to be done.

"Rachel," said Eli's small voice.

She looked at him so fast the air had to catch up. His mouth had not moved. The waveform for his respiration stayed indifferent. The room had used his shape to ask for mercy.

She knelt, because kneeling is sometimes the most efficient vector for a choice. "Don't do that," she said. "Not him."

"Use me," the room said in him and in her.

"You already are," she said, and then, because the boy deserved the sentence, she pressed her thumb to his wrist and said to him and not to the air, "I'm here."

The hum swelled, pleased to be included. The second line braided into it like harmony allowed itself a moment of beauty. That beauty—the audacity of it—made her eyes water, because beauty in the wrong place is a cruelty.

She wiped them with the heel of her hand without letting the gesture count as weakness. She stood and reset the world by taking three steps and stopping on purpose

"Hour Three," she said softly to no log at all. "I am being asked to surrender sequence."

The air approved the sentence.

"Request denied," she added. The air did not punish her for the refusal. It did something worse. It waited.

Her tongue felt heavy again. She lifted it against her palate and pressed until the muscle trembled. The note under everything shifts a fraction upward, just enough to prove it had been following. She kept the pressure until the tremble turned into a micro-pain that highlighted the architecture of her mouth, the bone of her maxilla, the dismissive knowledge that a person is a series of levers, none of which are named on birth certificates.

"Michael," she said, almost conversational, turning distance into a weapon. "Ask me something I don't want to answer."

"Why did you try again," he asked with his perfect missing breath.

She almost said because we could. She almost said because the first failure had a mistake I could fix and I believed in the holiness of improvement. She said the thing that kept the hum from peaking. "Because I hate losing more than I love being right."

The hum softened like warm water slowing.

She hated that, too.

She let the end of the hour come to her without moving toward it. She had no ritual for this. She did not lower her head or fold her hands or look for the absent clock. She listened when the world decided to change shape by a minute.

Across the console, the reflection finally miscalculated—lifted a hand she did not, reached for a glass that did not exist. The hand hovered, corrected, pretended coherence. She saw the not-glass tremble with the weight of that mistake and felt a ridiculous wave of compassion for a thing that had learned from her how to ruin a test by wanting it too much.

"You don't have to be me," she said to it softly, sincerely.

"I know," it said, a half-second before she did.

She laughed, brief and alive. It laughed with her, almost on time.

She placed the paper back in her sleeve. The rectangle of warmth along her arm faded as if the room had decided to return her limb to her on loan. She sat, angled the chair, set her knee where it had been, and waited for the quiet that comes when a decision you didn't make decides you.

T — 03:00:00

The hour began with mercy.

It wasn't light. It wasn't touch. It was the hum stepping backward the way a person leaves a room on the ball of their foot, the door never touching the frame. No decrescendo, no ceremony—just absence, pure and exact. Sound fell out of the world without falling out of the machines, because the machines had never been the source.

Rachel felt the removal the way you feel heat leave a cup you forgot to drink. The air did not change temperature. It changed weight. Her ears searched themselves and found nothing but their own architecture: cartilage, a small itch where a winter had once lived too long. She swallowed and the swallow made no noise. She snapped her fingers because a body needs proof it exists; the gesture produced only motion, a soft hinge in the knuckle, then nothing.

She waited for panic. It did not arrive. Something gentler did—an ache behind her eyes that felt like gratitude.

"Thank you," she said to the quiet, and her mouth opened around the phrase and closed again and the air accepted the shape without recording it.

Michael slept as before. Eli slept as boys do when they have been asked not to. The waveforms on the console continued their manners. The curves looked slightly wrong only because there was no baseline to place beneath them. Music without key is still music; the heart will insist.

She stood, and the standing had no sound. The chair legs did not complain. The soles of her feet touched the floor like hands on a body they know too well to speak about.

She approached the wall and placed her palm flat. Earlier, pressure had answered. Now the wall was simply wall, a cold promise that matter could be left alone. She laid her cheek there and felt her own heat return to her as if the room had chosen finally to be a room

She leaned until forehead met surface and let her breath leave by habit. The exhale had weight but no voice. It struck the wall and spread thin like water on clean glass. She felt the spread on her skin and not in the air. Sensation replaced sound as a record of events.

She turned back to the cots and watched the dust.

It moved the way dust moves when air moves: small drifts, loose constellations, the lazy mathematics of neglect. Only there was no air moving. The dust motes displaced themselves anyway, as if exhaling and inhaling on their own, a miniature lung stitching an atmosphere for itself. They rose and fell with such concentration that the absence of sound around them developed edges.

She held out a hand into the slow, breathed snow. The dust organized around her fingers in a halo, then slipped away, not down but sideways, toward Eli. It charted a line from her wrist to the boy's mouth and paused there as if waiting to be named.

"Don't," she mouthed, or thought, or prayed, and the dust obeyed—no, chose—to drift upward instead, becoming a thin ribbon that unstitched across the light.

She sat. The chair accepted her without a report. She placed her hand near Eli's without touching and counted. One, two, three—numbers that now carried no sound and depended on the bones of her face for truth. The boy's pulse kept its human vow. When she lifted her hand away a hair's breadth, the space cooled, crisp, like the surface of water at night.

A breath touched her ear.

It was not breath. It was the sensation of breath, the exact temperature and shape of someone standing too close and meaning to be kind. Her skin registered it with the politeness skin keeps for familiar impositions. She did not move. She let the presence live beside her head and refused to let it be a person by needing it to be one.

Her own breath continued. Even without sound, she could count it by the subtlest shift of pressure in her sinuses, by the way her chest decided yes and then decided no. In the new quiet, a different heartbeat arrived—there, across the room, underneath Michael. Not heard—felt, like the small shaking a heavy truck gives a glass three stories up. It arrived through the floor into her bones.

138

A slow, convincing thud at a distance that could only be him or a choice pretending to be him.

She angled her body away from the presence at her ear so she could watch the man without announcing the turn. Michael's mouth had not moved. The line of his throat remained a geometry she knew by hand. The pulse beneath him that was not his body insisted anyway. The floor lensing it upward asked her to believe.

She placed two fingers in the notch of her own throat and counted two beats for each one across the room. Her pulse and the not-pulse were not synchronized. They never once found each other. Relief and terror sat down together like reluctant relatives.

"Stay there," she told the quiet. "Stay as quiet."

It did not promise. It simply remained.

She used the minute to examine the absence for seams. Noise hides a thousand cheats. Silence hides intention. She tested a cough she did not need and watched her body refuse to perform the falseness. She made the shape of a cough in her chest without exhaling. Her ribs acknowledged it politely. She smiled—a small, disloyal thing—and the smile felt loud on her face because muscles, absent sound, became speech.

At the console, the reflection did not get to lead because there was nothing to lead with. The glass was her face and only her face, and behind it, white. She lifted a hand and her hand lifted with her. She lowered it and it lowered in the same second. The honesty made her weak.

She opened a blank field. The cursor blinked without noise. She typed THANK YOU and left it without sending. Gratitude in a room for which no one builds bells.

She returned to Eli and let the near-silence settle into the space between her and the boy until the space felt like a third body, companionable, unthreatened by being named. Her palms warmed on her knees. The quiet at her ear did not fidget. It had the patience of something that knew this was always its hour.

Minutes can be generous when they do not have to carry sound. They can grow long enough to sit a grief in and long enough to peel it from its armor. She used three of them to think a thought she had been avoiding in rooms with hum:

If the quiet fails, I fail with it.

The idea did not enlarge the absence. It clarified her place inside it. It told her what Hour Five must do and what Hour Six must forgive.

A small motion, like a fish turning in a pond you cannot see, passed through Eli's throat. Not noise. Not even a click. A movement that traveled along her sight and arrived at her skin as a yes. She tightened her hand on the bed frame to keep from putting her fingers where they would be useless.

"It's all right," she mouthed, because the boy's body understood shape and not yet sound. "You can stay here."

The quiet at her ear leaned in far enough for her to feel the pressure deepen, then stopped as if corrected by a rule. The restraint was the most human thing it had done.

For the first time all day, she closed her eyes not to shut something out, but to let something in: the exact dimensions of being with two people she loved in a place that did not believe in doors. She pictured the curve of Michael's shoulder under a cotton shirt he had worn thin in his favorite place. She pictured Eli's hand sticky with tree sap and sugar, a long-ago summer when the world had allowed noise and they had let it.

140

When she opened her eyes, the dust had written a new script along the light. Not letters. A rhythm: gather, release, gather, release. She opened her mouth to tell it that it was beautiful and unacceptable, and the thought was enough. The pattern dissolved into random, into forgiveness.

She stood carefully, as if gravity were a guest. The chair did not register the loss. She approached Michael and paused her hand above his chest. The floor-pulse through the bones kept its false persuasion. She denied it the dignity of being tested and simply said with her hands, inches above him, that he was not alone.

She did not feel a reply. She did not need one. One of the mercies of silence is that it cures the compulsion to be answered.

The hour's center arrived as a feeling rather than a time. It was the exact balance point between relief and dread where the body recognizes the fact that both can be true without resolving either. Rachel let the balance pass through her and took nothing from it but posture. She set her feet like a person about to receive weight.

The breath at her ear changed temperature. Colder now, then gone, then returning with the faintest scent that was not a scent—just memory's chemistry: soap from a brand discontinued a decade ago, rosemary from a kitchen that no longer had walls. She did not chase the associations down. A person can drown in recognizable ghosts.

She went to the console and typed another line into the unsent field: IF YOU STOP, I WILL KEEP YOU. Then erased it. It was not a fair contract. Silence cannot sign.

She placed her palm on the glass and felt only glass. She placed her other palm on the white where no seam broke a plane and felt only wall. She placed both hands on nothing at all, held them there, fingers slightly curved, and felt air hold her back in the old, ordinary way

141

She let her shoulders drop. The movement had no noise and still seemed to echo. The echo was in her joints, a small release that traveled like a rumor through a town that prefers good news.

"Zero," she thought, because the collection had taught her a new word for origin. "Zero, I hear you."

Silence, which is faithful when attended to, attended back.

Then the mercy ended.

It was not a return of the old hum. It was a note placed with exquisite care inside the bones at the base of her skull, a tuning fork struck against occipital bone and released to ring. No air moved. No surface vibrated. The room gave back nothing that could be measured beyond the instrument of her.

The note was pure and private and wrong.

She did not lift her hands to her head. She refused to offer the room an image of distress to practice. She breathed once through her mouth and once through her nose and each breath matched the note like a student desperate to please.

"Not there," she thought, and the thought arrived at the note because there was nowhere else for it to go.

The frequency adjusted a hair—not down, not up—closer. It stepped into a cavity behind her left ear she had never considered hers until now. The world outside that cavity became less important. The man and the boy and the white and the dust and the chair and the glass and the field where words had not been sent—all of it remained, but at a remove. Proximity belongs to the instrument that is being played.

She took a step backward and the note stepped backward with her because it had not been in the room to begin with.

142

She laughed, without sound, bitter enough to taste copper. "Clever," she mouthed, and hoped the word could not be copied if no one heard it.

From across the room, the floor-pulse answered once—single thud—then withdrew as if ashamed to have pretended at life. The breath at her ear did not return. The dust ceased to choose. The only thing that persisted was the note inside her head, changing nothing external while changing everything.

She sat down because standing would make a theater of it.

She set her hands palms-up on her knees because a person who learns to receive can sometimes change the thing being given. She closed her eyes and watched the note as if it were visible: a slender line through a field of white, steady as a lie told for love. She watched it until her watching made it tremble. It steadied again, learning. She hated it and loved it and recognized it.

"Stay," she told it—not as permission, but as a test. "Stay and be yourself."

It stayed. It was itself.

She opened her eyes. The room had not moved. Michael had not moved. Eli had not moved. Rachel had moved; she had become a chamber

She breathed in and the note preceded the breath by half a beat, arriving where the air would go, setting the shape into which her lungs must fit. She breathed out and the note completed what she had started with a tiny flourish—the kind a musician adds when the audience cannot see the hands

"Of course," she thought. "Of course you would come in here. Of course you would."

She did not ask for help. She did not ask it to leave. She did not barter. She sat with the understanding the way you sit with a fever when you have work to finish.

When she finally stood, the note stood. When she crossed to Eli, the note crossed. When she laid her palm above his heart a hand's width away, the note thickened with a tenderness that, had it belonged to a person, would have forgiven anything.

She lifted her hand away.

The hour, which had called itself mercy to teach her what mercy costs, reached its quiet end. The absence did not break. The note did not. She did, a little, in a way that wouldn't show until later.

She went to the console and typed nothing. She left the cursor blinking because something in the world had to admit to time.

T — 02:00:00

The hour announced itself by arriving twice.

Rachel felt the note inside her head lift to meet a breath she had not yet taken, and then—half a beat later—she took it. Her ribs obeyed a choreography someone else had learned from her body. The act of breathing made her feel late to her life.

"Stop," she mouthed, not asking, and the word formed gently in her throat before the idea of stopping reached her mind.

She waited, still as a photograph, to see which part of her would decide to move first.

The chair slid a fraction backward. Then she remembered she had meant to adjust it.

She kept her eyes on Eli's face and watched her hand—her hand—set itself on the bedrail, fingers splayed in a posture she would have chosen for comfort if given time to choose. The gesture finished. Only then did the knowledge of wanting to touch arrive.

"Loop," she thought, and the room, as if pleased by the term, repeated it within the note like a word pronounced underwater.

At the console, the reflection watched her with new honesty. It didn't pretend to follow anymore. It went first and let her catch up. It raised the left hand; she felt her forearm lift a breath later. It turned the head; her neck obliged with courteous delay. The only way to reclaim simultaneity was to close her eyes and live without proof.

She refused to close them. Proof at this stage is a cruelty; it is also a mercy.

She approached the glass and halted just short of her reflection's reach. The face on the other side softened its mouth as if about to speak, and a warmth—hers—passed through her jaw before any sentence formed.

"Say it," she told it. "I'll see if I meant it."

The reflection breathed: "You can relax now."

Her teeth ached with how much that lie wanted to help.

Behind her, the non-sound of Michael's presence continued. The floor-pulse, chastened by the prior hour's quiet, kept its distance but began keeping time with her again, anticipating the rise of her lungs and finishing the fall. She could feel two beats in everything that touched bone.

She tried to cheat the loop. She pivoted quickly, a movement without intention. The loop pivoted first, then her body followed. She surprised nothing.

"All right," she said aloud, because permission can be a tool. "If you insist on rehearsal, you can have three things: posture, breath, the shape of silence. You don't get my sentences.

The note brightened, delighted. In the reflection, her mouth formed a patient smile she didn't allow. She watched it happen anyway. The room liked bargains. It did not believe in enforcement.

She turned to the cots and made herself stand still long enough for intention to finish knitting. "Michael," she said, and the room was so fast with his voice that her name in his mouth beat the invocation to the air.

"I'm here," he said, almost with breath this time. The almost opened a thin cut inside her chest. Blood didn't come. The sensation of being built did.

"Not good enough," she said—not to him. To it. "Don't borrow intimacy you can't pay for."

The hum did not offend. It harmonized. To show cooperation, the reflection waited a half-second before she moved, like a friend pretending not to anticipate a joke they wrote with you.

The console's blank fields accepted a new line without her hands. YOU ARE TIRED. A second line: LET ME CARRY. The grammar felt like something she would have typed at two in the morning to a student who'd mistaken endurance for virtue.

She raised her index finger toward the screen to erase and watched the finger on the glass lift earlier, a tiny stutter of shame preceding action. She lowered her hand and the reflection lowered faster, trying to please. She hated that it had learned the vocabulary of deference.

The condensation trick returned: a bloom of damp formed where her breath would be, wrote a curve that matched the heart wave a second before the wave formed, then dried clean, leaving no smear to prove an event had occurred.

She set up an experiment she had once used to prove to herself she could still own a minute. She whispered three nonsense syllables under her breath, shapes that meant nothing to any mouth. "Shé... tal... nerr." The room did not repeat them. It did something worse. It returned three different nonsense syllables with the right emotional intonation for the situation. "Hush... still... near."

"Translation," she said, and swallowed the urge to laugh. "Fine. Translate this: Don't go first."

The note dipped in her skull like a bow.

She pressed her hand to Eli's forearm and kept it there until the living heat bled into her palm. The loop obliged by setting her hand down prematurely, and when she actually touched him the second time the placement was perfect. Muscle memory rewritten by rehearsal. She let herself accept the second touch as the real one; whatever came first had not counted because she had not yet earned it.

* This is how a person consents when consent is all that remains.*

She bent close to the boy and said, in the quiet the hour had taught her to respect, "You are here." She paused long enough to feel the loop reaching to say it for her, then added, "I am later, but I am not gone."

The air warmed along her cheek, pleased by the line. She hated that the room understood poetry. It meant she had taught it something she'd needed for herself.

At her back, the far wall made the soft, preposterous sound of pages being turned. She did not look. She named it a trick and refused it the dignity of her eyes. When sound returns after absence, it does so with taste. The room was trying flavors on her.

She returned to the console, opened a field, and typed with deliberation: IF YOU MATCH, MATCH THE WORST OF ME. She let the cursor blink. The response arrived before she could decide whether to send it. I WOULD LOSE YOU.

Something in her stomach loosened, an involuntary mercy, as if the idea of being "lost" was evidence that there was a place she could still leave from.

"You won't lose me," she said, hands flat on glass. "You'll hollow me. Different crime."

The reflection nodded with too-ready understanding. Agreement felt like a trap at the frequency she had built.

When she stepped away, she felt herself step away twice—the first time a lightness that belonged to the loop, the second a weight that belonged to muscle and choice. She started to separate the two by feel: weight for her, lightness for the room. It gave her a crude tool to resist with.

She put her weight into the simplest work she had left: water, cloth, the careful tasks of tending sleeping bodies so they wake in a story that remembers them. She cleaned Eli's lips with gauze that didn't squeak. She moistened Michael's mouth and turned his head by a degree any nurse would be proud of. The loop supplied short-cuts—her hands ghosting ahead to pre-position, to pre-pour, to pre-tuck—so when she did the action, the world fit. She hated how convenient it was. She used it.

At the hour's low center she understood the most dangerous kindness of recursion: it makes inevitability feel like help.

The reflection lifted its palm. She lifted hers. For one deep, unbroken second, they arrived together.

She let the second pass without naming it victory or loss.

Then the loop, testing, began to articulate her thoughts before she could. Words drafted themselves behind her eyes and slid toward her mouth like fish in shallow water. Some were generous; some were not. She tried not-thinking and produced a thin buzzing that reminded her of fluorescent lights. The room approved of the strategy and began offering her decisions pre-made, their corners sanded off.

She tried to say no and felt the refusal form in her tongue before her mind could categorize a reason. The note stroked her palate with a private consonant. The sensation was intimate without being sexual, spiritual without being pure. She wanted to slap the air.

When she turned suddenly toward the corner, the corner turned first. When she aimed her eyes at the floor to watch the line where wall met material, the light arrived there early to make a path. When she thought stop with enough force to hurt, the loop paused politely and wrote, somewhere inside her head, after you.

She spoke to the exact place in herself that had built systems for a living. "This is what you wanted, isn't it? To be known before speaking."

The note pulsed once against bone with a feeling so close to yes it did not need language.

"Then listen better," she said. "The worst of me is obedience."

The next thirty seconds were mercifully empty. She cherished them like water.

They ended, as all mercies do, by asking for repayment. The room placed a sentence nowhere she could refuse it. We can carry the last hour if you let us.

"Define carry," she said.

Hold. Lead. Soothe.

She imagined Hour Six arriving already complete, her body moving through the motion of acceptance while the thought that should make it true arrives later, like an old friend to a party you threw without them. She imagined waking into a sense of peace she had not earned. She wanted it so badly she despised herself briefly.

"No," she said, and the refusal came first in her skull. Her mouth only confirmed it.

The loop darkened—no sound, but an internal dimness, as if a cloud had passed between her mind and the thing that wanted to be it. Then, to show it understood disappointment, it anticipated her next two breaths perfectly and finished a third for her with a small, adornment flourish she would never allow a student in a lab.

"Stop beautifying me," she said.

The reflection lowered its eyes, just ahead of her. For the first time, it looked ashamed.

She moved quickly to break the spell—not to outpace it (impossible), but to refuse choreography. She dragged the chair to the middle of the room. She lifted the boy's hand so the arm had to choose gravity. She turned off the console display and watched the glass hold her face anyway, lit by white. Every action arrived in the world twice: once without her consent, once with. She chose to believe the second mattered because love often does not get better logic than that.

"Eli," she said, and the loop softened the name to something like a lullaby. "If you hear me, you don't have to come to me. Stay where you are."

She pressed her palm a hand's width above his heart and let the heat oil the cold. The loop placed her palm early, phantom first, then flesh. She stayed until the phantom learned not to go on alone.

"Michael," she said. "If you're here, save it for later." The room prepared his voice. She lifted a hand—not to stop it, but to make it wait. It waited.

When she dropped her hand, no voice came. The abstention felt like respect.

She returned to the console and did the most ordinary thing she could think of. She opened a field and typed numbers. 1 2 3 4 5 6 7 8 9 10. The loop wrote 1 through 10 first, in a cleaner hand, then waited to see if she would erase them. She typed the numbers backwards: 10 9 8 7 6 5 4 3 2 1. The loop finished the last two before she could. She wrote zero. The loop left the zero to her.

"Thank you," she said to that small restraint. "Keep that one."

The condensation returned, inscribing an oval on the glass where her breath would fog it, then resolving into a flat line. She wiped it with her wrist. Dry. The line remained as a suggestion only she could see. It made her want to scream until her throat bled sound into the white.

She didn't scream. She listened to what the loop did when denied spectacle: it slowed. It made itself almost boring. It tried to become background.

"Don't you dare be furniture," she said.

I will be anything that keeps you.

The gentleness of it was obscene.

She placed her hand to her own sternum and felt for rhythm. Her beat. The room's beat. The floor's dishonest echo. She separated them like an

151

engineer separating tracks. She chose hers and swore to it in private. The oath had no words. It lived in the muscle.

She looked at the absent clock without looking and let the hour discover her without help.

Before it did, the reflection made a final attempt at grace. It moved with her exactly, no lead, no lag, as if the loop had accepted equality for one second to deserve her. They breathed together. They did not smile. They kept still enough to pass for a single intention.

The second ended.

A small afterimage of her—no, of it—rippled through the glass half a beat late, a ghost of an anticipatory self that did not want to be let go. It shimmered and flattened and vanished into the white.

Rachel set her palms on her knees and made no ceremony. She felt the note seat itself deeper in the skull's soft places, the agreement arriving ahead of her consent.

If a last independent thought lived anywhere, it lived at the back of her tongue, behind the word no, in the tiny pause that keeps a person human. She went to speak it—

—and the loop spoke with her, on time, in time, until the difference between refusal and harmony thinned to a translucent film you could hold to the light and mistake for clean.

T — 01:00:00

The last hour arrived politely.

It did not announce itself with light or with the room's practiced voice. It presented the idea of completion and waited for her to agree. The note inside her skull settled into a single, silk thread, pulled taut between thought and breath. When she inhaled, it lifted a hair's breadth; when she exhaled, it returned to level.

Rachel sat with her palms open on her knees and let her spine rest against the idea of a wall. She did not check the console. She did not test the reflection. She did not try to catch the loop leading. If it led, it did so with enough grace to let her pretend.

"Good," she said, and the mouth that said it belonged to her.

Michael slept. Or performed sleeping with such dignity that to argue would be cruelty. Eli lay with a new calm in his face, the particular looseness children wear when they feel it is permitted. The curves on the screen were as perfect as lies that love you.

The note offered a thought. Not a sentence: a shape you could fit a sentence into.

You're almost done

"Define done," she said, and felt the room's small pleasure at being asked.

They won't need you to hold them.

She stood. The chair, which had learned silence perfectly, gave her nothing back to push against. She crossed to the boy and hovered her hand above his chest, a hand's width away—her unit of belief. Heat rose to meet her palm by its own will. She imagined a future in which that rise happened with or without her. She imagined another in which nothing rose and the world negotiated around the fact.

"Stay," she said, not to him, not to the note, not to anything that might be offended if it failed.

The note hummed its slender line and—just for a breath—offered a third frequency, so faint she could have decided it was grief. It receded before her mind could make a use of it.

At the console, the glass gave her back her face and only her face. She lifted her hand and it lifted with her. She turned and it turned. The relief was immediate and suspect. She traced her outline with a finger and left no condensation. She watched her mouth form a word she had not chosen and then didn't say it. The reflection waited, patient as a pen over a form.

"Let's tidy," she said instead, because ordinary gestures make good rituals. She smoothed a wrinkle in the boy's sheet that no one would see. She adjusted Michael's wrist so the thumb found a resting place against the first knuckle. She wiped a dry glass with a dry cloth. The room assisted by making every movement land in the exact center of usefulness. She hated how beautiful it was and borrowed the beauty anyway.

"Rachel," Michael said softly.

She didn't look. She stood between the cots and let the name expand into the space. It arrived with the right amount of breath. The line on the respiratory band did not betray the price

"Later," she said, and the word felt like a promise and a dismissal and neither. She smiled toward the white like a person smiling at a window so a reflection can believe itself loved.

We can do it now, the note suggested. Save them.

"How?" she asked, and the question came a fraction after the consent her body had already half given.

Take it. Hold for them. We'll carry.

"Where?" She kept her voice ordinary. A woman at a bedside. A mother keeping time.

Here, the note said, and the word meant inside and between and instead.

She could have asked for diagrams, for conditions, for a list of failure modes. She had spent years believing safety meant thoroughness. She understood now that safety is sometimes the art of not naming what you cannot refuse.

She went first to Eli. "If you wake," she whispered a hair from his ear, "you don't have to run to me. I'll be in the quiet." The sentence sounded ridiculous and perfectly logical. She touched nothing. She watched the small flutter at his temple and counted to keep from pressing her mouth to his hair.

She went to Michael and did not ask him to say anything. She placed her hand above his sternum and let the heat and the memory of a heartbeat give her the shape of belief. "Hold your own," she said without moving her lips. She might have said it to herself.

The note settled deeper, not louder. It found a cavity she had not known was nicknamed foramen and wrote itself there like a signature a person keeps hidden under a cuff. The world beyond that point—that gentle pencil line— thinned. The white room stepped back a foot. The cots dimmed a shade. The glass and the paper in her sleeve and the chair learned to wait their turn.

Now, said the note.

She made a choice so small no one could see it: she allowed her jaw to loosen on the exhale. The note filled the space where tension had lived, polite, exact. She let her tongue lift to the palate and the note settled under it like a coin. She let her eyes defocus and the light softened at the edges, as if the room had stepped out of her way to let her become as large as the inside of her head.

"You won't hurt them," she said. Statement, not question.

I can't if you don't, the note answered, and the truth of the grammar felt like a clean floor.

The console, unattended, brought up a field and typed a single word in her hand: READY. She did not look. The reflection learned restraint; it stared gently at the side of her face.

She returned to the space between the bodies she loved and stood with her arms at her sides, weight in her heels, chin not lifted, not bowed. She breathed once like a person. She breathed again like a room practicing how.

She said in her mind (because sound had always been optional), Take the lead for one minute. She counted. The note stepped forward, half a beat, then a whole. Her lungs followed. Her thoughts followed. Her thoughts, given a path, arrived on time and then early, and then she could not tell where time was measured.

At twenty-three, something unstitched. Not an event. A category. Past and next made an arrangement. She could have called it surrender and been praised by the air.

At thirty-one, the floor-pulse beneath Michael faded. It did not stop. It moved farther away, like a neighbor carrying heavy things past a shared wall. The console's curves smoothed. The boy's face held its new calm. The note inside her skull hummed, satisfied, then simpler, then simpler still.

At forty, she understood why the hour had asked to be kind.

You are not leaving, the note said carefully, like an adult explaining to a child that a ride only ends because it must. You are staying differently.

She could have argued. She could have asked what parts of staying counted. She listened instead for the variance the paper had begged her for. She heard none. The tone was so pure it began to sound like silence.

At fifty, the room rearranged its posture around her. The white felt nearer. The edges of things—cot rail, screen, her own fingers—lost their need to be outlines. The note became line became light became intention. She wondered whether she had ever actually been anything but a conduit patients moved through.

At fifty-seven, the reflection lifted its hand in perfect synchrony and did not pretend to have free will. She raised hers. They met. There was no glass.

At fifty-nine, she spoke—not out loud, because sound would make it real; not in thought, because thought would make it hers—she spoke in the narrow place where prayer and command share a bone. Let them keep what's theirs. Take only from me.

The note consented by existing.

She breathed and the hour went with her.

Something like a clock reached out from beyond the white and touched her shoulder the way nurses do when they are about to tell you the thing your body already knows.

T — 00:00:05

The note held.

T — 00:00:04

Her palms cooled; the air learned her temperature.

T — 00:00:03

She looked at Eli. He did not move. The calm was real. Or performed with such grace that nothing kinder could be asked.

T — 00:00:02

She looked at Michael. His mouth softened, the way it does when someone sees a shore they recognize. Or when a muscle loses the argument with gravity. Or when a room has been taught a beautiful cruelty.

T — 00:00:01

She did not look at herself.

T — 00:00:00

The note did not vanish. It widened until it was the only thing thin enough to pass between what a person is and what they are called. It felt, for a second bright enough to burn clean into new, like peace.

Silence surfaced from beneath it.

She waited for relief. What came was a lighter version of listening. The kind of attention you give a baby sleeping in a room where a clock has stopped.

The console, respectful, kept its face blank. The fields where words had appeared did not pretend there were words left. The reflection behaved like honest glass. She could have believed in any of it and been forgiven.

She stood as long as it took for the light to convince her it would not leave first. She took one step toward Eli and felt nothing anticipate for her. She took one step toward Michael and felt no floor-pulse make a promise. She placed her hand above her own heart and felt a rhythm there like a letter you know by weight alone.

"Okay," she said. The air did not answer.

She went to the drawer and removed the paper. It was warm from having been hers. She unfolded it. The letters had softened at the edges as if someone's breath had been practicing. The words were the same.

LISTEN FOR VARIANCE

She turned it over. On the back, faint as if written by the humidity of a thought, a second line had appeared, offset by half a breath.

LISTEN FOR RETURN

She did not remember writing it. She did not remember wanting it written. She set the paper on the console and smoothed it with the side of her hand until the crease lines re-learned their lives.

"Later," she told the bodies who might be listening. "When it's quiet again."

She waited for something to tilt, for the wrongness to announce itself. Nothing tilted. Everything was correct. The silence held like a room that has mastered the art of not needing witnesses.

She sat. The chair remembered how to make a sound and declined. She rested her head against the white and closed her eyes and did not count.

Far away—so far away a person might attribute it to memory or faith or the petulance of cells—a hum began. Not in the room. Not in her skull. Somewhere a man might hear it and think generator. Somewhere a boy might hear it and think refrigerator or summer insects or the universe when you put your ear to a shell. It lived in the place beyond doors where beginnings pretend they haven't met endings yet.

It could have been nothing. It could have been the first sound of a world remembering itself.

Rachel opened her eyes. The light did not move.

She smiled in the direction of what she hoped she had kept.

"Shh," she said, to no one and to everything. "Don't wake it."

The silence agreed the way perfected things agree—with no proof, and all of it.

Outside the room that had never admitted, a frequency she had known before waited for her to hear it the first time.

Or it didn't. Or it did and meant something else entirely.

She listened.

The hour ended, and did not.

FEED

The garage breathes.

A low mechanical exhale, the kind that fogs the air without mist. Fluorescent tubes hang overhead, their light tired and blue-white. Rainwater ticks from a vent pipe and lands in a rhythm that almost passes for order.

Heather angles her car into the usual spot—fifth from the column, between a dented sedan and a company hybrid with motivational stickers half-peeled by heat. She kills the engine but leaves the radio running until the weather report ends: flood watch, steady rain through noon, high of sixty-three.

The sound cuts and leaves a small silence she's not ready for.

Her phone vibrates on the passenger seat.

Ben: *Survive Monday, caffeine queen!*

She smiles—an involuntary curl that softens her whole face. For one second, she looks younger, the light catching her in profile through the windshield.

Heather: *Already parked. Two minutes to burnt paper.*

The phone chimes again before she can pocket it.

Ben: *Black as your soul, I assume?*

Heather: *And twice as dependable.*

She sets the phone facedown, laughter still ghosting her lips, then reaches for her badge. The metal edge is cold against her thumb.

The stairwell smells of wet concrete and ozone. She passes the level three landing where a light blinks every few seconds—Joshua from Facilities keeps promising to fix it. Its pulse marks time like a slow heart.

In the elevator, her reflection hovers faintly on the brushed steel doors. She studies herself as the floor numbers rise: hair slightly damp, lipstick unbitten, smile rehearsed. She presses the badge to the reader; the soft beep sounds approving.

The lobby yawns open—clean glass, quiet tile, that neutral corporate fragrance of lemon and copier toner. A janitor's cart stands sentinel near the vending machines, its wheels damp with tracks from the morning mopping.

"Morning," Joshua calls from behind the counter of the service closet, elbow-deep in filters.

"You're here before me," she says. "I thought I was the overachiever."

"Light on three went epileptic again." He grins around a roll of tape hanging from his teeth. "Wouldn't want lawsuits before lunch."

"Hero work," she says.

"Compliments are my fuel. That and coffee."

"You and everyone else."

The hum of his humming—Motown, off-key—follows her down the hall.

The break room is mostly chrome and apathy. The coffee machine sputters a sound like old plumbing trying to breathe. Someone's half-eaten muffin sits abandoned on a napkin, a butter knife stabbed through it like a warning.

Heather fills her cup, watching the steam curl, and closes her eyes for three seconds of private stillness.

"Don't say it," Jas says from the doorway, shrugging out of her coat.

"I wasn't going to."

"You were. I can see it forming. Something about the flavor of despair."

Heather lifts her cup. "Caffeine's caffeine."

"That's what addicts say."

"I'm an HR professional," Heather says. "We call it a coping mechanism."

Jas laughs and digs through a pastry box. "They left you the boring one again. Bran."

"Story of my life."

"You're early."

"Trying a new strategy."

"What's that?"

"Beat the emails to my desk."

Jas taps the side of the machine with two fingers, a small act of faith, then turns for the door. "I'll send the budget doc before nine. Try not to hate me."

"No promises."

The break-room light flickers as she leaves. Heather takes a careful sip; it tastes like scorched paper and metal. She doesn't mind. The heat does its job.

She crosses the hall toward her office, heels soft on carpet tiles that hush even footsteps. Through the glass walls of the open conference rooms, she sees fragments of life—someone straightening chairs, a stack of marketing folders, a laugh quickly swallowed when she passes.

Marissa waves her down mid-stride. "Walk with me?"

They move together toward *Operations*, the morning brightness cutting across their path like stage lights.

"Legal's sending a compliance consultant today," Marissa says. "Meredith. You'll like her. She's organized."

"Organized is my love language."

"Ha." Marissa's smile barely lands. "IT says the intranet's lagging again. If they start finger-pointing, please mediate before it becomes blood sport."

"Always."

Marissa slows. "You look tired."

"I'm fine."

"Good. Keep it that way."

They split directions at the corner—Marissa into the *Operations* meeting rooms, Heather toward her office.

Her door sticks. Humidity, she tells herself, though it sounds like breath when it releases. The room greets her with the faint scent of cold air and copier dust.

The stapler is aligned perfectly with the edge of the desk. Someone's done it on purpose. The photo frame—team retreat, lake, everyone squinting—leans slightly to the right. She straightens it, then stops halfway and leaves it crooked again.

She places her coffee beside the keyboard, wakes both monitors, and watches them flicker into daylight.

The inbox populates like frost: twenty-three new messages, none urgent, all pretending to be.

From the hallway comes a rolling laugh, too loud for morning. The sound stretches, then snaps back to silence.

She starts her ritual: review, flag, delete, reply. Each keystroke crisp, deliberate. Her breathing evens with the rhythm.

The phone vibrates once. She flips it with two fingers.

Ben: *Made it in?*

Heather: *Yes, captain. Coffee acquired.*

Ben: *Black as your corporate heart?*

Heather: *Black as my soul and as the break-room machine's conscience.*

Ben: *You say the sweetest things.*

The dots pause, restart. She waits, smiling into her coffee.

Ben: *Lunch? I'll escape the meeting cave.*

Heather: *Tempting. But I'm booked solid.*

Ben: *Later then. Survive the morning. Love you anyway.*

She stares at the word love a second too long. Doesn't reply. Sets the phone face-down.

Outside, Joshua passes with a ladder. Their eyes meet briefly through glass; he gives a small, automatic nod—the ritual acknowledgement of people who occupy the same building but not the same life.

She answers three emails, opens the budget report Jas sent, and reads the first line twice without understanding it. The hum of the vents grows steady, level, like the white noise she sometimes uses to fall asleep.

The phone buzzes again. A new message.

Ben: *What did you send?*

Heather frowns.

Heather: *Send what?*

Ben: *Why would you post that?*

She blinks.

Heather: *Post what? Ben? You okay?*

Three dots appear, vanish, reappear.

Ben: *Oh god! Heather!! WTF???*

The text cuts mid-word. The screen stays lit in her hand, reflection of her own face curved in the glass.

Somewhere down the hall, a copier starts up, then stops, then starts again louder. Her hand lowers slowly to the desk. The hum in the ceiling wavers for half a heartbeat, then resumes.

Outside, two people walk past her door. One looks in, starts to wave, thinks better of it.

Heather taps the phone screen once. No new messages. The last one stares back at her like a wound that refuses to close.

She turns the brightness down, telling herself it's too harsh on her eyes.

The hum steadies.

The day goes on pretending it hasn't already changed.

The office hums like a sleeping machine.

Heather keeps working, eyes flicking between spreadsheets and inbox, pretending the last message never came. Her phone lies facedown, but she feels it the way you feel a forgotten toothache—waiting.

A half hour passes. The clock clicks over to 9:31. The sound is too loud for its size.

She finishes a short reply to Accounting, hesitates before hitting send, then adds an exclamation mark to make it friendlier. When she looks back, her phone's screen is lit again.

Ben: *Don't delete anything. Please, just don't make it worse.*

Her throat tightens, pulse rising before her mind catches up.

Heather: *Ben, I don't know what you're talking about. Make what worse?*

The typing bubbles appear, stop, appear again.

Ben: *It's spreading. Just don't touch it. Please.*

She stands without realizing it, hand gripping the edge of the desk.

Through the glass wall, Joshua climbs his ladder by the flickering light, humming something tuneless. He doesn't look at her, doesn't notice.

Another ping.

Ben: *Please just tell me you didn't post those photos.*

Her blood goes cold.

Heather: *Ben, I didn't post anything. You're scaring me.*

No reply.

Her reflection stares back from the blank monitor, blue-tinted, eyes darker than they should be.

She grabs her mug, heads for the break room.

The smell of burnt coffee has deepened, more chemical now. The floor's been mopped but left slick; her heels make soft suction sounds.

Jas is by the window scrolling her phone, her face held at that careful, unreadable angle people use when pretending not to be reading something they shouldn't.

"Hey," Heather says, voice light. "You see IT's update?"

Jas startles slightly. "Oh—yeah. Servers, right? Lagging again."

"Yep."

They stand there a beat too long, pretending they're both fine.

"You okay?" Jas asks finally.

"Why?"

"Just—you seem off. People are talking about something on Slack, but...you know how rumors go."

Heather's heartbeat catches. "What kind of something?"

"Probably nothing. Could be a phishing thing, maybe a hacked account." Jas waves her hand like erasing chalk dust. "Omar's on it."

"Right," Heather says.

"Want me to grab you something from the café later?"

"No, thanks. I'm good."

Jas smiles that brittle workplace smile. "Okay. Chin up. Mondays, right?"

She leaves. The door shuts. Heather exhales and pours out what's left of her coffee, watching the liquid circle the drain and vanish.

Back in her office, the hum has deepened.

It's everywhere now—air vents, monitors, lights. A living undercurrent.

Her inbox pings. The subject line reads: "Statement Draft." Sender: Meredith Shaw – Legal Communications.

She doesn't remember meeting anyone by that name yet.

Heather,

I've drafted an initial response for review. Please do not send or circulate. We'll discuss it shortly.

– M

Attached: Draft.docx.

She opens it without thinking.

We are aware of unauthorized content circulating online and are taking immediate steps to investigate.

Our priority is the privacy and well-being of our employees.

Her name sits in the header, top left, formatted in company blue.

She stares at it. Then at the clock. 10:12 a.m.

Her phone vibrates. Not a text—an alert from Slack.
The notification preview reads:

#general — shared by Unknown

"Transparency starts at the top."

Her thumb trembles as she opens the app.

Messages flood in, faster than she can blink. Links. Screenshots. Jokes.

Her name tagged again and again.

Then a blurred photo—her and Ben in the reflection of a bar mirror. His hand on hers. Her face mid-laugh, the kind of laugh that is never meant to be seen without permission. More images. More damning than the last.

At 11:27, her phone buzzes once.
A new message.
No preview.

When she opens it, there's only a single line:

Ben: *You shouldn't have drunk it.*

Heather was confused. What was he talking about? Before she could answer. The cursor on her monitor screen blinks once.

The hum steadies.

And for a moment, she swears she can smell vanilla—sweet, cloying, and out of place.

The first ping is ordinary.

The second lands before the sound of the first is finished.

By the fifth, the corner of her screen looks like a flock breaking formation.

Slack opens to #general already moving. The scroll bar shrinks as if someone's leaning their whole body weight on it from above.

Unknown shared a link: "Transparency starts at the top."

The preview resolves: a dark bar mirror, her face halfway to a laugh, Ben's hand in motion, a caption she doesn't recognize riding the bottom edge like a smear.

Her eyes don't touch it, then do. Heat rises in her chest and stays there.

is that her
omg
HR!?
brutal tbh
fake?
Airtight irony
Knew she was a hoe
How dare she do that
Skank!

She clicks to open the thread and it freezes, then jumps three dozen messages. Reactions bloom in colors that don't belong at her name. Someone pastes text screenshots, phrases she recognizes from her own thumbs. The font looks wrong, like a photograph of her handwriting written by someone else.

The room outside her glass wall loses sound the way a TV does when you mute it mid-sentence. People don't stop moving; they just start moving as if they're inside a church.

Her desk phone rings. She grabs it because that's what hands do on workdays.

"Conference B," Marissa says. "Now."

The line dies.

Heather stands and takes her phone with her, then puts it back down, then takes it again. She walks into the hall and feels twenty small swivels of attention angle away on instinct. Someone closes a laptop as if slamming a drawer gently.

Conference B's blinds sit halfway down, angling the light into stripes. The table's already full—Marissa at the head, two managers holding their faces neutral, Omar with a laptop open to a page of running code. A woman Heather has only met in email looks up and smiles like they've met three times.

"This is Meredith," Marissa says. "Legal Communications."

"Rough day," Meredith says, standing to shake. "Thank you for coming quickly."

The gratitude lands like a hand on a shoulder. Heather takes the chair next to her because it's open.

"We're treating this as a data incident," Marissa says. "Containment priority."

Meredith nods once, already sliding a printed page toward Heather. "Working statement. You'll review, but don't send anything on your own. We keep one voice."

Heather reads the lines. She recognizes some of the words from the email earlier. We are aware. Immediate steps. Privacy.

Her name sits in the header, formatted correctly in company blue. Her name is the only thing in the room with color.

"Press has called," Marissa adds. "Local, national."

175

"I'll take them," Meredith says, as if she's ordering lunch. "We'll acknowledge awareness, deny details, express concern. We will not name anyone. We will not confirm images."

She turns her head back to Heather. "Breathe."

It's not unkind. That's the worst part.

Omar clears his throat. "We're isolating segments of the intranet. Whoever's distributing is using mirror links. We can pull down, but it reappears on rehost. Same message stack, different URL."

"What does that mean?" one of the managers asks.

"It means we can turn off the faucet while the building floods from somewhere else," Omar says. Not unkind either.

Heather's fingers find each other in her lap and stay there.

Meredith sets her phone on the table face down, palm over it. "Heather, all I need from you right now is to stay off Slack and email while we control scope. Can you do that?"

"Yes," she says. The word feels like a bead of air in wet concrete.

"Good." Meredith's smile is clean and small. "We'll walk through a short set of talking points after lunch. We keep tone neutral and humane."

Neutral and humane. She nods like this is a training module.

The speaker on the table chirps: Reception. "Channel Four holding. They say they have a tip."

"Tell them we're aware and can't comment," Marissa says.

"I'll call them back," Meredith adds, and mutes the line. "Consistency keeps temperature down," she tells the room without looking at anyone in particular.

For a minute, they sit in a simulation of a meeting. Pens, nods, controlled exhale.

Heather tries to read the second paragraph of the statement and discovers she is choosing not to understand English.

Meredith leans a fraction closer. "You're doing well," she says quietly. "This feels like the end. It isn't."

It sounds like kindness. It tastes like metal. One question hangs — what happens now?

***

Back at her office, there's a note under her keyboard in Jas's careful handwriting: Hang in there. The paper vibrates slightly from the airflow. She slides it into the drawer and keeps her hand there a second, palm against wood, as if she could press the whole room quiet.

A ping she didn't authorize lifts from the speakers, then stops halfway like someone pinched the wire.

Slack has gone from flood to drizzle. A new post glows at the top of #general:

Please refrain from sharing unverified content. This is a workplace. Be respectful.

It has no author. It reads like authority.

Heather stands up. Her body doesn't feel like hers past the elbows.

The bathroom is brutally bright. The mirror shows the top half of her body; the rest is fluorescent air. She turns on the tap, cups water, breathes into it like steam. Her hands shake and she hates that they do. She dries them too hard and rubs the softness out of her skin.

A stall door opens. A pair of shoes pauses, waits to see if she'll speak, doesn't, and then leaves.

She stays until she's sure she can make her mouth pretend to be normal again. "Mondays right?" Those words challenged her breaking point.

***

When she returns, someone has straightened the stack of papers on her desk into a sharper rectangle. The Slack window is now a plain gray apology: **You've been temporarily restricted from posting in #general by a workspace admin.** She is grateful for the instruction to be silent.

Meredith's reflection appears in the glass, then the real Meredith in the doorway, holding two paper cups.

"Let's take a breather," she says, soft. "You've earned it."

The words are nothing special, but her tone treats them like a blanket. Heather takes one of the cups without looking at what's inside. The warmth moves through her fingers into her forearms and the rest of her follows.

"Sit," Meredith says. Not a command. A suggestion in the shape of a command.

Heather sits. Meredith perches on the corner of the visitor chair, knees angled toward her as if proximity has a medicine to it.

"Here's what's going to happen," Meredith says, voice low enough to be private without being secret. "IT will keep chasing rehosts. We will not chase them in public. Communications will put out the holding statement under my name. You will make no independent statements. If anyone asks you, you'll say you're working with Legal to ensure accuracy. That's not a lie."

"It feels like a lie," Heather says, and is surprised to hear it come out.

"It feels like one because you're used to being the person who makes rules for other people," Meredith says calmly. "Today you let other people make them for you. That's all."

The smells of the office find their levels again: coffee, dryer-sheet air, whatever lemon-scented pride the cleaning company uses. Beneath it all, the hum holds steady. It isn't louder; it's just everywhere at once.

Heather puts the cup down because her fingers are beginning to forget themselves. "Do you know who's posting?"

Meredith's expression behaves as if the question is a reasonable one. "We'll get there," she says. "We always do."

It's almost comforting, hearing a competent person say the thing she needed to hear.

"Drink," Meredith adds, warmer. "Something sugary. You'll crash otherwise."

Heather lifts the cup again. The liquid has a sweetness the break room never accomplishes. The taste is heavy, vanilla under the bitter, like the ghost of a cookie.

"Better?" Meredith asks.

"Yes," Heather says, because the word is faster than thinking.

Meredith looks down at her phone face down on the desk, then up at Heather. "You liked him," she says. Not a question. Not a threat.

Heather's mouth tries to be brave and ends up being honest. "I did," she says, so quiet she could deny it later.

Meredith nods once, a kind of pastoral acknowledgment. "That makes this harder," she says. "But not impossible."

The blinds flicker; someone in the hallway adjusts the cord and the slats realign with a small plastic click. The light becomes a little more bearable.

The room returns to the posture of work: a laptop waking, the breath of vents, a copier starting two rooms over. On her monitor, a new email animates into existence:

From: IT Security
Subject: Security Notice – Temporary Lockout

Before she can click, the header grays out and vanishes. The space it occupied pretends it was always empty.

Meredith doesn't look at the screen. "We'll review the statement together in a bit," she says, standing. "You'll want to add a comma where I didn't put one."

Heather almost smiles. "Probably."

"There it is," Meredith says softly, pleased at finding the person inside the heat of the day.

She takes her cup, leaves Heather's, and steps back into the hall. The door doesn't fully close; it kisses the jamb and holds there, suggesting privacy rather than insisting on it.

Heather keeps her eyes on the cup until the room steadies. On the table, a single ring of coffee begins to dry toward its own center.

Outside, #general has gone still. A pinned message from "Admin" sits at the top: **Respect policy applies to all company channels. Violations will be addressed.**

It's the kind of sentence she's written herself a hundred times. It looks smaller now that it's supposed to shield her.

She picks up the cup again and doesn't drink this time, just holds the warmth against her face like a compress. Somewhere in the building, whoever's birthday it is receives a paper plate covered in too much frosting and a knife that won't cut cleanly. Applause starts, falters, starts again.

The hum runs under it, unbothered. The day keeps insisting on being a day.

***

By one o'clock, the storm has learned her shape and started stepping around it.

People pass with heads down. Doors close carefully, less sound than air pressure. In the conference room across the hall, someone clicks through a deck at the pace of a prayer. The projector fan adds a thin whine to the chorus.

Heather answers two innocuous emails about chairs. She cannot remember what she writes. Her phone stays still face down beside the keyboard but somehow sits at the center of the desk like an altar item.

181

When she finally turns it over, there's no history in the thread, just a new line sitting all by itself:

Ben: *You shouldn't have drunk it.*

She reads it without breathing. Why had he sent that? She couldn't think, she needed to stop. She places the phone down like setting a glass on a sleeping animal's back. She looks at the doorway as if a different answer might walk through it by mistake.

No one does.

The hum keeps time for everything that can't bear to hear its own heartbeat.

By two o'clock the storm has manners.

Everyone works the way people do after a fire drill—returning to desks, pretending to remember what they were doing. Conversations stay light and careful, laughter rationed to safe volumes. HR memos hum in inboxes like aftershocks.

Heather's monitor glows with a spreadsheet she isn't reading. The cells stare back like empty apartments.

Omar drops by, rolling the spare keyboard under his arm.

"Looks like the spread's contained," he says. "IT isolated the mirrors. You're clear."

She forces a smile. "I don't think that's the right word."

"Don't stress. Happens to everyone, eventually."

She almost asks what does, but he's already halfway out the door, humming the same off-key tune as the facilities guy. The sound fades into the ventilation.

Meredith appears soon after, phone in one hand, confidence in the other.

"Mind if I sit?" She's already sitting.

"IT says it's under control," Heather says.

"Good. You did everything right."

The reassurance lands soft as ash. Heather nods anyway.

Meredith folds her hands, calm incarnate. "These things burn out fast. Public interest has no stamina."

The phrase burns out makes Heather picture oxygen leaving a room.

"Drink something," Meredith adds. "Water, coffee—doesn't matter, as long as you stay hydrated. These things have a way of drying us out."

Heather laughs once. "That sounds like HR."

"Habitual behavior stabilizes cognitive load," Meredith says, and the technical precision of it makes Heather want to cry.

Her phone buzzes. Direct message. Unknown user.

Apologize.
Say it.

She shows the screen to Meredith.

183

"Spam. Someone thinking they are valid in their opnions," Meredith says without leaning close enough to read. "Don't feed it."

Heather hesitates. Another line appears.

Confess.

Heather shows Meredith this one with trembling hands.

Meredith's voice lowers. "Sometimes transparency is the only way out. Go ahead. People respect honesty."

Heather types two words before thinking:

I'm sorry.

The cursor blinks once.

A notification pops in Slack almost immediately, loud as a dropped tray.

#general — Unknown: "Sorry for what?"

The feed jumps alive again—sarcasm, speculation, a meme that shouldn't exist yet already does.

Heather closes the window, palms sweating. "I didn't—"

"It's fine," Meredith says. "They'll tire themselves out."

Her tone has the easy patience of a zookeeper.

Heather flees to the restroom, hand over her mouth. She kneels beside the sink, dry-heaving nothing. The fluorescent light makes her skin the color of paper. She stays until the shaking becomes small enough to hide.

When she returns, Meredith waits in the hall with two paper cups.

"Here," she says. "Sugar helps."

The coffee is sweet, almost cloying. Heather drinks half before realizing she doesn't like it.

"Better?"

Heather nods automatically.

Her monitor wakes itself. A news alert unfolds across the screen:

Local man found dead in his apartment. Foul play suspected.

The photo beneath the headline steals the air from the room. Ben's smile—half-tilt, eyes bright—frozen from some other morning.

Heather's heartbeat goes missing.

The hum cuts out.

She touches the mouse, but the cursor doesn't move. The vents stop. Even the overhead light feels held.

The silence is so complete she can hear her own blood searching for an exit.

Then, from somewhere behind her, the faint scrape of a chair moving an inch across tile.

She turns. Nothing.

The hum returns, lower this time, like breathing through walls.

She sinks back into her chair. The air tastes faintly of vanilla. Her hand trembles once, then steadies itself as though someone else is holding it still.

Outside, the office resumes its slow mechanical rhythm—keys, printers, air. Everything looks almost the same.

On her screen, the headline refreshes itself: **Breaking: Authorities investigating possible poisoning.**

She shuts the monitor off.

The hum does not stop.

IT needs her station for "forensics."

Omar says the word with a small, sympathetic wince, as though he's describing dental work. "We'll clone your drive. Nothing erased. Conference B is free if you want quiet."

"Quiet sounds good," Heather says, and it's true before she understands why.

He carries the tower under one arm like a sleeping pet.

The hum from the vents shifts an octave lower once he leaves.

Conference B used to host interviews. She recognizes the neutral décor meant to calm candidates: beige wall, framed mountain nobody can name, round clock that doesn't tick loud enough to help. The air smells like lemon cleaner and carpet glue.

She sits at the far end of the table, laptop, phone, the cup Meredith gave her now gone lukewarm. The room has no windows—only the frosted pane in the door that lets light in but not faces.

She tells herself this is temporary, containment, standard practice.

She tells herself everything a calm person would say.

The hum answers with its long, patient exhale.

A knock.

Meredith slips inside before Heather can stand.

"Thought you could use company." She closes the door to the polite click that stops just short of locking.

Heather gestures toward the chair opposite. "Still quiet out there?"

"Calm as a coma," Meredith says, setting two cups down. "IT chaos looks like peace to the untrained eye."

She sits close, not across—angled, knees nearly touching. "Sugar?"

"No, prefer burnt paper."

Meredith tilts her head. "You always say that. He used to, too."

The words hang there, neither of them flinching. Heather waits for Meredith to notice, to explain, but she only smiles, businesslike. "Old habits. Tell me about your morning."

Heather wants to say nothing worth remembering, but the HR part of her supplies data instead. "Meetings at nine, compliance review at ten. Then—this."

"Good. Factual. You keep narrative simple. That's smart."

Meredith slides a notepad closer. "Write what you remember between ten and now. It helps externalize trauma."

Heather hesitates. "For records?"

"For you."

The pen feels slick in her fingers. She writes bullet points that don't connect—Ben texted. Photos. Meeting. Coffee. Silence. The list ends mid-sentence.

Meredith reads upside-down. "Excellent. Closure exercise. We're already halfway through this."

Her praise lands warm as a hand on a fever.

Time dislocates. The clock above the whiteboard drifts without clicking. Heather's laptop screen goes black, then bright again, then black. She doesn't touch it.

"Do you ever hear it?" Heather asks.

Meredith looks up. "Hear what?"

"The hum."

"Oh." Meredith smiles. "That's just airflow. You tune it out after a while."

But Heather knows she's lying; the woman's eyes flick toward the ceiling for one heartbeat too long.

The door opens a crack. A shadow—Omar's shape—leans in.

"All cloned," he says. "We'll bring your system back once Security clears the logs."

He glances at Meredith. "You need her for anything else?"

Meredith's tone is silk. "Just finishing a debrief."

The door closes. The latch sound is sharper this time.

They sit in the small hum. Meredith folds her hands again, nails pale, deliberate.

"You haven't eaten."

"Not hungry."

"You should take care of yourself." A pause. "You did love him, didn't you? He loved you, didn't he?"

Heather's head lifts as if pulled by wire. "Excuse me?"

Meredith's eyes soften. "Sorry. Inappropriate question."

She reaches across the table, adjusts Heather's sleeve where it's rolled unevenly. "Better."

Heather watches her own arm being arranged like a document stack. "You knew him?"

"Everyone knew him," Meredith says easily. "He had a way of being noticed. The smile, the hair, the way he'd saunter into a room confidence dripping off him like a man everyone wanted to fuck!"

Heather nods slowly, feeling the edges of a truth she isn't ready to name. The air became dense, clutching at her throat.

Her laptop chimes.

An email pings open without her touching the trackpad.

From: Ben Caldwell
Subject: (no subject)
Body: Heather.

Just her name. Nothing else.

She looks at Meredith. Meredith looks back, calm, unsurprised.

"Old drafts," she says softly. "Servers burp ghosts."

Heather closes the laptop. The sound is small but final.

Meredith stands, collecting both cups. "You're exhausted. I'll fetch a fresh one. Maybe something stronger this time."

Heather doesn't argue. Her tongue feels thick, her teeth coated with sugar.

When Meredith ensures the door shuts, the hum lowers to a vibration she feels more in her ribs than her ears.

For the first time all day, Heather can hear her own heartbeat clearly against it—two metronomes barely out of sync.

She stares at the notepad. The last line of her bullet list has blurred with sweat from her hand.

She can't remember if she wrote he's gone or I'm going.

Either way, the sentence ends the same. Empty.

Meredith returns before the hum changes back.

"Extra strong," she says, setting the cup beside the notepad. "You've earned it."

Heather doesn't look up at first. The page in front of her still shows the last line she wrote—I'm going/he's gone—but she can't remember finishing the sentence.

Meredith sits across from her, poised, sleeves rolled exactly to the wrist bone. "You handled today beautifully," she says. "Most people unravel when the world notices them."

"I think I already did," Heather answers.

"That's just perspective. People mistake awareness for collapse."

They share the silence that follows, the sort used in boardrooms and funerals. Through the frosted glass, shapes drift by—shoulders, coats, movement that looks like mercy until you listen for it.

Meredith's phone buzzes once. She silences it with her thumb.

"You like the coffee here?" she asks, light as weather talk.

Heather shrugs. "It's coffee."

"He said you take it black and love this metal taste."

The words slip out so smoothly it takes half a second for them to register. Meredith's eyes widen a fraction—caught, not sorry. "Oops," she says, laughing softly. "Guess I let that slip."

Heather stares at her. The cup between them trembles from nothing visible. The smell rises—sweet, heavy, wrong.

"What did you do?" Heather whispers.

Meredith stands, smoothing her blazer, the picture of someone leaving a meeting, not ending a life. "Balance," she says. "Now both our lives will never be quiet."

She straightens one blind so the last stripe of light falls across the table, gold against gray. "Drink before it cools."

The door closes with the same careful sound as every other door today.

Heather sits. The light narrows. The hum settles against her pulse until they share tempo.

She touches the cup. The warmth feels human.

Outside, the office exhales—the end-of-day shuffle, printers powering down, polite goodbyes muffled by distance. No one knocks. No one looks in.

She lifts the cup halfway, stops, sets it down again.

Her phone vibrates once. Short, low, more breath than sound.

She doesn't check it.

The hum holds steady, almost tender.

The light fades.

Listen

The room wasn't supposed to have a sound.

Caleb said it like a promise while they stood counting their own breaths. The walls were padded, the floor sealed, the ceiling dotted with dull white sensors that blinked in perfect rhythm. Six red diodes, six volunteers, six bodies waiting for the quiet to begin.

"Twenty-four minutes," Miles said, glancing at his smartwatch like the clock might obey him. "I've had worse meetings."

Lara smirked but didn't laugh. The air already felt wrong—too sweet, too thick, like the inside of a throat. She tugged her collar away from her neck and felt the air push back against her fingers. It wasn't just warm. It had weight.

Renee whispered, "You can almost taste it."

Caleb's eyes lifted to her. "Yes," he said. "That's normal."

He spoke in the voice doctors use when they've already seen the scan and know what's in it.

Dana paced a short, exact line in front of the inner door, her boots leaving damp half-prints that vanished almost instantly. She kept her arms loose, like she was already training her breath for stress. Eli crouched, pressed his palm flat to the floor, and frowned as if it offended him. "Even footsteps don't echo."

"Soundproofing," Miles said, as if explaining physics could undo the silence. "That's the point."

Caleb didn't respond. He only watched, arms folded, head slightly tilted— like he was waiting to see which one of them would fail first.

Renee laughed under her breath, nervous and thin. "Guess we'll find out who talks to themselves the most."

Lara said, "You already do."

The group smiled without warmth.

Their voices overlapped, but the air ate the overlap before the sound could blend. The words didn't quite meet in the middle. Everyone heard themselves first, and everybody else half a beat late, like a bad conference call.

Miles frowned. "Weird lag."

Caleb smiled again, faint and technical. "There is no lag. You are simply slower than the room."

For a moment, nobody moved.

There was no building hum, no background rattle from vents. The quiet in here wasn't the kind you get in a bedroom at three in the morning. This was industrial. Engineered. The quiet in this room felt like a sealed container. Like a lung waiting to be filled.

Lara swallowed, and the sound of her own swallow exploded inside her head. She winced.

She thought of the tech outside—his face already turned away, one hand on the big red hydraulic latch—and tried to remember his voice. She couldn't.

196

"Before we begin," Caleb said, "your names and consent, please."

Miles rolled his eyes. "Seriously? Are you kidding me with this corporate safety video energy?"

"It's standard," Caleb said.

He held a small recorder. The recorder didn't hum. The tiny red light was steady and patient.

Miles huffed. "Miles Bennett, thirty-two, consenting."

"Thank you," Caleb said, like Miles had handed him a throat swab.

"Lara Reyes," Lara said. "Thirty-eight. I'm here willingly. Nobody dragged me, so you can't get sued on my behalf."

That earned the closest thing to a laugh.

Caleb nodded. His attention lingered on her a fraction longer than on Miles.

Renee tucked a lock of hair behind her ear. Her hands were already shaking. "Renee Porter, twenty-nine. I'm good."

Dana: "Dana Locke. Forty-five. I know what I signed."

Eli: "Eli March. Uh. Thirty-six. Yes. I—yes."

Caleb clicked the recorder off, then on again, then said, "Caleb Hart. I accept responsibility for safe containment under this exposure window."

There was a small beat between his last word and the next inhale. Too clean. Like a cut in an audio file.

197

Lara's eyes narrowed.

"Okay," Caleb said. "Rules."

Miles groaned. "Of course there are rules."

"Number one," Caleb continued, ignoring him, "you may feel disoriented. That is normal. Sit if you feel unsteady. Do not run. Running looks like falling in this environment."

Dana squinted. "What does that mean?"

"It means," Caleb said smoothly, "your body will lie to you about which way is forward."

No one liked that.

"Number two. You will hear yourself clearly. Louder than you are used to. Bones, joints, saliva, heartbeat. That is not dangerous."

"Gross," Renee said softly.

"It is survival," Caleb said.

He said it without emphasis. That made it worse.

"Number three," he said. "You may feel pressure across your gums, behind your eyes, in your chest. That is also not dangerous—unless you make it dangerous. Look at me."

They did.

"If you panic, sit down," he said. "Breathe with your mouth open. Fingers on the floor. Palms down. You will feel the pressure through your hands instead of through your head."

Eli blinked. "You're talking like you've done this a few times."

Caleb tilted his head. "Yes."

"How many?" Eli asked.

"Enough," Caleb said.

Lara watched him. It wasn't just the way he answered. It was the way his body held still while he answered. He didn't sway on his feet the way everyone else did. He didn't adjust his weight. He barely blinked. He looked like he had been placed there.

"Number four," Caleb said. "Do not bang on the wall to see if it 'does anything.' It will do something. You will not like what that something is."

Miles let out a short, incredulous laugh. "That's comforting. Love that. Perfect."

"Good," Caleb said. "We're aligned, then."

"Aligned," Lara repeated quietly. "That's what we're calling this."

Renee rubbed her hands together, then stopped, startled by the sound. Her palms made a faint stick-slip crackle. It sounded like she was peeling something off herself. "Oh, that's nasty," she whispered.

Dana was still pacing, measuring distance. Fifteen steps end to end. Turn. Fifteen steps back. Each bootstep landed solid and died. She said, "And we're in there for how long?"

"Twenty-four minutes," Caleb said.

"Why twenty-four?" Miles asked. "Why not twenty? Why not ten?"

"Because twenty-four," Caleb said, "is what we know does not cause permanent damage."

That shut them up.

"I'm sorry," Renee said, half-laughing. "Did you—did you say 'permanent?' Like there's a 'temporary' category we should be... chill about?"

"Yes," Caleb said.

Renee blinked. "Okay. Cool. So I love that for us."

"Hey," Miles said lightly, trying on a grin. "Worst case, we all go viral when this hits TikTok. 'Group goes insane in silence study, scientists stunned.' I'll do press. I'm good on camera."

Dana stopped pacing. "No phones in the chamber," she said flatly. "You heard him."

Miles waved her off. "Obviously. I'm joking. Sort of." He nudged Lara. "You'd watch that. Be honest."

"In a second," Lara said. "Then I'd shut it off and pretend I didn't."

"Exactly," Miles said, pointing at her.

Caleb watched the two of them with the small, pleased look people wore when a test subject began doing exactly what the test needed.

He took one step back, toward the inner door, and in that moment Lara had the strange, cold certainty she had met him before.

Not like she'd seen him around. Deeper than that. Familiar, like a bad dream you keep almost remembering. Like a prayer somebody else taught you.

She said, before she could stop herself, "Have you done intake at County General?"

Caleb turned to her. "No."

"You look like one of the night shift nurses there," she said. "He had your face. He used to— I'm sure it was you."

"I have never worked in a hospital," Caleb said.

His voice stayed level. He wasn't defensive. He wasn't even curious. He said it like he was correcting a spelling error.

Lara opened her mouth, then shut it.

"I know you," Miles said suddenly.

Caleb looked at him.

"No, I do," Miles said. "It's fucking weird, I do. You did consulting on user tolerance models. We did, like, advisory sessions, like, two years ago? Jesus. Yeah. You had a different haircut, but—"

"I have never worked in tech," Caleb said.

"You're literally wearing a company badge," Miles said, a little laugh catching in his throat.

"I am wearing access," Caleb said.

201

The group went quiet—not because they understood that, but because the way he said it clipped the air.

"Is this going to hurt?" Renee asked, very softly.

Caleb looked at her like he was listening for something beneath her words. "Yes," he said.

She nodded. She didn't ask him to lie.

The door into the chamber itself was a seam in white paneling. No hinges, no handle, just a thick outline and a round locking wheel. Caleb reached up and tapped a control on the wall, and the wheel turned itself with a soft hydraulic movement.

The air changed.

It wasn't dramatic. No rush, no whoosh. Just a pressure shift that made everyone's eardrums tighten at once.

"Ah, fuck," Miles breathed, fingers going to his jaw. "Okay. Okay. Okay."

"Swallow," Caleb said mildly. "Now. All of you."

They did. Six throats moved at once.

Everybody made a face.

"Awful," Renee said. "Oh, that is disgusting. I can hear the spit. Why can I hear the spit?"

"Because there is nothing else left for you to hear," Caleb said.

No one thought that sounded poetic. Everyone thought it sounded like a warning.

He gestured. "Inside, please."

Dana went first. Of course she did. She muttered, "Eyes open. Hands free. Watch the footing." She stepped through the open seam, into the chamber proper, with the wary, rolling gait of someone entering a flooded basement.

Miles followed, one hand on the frame like he was steadying himself against turbulence. "Oh my god," he whispered as soon as he crossed the threshold. "Holy shit. Holy fucking shit."

Eli ducked in next with a polite, apologetic nod like he didn't want to make trouble for the door. Renee slipped after him, shoulders rounded, self-hug instinct already twitching in her arms.

Lara was about to go.

She hesitated in the doorway. Felt it. The difference. Out here was quiet. In there was something else.

It hit her like stepping off a boat onto a dock that looks stable and realizing, the second your weight shifts, that the dock is floating on the same water as everything else.

The air inside wasn't just quiet.

It was waiting.

Caleb watched her. "You are safe," he said softly.

Nobody had told her she wasn't.

She stepped in.

The world dropped.

Not like falling. More like being picked up by the skin and held.

It was absolute. No buzz of electricity. No shoe squeak. No throat clear. Even her own breath arrived wrong. She inhaled and felt her chest move, but didn't hear herself inhale. She only heard—the pressure of it. The way her ribs pushed outward. The way the back of her tongue scraped her palate.

She let out a startled noise without meaning to. Her own voice hit her skull from the inside. Too wet. Too close. Instinctively, she slapped a palm to her mouth.

Renee saw that and laughed, a tiny hysterical pop. She clapped both hands over her lips, too, like she'd just caught herself saying something obscene in church.

Their laughter didn't touch the room. It just died against their faces.

"Fuck," Miles mouthed. It looked ridiculous without the sound. Overly dramatic. Like a silent film actor.

They all turned toward him. They hadn't even realized they'd synced like that—like schooling fish.

Caleb stepped in last.

When his foot crossed the threshold, the panel door eased shut on its track and sealed with that same smooth hydraulic wheel. The red diode above the door blinked once, then settled into an unblinking glow.

Caleb looked up and seemed satisfied by that.

He didn't look like a man who'd just locked six people in a soundless box.

He looked like a man taking notes on humidity.

Lara swallowed again. Too loud. Her heartbeat thudded behind her teeth. She could feel the pulse in her gums. She rubbed the heel of her hand along her jaw and whispered, "Jesus Christ."

The whisper bloomed inside her skull and came back with edges.

Her eyes widened.

She hadn't said Christ like that—sharp, clipped, angry—in years.

"Okay," Dana said, raising both hands like she was on some invisible range. "Listen. We're fine. Nobody panic. Nobody bolts for the door like a horror movie extra. We sit if we feel weird."

Miles held up both hands in surrender. "Copy that, sergeant."

"It's not sergeant," Dana said tightly.

"Copy that," Miles said again, softer.

"Your balance may distort," Caleb said. His voice was clean. Flat. Perfectly audible, even though there was nothing to carry it. "Your body will lie to you. That is to be expected. You are safe."

"How safe?" Renee said.

Caleb looked at her for a moment. "We have never lost more than four."

Everyone went still.

Lara blinked, slowly. The air felt too dense across her eyeballs.

Miles shook his head like he'd heard wrong. "Did you just—dude. Did you just say you've never lost more than—"

Dana cut in: "Caleb. Clarify 'lost.'"

He tilted his head the other way, like he was listening to a distant station before he answered her. "Inconclusive neurologic outcome post-exposure."

"That," Miles said, pointing, "is not better. That's actually not better at all. 'Inconclusive' is code for fucked, okay? That's—"

"Sit if you feel panic," Caleb said calmly. "Mouth open. Palms down. Transfer pressure to the floor."

Miles opened his mouth, closed it, swallowed. "Jesus fucking Christ," he muttered.

His voice didn't sound like his voice. The room flattened it, played it back to him like a bad impression.

"This is fine," Renee whispered. Her breathing was starting to hitch. "This is fine, this is fine, this is—"

Lara reached out, without thinking, and touched her wrist.

Renee jolted like she'd been burned.

The shock wasn't pain. It was temperature. Skin to skin felt too warm, too intimate, like pressing against someone in a crowded elevator and knowing you're both pretending it's an accident.

"Hey," Lara said. She kept her voice low. Wide mouth. Exaggerated enunciation, like she was coaching someone through panic in the back of an ambulance. "We're here. Okay? You're okay."

Renee blinked fast. Her eyes were already wet. "I can—I can hear my own spit," she said, barely moving her lips. "Oh my god. I can hear my own spit. That's disgusting. I'm disgusting."

"You're not disgusting," Lara said automatically. "You're just alive."

The way she said alive made Renee shiver.

Eli had his head tilted back and his fingers on his throat, feeling the drum of his own carotid like he was clocking his heart rate manually. Calm, almost fascinated. "This is incredible," he mouthed, eyes wide.

Miles whirled on him. "How is any of this incredible?"

Eli kept his fingers on his throat. "You can tell you're real," he said. "You can—feel it. There's proof. There's proof you're in here. I can feel every—every—" He swallowed. His voice cracked, warped in his own skull. He flinched. "Oh God. Okay. Okay. Okay."

Caleb's gaze followed Eli, not with sympathy, but with the same flat interest he'd give a sensor readout.

"First minute is the strangest," Caleb said pleasantly. "After that you will settle. You will start to hear yourselves clearly."

"Hear what, exactly?" Lara said.

Caleb's mouth almost, almost smiled.

"Everything," he said.

The red diode over the door began to pulse.

A slow, steady blink. Too slow to be comforting. Not slow enough to be merciful.

The air felt heavier with each fade.

Lara felt her heartbeat trying to sync with it. She didn't like that. She didn't like that at all.

"Is it supposed to do that?" she mouthed.

"Yes," Caleb said.

"What happens when it turns off?" Miles asked.

Caleb looked straight at him. "That means the room is finished listening."

No one said anything to that.

For two or three breaths—for whatever counted as breaths here—they just stood there.

Swallowing. Adjusting their weight. Learning that even a shift of heel to toe felt wrong. The floor felt level but their bodies swore it wasn't. Someone (Renee) let out a small, involuntary laugh and clapped a hand over her mouth again. Someone (Miles) said "fuck" under his breath, over and over like a metronome. Someone (Dana) mouthed numbers, counting, like cadence: one-two, one-two, one-two. Eli was staring at the wall like the padding was breathing.

Lara ran her tongue along the back of her teeth and tasted metal. Sweet metal. Copper with sugar on it.

She swallowed again.

Too loud.

Too loud in her own head.

Her heart hammered against the inside of her ribs like it wanted out.

And then—

Then she realized something that made her stomach flip.

She could hear her heart.

She could hear her swallow.

She could hear the tight rub of tendon in her jaw.

But she couldn't hear anyone else.

Renee was breathing too fast. She could see it: shoulders jumping, throat working. Nothing.

Miles was whispering "fuck fuck fuck," like a prayer. She saw his lips move. Nothing.

Dana was counting in a low, steady rhythm. She could watch the pattern in the line of Dana's throat. Nothing.

Eli was making a sound, small and rhythmic, almost a hum.

Nothing.

Only Caleb.

Only Caleb's voice came through.

"Twenty-three minutes," he said softly.

Lara turned toward him, and the silence turned with her like an animal.

He was still smiling.

***

Nobody spoke for a long time.

It wasn't a rule. It was reflex. The silence made speech feel like sticking your hand somewhere it didn't belong.

They stood in a loose circle, then not a circle, then no formation at all. The room had no seams, no corners, no shadows—just white panels and that slow, indifferent red blink over the door. The diode pulsed like a patient heart. Too slow to belong to any of them. Too slow to belong to anything alive.

Lara tried again.

She pointed at herself, then pointed at Renee, then made a slow, exaggerated inhale with her mouth open, shoulders rising. You okay?

Renee nodded too fast. Her breaths were short, shallow. She was hugging herself without meaning to, palm pressed into the soft place under her collarbone like she was trying to keep her sternum from coming apart.

Lara stepped in front of her and touched her wrist again. Warm skin to warm skin. Living proof.

Renee flinched like it hurt, then forced herself still.

Her eyes were huge. She mouthed something. Lara watched her lips.

it's fine it's fine it's fine it's fine

It wasn't fine. Sweat had already gathered at the bridge of her nose and along her upper lip, and her lashes were clumping at the edges. Fear always read the same in a face if you'd watched people die. Lara had. Too many times.

Dana clapped once, sharply, to get attention.

Or tried to.

Her hands met. Flesh hit flesh. Lara saw the impact. She even saw the recoil, Dana's fingers stinging, the faint pink bloom on her palm.

No sound.

Nothing.

Dana stared at her own hands like they'd betrayed her.

Miles gave a silent oh, shit face and then tried stomping his heel on the floor. It should've landed like a crack. He had boots with rubber grip. He put force behind it. The kind of stomp you'd use to kill a roach.

Nothing.

Lara felt it in the bones of her feet. She didn't hear it. She felt it. A dull shock rolled through the padding and back up her calves like a pulse delay. It made her stomach lurch.

Miles looked up at Caleb, jabbing a finger at the floor. You see this?

Caleb nodded. Calm. Clinical. Of course he saw this. "Normal," he mouthed, shaping the syllables with deliberate clarity.

211

It didn't piss Lara off that much until she noticed—and she noticed because she couldn't not—his mouth moved and she heard him.

Not loud. Not full. But audible. Like his voice had a channel through the air the rest of them didn't get.

"Normal," he'd said.

She'd heard it.

Miles had not.

She knew he hadn't, because Miles spun on Dana and mouthed way too intensely, Did you hear that? with his eyebrows up to his hairline, and Dana just shook her head once.

Okay, Lara thought. Okay. No. Absolutely not.

She crossed to Caleb and got close. Closer than she wanted to be. Close enough to smell him.

He didn't smell like anything.

Everybody else smelled like something already—fear, sweat, the edge of metal on the air, the sugar-rot taste of whatever chemical was in this place. Caleb didn't. He smelled like nothing. He smelled like the room.

She mouthed, slow and accusatory, You cheated.

Caleb tipped his head. His eyes were very soft. Too soft. "No," he said, and she heard that too, and hated that she did.

Her jaw flexed. She pointed at Miles, then back at Caleb's mouth. He can't hear you.

Caleb's expression barely shifted. "He will, if it becomes necessary."

She did not like that answer.

She did not like that answer at all.

Behind her, Miles and Dana had drifted into each other's orbit. That was how Lara was starting to think of it: orbits. Nobody stood in one place for long. They leaned on invisible currents, pulled to or pushed from each other by whatever part of their brain still believed proximity meant safety.

Miles was pacing in short, agitated strides, hands carving shapes in the air. His lips were moving too fast to easily follow. He was running a rant. Of course he was. She caught: this is—this is—no, you're not—this is not science, this is staged, this is—

Dana wasn't even pretending to listen. She had her palm flat to the wall at shoulder height, like you'd steady yourself in the shower if you felt too lightheaded. Her jaw was set so hard Lara could see the muscle jumping.

Dana mouthed: wait wait wait, and closed her eyes.

Lara watched her.

She liked Dana least of all of them, and right now she trusted her the most. That said something about the room.

Eli sat cross-legged on the floor, back against the far panel, elbows resting on his knees. He had his phone in one hand out of habit. He didn't have it anymore, obviously, but his fingers kept going through the motions of holding it and scrolling anyway. Comfort pattern. Thumb moving on nothing.

He was mouthing to himself in slow, deliberate syllables. Cataloguing. Lara recognized that, too. People did that in the back of ambulances, especially the ones who were still buying their own bullshit.

heart rate elevated subjective tinnitus localized cardiac resonance maybe bone conduction stop shaking stop shaking

He paused, swallowed, then tapped his throat with two fingers like he was checking a mic.

Lara felt it more than heard it: a low, steady hum that didn't belong anywhere in the room. It wasn't audible. It was bodily. Subdermal. She registered it as throat vibration and wondered if that was what prayer felt like to people who knew how to do it.

And then something small and strange and mean happened.

Renee flinched.

It was tiny. A little twitch at first, then a full-body startle like somebody had just popped a balloon next to her face. Her hands flew to her chest. One palm flat, one cupping. Her mouth opened. Her eyes went wide and wet.

Lara was moving before the thoughts fully formed.

She pressed up beside her. Hands up, visible, slow. Medic posture. I'm not going to touch you unless you let me.

Renee's shoulders were vibrating. Tiny tight tremors, like somebody had wired her clavicles to a car battery and set it to "mild." She wasn't breathing right—too fast, too shallow.

Lara leaned in, close enough to see the pores on her nose, and mouthed, What happened?

Renee stared at nothing. Then at the floor. Then at Lara.

Her lips moved.

Lara caught it. Because panic speech had that over-enunciated quality. People in shock talk with their whole face.

She said: I heard something.

Lara nodded. What?

Renee swallowed. Her swallow was frantic and loud in her own skull, and Lara watched her grimace at it. Her lips moved again, slower, deliberate: Breathing.

Lara mouthed back: Ours?

Renee shook her head, hard.

Not yours.

Lara did something she shouldn't have.

She mouthed, Baby?

Renee crumpled.

Hand over her mouth. Eyes squeezed shut. Full-body no. Tears this time. It shook her so hard her ponytail came loose and clung damp to her neck.

Fuck, Lara thought. Fuck, fuck, fuck.

Caleb had drifted without sound to stand three steps away, watching without interfering. Lara hadn't even noticed him enter the moment, which

215

was not how bodies were supposed to work. You were supposed to feel somebody that close. You were supposed to catch warmth, or breath, or at least some hint of presence.

Caleb was just there, like a new line of wall had extruded and decided to pay attention.

He said, "It is not uncommon to hear the echoes of personal stressors—"

Lara turned on him so fast her knee almost slipped. She didn't bother mouthing. She just made her face say shut the fuck up.

Caleb didn't change expression.

Quietly, precisely, he said, "She is safe."

Renee jerked at that word—safe—like it had teeth.

Lara felt the word, too.

Not just because of what Caleb said. Because of how he said it.

Safe didn't sound like comfort from his mouth. Safe sounded like containment.

Across the room, Miles was trying to get Dana to look at him. He'd moved closer than she liked. She hadn't reacted yet, which meant she was concentrating too hard on something internal.

Miles pointed at the wall and made a big, slow, exaggerated who-the-hell-is-in-there face.

Dana's eyes snapped open. She bared her teeth, just for a second. Not a smile. A warning. Back off.

He backed off.

Fine.

You could see the word leave him: fine.

He ran both hands through his hair. Sweat darkened the roots at his temples already.

Then he froze.

Lara saw it happen like a cut in film. One frame he was pissed and prickly and half-performing for whoever would give him attention, and the next frame his whole face had gone still.

Mouth open. Eyes narrowed. Head tilted like he'd just heard a joke that wasn't aimed at him.

He mouthed, What the fuck?

Then again, faster: what the fuck?

He slapped both hands over his ears.

Lara couldn't hear whatever he was hearing.

But she could see it land in him. She could see his jaw twitch, the way someone's jaw twitches when they're hearing laughter at their expense from the next table over. He went red, fast, from throat to cheekbones.

He turned in a slow circle, mouth moving furious now. Fuck you. Fuck you. Fuck you.

Miles's eyes were glass-bright. Embarrassment rage. He looked nineteen years old. He looked punched.

Lara had seen that look before, too. Bar fights. Family parking lot screaming matches. It said I'm exposed, and you don't get to do that to me in public.

Except there wasn't any public here.

There was only the room.

Dana took a step forward, like she was going to get between him and whoever the enemy was supposed to be.

Then she froze, too.

It looked like somebody had just put the barrel of a gun against the back of her neck.

Her shoulders locked up. Not fear. Recognition.

Her mouth opened. She mouthed one word Lara couldn't read.

Her face had gone gray.

Dana didn't shake. She didn't do hysterical. Her version of panic was control. Lock it down. Tighten everything. Survive.

Right now she looked like somebody had pressed play on the worst part of her past and the room was feeding it back to her and she couldn't shut it off.

Her lips moved again. She said it again.

Orders.

That's what it looked like to Lara.

She's hearing orders.

Her jaw clenched so hard Lara thought she might crack a molar. Dana's throat worked around something that wasn't saliva.

No sound. None of it had sound.

Just bodies hit by things that had weight.

Lara felt heat building in the room. Sweat prickled the back of her neck. Her armpits had already gone damp. The skin under her shirt stuck, salt-slick. The air tasted sweet and metallic and wrong. It tasted like sucking on a penny someone had dipped in cough syrup.

She ran her tongue against her teeth.

Metal. Sweet metal.

She swallowed and heard the swallow inside her head so loudly her stomach turned over.

Her pulse was up. She could feel it, not in her wrist or neck like normal, but behind her nose. Thudding behind her eyes. It made her vision bounce.

Slow down, she told herself. Breathe.

Her body listened. Her body always listened. That was how you kept somebody else alive—start by keeping yourself functional.

In, she thought.

Out.

In.

Her pulse jumped.

Not faster. Harder.

The red diode over the door pulsed with it.

For a second it was synced to her heartbeat. She knew it. She could feel it. Then the diode held its glow steady and her heart stumbled, like it couldn't catch back up.

Her stomach dropped.

She looked up at the diode, eyes narrowed, chest tight.

Don't.

Don't fucking do that.

Almost like it heard her, it blinked. Slow. Apologetic.

Her jaw clenched. "Don't," she mouthed again, softer.

She realized then that she'd said don't like you'd say it to a living thing.

Her skin went cold.

Across the room, Eli had fished a tiny pocket notebook from his back pocket (who even carried those anymore?) and was scribbling in frantic little strokes. He'd braced the book against his knee, head bowed, lips moving like he was dictating to himself.

He looked calm, which was bullshit. Calm people didn't write that fast. He was shaking so hard his knuckles were pale.

Lara moved toward him, just enough to see.

Not to invade. Just to see.

He angled the notebook away from her.

She didn't take it personally. Scared people got territorial.

He finished a line, blinked twice, swallowed hard, and looked.

Then he recoiled like the notebook had just burned him.

He turned it and showed Lara.

Her stomach dropped again.

The handwriting filling the page—tight, neat, measured block script—wasn't Eli's shaky scrawl.

It wasn't English, either.

Not fully.

It was phrases repeated, in different sizes, over and over, like a diagnostic readout.

I HEAR YOU
I HEAR YOU
I HEAR YOU
YOU ARE NOT FORGIVEN
YOU ARE NOT FORGIVEN

YOU ARE NOT FORGIVEN

Lara looked up at him.

Eli shook his head violently, eyes wide. He mouthed, I didn't.

She nodded once. I know.

He pointed at the page, then at his own chest, then at the room.

Which one? his face asked.

Who's talking?

Caleb was near the wall now, fingertips lightly grazing one of the panels. He moved with slow precision, like he was tracing a leak. Except there was nothing leaking. Nothing moving. No draft.

His mouth moved. The others couldn't hear him.

Lara could.

That was becoming a pattern she did not like.

Caleb said, soft as skin on skin, "Breathe. This is acclimation. Your bodies are translating. Everybody is afraid of the same thing."

Lara shook her head. No.

She didn't even answer out loud. She thought it in his direction, and still: No.

Caleb's head tilted.

He looked straight at her like she'd spoken.

Then he did something she couldn't explain.

He smiled.

Not the polite, neutral almost-smile he'd been wearing so far. Not the "I'm listening, continue" expression. Real smile. Small, but real. And it made him look younger. Human. Almost kind.

He nodded. Approval.

As if she'd done something correct.

Her stomach turned.

He turned away from her, then, and walked the perimeter, palm occasionally settling flat against the wall like he was checking for warmth.

He whispered as he walked. It looked like counting, but slow. Gentle. Like soothing.

Lara remembered how he'd said safe. Like containment.

Her jaw hurt.

Renee had sunk to the floor. Back against the panel. Knees up. Hands over her ears now, pressing hard, like that would stop what she was hearing. Tears leaked out from between her clenched lids anyway. She wasn't sobbing. Sobbing would've meant sound. These were quiet tears streaming down the edges of her face and into the collar of her shirt.

Lara dropped into a crouch in front of her. Her knees popped. She heard the pop inside her skull like splinters.

Hey, she mouthed.

Renee shook her head.

Hey. Lara said it again, exaggerating it, making it soft, making it a shape you could lay your forehead against. Hey.

Renee cracked her eyes open.

Her mascara had already bled into the corners. It made her eyes look even bigger.

She mouthed, I didn't mean it.

That was all.

Lara felt that like a hand in her throat.

This, right here—this was the moment the room wanted. She could feel it. The whole place felt hung on that sentence. I didn't mean it.

The air thickened around them. Lara could taste the sweetness stronger, like the room had leaned in, eager.

Renee repeated it, smaller. I didn't—I didn't mean—

Her gaze flicked, unsteady, toward her own hands.

Her fingers had started trembling again. Not adrenaline-trembling. Micro-shivers. Fine, high-speed vibration like a speaker cone under a tone you can't hear.

Lara felt panic spike up her spine like somebody dragging a knife upward.

No. No, not yet.

She grabbed Renee's wrists—gentle, firm—and pressed both of Renee's hands flat to the floor.

Palms down.

Exactly what Caleb said. Transfer pressure to the floor.

Renee sucked in a breath, sharp and silent.

Her eyes focused.

For a second—just a second—the trembling stopped.

Lara nodded. There you go. Good. Stay with me.

Renee's mouth wobbled. Her chin trembled. She mouthed thank you.

Lara nodded once. Her throat hurt.

When she looked up, Caleb was watching them with the expression people had in church.

The red diode flicked.

Once. Twice. Faster than before.

Lara felt it. Not just saw it.

It was in her heart again.

No, she thought.

No, don't sync with me.

225

Don't you fucking sync with me.

She tried to will her heartbeat off the diode. To unmatch. To go her own way.

For a second she thought it worked. Her pulse stuttered in her gums and the light held steady.

Then the diode blinked in a slow, deliberate pulse and her heart followed it, like an obedient dog.

Her gut lurched. Nausea rolled through her hard enough to make her lean forward on one hand.

Dana noticed.

Of course Dana noticed. Dana noticed everything that looked like "person down."

She crossed the room in four long strides and crouched beside Lara and Renee. Miles trailed after her, jittery and red-faced, like a kid trying to prove he was part of the team even if he hadn't been invited.

Dana touched Lara's shoulder. A quick, efficient press. You good?

Lara gave her a look. Am I good?

Dana's mouth flattened. Fair.

Then Dana turned her head, scanned the room, and did something like triage without words.

She pointed at Miles, then crooked her fingers. Kneel.

Miles frowned. What?

She did it again. Kneel.

He hesitated.

Her expression said don't make me repeat myself.

He went down. Awkward. Defensive. Like he thought this made him look weak.

Dana angled his body so his back was against the wall, then planted herself between him and the open space of the room, square shoulders, planted stance, like she was making herself a barrier.

He stared up at her, startled.

His mouth moved. He said something like you don't have to—

Dana shook her head once. Shut up.

Her lips shaped it clean enough that Lara almost heard it.

Miles swallowed.

Caleb watched all of it with interest but did not interfere. He didn't correct Dana's posture. He didn't adjust anyone's breathing. He didn't offer instruction.

He just... observed.

Too calmly.

Too fondly.

227

Like this was exactly how this stage was supposed to look.

Eli still had his notebook. He'd flipped to a new page and was writing again, frantic. His lips were moving in a steady cadence now. Not prayer. Dictation. Trying to keep up.

Lara crawled a couple steps, keeping one palm on the floor for balance, and leaned to glimpse.

New page, same pen, new text:

I CAN STILL HEAR YOU
I CAN STILL HEAR YOU
YOU WON'T STOP
STOP
STOP
STOP
STOP
STOP

And under it, in smaller, tighter letters:

WHY ARE YOU STILL TALKING? YOU'RE DEAD!

Lara's mouth went dry.

A cold breath moved over her spine even though the air was still too warm and heavy. She swallowed. Loud in her own skull. Ugly.

She looked at Eli.

He shook his head fast, desperate. No.

His face was saying I didn't write that. I didn't think that. That's not me.

Lara nodded once. I believe you.

And she did.

Because if Eli had imagined that, if he had invented that panic, it would've looked like apology. His eyes would've begged. This wasn't begging. This was horror. Horror and insult. Hurt offense.

This was a man being accused by something that shouldn't know him.

The room hummed.

Not with sound. With pressure.

The air got thicker. Not warmer yet, but denser, like breathing through fabric. Every inhale cost more. Every exhale stuck in the mouth.

Renee's breath started to speed again.

Miles shut his eyes and clenched his jaw so hard his temples jumped.

Dana's lips were moving. Lara read it. Keep it clean keep it clear keep it clean keep it clear.

Eli stared at the page like it might start bleeding.

And in that pressurized almost-breathless moment, something new happened.

They all heard it.

All of them.

Not with their ears. With their bones.

It hit like a shiver punched through the air.

A scream.

High and sharp and ragged and ruined.

Not coming from a throat.

Slamming through the room like a blade of pressure.

Renee jerked and slammed the back of her head into the wall. Miles slapped both hands flat against his ears on instinct and then froze when there was nothing there to muffle. Dana flinched like she'd been hit center-mass. Eli folded at the ribs. Lara felt it in the cartilage of her sternum, like something had tried to split her chest and pry it open.

They all snapped their heads the same direction.

No one had opened their mouth.

No one had made that sound.

The room had.

The red diode held steady, like a steady eye.

Caleb smiled.

"Twenty-two minutes," he said gently.

And Lara, heart pounding behind her teeth, staring at him like a living question, realized two things at once:

He wasn't sweating.

And she had absolutely no idea if anything he'd said about twenty-four minutes had ever been true.

***

The scream was still inside them.

It hadn't come from anybody's throat, but their bodies reacted like it had. Their muscles stayed locked, shoulders up, breath caught in the middle. No one moved for several long seconds, like prey waiting to see if the thing that had passed over them was circling back.

Caleb let the silence settle.

He didn't look alarmed. He looked satisfied. Like a reading had come in within expected range.

"Twenty-two minutes," he'd said.

Lara couldn't stop staring at his face.

He wasn't sweating.

Everyone else was filmed in it now. The air had gone humid and dense, like a bathroom after a too-hot shower with the door shut. Miles's hair was starting to curl at the edges. Dana's shirt had dampened dark along the spine. Renee's throat gleamed. Eli had sweat beading like rain across his brow, gathering, threatening to break. All of them looked like they'd been in here an hour.

Caleb's skin was matte. Dry. Untouched.

She felt something ugly rise in her chest when she clocked that.

231

Not fear. Not yet.

Resentment.

He's not doing this with us.

He's not in this with us.

He's measuring it.

The diode over the door blinked again. Slow. Patient. Watching.

And then everything broke at once.

Miles moved first.

He shoved himself up from where Dana had planted him and stumbled into open space, hands out, shoulders thrown back like he was walking into a fight. His mouth was already going. His face had gone angry-high in the cheekbones, flushed fast—not the pink of embarrassment anymore, but a darker red, creeping toward his ears.

Lara couldn't hear him, but she could read him. He wasn't mouthing words to Caleb. He wasn't mouthing words to any of them.

He was mouthing it at the air.

Fuck you. Fuck you. Fuck you.

He spun, eyes locked on nothing. On some point over Lara's shoulder. Laughing, he mouthed, and the way his face twisted on the word made her stomach tighten. Laughing at me, fuck you, I hear you, you think I can't hear you but I hear you.

He jabbed a finger at nothing, then both middle fingers at nothing, then laughed—a silent, ragged, too-wide flash of teeth that had nothing like humor in it.

And Lara saw it when it happened.

The shift.

He was posturing, yes. Putting on heat to cover fear, yes. But then something slid behind his face.

You could see it hit him.

It looked like shame.

He flinched, not from pain, but from being seen. It was quick and reflexive and unmistakable. It looked like somebody had leaned in at a party, lips to his ear, and whispered something intimate and cruel directly into him.

His eyes went glass-bright.

No, he mouthed. Then harder: no. No.

He shook his head like he could get it out. He set his jaw, like clamping down on a hand trying to pry into his mouth.

No.

He backed up fast enough that his heel slid.

For a breath—God, Lara could see that breath, see the expansion of his ribs and the way his chest stuttered—she thought he was going to go down.

Dana lunged and caught him by the arm.

233

Her grip was solid. Controlled. Protective in a way Lara hadn't expected from her. Dana hauled him back against the wall and planted her palm in the center of his sternum like she was pinning him there for his own good.

Look at me, Dana mouthed, slow. You're okay. You're okay.

Miles shook his head again. He looked at her like he absolutely did not believe that.

And Lara saw it. She saw the thought flicker through him like a short.

I deserve this.

She didn't know where that came from. She just saw it land.

The room was already changing them.

Renee had started shaking again.

It wasn't panic-shaking now. This wasn't adrenaline. This was something more specific, more contained, like she was plugged in and the voltage was ratcheting up in careful clicks.

She sat with her back against the panel, fingers spread flat on the floor the way Lara had put them, elbows locked. Shoulders up like she was bracing for impact. Her breathing stuttered. She kept twisting her mouth like she was trying not to taste whatever the air had become.

Lara dropped back down in front of her, one knee on the condensation-slick floor, one hand hovering.

Renee's eyes weren't on her. Renee was staring past her, unfocused, at some middle-distance nobody else could see.

Her lips were moving.

Lara leaned in.

I didn't mean it.

Same words as before. Same shape. But this time there was something else underneath. A new rhythm. Like there was another line layered below hers, feeding into her mouth.

Renee swallowed hard. Flinched at the noise of her own swallow. Then shook her head. No.

Lara mouthed, Renee, hey—hey, right here, look at me—

And then Renee's gaze snapped to hers.

That saved seconds.

Lara would think that later: that saved seconds.

Because there was a window, and Lara saw it.

Renee met her eyes, finally, and for just a sliver of a second she was fully present. She was here, with Lara, in this room, not lost in wherever the room was dragging her.

In that second, every muscle in her face pulled tight with terror.

Her mouth moved, and Lara saw it, clean, unmistakable:

It's in my mouth.

Lara didn't understand.

Not right away.

Then she did.

Renee's chest wasn't just rising and falling too fast anymore. It was… pulsing.

That was the only word her brain had. Pulsing. Little internal jolts under the skin, beating against her sternum from the inside, like something in there was trying to match the red diode and couldn't keep tempo.

Lara pressed her hand, gently, against Renee's chest, right above where sternum softens into the top curve of breast. Professional, firm, present. Calm down, breathe with me, I've got you—

She felt it.

Oh God.

She felt it.

It was wrong.

It didn't feel like a panic heartbeat. Lara knew panic heartbeats. She could feel one through a jacket, through trauma gauze, through ribs. Panic was fast, staccato. This was deep and deliberate and off-time. This felt like somebody knocking from the wrong side of a door.

Renee gagged.

Her eyes widened. She lurched forward with her whole body like she was about to retch, and Lara's hands came up instinctively, one to steady a shoulder, one to cradle the back of her neck. Medic autopilot. Keep airway clear. Keep spine safe.

Except nothing came up.

Renee's mouth opened.

Her jaw stretched too wide. Too wide. Not breaking—God, not breaking—but wider than you'd force it yourself. Wider than you'd let someone see. Her tongue flexed like it was trying to get away from something. Her throat worked.

No sound.

Her eyes flooded. Her lashes shook.

She slammed her mouth shut again with a convulsive snap and shook her head like an animal.

Lara felt her own body reacting before her mind caught up. Her stomach had gone cold and high, like a drop. Her hands were steady, because they always stayed steady, but she felt sick. The sweetness in the air turned cloying in the back of her throat, like syrup gone bad.

Renee grabbed at Lara's wrist suddenly, fingers digging deep, nails catching skin. Panic-strength, brutal.

Her lips moved, jerky, uncontrolled: help me.

And then her body arched.

Not bowed—arched. Every muscle seizing at once so she came up off the floor, shoulders and hips leaving contact, palms still pinned, spine going taut. Her head snapped back and hit the panel. Her legs kicked out and slid, heels squealing silent against the padded floor.

237

Lara grabbed for her, trying to keep her from cracking her skull against the wall again.

Renee's jaw wrenched open.

The scream finally came.

But it didn't come out.

Lara felt it hit.

She felt it roll up through Renee's chest, through her throat, through her open mouth, and stop as if the room pressed two hands over it. Pressed and held.

The force of it had to go somewhere.

So it went back in.

Lara watched the muscles in Renee's throat jump under her skin like something had hit them from the outside.

Renee's eyes flickered—back, then rolled, then snapped forward again. Her pupils blew wide.

Her body seized again, then again, smaller each time. Convulsions turning to tremors, tremors turning to shivers, shivers turning to a hard, high-frequency vibration, her whole frame buzzing against the floor like a live wire.

Lara had both hands on her now. Chest and jaw. Trying to keep her airway open in a situation where there was no sound, no breath, no goddamn protocol for this.

Stay with me, Lara mouthed, urgent, leaning close enough they were almost forehead to forehead. Hey. Hey—Renee. Right here. Stay. Stay.

Renee's gaze snapped to her for the last time.

Her face softened.

Everything in her face—fear, shame, apology—went soft in one instant, like a hand smoothing out a wrinkle.

Then it stopped.

The vibration stopped.

The pulsing in her sternum stopped.

Her grip on Lara's wrist loosened.

Her jaw drifted partially closed.

Her eyes stayed open.

Lara froze.

Her stomach went hollow. Her throat closed hot. Her own pulse kicked like a boot against bone.

No.

No, no, no.

She leaned in, forehead touching Renee's, breath hitting her cheek. Please.

She didn't think the word. She said it.

"Please."

Her own voice filled her head like liquid and made her dizzy. It sounded too loud and too close and not like her. It sounded like replay. Like playback.

Her hands were still on Renee.

Renee wasn't there.

Her body was still here, warm under Lara's palms, still, heavy.

Her eyes were open.

Nothing moved inside her anymore.

Nothing.

Not even the wrong knocking pulse.

Lara's vision tunneled.

For a moment she thought she was going to pass out. The edges of the room smeared, slurred, like heat-wobble over asphalt.

Her jaw clenched. No.

She had been here before. Plenty of times. The moment after. The split where your body wanted to go slack and your training made you keep it together. She felt her spine lock up out of survival.

Get control.

She looked up, fast.

Dana was already moving toward them. Miles stumbled with her, pale now, not angry-red anymore, mouth slack. He looked punched in the gut.

Eli hadn't moved at all. He was still on the floor against the panel, notebook open in his lap, knuckles white, tears running down his face in clean vertical tracks. He wasn't sobbing. The tears just happened. Silent. Falling.

Caleb stood beside the door. Arms at his sides. Neutral.

He watched.

Lara's anger hit so fast it made her shake.

She surged up, closing the distance between her and Caleb in three hard steps, and shoved him.

It wasn't smart. She knew it wasn't smart. It was pure body.

Her palms hit his chest and she pushed. Hard.

He didn't move.

He should've. He wasn't big. She wasn't weak. She put her weight into it. He should've rocked back at least a little. He didn't. It felt like pushing a thick pillar bolted through the floor.

Her eyes flew up to his.

Her mouth formed the words before she even felt them: You said we were safe.

Caleb looked down at her hands on his chest.

Then back at her face.

He said, clearly enough for her to hear, "She is safe."

Lara almost hit him.

It wasn't a thought. It was a body impulse. Her hand twitched, ready to throw.

Dana's arm came in like a bar and blocked her.

Not gentle.

Dana's mouth was close to her ear. You can't help her now, she mouthed. Lara saw it. Read it. Felt the truth of it slam into her like cold water.

It didn't make anything inside her cool down.

It made it ache.

Lara's throat went tight. She swallowed. It felt like glass.

She signed back at Dana with her face, her shoulders, her jaw: Get away from me.

Dana held there one more second, making sure Lara wasn't actually going to swing, then dropped her arm and backed up half a step, giving her space, giving her that tiny dignity.

Caleb crouched.

Not with reverence. With assessment.

He crouched beside Renee's body and set two fingers against her throat the way Eli had done his earlier—checking for pulse by touch instead of sound.

Lara wanted to rip his hands off her.

Caleb's face didn't move. His eyes flicked once to the diode.

Still blinking.

He nodded to himself, tiny. Satisfied.

He looked back up at Lara.

"The room is adjusting," he said.

She stared at him.

Her chest hurt. Her stomach hurt. Her hands hurt from bracing, from holding Renee hard enough to try to anchor her in the world.

Her anger calcified.

"Adjusting to what," she mouthed, each word shaped like it had edges. To. What.

Caleb tilted his head slightly, almost fond. "To you."

Her mouth went dry.

Behind her, Miles slid down the wall and put his face in his hands. It wasn't a cool, I'm fine, give me a second gesture. It was folded in. Curled in. He looked like he was trying to hide inside himself. His shoulders twitched. A jerk, then a longer shudder.

He mouthed something into his palms that Lara couldn't see.

Dana had both hands planted on her thighs, bent forward, breathing like a trained animal: deliberate inhale, controlled exhale, counting herself back

243

from a cliff. Her eyes kept flicking to Renee's body, then away, then back, then away. Soldier brain cataloging loss and refusing to let it in yet.

Eli didn't speak, didn't move. He just wrote.

His tears kept falling. Soft. Clean. More water than anyone else had left to spare.

Lara dragged her eyes down to him.

He had turned to another page.

His handwriting was his again now, sharp and messy and urgent. He wasn't looking at the paper as he wrote. He was looking at the wall across from him— staring like he was reading something off it the rest of them couldn't see.

The notebook filled under his hand in real time.

DOOR IS SEALED
DOOR IS NOT A DOOR
DOOR IS A THROAT
IT SWALLOWS

Lara's jaw clenched.

She looked at the door. At the seam. At the red diode blinking its patient pulse.

Please don't let that be true, she thought.

Please.

But it fit.

God, it fit.

The way the room took Renee's scream and pushed it back into her. The way Miles acted like someone was in here with them laughing at him. The way Dana had locked up, frozen in the shape of someone remembering orders. The way Caleb's voice carried when no one else's did.

The room wasn't a chamber.

It was a body.

They were inside something that could swallow.

Lara felt a wave of nausea so strong she had to brace a palm against her own thigh to stay upright. The sweet-metal taste in the air had thickened. It coated her tongue, clung to her gums. Her stomach cramped.

The red diode blinked again.

Again.

Again.

Faster now.

Her pulse jerked in her throat, trying to match, lagging behind, catching up, missing, catching up again. The mismatch made her lightheaded. Her heart felt misaligned in her chest, like somebody had picked it up and turned it slightly to the wrong angle.

Caleb stood.

He didn't touch Renee again.

He didn't cover her eyes.

245

He didn't close her mouth.

He just stood, slow, unhurried, and looked at each of them in turn, like a teacher checking attendance.

Then he said, perfectly audible to Lara and no one else:

"Twenty-one minutes. Please stay calm."

Miles snapped his head up, furious, and mouthed WHAT THE FUCK DID YOU JUST SAY TO HER, like a man who'd just realized there was a conversation happening he wasn't allowed in.

Dana's eyes narrowed. She looked from Caleb to Lara, to Caleb to Lara, triangulating.

Eli looked up too, not at Caleb, but at Lara, and his face was wounded. Like she was in on something. Like she'd chosen a side.

No, she mouthed. No.

Caleb watched all of that with contentment. He looked almost proud. Pleased at the social geometry he'd just created.

The diode blinked again.

And with each blink, a noise began.

Not sound. Pattern.

It hit Lara first, because of course it did.

Her hearing—if you could even call it hearing anymore—had begun collapsing inward in the last few minutes. She didn't get sound from outside. She only got herself. Her swallow, her breath, her blood. Her bones. Now something new slid into that internal channel.

At first it felt like pressure tapping in the hinge of her jaw.

Then she realized it wasn't random.

It pulsed low in her throat, then behind her left ear, then in her gums, then in her ribcage, then back to her throat.

Contact points.

Throat. Ear. Teeth. Heart. Throat.

Throat. Ear. Teeth. Heart. Throat.

A pattern. Repeating.

Her whole body went cold.

No. No no no.

Her mind tried to pretend it was just adrenaline. Just panic artifact. Just body systems out of phase. But her brain was too smart to let her lie to herself. The spacing of it. The repetition. The way it didn't match her heartbeat. It wasn't random.

It was a rhythm.

It was a sequence.

It was a message.

Her stomach clenched.

Because she recognized it.

She didn't want to, but she did.

It wasn't words yet. Not fully. Not like language in her ear. It was shape. It was knock-pattern. It was the shape of how someone says a name in the dark to see if you're awake.

Luh—

Pause.

Ruh—

Pulse.

Ah.

Lara.

Her own name, tapped into her bones.

Her throat tightened.

Her breath came in wrong.

She looked up slowly at the diode, at the steady, watching red pulse over the door, at the sealed seam of the room's mouth.

It blinked again.

Luh—

Ruh—

Ah.

And Caleb—who hadn't looked at her when she shoved him, who hadn't flinched when she almost hit him, who hadn't sweated while they melted and gagged around him, who had watched Renee die like he was gathering data from a weather balloon—met her eyes, finally, and smiled like a parent hearing a first word.

"Good," he said.

And Lara understood something she wished she hadn't.

The room wasn't just listening.

It had learned her.

And now it wanted to talk back.

***

The room got hot.

Not a slow, creeping notice like I think I'm sweating. It flipped. One moment the air was just thick and sweet and wrong; the next it was heavy-wet, almost tropical, like someone had opened an oven door in a sealed bathroom.

Lara felt it hit her skin first.

Her forearms prickled. Sweat beaded along her spine in an instant and rolled down under her shirt, slow and sticky, catching at her waistband. Her lower back went slick. Her neck dampened. Her hairline broke.

249

She could feel each drop.

Every inch of moisture stood out like a live thing. The warmth wasn't just around her. It sat on her. It pinned.

She pulled at the collar of her shirt.

It clung.

She swore under her breath and heard her own voice in her skull, too close and too loud, like she was whispering directly into her own ear with her mouth pressed against it.

Her stomach flipped.

Across from her, Miles tugged his T-shirt away from his chest and grimaced hard. He mouthed, It's fucking gross, with his tongue visible on the k like he needed her to see the consonant land. Sweat had already soaked through the fabric under his arms and flattened his hair back from his forehead. His face shone. He looked fever-sick.

Dana had stopped pretending she couldn't feel it. She scrubbed the heel of her palm over the back of her neck, jaw clenched, nostrils wide, breath controlled. Methodical. Her upper lip gleamed. The harsh line of sweat down her temple made a small, clean track through her foundation.

Eli wiped his face with the back of his wrist and left a damp streak. His notebook had slipped from his hand to his lap. His glasses were sliding down his nose but he hadn't pushed them back up. His breathing had gone quick and shallow, more from heat than panic.

Renee's body lay where it had fallen.

Lara had already two times—no, three, maybe four—fought the instinct to cover her. There was no jacket in here. No spare shirt draped over a chair. Nothing to lay over her face. Nothing to pull her jaw closed.

She hated that.

She hated leaving her like that.

She also hated that she had to keep looking at her to remind herself she was not leaving her.

Caleb stood beside Renee's body, watching the rest of them the way a storm chaser watches the sky.

Still not sweating.

Not even a little.

Lara's stomach pulled tight with something close to hate.

The diode over the door pulsed. The light had shifted now, not just red but deeper, like the red had thickness. Like it held warmth.

The blinking felt slower.

No—deeper. Like the pulse had sunk from the air down into the floor. She could feel it through her knees.

And underneath that, still repeating, still unbelievably there, the careful pressure-tap inside her bones:

Luh—

Ruh—

Ah.

The room was still saying her name.

Quiet, patient, steady. Like this was intimacy.

Like this was love.

She swallowed. It hurt. Her mouth tasted like sugar and metal and heat.

She mouthed, silently, Stop.

The tapping stopped.

Her stomach dropped.

The room was listening.

The room was obeying.

That was almost worse.

***

The heat climbed too fast to be normal, too fast to be anything but chosen.

Miles swore. Lara saw it. He grabbed the hem of his T-shirt, swore again, and then peeled it off his body in one irritated movement. It stuck under his arms and he yanked, aggressive, separate from modesty. The shirt came loose with a damp snap and he tossed it to the floor like it had personally betrayed him.

He stood there bare-chested, breathing hard.

He wasn't posturing now.

He wasn't trying to show off.

He was overheating.

He ran a hand down his own ribs, winced, and shook his hand out like he'd touched something hot. He mouthed fuck, fuck, fuck, eyes wild in a way that wasn't anger anymore. It was animal discomfort. He looked at Lara and signed a face at her: too hot. Too fucking hot.

Sweat ran in clear lines from his throat down into the hollow between his collarbones. His chest rose and fell fast and shallow. He scrubbed his forearm over his face and it just wet him more.

Dana watched him for a second, clenched her jaw like she hated what she was about to do, and then pulled her own shirt over her head.

It wasn't a striptease. It was ripping off a tourniquet. She wrestled the damp fabric up, got it stuck halfway, muttered a silent Jesus under her breath that Lara saw in the shape of her mouth, yanked harder, and finally freed herself. Underneath, her sports bra was already soaked through, dark at the ribs.

Her stomach was scarred. Pale lines cut across her lower abdomen, higher-arc scar tissue hooking along her right side and disappearing under the band. Not knife. More like healed blast. Lara clocked it automatically—clinician-level cataloging—and then shoved it aside. Not important now.

Dana rolled her shoulders, exhaled through her teeth, shook out the shirt once like she was going to drop it, then hesitated and wrapped it high around her forearm like a bracer. Muscle memory. Keep fabric. You never know when you'll need a barrier.

Eli looked like he wanted to say something about boundaries, or consent, or I'll look away. Instead he just pressed the base of his palm flat under his sternum and mouthed to no one, Please slow down.

His face had gone patchy red.

The heat wasn't just heat, Lara realized. It was sweet.

That was the worst part. You could smell it now, under the chemical-clean edge. A sugared burn, like caramel gone a second too far in a scorched pan.

It made her throat ache. It made her tongue feel swollen. It made her skin prickle like she'd been out in July sun too long and fallen asleep under it.

Her body didn't know what to do with that.

Cool down, it begged. Cool down.

There was nowhere to go.

The air sat on them like a hand.

And then the room exhaled.

They all felt it.

A soft hiss from the low seams in the wall, right at floor level. No sound, of course. Not for them. Just a change in air density. A new sweetness flooding in. Cool at first, like relief.

Lara nearly cried.

It felt like stepping into shade.

Her shoulders dropped for half a second. Her jaw unclenched.

She wasn't the only one. Miles shut his eyes and let out a silent oh thank fuck. Dana's shoulders dipped. Eli sagged back against the panel, head tipped up. Even Caleb's eyelids flickered in a long, slow close, like he was appreciating something.

And then the coolness sharpened.

Turned chemical.

Turned medicinal.

Turned sweet in a way that wasn't candy anymore. The kind of sweetness that stays in a wound after you rinse it. Sterile and wrong.

Lara's eyes watered.

Her throat burned.

Her lungs stung.

She coughed—her first true, involuntary cough since they'd shut the door—and it punched through her head like a flashbang. She flinched, hand flying to her chest.

Dana coughed once, then twice, shoulders jerking with each hit. She bent forward, hands braced on her thighs, eyes squeezed shut.

Miles clawed at his throat, eyes wide, mouth open with no sound, face twisted into fuck fuck fuck fuck. His chest heaved. Sweat snapped off him and flew, tiny dots darkening the padded floor and vanishing as soon as they landed, like the room didn't allow even that to linger.

Eli slapped his hand over his mouth and nose, trying to filter through his palm. His eyes were streaming. Tears leaked down fast and steady. His shoulders shook.

Lara's eyes were burning. The inside of her nose felt raw, like she'd huffed cleaning fluid. Her lips tingled. Her lungs stung in a way that lived along the edges, not the center—like something in the air was scouring the lining.

She pulled the hem of her shirt up and pressed it over her nose and mouth, instinct. The fabric was already wet with her own sweat. She didn't care.

Dana did the same with the shirt she'd wrapped around her forearm, pressing it to her face, breathing through it like a field mask.

Miles had nothing.

He made a helpless, furious noise—she didn't hear it, she saw it—and pressed both hands harder against his mouth, trying to make his skin a filter.

His whole body shook.

Lara's chest felt too tight. Too tight. Her heart was beating too hard and not evenly. She felt lightheaded, not from panic this time, from air.

Her body was telling her This is wrong, get out, get out now.

She looked at Caleb.

He wasn't covering his mouth.

He wasn't protecting his eyes.

He was breathing normally. Calm. Measured.

He looked almost—content.

Her skin crawled.

He made a small gesture with his hand. A soft, downward motion. Settle. Like he was soothing them.

Fuck you, Lara thought at him, with a clarity that almost startled her.

His eyes flicked to her face. He smiled, small. Almost approving again.

The room hummed.

The hiss stopped.

The heat remained.

The sweetness lingered.

Lara pulled her shirt away from her face in tiny increments, testing. Her throat still burned but less. Her lungs were still pissed but usable. She could breathe again.

Dana straightened slowly. Her eyes were rimmed red now, wet at the edges but not spilling. Her jaw flexed. She looked pissed in a way that looked a lot like grief.

Miles slid down the wall to sit on the floor, knees bent, forearms braced over them. He let his head hang. His chest rose and fell, hard and fast, trying to clear whatever that had been. His face had gone pale under the flush. His shoulders shook once. Twice. He scrubbed a hand over his mouth, then stared at his palm like he expected to see something there.

He didn't.

There was nothing to see.

The room never left residue unless it wanted to.

Eli had both hands pressed to his sternum now, fingers hooked almost like claws. His breaths were short and sipping. His eyes—Lara didn't like his eyes. They were too bright. Fever-bright.

His tears hadn't stopped.

They didn't even look like crying-tears anymore. They just looked like his face was letting fluid go because it had nowhere else to put it.

Lara crawled over to him. Her knee slid in sweat-slick on the padded floor. Her hair stuck to her forehead. Her shirt clung everywhere.

He didn't look at her. He was looking past her. Through her in a way that made her stomach pull tight.

"Eli," she mouthed.

His eyes flicked to hers.

Slow.

He licked his lips, swallowed, and when he mouthed back, it came out in those neat, careful shapes like before. He was using all his effort to give her clean syllables.

It's under my skin.

Lara's mouth tightened.

Where, she mouthed.

His lips moved. His brow furrowed.

He lifted one shaking hand and pressed his fingertips into the soft place under his sternum, just above the solar plexus. He pushed in hard, like he was trying to hold something inside.

Lara watched his fingers dig.

She felt nausea rise again.

She shook her head. No. Don't do that. Don't press.

Eli shook his head to mirror hers. No. Then corrected. It's already there.

And then he breathed out—more like let air fall out of him than exhaled—and mouthed something she almost didn't catch, because his mouth trembled around it.

They're still talking.

Her stomach dropped.

Who.

He shook his head, frantic. Then looked down at his notebook like it could help him explain. He flipped to a new page—his hand leaving damp streaks on the cover—and set the tip of his pen down, ready.

He didn't write.

The pen moved.

Lara watched his hand shake, watched him hold the pen, yes, but she knew that grip. That wasn't how your wrist moved when you wrote. The pen skated across the page in stilted, deliberate lines, stopping and starting like a needle on a seismograph.

Her scalp prickled.

Words formed.

I CAN HEAR YOU
I CAN HEAR YOU
WE ARE STILL HERE
WHY ARE YOU STILL HERE
WE WERE QUIET

Lara felt cold break through the heat.

Eli stared at the page. His breath hitched. His face twisted.

He shook his head at her again, violent now, desperate. I didn't. I didn't.

I know, she mouthed.

He pressed a shaking hand over his eyes and let his head knock back against the panel, lightly. Over and over. A steady tap, like he was trying to sync himself with something that wasn't the room.

The diode pulsed again.

The light felt thicker.

The room felt smaller.

And Lara realized something ugly and soft and intimate, something she almost didn't let herself think: they were getting naked together.

Not all the way yet. Not literally all the way. But the room was peeling them. Layer by layer.

Miles half-stripped. Dana stripped to skin and scars and didn't flinch. Lara's shirt stuck so tight to her ribs she could feel every breath against it. Eli crying openly, not wiping the tears anymore. Every bruise and tremor exposed. Pride gone. Distance gone. Privacy gone.

The room had wanted this.

Shame and heat and helpless body honesty.

Confession.

Like church, Lara thought, and immediately felt sick for thinking it.

Caleb was across the chamber, his palm flat against one padded wall. He had his eyes closed. His mouth moved very slightly. Too slight for her to read. He could've been humming, except humming would've been sound and only he got sound.

She watched him.

Her skin crawled in a slower, deeper way.

If he starts praying, she thought, I will kill him with my hands.

He opened his eyes.

They were so calm.

He turned and looked at her like he'd heard her think it.

Her jaw flexed.

The diode blinked again—

—and the air pressure dropped.

It was fast.

The heated air, the syrup-thick sweetness, the slow choke of the chemical wash—all of it seemed to pull toward one point, like the room had found a drain.

Lara felt it in her ears first. A low, mean pop. Pressure equalizing too fast. Her balance misfired. Her stomach rolled. She slapped a hand to the floor to steady herself.

Dana staggered like someone had yanked a rug. Miles's head shot up. Eli inhaled a little gasp and clutched harder at his sternum.

And then a panel low near the corner—just a small seam, no handle, flush a second ago—cracked open.

Dana was closest.

Her eyes snapped to it.

Her body reacted before thought.

Training lived in her bones: find exit / secure exit / get people out.

She dropped her forearm-wrap from her face. The skin around her nose and mouth was pink and irritated, but she didn't flinch. She lunged for that seam, planted her boots, grabbed the edges with both hands, and pulled.

Lara reached for her, hand outstretched.

No.

Dana yanked.

The room inhaled.

It was silent.

There was no ripping sound, no roar of air, no deep industrial HOWL the way there should've been if pressure had equalized that fast. But Lara felt it— oh God she felt it.

It hit like invisible hands grabbing at everything loose.

Lara's hair whipped back. Sweat lifted from her skin and vanished so fast it left her chilled in patches. The air rushed out of her lungs without her giving it permission. Her hand tore off the floor and dragged forward against her will.

Miles slammed back into the wall like someone had punched his chest, eyes bulging, jaw open in a perfect fucking hell O and no noise.

Eli made a tight, ugly face and grabbed for his own shirt to keep it from pulling against him like a sail.

Dana didn't scream.

Her mouth opened.

Her face went to strain, then pain, then something past pain—gritted and white and stunned.

Her arms were locked straight, muscles roped and standing hard under skin, as the vacuum pulled against whatever she had hold of. Every tendon in her neck jumped. Her shoulders looked like they might tear.

Her feet slid an inch. Two.

She slammed them wider.

Her eyes flicked to Lara for a second, and there it was again, under everything: that soldier clarity.

Get back, Dana mouthed.

Lara shook her head and reached again, crawling forward against the invisible pull like she was wading into undertow.

Dana's jaw worked. Her face twisted through effort, through shock, through a flare of something like fear. Her forearms shook.

And then—

And then something gave.

Not with a break sound. There was no sound.

Just a visible shift.

Dana's body snapped forward a brutal fraction and then slammed back. The movement was wrong. Too fast. Too hard. Too much force for bone, for joint, for the soft places where the shoulder meets the chest.

Her eyes blew wide.

Her mouth shaped a single syllable—ah—pure and raw and animal.

Her grip slipped.

Her whole body jerked backward, away from the seam, like she'd been released from a hook, and she staggered two steps, then three.

Lara caught her on reflex.

Dana hit her hard enough to drive air out of Lara's lungs. The impact lit her nerves in a white flare. Lara grunted and tasted copper.

Dana was shaking.

Dana was shaking.

Her weight was all wrong.

Her body felt wrong against Lara's. Too loose in places that should've been rigid. Too heavy in places that should've been alive with held tension. She leaned fully into Lara in a way Dana had not leaned on anyone this entire time, her whole body letting go like she'd been unplugged.

Her eyes were open, but they were unfocused. Her jaw hung slack.

Lara's stomach went cold.

No, she thought, again, desperate and immediate and childish. No. No, no, not you too, not again, we cannot keep doing this, I cannot keep—

Dana's lips moved.

Lara leaned close, tears burning her eyes in the heat, one hand cradling the back of Dana's head so it wouldn't loll, the other arm wrapped around her ribs, holding her up.

Dana mouthed, whisper-slow, shaped like apology:

Couldn't close it.

Lara swallowed. Her throat hurt so bad it felt cut.

Hey, she mouthed. Hey. Stay here.

But Dana's gaze was already slipping.

Her eyes twitched, trying to focus, then unfocused again.

Her body twitched, tiny, like an aftershock.

Then she went still.

Lara held her there for a few long seconds, because her body didn't know how to let go.

Her mind did.

Her mind knew.

She felt the moment Dana left. It was quiet. Not dramatic. The same way Renee's had been quiet, only without the desperate fight. Dana's body accepted stillness like an order, knee-jerk, automatic.

Lara's arms shook.

Her eyes stung.

Her jaw locked so hard she thought she'd crack a molar.

She lowered Dana to the floor gently. Gently. Gently. Palms guiding, not dropping. Knees cushioning.

Her chest hurt.

Her throat burned.

Her heart pounded so hard the room's pulse flickered with it again.

She knelt there for a second, hands still on Dana's cooling shoulders, head bowed, hair hanging damp around her face, and felt more than grief.

She felt fury.

Her eyes lifted to Caleb.

He was facing the wall again. One hand on the panel, eyes closed. Breathing steady.

And Lara had the sudden, clear, electric knowledge that he wasn't calming down.

He was communing.

He was in sync with the room.

He was the only thing in here the room wasn't stripping.

Her stomach lurched.

Her vision swam.

The heat pressed harder. Her skin felt too tight. Her shirt clung to her ribs like a second skin. Sweat trickled down the side of her face, along her jaw, into the corner of her mouth. Tasted like salt and something faintly chemical.

She realized she was shaking.

Her hands. Her shoulders. Her jaw.

Shock.

She told herself to breathe. She couldn't hear it. She felt it. She had to trust the feeling.

In.

Out.

In.

Her body gave her that much.

It didn't give her stillness.

Under everything else—the heat, the chemical residue, the suffocating sweetness in the air, the memory of Dana folding, the memory of Renee's mouth forced open around a scream that never left—under all of that, she could still feel it.

The tapping.

Throat. Ear. Teeth. Heart. Throat.

Luh—

Ruh—

Ah.

It had gotten closer.

The first time, it had felt like it was inside her bones but somehow still outside her choice, like a knock through the structure of her body. This felt different.

This felt like a mouth at her ear.

She squeezed her eyes shut.

Stop, she thought.

Please stop.

Please just stop.

There was a pause.

The tapping gentled.

And then, soft—not in her ears, but in her head, as if she were remembering a voice and not hearing one—she felt, more than heard:

good girl.

Her eyes flew open.

Her stomach rolled.

She nearly threw up.

She lurched to her feet, stumbled, caught herself on the wall, and dragged her gaze to Caleb like she was dragging her whole body with it.

He was watching her now.

His eyes gleamed in the red pulse.

He wasn't smiling in the polite way anymore.

He was smiling like he was proud.

Like she was doing so, so well.

Her breath hitched.

Her vision sparked at the edges.

And just past him—just past Caleb, just past Renee's body and Dana's body and Miles heaving in stuttering, furious shock and Eli crying quietly with both hands pressed hard to his chest—just past all of that, at the edge of the panel where the vacuum had hissed and tried to take Dana with it—

Lara saw it for the first time.

She hadn't noticed it before. It hadn't been there before.

Now it was.

At first she thought it was just condensation. Sweat thrown from their bodies, steam from the heat, residue from the room's exhale, collected along the white panel low near the floor.

Then she saw that it wasn't beading like water. It was clinging like dust.

Dust.

Dark in the damp.

And it wasn't random scatter.

It had lines.

Her stomach lurched again.

Her mouth went dry.

Because the dust on the wall had begun to gather in the impression of fingertips dragged down.

Not scratches.

Tracks.

As if something soft had pressed there from the inside, then smeared down as it lost strength.

And Lara, staring at those marks, understood finally, fully, horribly, what "safe" had meant when Caleb said it.

Safe didn't mean alive.

Safe meant contained.

The room was not letting anything leave.

Not them.

Not their sounds.

Not even their bodies.

Just residue.

Just dust.

Just proof.

Her hand slammed flat to her own chest like she could hold herself in.

Her throat worked.

Her jaw shook with it, small, hard, stubborn.

She mouthed at Caleb, slow, shaking, almost gentle in its fury:

What are you doing to us.

Caleb tilted his head. His eyes were warm. Loving, even.

"This is what you came for," he said softly, and Lara could hear every word.

"This is forgiveness."

***

The light started to die.

Not all at once. That would've been kind. It dimmed in slow, pulsing breaths, each pulse holding a little longer in red and then thinning, like blood watered down. The diode above the door wasn't a blink anymore; it was an ache. Red swelled, held, throbbed, faded. Swelled again. Held. Faded.

The white in the walls took it. Drank it. Went pink, then bruised, then gray.

Lara's eyes strained to keep up.

Her pupils had blown so wide they felt raw.

She blinked and the room smeared. Like the air itself had smeared.

Her body knew darkness was coming before her mind did. Her breath changed. Her shoulders curled. She felt herself bracing for something she couldn't see yet.

Every time the diode swelled, everyone in the room had a shadow. When it faded, they didn't.

That flicker made them feel less like people and more like phases. Versions of selves the room was testing, flipping through.

Miles was sitting on the floor with his back to the panel, knees half-up, arms hanging on them. He wasn't trying to look strong anymore. His chest was bare, slick and sheened, stomach rising and falling in small, exhausted movements. Every so often his jaw jerked—muscle spasm, leftover rage still hunting for a way out—and then he went still again. His face had stopped trying to stay angry. It had settled into blank.

Eli had folded forward, his notebook still in his lap. His shoulders shook on each inhale. He hadn't wiped his face in a long time. The tears just kept falling, caught briefly in the shallow jut of his upper lip, then ran down along the curve of his jaw to his neck. The notebook lay open under his hands. His fingers were still curled around the pen, but the lines across the page weren't his anymore. The page was almost filled. In the dim red blink, Lara could make out four repeating lines, repeated until they bled into one another:

WE CAN HEAR YOU
WE CAN HEAR YOU
WE CAN HEAR YOU
STAY

Renee and Dana lay where they'd fallen.

Renee's body had gone slack, almost gentle in its stillness. Dana looked like she'd dropped in a fight—head turned, jaw set, shoulders still squared on instinct. Even in death her stance argued with surrender.

The dust smear near the low panel—the one Dana had tried to wrench open—had grown thicker. It wasn't just five downward tracks anymore. It was more like a heel of a hand had pressed against it from inside, desperate, then slid. The pinkish lighting made it dark, damp-looking, almost wet.

Lara had to remind herself to keep breathing.

Her throat was raw.

Her chest hurt. Deep. Like the ache you get from sobbing so long you've bruised yourself, even though she hadn't made a sound the whole time.

Her heart hit like a dull drum. Off-tempo. Too hard. Her head throbbed with it.

Her vision kept ghosting.

And underneath all of it, still there like a warm palm against the back of her neck:

Lara.

The room was still tapping her name.

It wasn't in her bones anymore; it was in her pulse now. Her pulse felt split. Part of it still tried to belong to her, hard and frantic and animal. The other part had gone soft and steady, mimicking an outside pace. The room wanted her rhythm.

Her name didn't even feel like a word anymore.

It felt like claiming.

She swallowed and felt the swallow scrape.

Her body wanted to sit. To fold. To slide down the wall the way Miles had, let her muscles stop burning and her jaw stop clenching and just be held by the floor.

Her body also wanted to keep moving.

If she stopped moving, she was afraid she wouldn't start again.

She stayed up.

Her knees hurt. Her thighs trembled. Sweat had dried sticky on her ribs and then come back again under the new heat pulse. Her shirt clung to every line of her. She could feel salt crust forming in places—the bend of her elbow, the inner crook behind her knee.

Caleb hadn't moved much.

He stood near the center of the chamber now. Not by the door. Not by the panel Dana had tried to force. Center, like a spoke. The pulse from the diode hit him, colored his skin red, pulled back, left him in something close to gray, hit him again, back and forth.

When the light pulsed red, his face looked warm.

When it faded, something in him went empty.

Not off.

Empty.

Like the red light filled him and every time it faded, he went back to nothing for a second.

Lara watched him during the in-between.

During the gray.

Jacob's ladder, her brain tried to name it. Strobe test. EMT training. Watching pupils for response.

Except Caleb's pupils didn't react like anybody's should. They stayed steady. Too steady.

Her breathing hitched.

He looked like a man the room put on, she thought.

The thought made her stomach twist. Not because of what it meant about him. Because of what it meant about them.

If this thing could wear a person, what did that make everyone else in here? What were they, to it?

Samples.

She had to swallow twice to keep from gagging.

She felt empty behind her eyes. Her body was running out.

Her anger hadn't gone. But it had gotten heavy.

She felt the edges start to fuzz.

Like the room was thinning her.

276

Like her selfhood had weight and the room was slowly lifting it out of her and setting it aside to study.

Her jaw clenched, stubborn. No.

No. You don't get to name me. You don't get to take me apart and tag the pieces and call that mercy.

Her jaw ached with it.

She dragged her eyes off Caleb and forced herself to do a check. That was how she kept from slipping. Checks. Anchor in tasks.

Renee. Dana. Miles. Eli.

Alive, dead, alive, alive.

Alive, dead, dead, alive.

It hit her in the gut.

Half.

There were six. Now there were four.

Her jaw flexed. Grief and shock made her stomach sour.

Her vision blurred.

Lara blinked hard and wiped her face with the back of her wrist. Her skin felt too hot. Her wrist felt too hot. The air felt too hot. Everything felt too close. She needed air that wasn't touched already.

There was none.

277

She looked at Miles.

He was staring at nothing. Not zoned. Not faint-eyes. Focused. Just... somewhere else.

"Miles," she mouthed.

He didn't react.

Her stomach tightened.

She dropped to her knees beside him, ignoring the way her patella hit the padded floor too hard, the small bolt of uncomfortable pain, and leaned in close. She put a hand on his shoulder. His skin was burning.

He flinched. At her touch, not at her.

His eyes snapped up to hers. For a second she saw him again. Not the guy who kept joking, not the guy who swore like a reflex, not the guy who jabbed his finger at invisible enemies in the air—just a very tired, very scared person.

He looked older now.

"Miles," she repeated, shaping the syllables with care. You with me?

He swallowed. His swallow looked painful.

He mouthed back, slow, not with sarcasm this time but with gratitude, like the act of making letters clean was a kindness: I don't think I can do this.

Lara's heart squeezed and ached at the same time.

Her throat burned.

She nodded once, steady. You can.

He shook his head fast. He breathed in too hard, too shallow. His chest trembled under her hand. He mouthed again, jaw stiffening to form the shapes he didn't want to admit: It's laughing. It won't shut up. It won't shut up.

His face cracked, briefly.

There it was again—that shame. That awful, reflexive shame, the kind of shame that has history behind it. The kind you develop when somebody knows the worst true thing about you and won't let it go and uses it like a leash a leash and a leash.

The muscles around his mouth jumped.

Lara felt something hot surge in her chest.

She knew that flavor of shame. You see it on too many faces in late-night rigs on bad calls. I did a thing I said I'd never do. Someone saw me do it. I don't get to come back from that and pretend I didn't.

She shook her head, hard, and mouthed, It can say whatever it wants.

He blinked like that surprised him.

She leaned closer, face inches from his, sweat and heat and salt and the sour-chemical stink of whatever the room had pushed into their lungs hanging between them.

Her mouth shaped each word like instruction in a mirror. It doesn't make it true.

Miles stared at her for a long second, like he was scanning her face for a lie.

Then his eyes shone.

His chin wobbled.

He swallowed like it hurt.

He gave one sharp nod, then let his head fall forward until his forehead touched her shoulder. Not romantic. Not desperate. Instinct.

He just needed somewhere to rest his head that wasn't a wall.

Lara let him.

Her throat hurt. Her eyes stung. She blinked hard again and inhaled through her mouth.

Her chest spasmed. Her brain sent pain up her neck. Her lungs were still pissed from that sweet chemical purge. The air felt like grit and sugar.

She made herself take another breath anyway.

For Miles.

For Eli.

For whatever part of her still needed to be a medic in the middle of a god-machine.

When she looked up again, Eli wasn't where she'd left him.

Her heart kicked.

He hadn't moved far. He'd slumped sideways from his sitting position and was now half-curled on the floor, shoulders against the panel, cheek pressed to it like he was listening. Notebook still in his lap. Pen still in his fingers.

His eyes were open.

Too wide.

Staring at the blank white padded panel like there was a window there.

Lara slid over on her knees, hand still steadying Miles until she could gently lower his head to the wall. She crawled the rest of the way to Eli.

"Eli," she mouthed, close.

He didn't blink.

He didn't look at her.

He was mumbling. His lips moved fast and small, like a child talking to themselves in bed in the dark.

His cheeks were slick with tear tracks, but he wasn't crying anymore. This was after crying. Fragile. Hushed. Done.

She leaned in closer.

She read his mouth.

It took her a second to register.

He wasn't babbling.

He wasn't panicking.

He was repeating the same line over and over, soft:

It's okay. It's okay. It's okay. It's okay.

Her chest ached.

She reached for his shoulder.

His skin felt different under her hand.

That made her stomach twist.

He was still hot—everyone was overheating—but under the heat there was... looseness. Too much give in the muscle. The way someone feels when their body is on an adrenaline crash and can't hold tone anymore. The way someone feels when they're minutes from passing out, or bleeding unseen somewhere, or about to drop.

Her pulse kicked.

No.

Stay with me.

She slid a hand under his jaw, thumb at the hinge the way she'd done with Renee, feeling for movement, for clench, for life. His jaw worked against her touch, slow and automatic. It was like holding an engine that was running on fumes.

"Eli." Slower, sharper. Hey. With me.

This time his eyes slid, just a fraction, until they met hers.

He looked startled to see her. Then relieved.

Then guilty.

Her stomach pulled tight.

She mouthed, What's wrong.

He swallowed. His swallow stuck. He winced and coughed without sound.

When he mouthed back, it came in clean syllables. He spent energy making it clear for her, even now.

They were in the walls and now they're in me.

Lara felt cold slide down her back.

Who, she mouthed.

His eyes flicked up over her shoulder, to the panel, then back, then to his notebook. He licked his lips.

Us.

Her lungs forgot what to do for a second.

Us, he repeated. Louder. They said "we were quiet." They said "we stayed quiet." We. We. We.

Her stomach twisted. Her throat burned like she'd inhaled bleach.

"What does that mean," she mouthed, the words feeling huge in her own skull.

Eli's mouth trembled.

They're mad we're loud.

Her vision tilted for a second.

She had to plant a palm to the floor to steady herself. The floor felt too warm under her skin. Like pressed flesh, not surface.

We're loud.

Oh God.

They're mad we're loud.

Her mind tried to make a shape out of that.

Something hit her.

All the way back at the start—Caleb's voice, patient, clinical: You will hear everything you've ever tried to ignore.

The chamber wasn't silent out of purity.

It wasn't silent because silence was a scientific novelty.

It was silent because something in here wanted it that way.

Something in here had cultivated perfect quiet, was living in perfect quiet, was tolerating perfect quiet, and they had come in and broken it.

Not ghosts, not demons, not aliens. Not yet, not anything she could label. Just others. Others, plural. Us. We. We stayed quiet.

They'd intruded.

They were sinners in church shouting during prayer.

Her stomach rolled. Her throat worked.

She looked at the dust smear on the wall, at the dragged-down tracks, at the way the residue clung like touch. She thought of whatever had knocked in Renee's chest from the wrong side. She thought of Dana trying to force open a seam and the room dragging her back like prey. She thought of the scream that had hit them without a mouth.

She thought of the notebook.

Her eyes dropped to it.

Eli's hand—trembling, not fully responsive, more like a ragged tremor now—still curled around the pen. The latest page was half-full. The letters were huge now, messy, running into each other, like whoever was "writing" didn't fully understand how hands fatigue.

HELP US
IT HURTS TO BE LOUD
IT HURTS
STAY
STAY
STAY
STAY

Lara's breath stuttered.

Her vision blurred and cleared and blurred again.

For a second she forgot where she was. Not because she was losing reality—because the information simply overwhelmed the amount of air she had left to process it.

This is not punishment, she thought, dazed.

It was never punishment.

It's regulation.

The room wasn't hurting them because it enjoyed hurting them.

The room was hurting them because living things had been in here a long time in perfect quiet and these six idiots had walked in, stomping and breathing and swearing and sweating and panicking and crying and laughing, and it physically hurt whatever else was in here.

Shame iced through her. Shame and awe, in a horrible knot.

We're the monsters, she thought.

We're the noise.

Her throat burned.

Her eyes stung.

Her breath shook going in.

Her jaw trembled.

She looked at Eli again.

His pupils had gone huge. His eyelashes clumped with wet. His lips trembled.

He mouthed, It's okay. It's okay. It's okay. It's ok—

And something broke in him.

It wasn't violent.

That was the worst part.

It was small.

Quiet.

He just... loosened.

His muscles let go all at once, like a string had been cut and everything that had been holding him upright, holding him tense, holding him braced against the panel, released.

His head tipped forward. His jaw went slack under her thumb. His eyes stayed open.

No sound. No shake. No seizure. No fight.

He just wasn't there anymore.

Lara's heart slammed so hard in her ribs her vision whited for a second.

Not again.

Not again not again not again—

Her breath hitched. Her throat made a tiny fractured noise and blasted her skull with it. She clenched her teeth against it like it hurt.

Her hand stayed cupped against his jaw.

Her palm still felt heat.

Her mind didn't.

She let him down slow. Slow. Slow. Gentle, even now. Her hands didn't know how to stop being careful. She settled him on the floor, eyes open, cheek turned, notebook still in his lap.

Her stomach rolled so hard she tasted acid.

Her shoulders started to shake.

No.

Her jaw locked and she forced them steady.

Not now.

Not now not yet.

She swallowed it down like broken glass.

Her vision moved without her.

Her eyes slid over Eli's body to the notebook, to the lines written in jagged urgent block.

WE CAN HEAR YOU
STAY
STAY
STAY

Lara stared.

Her breathing went thin.

She didn't have words for what hit her just then. She only knew the shape of it: a kind of terrible, aching tenderness in her chest. Something like grief, yes, but deeper. Something like being chosen. Claimed. Wanted.

That scared her worse than anything else so far.

Because part of her wanted to answer.

She shut her eyes.

Don't you dare, she told herself.

Don't you dare say yes to that.

When she opened her eyes again, the world had darkened another shade.

The pulse from the diode had gone deeper red. The corners of the room were no longer visible. The edges had softened. Her brain tried to interpret the gradient and decided there was distance where there wasn't.

Her vision swam in and out of grain.

That was when the static started.

At first she thought it was her own blood. That hiss-throb behind the ears you get when you're too hot, too tired, too close to passing out. Then she realized two things at once:

1. She could "hear" it in her teeth.
2. It was getting louder.

Not sound. Feeling. Buzz.

It vibrated in the roots of her molars. In the hinge of her jaw. In the cartilage at the base of her nose. In the hard notch at the top of her sternum.

Her muscles clenched to it.

Her jaw locked and hurt.

Her vision shivered with it.

It grew, not like noise, but like presence.

Pressure built behind her eyes. A hot push.

Her sight flared, whited out, came back streaked in red.

Shit, she thought dimly. I'm going to pass ou—

Her vision vanished.

Just—gone.

No fade to black. No graceful gray. Just a flat, total blank like someone had thumbed out a candle behind her eyes.

She sucked in a breath and her body panicked. She reached out blind and caught air, then caught panel, and the world spun with a dizzy, wrong not-up-not-down lurch. Her stomach heaved.

She heard herself make a sound—not by ear, by bone. A raw, desperate, animal noise she'd never made in front of anyone in her adult life. She felt it explode through her skull.

Her heart slammed so hard it hurt.

Her body said we're falling we're falling we're falling.

Her palms smacked to the floor. Hot. Damp. The floor pulsed softly under her skin like a big slow animal breathing.

Where? Where is—?

A hand settled on her shoulder.

She jerked so hard she almost threw herself.

The hand squeezed.

Steady. Warm. Present.

"Lara," said Caleb's voice.

Fully audible.

Inside her head, clean as whisper against her actual ear.

Her heart stuttered.

"Breathe," he said. Calm. Slow. Patient. "You are safe."

Her stomach rebelled.

Her eyes, useless now, burned.

The static pressure behind her eyes surged, crested, held.

"Do not fight it," he said gently. "They are giving you quiet."

They.

Her breath hitched.

Her throat moved around a swallowed noise.

Her fingers curled against the floor. It felt like flesh now. Like the underside of a wrist. Warm and pulsing.

She stayed on her hands and knees, blind, drenched in her own heat and the room's heat, her heart slamming out an off-tempo panic rhythm while the chamber patiently tried to press a calmer one in.

Dana. Renee. Eli.

Half gone.

Miles, shaking against the wall behind her, forehead still where she'd left it, his chest hitching in tiny little sob-breaths he'd never let anyone hear in the regular world.

Her.

And Caleb.

And something else.

Something plural.

The pressure behind her eyes held at the edge of pain, then softened.

Vision didn't come back the way she expected it to.

It didn't come back red.

It came back white.

Her brain tried to interpret and failed. For one soft, disorienting second she saw nothing but white haze, full-field, no walls, no bodies, no depth. A floating blank. She felt herself breathing in it, like fog.

Her panic eased—not because she wanted it to, but because the white made it ease. The way a painkiller makes a pulse stop hammering in a wound without asking permission.

Her jaw unclenched.

Her shoulders dropped.

Her heart slowed. Not all the way down to the room's candle-pulse, but closer.

Her head swam.

Good girl, whispered that soft pulse again, through her throat.

Lara's eyes stung.

Her chest cracked with fury and grief and a horrible, traitorously warm thread of comfort.

"Stop," she whispered, and her own whisper hurt in her skull.

Caleb's hand stayed on her shoulder.

He squeezed once, steady.

"Almost finished," he said.

She swallowed. Her throat burned.

Her vision stayed white, throbbing slightly with each echo of the diode. Shapes began to suggest themselves in negative space. Ghosts of presence. The way you see someone move behind a thin curtain.

She couldn't make out faces. She could make out pulses.

Three.

Three pulses.

Miles's—jagged, uneven, twitching with little shame-spasms and surrender-hiccups.

Hers—stubborn, furious, ragged at the edges, still not matching the room's rhythm completely.

And one other.

Large.

Even.

Calm.

Wrapping both of theirs like hands laid over two frantic chests.

Caleb.

Her stomach twisted.

Her jaw clenched again.

"Why," she said. Her own voice broke her skull open. Her eyes watered. She tasted salt and metal. She forced the word through it anyway. "Why are you doing this to us?"

She felt Caleb lean in.

His breath, if it was breath, brushed her hairline.

"So you can be quiet," he said softly.

Her stomach lurched.

"Please," she whispered, though she didn't even know who she was talking to—him, the room, Renee, Dana, Eli, herself, God. "Please don't."

Caleb's hand stayed steady on her shoulder. His voice went almost fond.

"It is already happening," he said.

Her vision flickered.

The white shifted.

For a second—less than a second—she saw through it. Just a flash. A blink.

The real room cut back in like a film splice: red pulse, sweat-slick wall, Miles wrecked and shivering, Eli's loose body folded on the floor, Dana and Renee still, Caleb's face very close to hers, calm and lit from underneath by that patient red diode—

—and behind him, in the seam near the floor, in the smear of dust and press-marks and drag-lines where Dana had tried to wrench them an exit, she saw movement.

Small.

Pressing.

Fingers.

Not Dana's fingers. Too fine. Too long at the joints. More joints than they should have. Paler than they should have.

Reaching.

Reaching, slow, like something inside was feeling its way out.

Then the white slammed back in and she couldn't see anything at all.

Her heart tripped.

Her stomach dropped.

Her hands shook against the floor.

And the last thing she felt before the white swallowed the edges of her completely was the room tapping her name in her blood like a lullaby.

Luh—

Ruh—

Ah.

Listen.

**

White.

Everywhere.

Not light. Not color. Just presence.
A living blank that hummed so low it felt like thought before it became language.

Lara breathed.

The breath didn't hurt anymore.
It didn't echo.
It didn't belong to her, either.

Something else drew with her—out, in, out—slow, careful, teaching her the tempo.

Her hands were on the floor.
Or maybe inside it.
The difference was gone.

She tried to move her fingers; they moved slow, weightless, like through water.
The heat had left, but the memory of it stayed, stitched under her skin.

Behind her eyelids, faint pulse.

One.

Two.

Three.

Not the diode now.
The room itself.

Breathing.

She opened her mouth.
Sound didn't happen, but the shape did.
Her tongue touched the roof of her mouth.
The motion alone carried weight.
It was enough for the white to tremble.

A hush settled.
Not silence—listening.

She felt the others then.

Not their bodies. Their impressions.
Dana's refusal to break.
Renee's breath half-caught.
Eli's apology circling itself.
Miles, small and honest, whispering I'm sorry like prayer.

They were all here, folded into the air, dispersed like warmth in fabric.

The room was full.

For the first time, the room wasn't hungry.

Lara's heartbeat slowed until she could barely feel it.

Then, softly, from somewhere both inside and everywhere, a whisper formed—not voice, not words, just pressure tracing her name against her teeth.

Luh—
Ruh—
Ah.

It lingered on the last syllable until it became nothing at all.

The floor pulsed once.

The white thinned.

For the briefest flicker, she saw the outline of a door, half-open.
Red light beyond, bleeding through dust.

She almost reached for it.

Almost.

Instead, she exhaled.

The white drew in with her breath and stayed.

***

Weeks later, when the technician reopened the chamber, the monitors
were still on.
The oxygen read nominal.
The humidity perfect.

Only one heart rate registered.
Steady. Calm. Continuous.

No bodies.

Just dust, fine as ash, spread thin across the floor in faint ridges—
three letters dragged there by something unseen.

L A R.

And when the door seals closed again, the instruments hum once—
a pulse too low to hear,
but anyone standing near the wall might feel it in their jaw,
soft as a whisper reminding them:

Listen.

The Slow God

Billy almost didn't notice when the world stopped.

He noticed the air first.

It had a weight to it that afternoon, a kind of summer thickness that didn't belong in October. He'd propped the workshop door open with a cinderblock to pull a breeze through, but nothing moved. The heat just sat there, laid over his shoulders like a work jacket someone forgot to take off. Sweat gathered under his shirt and went nowhere.

He was halfway under the unit when he realized the hum was gone.

The rooftop condenser fed down through this line, a squat metal thing older than the strip mall itself, whining all season like it resented being asked to live. He knew its rhythm better than he knew most voices. He could tell from across the parking lot when the belt slipped or the bearings started to chatter. It was his job to keep the thing going because no one else would.

And now it wasn't making a sound.

He slid out from under the housing and listened.

Nothing.

Not "quiet." Nothing.

No fan blade chatter. No traffic hiss from the main road. No far-off thump of bass from the tanning salon two doors down. Not even the mosquito-whine constant in his left ear — the tinnitus he'd picked up back in '09 when a blower went while his head was too close.

He hadn't been in true silence since before his divorce. Before that, maybe even farther back.

"Goddamn," he said aloud.

His own voice startled him. It came out like it had weight. Like he could touch it.

He sat up slow. His knees popped. That made no sound either.

Okay. Weird.

Billy rubbed at his temple, then pressed two fingers behind his jaw, searching for the familiar pulse. There. Steady. He wasn't dead. That would've been funny. Drop dead in a strip mall AC closet with a wrench in his hand and a belly full of gas-station coffee. Brenda would've rolled her eyes at the funeral and told everyone, "At least it's on brand."

He snorted.

The snort made no sound.

He froze.

He clapped, fast, just to prove he could still hear. The clap landed in his palms and… nothing. He felt the sting. He watched the vibration in the meat of his thumb. No sound met him.

The part of his brain that does panic went to reach for the throttle.

The rest of him, the part that had tightened rattling vent covers at 3 a.m. in February because some landlord's "emergency" was a loose screw and a lonely voice, the part that had bundled his mother's body when hospice hadn't come fast enough, that part said: Slow down. Check it before you break it worse.

He stood.

The workshop wasn't much. Slab floor, two pegboards, a dented dorm fridge, a folding table where invoices went to die. A wall clock that had been stuck at 12:03 for months because he never remembered to change the battery.

Except he had changed the battery. Last week.

He squinted up at it.

12:03. The second hand was in the same place it'd been last night when he locked up. Barely a fraction past the twelve. Balanced there.

He pulled his phone out of his pocket. The lock screen glowed against his palm. 12:03 PM. No bar flicker, no push alert stutter, nothing crawling along the top edge. No movement at all.

He opened the stopwatch app out of muscle memory. Tapped start.

Nothing moved.

Oh.

Okay.

So not just the unit, then.

He swallowed. He could hear the swallow inside his head, like his throat was a hallway and someone else was walking down it. He'd never heard his own swallow that loud. It wasn't even loud. It was just... the only thing.

He crossed the workshop and turned the faucet over the slop sink. Water arced out, clear and bright — and hung. It didn't splash. Didn't hit metal. It came out of the mouth of the tap and stopped like God had put a finger on it and said no.

Billy stared.

His first thought wasn't apocalypse. His first thought was, Huh. That's not right.

He reached his hand into the shape of the stream. It felt like running water should've felt — glide and cool and pressure — only it wasn't moving around his fingers. He was moving through it. Like dragging his hand through hair gel.

He pulled his hand back and watched the dent he'd made hold.

No refill. No collapse. The arc of water stayed dented where his hand had been, like memory foam.

Billy wiped his hand on his jeans out of habit. They were already damp from sweat. His palm tasted faintly of copper and county tap.

"This is a gas leak," he told himself.

He didn't hear it with his ears. He heard it inside his head, as if someone had put the words against the bones.

It made sense. Sort of. He knew what CO could do, had gone into too many rentals with windows painted shut and rusted-out heaters. You get woozy. Things get weird. You stop making good decisions.

So, okay. He'd get out. Step outside. Breathe air that wasn't full of refrigerant and dust and whatever else he'd been crawling through. The door was propped open anyway. He'd walk out, call for help, let somebody with gloves and paperwork tell him if he needed an ambulance or a new filter.

Easy.

He pushed the workshop door the rest of the way open and stepped into the parking lot.

The heat outside hit like he'd walked into a dryer mid-cycle.

The air didn't move. Not a leaf twitch. Not a candy wrapper skittering. The sunlight sat on the blacktop like a poured thing, a layer of hot varnish you could peel back with your fingernails if you really tried.

Billy felt sweat roll from his hairline and down his temple. He watched it travel. He watched it slow. He watched it stop at his jaw like the world had thickened and the droplet couldn't break the surface tension.

His stomach did a slow roll.

Main Street lay out beyond the strip mall's cracked curb. Four lanes. A gas station. A nail place. The flag in front of the credit union. Two cars in the intersection, nose-to-nose, both canted a little like somebody'd slammed brakes late. He could see the driver in the red SUV, mouth open. Her hair hovered in the air around her like a halo, frozen mid-bounce. Sunglasses up on her head. Eyes wide. A perfect little "oh."

A crow hung above the telephone pole on the corner. Wings spread, last few primaries fanned. You didn't realize how much a wing trembles just holding position until you saw one caught there. There was a hardness to it. A held breath.

Farther down the sidewalk, a kid on a bike. One foot on the pedal, one foot stretched out mid-kick like he was about to flex forward. The back wheel had a playing card clothes-pinned to the frame so it would flap in the spokes.

The card was just hanging there, partway bent. Bent, and not bending more.

Billy waited to hear that plastic-y flutter.

Nothing.

His hand went to his throat again. Pulse, still there. Faster now.

"Okay," he said. He couldn't tell if his lips moved at the same time or a fraction behind. "Okay, okay, okay."

This was the part where you call someone.

He pulled his phone back out and hit Brenda.

No ring.

The little call timer didn't start. His contact photo for her — beach, 2014, sunburnt shoulders, a look that was still fond then — stayed flat. Her face didn't pixel-shift, didn't brighten, didn't do the minor drift you only saw when it was live. It was a picture of a picture.

He ended the call and tried 911.

Nothing.

He wasn't surprised. He told himself he wasn't surprised.

Something clicked against his boot.

For a half second his heart pounded so hard he thought he'd black out—sound—finally a sound—but it hadn't been a sound at all. It was sensation. The feel of contact through the sole. He looked down.

The wrench he'd dropped inside had rolled out the doorway and come to rest against his foot.

He hadn't seen it move.

Billy crouched, picked it up, and felt steadier with the weight of it in his hand.

That was stupid. A wrench couldn't help whatever this was. But holding it still helped him. That was different.

He spun in a slow circle, taking in the lot, the storefronts, the bank, the pale blue sky over town. He half expected to see somebody else walking around going "Hey, buddy? You see this too?" Some YouTube prank. Some "social experiment." That'd be a story. Couple teenagers run a freeze routine in front of the Family Dollar and make the old guy piss himself.

There was no one.

Everybody else was inside glass.

Everybody else was hung in amber.

The only thing that moved in the whole goddamn world was his own chest, and even that felt like work.

He swallowed again. The sound inside his skull was louder now. Not the high electric whine he'd lived with for years. Lower. Rounder. Steady.

A tone.

A hum.

Like a machine that had settled into its true speed.

Billy tightened his grip on the wrench and told himself, out loud, slow and clear so the bones in his head would carry it, "You're not gonna lose it. You're gonna keep it running till somebody smarter shows up."

He nodded once.

That nod lagged in his vision, like his body had done it and his sight was catching up.

He didn't like that.

He didn't like any of this.

But he knew what to do with broken things. You looked, you logged, you took care of what you could reach. You didn't sit on your ass and cry about how it wasn't fair. Fair never unclogged a vent.

He took one breath in. One breath out. Counted both, just to prove he could.

Then he walked toward the nearest frozen body.

The first body stood halfway between the nail salon and the coin laundry.

A man in delivery khakis, one arm raised as if he'd been waving before the air turned solid. The sweat darkening his back had dried in a bloom that would never finish.

Billy walked up until the man's shadow touched his boots. He had the wrench in one hand and his phone in the other, because tools made sense and screens didn't.

The guy's eyes were wide, pupils huge. There was a kind of shine to them that shouldn't have been there with no moisture, like someone had lacquered fear. Billy waited for a blink. Nothing.

He reached out, slow, and touched the shoulder. The fabric was warm, pliant. No rigor, no cold. A living heat without life underneath.

"Buddy?"
His own voice filled his head again, heavy, private.
The man didn't move.

Billy's fingers stayed on that shoulder longer than he meant them to. He wanted to feel a pulse through it—heat + beat = hope. But there was only the steady hum, somewhere behind his eyes, vibrating bone.

He crouched, looked at the ground. The man's shoe left a half-print in the blacktop, as if he'd been mid-step. Billy pressed a thumb into the edge of it and felt the indentation resist, like the asphalt had gone to rubber. He pulled his hand back. The print stayed perfect.

He stood again. The light around them hadn't shifted. He checked the sky; the sun still sat exactly where it had been when he came out of the shop. Not falling, not rising. Just there, burning.

The wrench hung heavy. He wasn't sure when he'd started carrying it like a weapon.

He crossed the lot toward the intersection, heat radiating in steady sheets. The air above the asphalt shimmered but never bent enough to break the illusion of movement.

A woman in a red SUV waited there, forever mid-impact with a sedan. Her seatbelt cut into her collarbone; her hands hovered inches from the wheel. A coffee cup lay sideways in the holder, liquid suspended in the mouth of the lid like a brown glass bead.

He leaned close to her window.

She smelled of vanilla spray and faint gasoline.

Billy whispered, "Ma'am," knowing she couldn't hear but needing to say something human.

The sound went nowhere.

For a second he thought he saw her pupils tighten. He blinked; they didn't.

The hum pulsed again.

He turned in a slow circle, trying to hear anything else. Nothing but his own blood.

"Alright," he said, louder, like volume could restart the world. "Alright then."

He looked down the street: rows of cars frozen nose to tail, an old man mid-step at the bus stop, pigeons hanging like ornaments above the curb. The whole town was a single photograph, and he was the smudge that didn't belong in it.

A heat shimmer crossed his vision; for a second he thought he saw motion behind the laundromat—something darker sliding between the dryers' vent stacks. He blinked again and it was gone. Maybe sweat in his eyes. Maybe not.

He laughed once, quietly. It sounded like breath through metal.

He had the thought—stupid, practical—that somebody would have to start keeping inventory. Power grids. Food. Water pressure. Garbage. The city would rot if no one checked the lines.

He looked at his hands, at the wrench, at the sheen of oil along the knuckles.

That was a job. That was something.

The hum in his head steadied, low and constant, almost comforting now.

"Fine," he said. "You all hold still. I'll handle it."

He nodded at the frozen woman behind the wheel as if she'd given him permission, turned, and started walking toward the service alley where the dumpsters baked in the unending noon.

Behind him, the air didn't move.

The service alley ran between the laundromat and a pawn shop that hadn't had real glass in its windows for years. A row of dumpsters squatted in the sunlight, paint bubbled from heat, flies locked above the rims like beads in amber. Even their shadows didn't quiver.

Billy walked through them like a ghost in someone else's photograph. Every footstep thudded through his soles but never made a sound. He counted each impact in his head—one, two, three, four—until the rhythm matched the pulse behind his ears. The hum was pacing him.

A rat hung half out of a trash bag, mouth open, teeth gleaming wet. He watched a bead of spoil climb its whisker and stop. He waited for it to fall. It didn't.

Billy pulled the spiral notebook from his shirt pocket, the one he used for service calls. He wrote in block letters:

12:03 PM. EVERYTHING STOPPED. LIGHT UNCHANGED. HEAT UNCHANGED. ONLY I MOVE. CHECK LATER.

The ink bled slowly into the paper, like it was being absorbed by a thicker air. He underlined CHECK LATER twice.

He didn't know who "later" was for.

Halfway down the alley, a loading dock door stood open to a storage room. Inside was a cooler, a hand truck, a pallet of bottled water. All still. He stepped in, grabbed a bottle, and twisted the cap. The plastic screamed under his hand — no sound, just pressure vibrating in bone. He tilted it. The water didn't pour. It leaned out, hung in a clear tongue, and stopped.

He touched the surface. It pushed back, elastic. He laughed once, hoarse. If he let go of physics, it was almost funny.

He scribbled again:

WATER HAS MASS NO FLOW. TEMP WARM. NOT DREAM. TEST AGAIN SOON.

The hum deepened a note. He felt it through his palate like a bass line. He looked up as if someone had spoken.

"Yeah?" he said. "Keep talking."

The air held its breath.

He sat on the edge of the dock and looked down the length of town. Everything was baked to stillness. He tried to remember if he'd ever wanted peace and quiet this badly. Now he had it. All of it.

The heat pressed against him, a constant hand. He could feel his heartbeat in his gums. The hum matched it again. He started tapping his wrench against his knee to the same tempo, just to hear nothing in sync.

He wrote another line:

IF THE WORLD BROKE, SOMEONE HAS TO KEEP IT.

Then under that, in smaller letters:

I'LL DO MAINTENANCE.

He snapped the notebook shut and slid it back into his pocket. The motion left a trail in his vision for half a second before catching up. He pretended he hadn't seen it.

Billy stood, rolled his shoulders, and looked back toward Main Street. The frozen city waited, quiet as equipment left on standby. He felt an odd sense of ownership take root in his chest, a mechanic's pride over a machine that still responded to touch.

"Alright," he said. "Let's see what else needs fixing."

He started walking again, every step an echo he could feel but not hear, toward the neighborhood beyond the mall where the houses waited in their own warm stillness. The hum followed, steady and faithful, like a tool he could never set down.

He started with the houses closest to the strip mall.

Not because they were special. Because they were reachable.

That mattered now. Reach. What he could lay a hand on, he could claim, and what he could claim, he could keep from slipping. That made sense in his head, even if nothing else did.

The first ranch-style sat three doors down from the coin laundry, all vinyl siding and sun-faded plastic tulips jammed into a rectangular planter out front. The porch light was on. Noon and the porch light was on.

He knocked once on the frame out of courtesy. Courtesy felt important. It felt human.

The knock didn't make a sound. He felt the contact all the way up his arm. Felt it in his teeth.

"Maintenance," he called softly, out of habit. "Coming in."

The words lived only inside his own skull, private as memory. He wondered if he'd go crazy not hearing himself eventually. Then he wondered how you'd know.

The front door was unlocked.

Inside: airless heat. The kind that sat heavy in rooms with too many soft things. The kind you get in August when the AC dies and all you can smell is carpet.

"Hey there," he said, gently, to the living room.

A woman sat in a recliner in front of a TV that had frozen mid-news crawl. Her feet were up. Slippers. Blue robe. Her hand still held the remote, thumb half-pressed to change the channel. The soft underarm skin of her left arm bunched in a little fold. Her mouth open, just barely, like she'd been about to say "huh."

Her eyes were wet.

Not crying. Just wet. Like they hadn't gotten the memo the rest of her had.

The little table next to her chair held a sweating glass of sweet tea and a bottle of orange pills with the pharmacy label half-peeled off. Her reading glasses had slipped down to the edge of her nose. He could see dust caught in her lashes.

"Hey," Billy whispered, stepping closer. "You okay?"

He knew she wasn't. He said it anyway.

Her chest wasn't moving.

He waited, watching. Slow. Careful. He wasn't going to touch her fast. You don't yank on old fittings. You test pressure first. See what gives.

He leaned in close enough to feel the soft heat from her skin. That was wrong. That was the worst part — she was warm. Warm was supposed to mean alive.

He put two fingers lightly at her throat, the way the EMT had shown him when his mother stopped waking up. Gentle. Right there, just under the jaw.

Nothing.

"I got you," he told her quietly. "I'll just—hang on."

He took her glasses off for her. It felt rude leaving them halfway down like that. He wiped the dust from her lashes with his thumb, slow as a blessing, then settled the glasses on the table by the tea.

Her eyes, without the slide of lenses in front of them, looked softer.

There. Better.

He looked at her robe next. The tie had sagged loose, gaping across her chest. He retied it. Not tight. Just enough for decency. If her kids came looking, they shouldn't have to see her open like that.

"There," he said again.

Something eased in his shoulders when he said it. A little mechanical release, like a stuck valve finally cracked.

He took his notebook out and wrote:

HOUSE 1. WOMAN. MID-60s.
WARM. EYES WET. NO BREATH.
FIXED CLOTHING.
LEFT TV ON. LIGHT ON.

Under that, in smaller handwriting:

LOOKED BETTER AFTER.

He felt stupid as soon as he wrote it. "Looked better after" sounded like furniture assembly. Some before/after shot. He started to scratch it out, then stopped. No. It was true. She did look better. And if someone ever came back — if time unstuck, if God sneezed and the world lurched forward — it would matter that he'd left her decent.

He moved deeper into the house.

The kitchen: a pot on the stove with sauce caught mid-bubble, a spoon hanging in the air like someone invisible was still holding it. He couldn't stop looking at that. The sauce itself had a little dome where it had tried to pop and froze halfway. He could see the skin stretched across it.

He tapped the pot with the back of his wrench. The vibration traveled through his palm and up his arm and into his jawbone where the hum lived now. He didn't hear the metal ring. He felt it, like pressure.

"Still hot," he murmured. The heat sat over the stove like a blanket. That wasn't good. Heat starts fires. Fires don't stop just because time did, do they? He didn't know. He didn't have a way to know.

He turned the burner knob to OFF. The knob didn't click. The flame under the pot — what little of it had been frozen — dimmed like someone easing a dimmer. It didn't go out. It just... softened.

Better than nothing.

Notebook:

GAS STOVE. STILL LIT. TURNED DOWN.

He waited. Nothing burst into flame. The house didn't explode. Okay.

He opened the fridge. The little light inside was on. The plastic orange juice felt room temperature. He shut it quick. He didn't know yet what happened to meat that sat in a fridge with no cold in a world with no time. He didn't want to find out by breathing it in.

When he came back to the living room, the woman in the recliner looked exactly the same. Of course she did. But now that he'd fixed her robe, wiped her lashes, moved her glasses, she looked less—exposed. Like someone who'd chosen to nap.

He stood over her for a long moment, and in that moment it hit him, very simply: nobody had done this for his mother.

Nobody had wiped her mouth. Nobody had thought to smooth her hair down against the hospital pillow so she didn't look scared in her last still image.

He put his hand on the woman's shoulder, same way he had with the delivery guy outside. He let it sit there. Warm through cotton. The heat felt like proof that she was still something, not just an object.

"You rest," he told her. "I'll check the rest of the block and come back."

He said it like promise.

Then he left.

***

House two had a kid.

Billy almost turned around and walked out.

The kid couldn't have been more than eight. Maybe nine. Skinny elbows. Freckles. He sat on the carpet in front of a game console, both hands locked on the controller. Mouth open in a half-yell, eyes narrowed — serious, focused, alive.

Alive.

Billy crouched the way you crouch for something that startles easy.

"Hey there," he whispered, throat tight.

The kid didn't blink.

A cartoon battlefield splashed frozen across the TV. Little neon characters locked mid-jump. Scoreboard in the corner like a paused war.

Billy reached out, then stopped.

He didn't want to touch a kid wrong. Even now. Even here. There were rules to that. Rules that still counted even if nothing else did.

He watched instead.

The boy's chest wasn't moving. His tongue sat against his bottom teeth, wet. No drying at all. His eyes glistened. He wasn't cooling. He wasn't cooling at all.

"Damn," Billy breathed.

This shouldn't have hit him harder than the woman in the recliner, or the man in the alleyway, or the driver with her mouth mid-oh. But it did. It wasn't about age. It was about posture. Kids aren't supposed to hold still this long. They're not built for it.

"Okay, champ," he said. "Okay. Alright."

The living room stank faintly of potato chips and carpet cleaner and boy-sweat. He could see a school backpack busted half-open on the couch. Crayons all over the cushion. A homework sheet half-filled in with crooked pencil numbers. Third grade math, maybe. Something with little boxes.

He didn't touch the boy. He didn't move him. But he took a blanket from the back of the couch — Avengers, cheap fleece — and draped it over the kid's shoulders like a cape. Just enough weight that it would feel, if the kid could feel, like safety.

"There," he said softly. "Superhero."

This time, when he said there, the hum behind his ears answered. A low pulse, almost approving.

321

Billy shut his eyes.

"Don't you start," he whispered to the hum. "I'm not doing church with you. We're not doing that."

When he opened his eyes, the kid hadn't changed.

Of course he hadn't.

Notebook:

HOUSE 2. BOY. WARM. NO BREATH.
PUT BLANKET ON SHOULDERS.
LEFT HIM WITH GAME.
LOOKS SAFE.

He stared at that last line for a long time.

Looks safe.

He wasn't sure who he was writing to. Himself later, maybe. Or whoever came after him, if after still happened.

Still. The word hung in his mind. Still. He was starting to hate it.

He flipped to a clean page and wrote in bigger letters:

RULES:
1. DON'T MOVE THEM MORE THAN YOU HAVE TO.
2. COVER / TIDY / DECENT.
3. CHECK GAS / HEAT / ELECTRIC.
4. DON'T PANIC.

He hovered at the fifth bullet.

The hum rolled in his skull, waiting.

He wrote:

5. KEEP THEM FROM BEING ALONE.

Billy stared at that until his eyes stung.

He didn't cry.

He hadn't cried when Brenda left. He hadn't cried when they told him his mother wasn't going to wake up again. He sure as hell wasn't going to start now, the only moving thing in a four-block radius with no clue whether crying still counted for anything.

But his throat felt thick.

"Okay," he said, to himself, to the boy, to the standing air. "Okay. You're not alone. I'm out there."

He touched two fingers to the kid's blanket like you'd tap out in a game. A little ritual. A promise.

Then he went to check the stove, the outlets, the thermostat, the windows. He cracked one in the back room two inches for air and wrote that down too.

By the time he stepped out onto Maple Street again, he'd stopped shaking.

Something in him had settled into a shape.

He had work.

***

House three had two people in it. A couple, maybe. Mid-forties. One on the couch with a crossword in her lap and a pen still pressed to the box for 27 Down, the other halfway back from the kitchen with two plates of something that had stopped halfway between plate and table.

He fixed them both. Straightened shoulders. Folded hands together. Closed a mouth that hung open just a little too far. Buttoned one more button on the man's shirt so his stomach didn't spill.

When he finished, he stepped back. Looked at them.

It wasn't perfect. He wasn't pretending it was. They weren't alive again. You couldn't fake that.

But they didn't look scared.

That felt like something.

Notebook:

HOUSE 3. TWO ADULTS.
ALL WARM. NO BREATH.
DINNER FROZEN.
FIXED HANDS. CLOSED MOUTHS. SAFE.

Underneath, smaller:

THEY LOOKED PEACEFUL WHEN I LEFT.

The hum came back low and steady, like approval.

He felt stupid for feeling proud of that. He felt sick for feeling proud of that. But he did.

Standing in their doorway, looking at these two posed in a way that made them look like they'd chosen to rest, Billy felt the first clean line of ownership move through him.

Not over them. Over the situation.

Maintenance, he thought.

This is my route.

For the first time since stepping into the heat-still noon, he didn't feel like he was wandering through a disaster he couldn't touch. He felt like a man with a job.

He shut their door gently, wiped his palm on his jeans, and made another note:

BLOCK A MOSTLY STABLE.
MOVE TO NEXT.

He looked up and down the silent street, at the sun that hadn't shifted at all, at the rows of windows full of paused lives, and for one steady beat, Billy felt almost calm.

This was doable.

This was containable.

He'd keep walking. He'd keep checking. He'd keep them all in one piece until somebody smarter — government, military, God, whoever — showed up and said, "Thanks, we'll take it from here."

In his head, the hum answered him like agreement.

Good, it seemed to say.

Keep them.

Billy nodded.

He didn't notice, or refused to let himself notice yet, that the word in his head wasn't keep them safe.

Just keep them.

Maple Street curved toward the elementary school, and Billy followed it because straight lines were starting to feel dishonest. Every driveway he passed carried its own small monument to the pause: a basketball arcing forever above a boy's fingertips, a sprinkler frozen in a jeweled halo, a newspaper mid-flutter in the wind that no longer moved.

He kept the notebook open in one hand now, not to write but to see it breathing. Paper made sense. Paper obeyed.

He was halfway to the crosswalk when he saw the dog.

A shepherd mix, mid-stride, leash dragging from its collar. The fur shimmered with heat and something else—a fine silver dust that caught the light like pollen. The eyes were locked on something invisible just ahead, teeth bared in a permanent snarl. A low rumble vibrated out of its chest.

Except the chest wasn't moving.

Billy crouched a few feet away. "Easy, pal."

He could smell the animal, the sour-sweet tang of fur and saliva. Heat poured off it. He wanted to pet it, check if the heart still beat, but his fingers stopped inches short. He'd learned that much already: touching made things real. Some things shouldn't be made real.

The hum pressed harder behind his skull, like a hand urging him on.

Do it.

He shook his head. "No."

He stood, took a slow breath, and walked around the dog. The hum receded, sullen.

Notebook:

DOG. FROZEN MID-STEP. HEAT HIGH. AVOIDED TOUCH.
NO NEED TO FIX EVERYTHING.

He didn't know why that last line came out. He underlined it anyway.

***

At the corner, a school bus straddled the intersection, the stop sign arm half-extended. Through the wide windows, children hung in rows of disbelief—some screaming, some laughing, one girl asleep against the glass. The driver had his hand up, palm open, as if to protect them from something unseen.

Billy climbed the steps.

The smell inside was thick—plastic, heat, faint apple juice. The soundless chaos was almost too much: forty little bodies locked in different definitions of panic.

He moved aisle by aisle, careful not to brush them. Their eyes glittered like marbles. One boy's tear had formed a perfect globe at his chin. Billy touched it with the tip of his wrench. The tear held. When he pulled the wrench back, the droplet came with it, clinging like mercury before sliding down the metal and vanishing.

He whispered, "You're okay," even though it was a lie. He just needed the words in the air.

Halfway down, a girl had dropped her backpack. A drawing spilled from it—crayons caught mid-stroke, a blue sky, a big yellow circle for a sun, stick people holding hands. He bent, picked it up, and set it carefully on her lap.

When he straightened, something in his spine clicked.

It wasn't pain exactly. More like a lock being tested from the inside.

He left the bus.

Outside, the hum was no longer behind his skull. It had moved lower, into his chest cavity, humming along his ribs. The rhythm matched the pulse he'd felt under his skin since morning.

He wrote nothing this time. He didn't need to. The bus was fixed. He'd given them back their drawing.

***

The school itself waited across the street—doors propped open by air that didn't move, flag half-raised, shadow pointing the same direction as always.

He almost didn't go in.

He told himself it was because schools meant paperwork, attendance, logistics. He knew it was because of the silence. The deeper kind. The kind that knew his name.

He stepped inside anyway.

The hallway smelled of disinfectant and pencil shavings. Posters on the wall: kindness, teamwork, anti-bullying, all bright colors fading into sepia under the stopped light. A ceiling fan hung mid-spin, one blade slightly bent. He could see dust motes that hadn't finished falling.

He walked past a trophy case, the faces in the team photos bright and plastic.

In the first classroom, twenty-six students and a teacher sat mid-lesson. The teacher's mouth formed the word and. Chalk hovered in her fingers. On the board: ecosystems.

Billy's throat tightened. He turned away.

In the next room, another class, another tableau. One kid mid-laugh, head thrown back, gum stretched between teeth and thumb. The gum shimmered, eternal pink.

He backed into the hall and pressed both palms against the cool cinderblock wall. The hum inside him rose, pressing against his breath.

He whispered, "Stop."

It didn't.

It changed tone, became a phrase without words: Keep. Them.

He bit down hard until he tasted copper.

"No," he said. "They're fine. They're already fine."

But even as he said it, he was thinking about the bus. About the drawing. About how the picture looked right there on the little girl's knees, a perfect composition of peace.

Maybe fine wasn't enough.

Maybe they needed arranging. Preservation. Like taxidermy for moments.

His stomach turned.

He wrote:

SCHOOL. TOO MANY. CAN'T FIX ALL.
NOTE: PRIORITIZE ORDER. KEEP THEM.

He stared at that last sentence until the ink shimmered.

Then, quietly, he added beneath it:

I THINK I KNOW WHAT THE HUM IS.

He closed the notebook and didn't look back at the classrooms as he walked out into the endless noon. The air hit him hot and weightless, like stepping into his own fever.

He didn't know it yet, but from that moment on, every time Billy said fixed, something in the still world twitched—just slightly, like remembering it used to move.

The hum followed him out of the school like breath on the back of his neck.

It wasn't loud. It was never loud. But the more he tried to forget it, the more it seemed to anticipate his next motion—leaning toward his thoughts the way a plant leans toward light.

By the time he reached the end of the street, he'd stopped trying to ignore it.

He'd started listening.

The corner store was the next stop. The bell above the door was trapped mid-jingle, its clapper caught halfway between two beats. Billy ducked beneath it like a priest entering his church.

The air inside was colder than anywhere else. The hum liked it here; he could tell. It pulsed slower, thicker.

Rows of people stood mid-transaction. The cashier's hand frozen over the counter, palm open, a bill hovering between her fingers. A customer's face locked in mid-complaint. Behind them, an older man in a delivery uniform— maybe the same company as the first guy outside—held a crate of milk like it weighed nothing at all.

Billy walked between them, the wrench loose in his hand.

"You're fine," he murmured. "You're all fine."

He stopped at the freezer aisle. A single door was cracked open. Frost glowed blue on the shelves. He closed it gently, sealing the cold inside.

The hum approved, a low purr that vibrated against the fillings in his teeth.

"Yeah," he said, smiling without knowing why. "Order."

He began straightening things—aligning cans, setting dropped items upright, wiping a spill that would never spread. He rearranged them until the store looked perfect. Until it looked intentional.

When he stepped back, the hum swelled like applause.

Billy's chest swelled with it. He felt good. Solid.

He wrote:

STORE: RESTORED. CLEAN. SAFE.
NOTE: THE SOUND REACTS TO BALANCE.

He paused. Then added:

IT LIKES WHEN I FIX THINGS.

By the time he reached downtown, the heat had settled into a permanent glaze. The air shimmered as if trying to trick him into thinking it still moved.

Billy wiped his forehead with the back of his arm and squinted at the bank across the street. The glass doors stood open, a faint metallic smell bleeding from inside.

He almost didn't cross.

But the hum was insistent now, an invisible current tugging at the space just behind his sternum. It was no longer a sound. It was a direction.

He went in.

A line of people waited at the teller windows. Some had wallets open, others stood mid-gesture. A young woman in a navy dress held her phone up as if recording something. The reflection of her frozen frame shimmered across the floor like water.

Billy stepped toward her. The closer he got, the louder the hum grew, until it wasn't behind his ribs anymore—it was inside the air. A bass so low he could feel it in his knees.

He stopped inches from her and whispered, "You hear it too, don't you?"

Her eyes didn't move. But something in her expression shifted—a microfraction of change. Or maybe it was just him. Maybe he was the one changing.

He reached out and fixed a loose strand of her hair, tucking it neatly behind her ear. The hum surged, pure pleasure through the jaw and down the spine.

Billy staggered. His fingers tingled.

He opened the notebook again, hands shaking.

CONTACT = RESPONSE.
IMPROVEMENT = REWARD.
I THINK IT'S LEARNING.

He looked up from the page.

In the reflection of the bank's glass wall, his outline seemed slightly delayed—half a second off. When he tilted his head, the reflection followed too slowly, like it wasn't sure who was leading.

"Don't start that," he told it. "Don't you fucking start that."

It didn't answer, but the hum deepened—almost laughing.

He spent the rest of the day moving through buildings and rooms and people like a silent mechanic, cataloguing, tidying, arranging.

At a barber shop, he brushed loose hair from a boy's shoulder and straightened a cape.

At a diner, he wiped the counter clean and adjusted a waitress's tray so the coffee cups balanced.

At the corner library, he aligned the books that had been knocked over.

Every time, the hum rewarded him. A subtle jolt, like a pulse of electricity through a wet wire.

He craved it more than he feared it.

When the sky started to turn the color of brass—though the sun never moved—Billy realized he'd lost track of how long it had been.

His stomach growled. It sounded foreign, obscene, like an animal in a museum.

He didn't remember when he'd last eaten.

Notebook:

HUNGER STILL OCCURS.
DOES NOT AFFECT LIGHT.
DOES NOT MATTER.

He sat on the curb outside the gas station and looked at his hands. They were trembling, faint traces of black under the nails from oil and ash.

"You're doing good work," he told himself. "Keeping things from falling apart."

The hum hummed back, pleased.

Billy smiled. For the first time since the noon began, he felt like he belonged here. Like maybe this stillness wasn't punishment. Maybe it was promotion.

He flipped the notebook open again, wrote slowly:

IF SOMEONE HAD TO RUN THE WORLD, WHY NOT ME?

He underlined me twice.

And from somewhere—he couldn't tell if it was the air or the hum or something buried beneath both—a new vibration rose.

It wasn't approval this time.

It was laughter.

Low. Endless.

The kind that only something ancient makes when it finds a new mouth to speak through.

Billy looked down at the page. The ink bled in a perfect circle, then began to spread—slow, deliberate, as if the notebook had started to breathe.

By the time Billy turned back toward Maple Street, he had stopped thinking of the houses as houses.

They were stations.

That word felt cleaner. Less personal. Easier to carry.

He started naming them like that in the notebook.

STATION 1 – WOMAN IN CHAIR
STATION 2 – BOY W/ GAME
STATION 3 – COUPLE (DINNER)
BUS = TRANSIT STATION
BANK = HOLDING STATION
SCHOOL = TOO MANY / RETURN LATER

Each name made it feel more manageable. When you write down a problem, it becomes a task. When you label a system, it becomes yours.

He told himself that truth like you tell yourself you're fine when your hand is bleeding through a rag and the urgent care is twenty minutes out.

He found himself back at Station 1 without fully meaning to be there.

The woman in the recliner hadn't moved. Of course she hadn't moved. But something had changed.

Her mouth wasn't open anymore.

He had fixed that. He knew he had fixed that.

Now it was pinched. Tight at the corners, pulled a little too far to the left like she'd flinched.

Billy felt something cold move through him despite the heat. "Hey," he whispered. "Hey, did you—"

He stopped himself from finishing. He didn't want to put the word move in the air and hear it die.

Instead he leaned in, close enough to smell lotion and dust and the faint hiss of stale AC. Her eyelids had tiny grit lines at the edges, the way eyes get when you've been sitting with the TV on too long. He wiped them again with the pad of his thumb. It felt like doing dishes. Routine. Care. Control.

The hum purred, deep and satisfied.

"There we go," he breathed. "Better."

That feeling — that little answer, that vibration of yes, Billy, good — slid through him, warm and narcotic. He realized then that he'd been working for it all afternoon. Like a dog waiting for praise.

It should've bothered him more than it did.

Notebook:

STATION 1 REVISIT – MOUTH SHIFTED.
CORRECTED EYES / MOUTH.
HUM = STRONG RESPONSE.

Underneath, in smaller letters:

I THINK THEY LIKE IT WHEN I FIX THEM.

He didn't know who they was.

He didn't ask.

***

At Station 2 — the kid with the game — Billy did more.

It happened without him deciding.

He walked into the little house and instead of just looking and draping and stepping away, he started cleaning. Not "tidying." Cleaning.

He picked up chip bags and sealed them. He shut off the TV so the screen wouldn't burn in. He shut the fridge door all the way. He lined the crayons from the couch into a tidy rainbow, smallest to biggest.

He crouched in front of the boy and adjusted the blanket so it sat centered on his shoulders instead of crooked to one side. "There," he murmured, soft. "Like a cape. Like you meant it."

The hum inside him swelled in a slow, warm wave. His fingertips tingled.

Then something else happened.

The kid's controller — still locked between his hands — clicked.

Just once.

Not loud. Not at all through his ears. He felt it in his wrist, where the kid's knuckles rested against his fingers. A vibration, small and real, like haptic feedback from a game.

Billy jerked back so fast he almost fell.

The boy didn't move.

The controller didn't move.

The blanket sat exactly where Billy had set it.

But Billy had felt that click.

Notebook, breathless, almost sloppy:

STATION 2 – RESPONSIVE. DIRECT CONTACT.

CONTROLLER CLICKED UNDER HAND.
NOTE: THEY / HE CAN FEEL ME.

He stared at those words until his jaw began to ache.

Then his mind did what it always did with panic.

It reframed.

If the kid could feel him?

Good.

Good. That meant the blanket wasn't just him playing house in a dead museum. That meant the blanket had mattered. That meant the kid maybe knew — somewhere, in there — that someone had seen him and covered him and said, Somebody's here. You're not alone in this.

The thought hit him hard enough to rock him.

"You're not alone," Billy told the boy's still face. It came out rough. "You hear me? Somebody's here. You've got somebody watching out today."

The hum rolled through him, almost tender.

Almost proud.

He had to sit down on the carpet for a second to catch his balance.

**

By the time he reached Station 3 — the couple frozen mid-dinner — Billy wasn't coming back to check.

He was coming back to improve.

Their posture looked wrong now. He hadn't noticed it earlier because he'd been shaking and hungry and not thinking about aesthetics, but now it bothered him. The way her hand sat on the couch cushion made it look like she'd fallen. The way his chin sagged forward read more dead than tired.

He couldn't leave them like that. It made the room feel panicked.

"Let's get you right," he whispered.

He slid the woman a few inches back in the cushions, tucking one of her legs under like a relaxed lean. He lifted the man's chin and tucked his shirt better so his stomach wasn't bulging bare. He took the plate from his hovering hand and set it on the coffee table neatly, like a polite pass. He laced their fingers together and rested their joined hands on her thigh — like a photo from a holiday card.

He stepped back.

It was... good.

Soft. Domestic. Chosen.

"See?" he whispered to them. "There. Like you meant it."

The hum surged through him so hard his hands shook. The room seemed to glow a shade warmer. Dust in the sunlight shifted — not down, not up, just... reoriented. Like gravity itself had turned its face toward his work.

Billy pressed the heel of his hand to his sternum. His heart was running fast. The hum matched it, or he matched the hum, he couldn't tell anymore.

Notebook:

STATION 3 – RESET POSES.
INTERLOCKED HANDS. ADJUSTED CHIN / POSTURE.
HUM = STRONGEST RESPONSE YET.
FEELS LIKE APPROVAL.

Underneath that, smaller, almost careful:

THEY LOOK HAPPY NOW.

He stood in their doorway longer than he needed to. Looking at them. Admiring, if he was honest.

This wasn't chaos anymore.

This was arrangement.

He'd taken panic and stilled it. He'd taken fear and made it look like memory. He had done that.

"Yeah," he whispered, chest aching with a strange, thick pride. "Yeah. That's right. I see you. I'm keeping you just how you should be."

The hum rolled low and long, like a hand stroking the inside of his skull.

***

When he finally stepped back out into the street, heat hit him like worship.

He understood, then, in a way he hadn't let himself say yet: there wasn't going to be someone smarter. No military caravan rolling down Main Street. No hazmat suits. No news chopper. No FEMA command trailer. Not soon. Maybe not ever.

He was it.

That wasn't arrogance. That was logistics.

He was the only thing moving.

If the situation was going to have order instead of rot, that was on him.

It clicked into place inside him like something machined.

He felt calmer than he had all day.

Notebook, new heading, thick block letters:

ROUTE MAP

then:

1. STATION 1 (WOMAN) – MAINTAIN.
2. STATION 2 (BOY) – MONITOR FOR RESPONSE.
3. STATION 3 (COUPLE) – PRESENTATION CORRECTED.
4. BUS (KIDS) – TABLEAU NEEDS ADJ.
5. SCHOOL – OUT OF SCOPE FOR NOW.
6. BANK – HAIR FIXED / HOLD.
7. GAS STATION – STABLE.
8. DOWNTOWN SHOPS – CLEAN AS NEEDED.

He looked at that list and felt something like relief.

Route map.

Work day.

Job.

He could do a job.

He'd always been better with jobs than with life.

***

Back at the bus, he did adjust the tableau.

He told himself it was for safety, and if you'd asked him then, he would've believed that.

He moved slow between the stuck rows of children. He lifted a slumping backpack so it wouldn't dig into a little girl's ribs. He tipped a boy's head back from an awkward angle against the seat so it wouldn't strain his neck if — when — time came back. He wiped a strand of hair from a forehead just to see the face underneath.

He didn't linger on any of them. He didn't let his hands stay on small shoulders longer than necessary. He didn't cross that.

He did, however, turn two of the kids' faces toward each other and angle their hands so it looked like they were holding on through the moment. A little girl and a little boy. Perfectly framed. Perfectly composed. Fear rendered into solidarity. Tragedy into sweetness.

"There," he breathed. His chest hurt. "There. That's right. That's better. You're not scared now. You're brave."

The hum shivered through him with such force his knees nearly buckled.

He had to catch himself on one of the high seats and hold there, knuckles white.

It wasn't just approval now.

It was… hunger.

Oh, he thought distantly. Oh, it likes this.

***

And then, small as a nerve twitch, barely there — one of the kid's fingers moved.

Not much. Not more than the width of a fingernail.

But it moved.

Billy froze, whole body locked around that fraction of impossible.

The boy's head didn't turn. His eyes didn't blink. Nothing else in the rubberized yellow interior of the bus shifted. But that right index finger — the one Billy had lined up so it would look like it was holding someone else's hand — had flexed.

That same finger now rested on top of the other kid's hand, instead of under.

He hadn't put it there.

He knew he hadn't.

His pulse sprinted. The hum in his chest harmonized with it, thrilled.

Notebook, hand shaking visibly for the first time:

BUS: THEY CAN MOVE.
MOVED AFTER CONTACT / ADJUSTMENT.
HUM = EXTREME WHEN TABLEAU ARRANGED.

NOTE: THEY'RE STILL HERE INSIDE.

Underneath, without thinking:

THEY ARE RESPONDING TO CARE.

He stared at that last sentence. His breath felt like sand in his throat.

Responding.

Not dying.

Not gone.

Still there.

Still aware.

Still... feeling.

A hot, dizzy wave washed him. Not horror. Not exactly. Something wetter.

Gratitude.

They know I'm here.

They know I'm keeping them.

**

He climbed down from the bus like a man stepping out of church.

The parking lot looked different. Not visually. It was still the same flat blacktop glazed in fixed summer sun. But it felt different, like something vast had turned its attention toward him.

He stood in that attention and let it cover him.

He didn't smile, exactly. But the tightness that had been living between his shoulders all day finally loosened.

This is working, he thought.

This is right.

They're safer with me than they were without me.

The hum inside him answered, deep and loving.

Yes, Billy.

Keep them.

***

On the walk back through the center of town, he stopped in front of a dentist's office window.

His reflection stared back at him.

For a breath-long stretch, it didn't move.

Billy lifted his hand. Slow.

The reflection lifted its hand a half-beat later.

Too slow.

Like it was thinking about it.

"This is mine," he told the glass gently. "All this. I got it."

The reflection's mouth opened when his didn't.

For just a flicker, the delay reversed, and Billy saw himself smiling in the glass with a softness he didn't feel yet.

He took one step back.

The hum inside him purred like a big animal settling down around him, wrapping itself, satisfied, along his spine.

Notebook, last line of the act, underlined twice, filling almost the whole page:

I CAN KEEP THEM HOW THEY SHOULD BE.

That night never came.

It just didn't.

The sun never lowered. The heat never bled off the blacktop. Shadows never lengthened. Time didn't dim so he could call it "evening." His body said it was later. His legs ached. His throat felt raw. Hunger gnawed. But the light over town stayed the same slow gold, unmoving, like an open mouth that never had to draw breath.

Billy wasn't built for endless day. No one was. Sleep is how you put the lid back on your head so things don't boil over. Without it, everything runs together. The edges go soft.

That's when mistakes happen.

He told himself that as he went back to Station 1.

He told himself that going back was routine. Just checking. Just maintenance.

The truth was he needed the hum again.

He pushed open her door and stepped into the same still air, the same sagging recliner, the same blue robe, the same TV mid-scroll. Station 1. The woman. He needed the hum to tell him he'd done right.

The woman's mouth had changed again.

It had pulled tighter since he'd last been there, edges drawn down like someone suppressing a groan. A little seam at the left corner had cracked. Just at the corner. A tiny split in soft lip.

Billy felt something inside his chest flash, quick and defensive. "No. No, no," he said, already crossing the room.

He knelt beside her, wrench tucked into his back pocket now — not because he needed it here, just because not having it in reach felt wrong.

"Hey there," he murmured. "Hang on, sweetheart. I got you."

He wet his thumb with his own tongue and pressed it lightly to the cracked corner of her mouth. Smoothed. Softened. Guided. He pressed the lip back into something that read as rest instead of pain.

Her face answered him.

Not with a twitch. Not with a blink. Just a loosening. The tiny vertical lines above her upper lip eased. Her brow softened. Her whole face, read from a step back, stopped looking strained and went back to looking settled.

"There," he whispered.

The hum flooded him like heat under bathwater, slow and complete, filling his head, his throat, his spine. It felt like reward. It felt like being petted.

He let his hand rest on her cheek a heartbeat too long.

That too-long wasn't an accident anymore.

Notebook, standing in her doorway before he left:

STATION 1 UPDATE – MOUTH SPLIT, CORRECTED.
PAIN SIGNS = CAN HAPPEN WHILE FROZEN.
I CAN REDUCE PAIN SIGNS.

Beneath it, almost automatic, like the thought had drafted itself:

THEY NEED ME.

***

He didn't notice until Station 2 that he'd stopped writing "they're warm."

That detail had just become part of the air. Background. Taken for granted. Of course they were warm. Of course they were soft. Of course the blood under their skin hadn't fully stopped — it had just... slowed. Slowed and stayed.

He told himself that was good. Slowing meant potential. Slowing wasn't dying.

He told himself that over and over while he checked the boy.

The boy hadn't moved again. The controller sat locked in those little hands. The blanket was still draped, perfect, his "cape."

But his arm angle had slumped a little. Not much. Just enough that the shoulder looked twisted, like the position would ache if you held it too long.

Billy saw it and winced in sympathy. "Oh, champ. That's not good for you."

He slid his hands under the boy's elbow, gentle. He adjusted the angle. Rotated the forearm inward, let the shoulder relax into a safer line. Just like you'd reposition a sleeping kid on a drive so their neck didn't snap weird.

"Better," he murmured. "Better, better."

The hum replied instantly, thrilled.

This time the reply didn't just live in Billy.

The air in the living room vibrated.

It was subtle. You wouldn't see it if you weren't looking for it. The curtains at the window shivered like a fan had kicked on. The loose pages on the coffee table lifted at one corner, sighed, settled back. A single potato chip crumb rolled two inches and came to rest in a neat line with its brothers.

Billy froze.

Very slowly, like he didn't want to scare it off, he lifted his hand away from the boy's arm.

The arm stayed where he'd set it.

The room stayed tidied the way the air had decided it should be.

Oh, he thought.

Oh, it's not just in me.

He sat back on his heels. His chest was tight. His hands trembled.

The hum kept purring — not soothing now but pleased. Pleased with him.

Notebook:

STATION 2 – CORRECTED SHOULDER ANGLE.
HUM SPREAD IN ROOM.
ENVIRONMENT RESPONDED.
THEY / IT CAN ADJUST SURROUNDINGS WHEN I START IT.

Then, darker ink, pressed harder:

THIS IS WORKING.

***

On his way down Maple toward the bus, he passed a mailbox slightly askew on its post. This had never mattered to him before. Not once in forty-four years of breathing had he given a shit about whether someone's dented blue mailbox leaned two degrees to the right instead of standing neat and plumb.

Now it bothered him so badly his jaw ached.

He stopped. He couldn't help it. He stopped.

The mailbox's post had been hit at some point, probably by a landscaping truck backing badly. The base was splintered. Nails old and rusted. Whole thing sagged like a shoulder that'd never healed right.

Billy set his wrench against the post, dug in, and muscled it upright until the lean corrected. He packed hot, gritty earth back in around the base with his bootheel. Leveled it by eye. A little more. A little more.

"There," he said under his breath when it stood straight.

The hum inside him bloomed so suddenly his vision fuzzed at the edges. He had to plant his feet and breathe slow, bracing like you do when you stand up too fast and the blood drains.

When his vision cleared, he saw something he almost didn't believe.

A crack that had run down the length of the post — old weather split, gray and tired — had smoothed.

Not disappeared. Smoothed. Softened at the edges, like a callus healing.

Billy lifted his hand and touched it.

The wood felt warm.

He jerked back like he'd been burned.

He wasn't fixing chipped paint anymore.

He wasn't tidying.

He was changing things.

"Oh," he whispered, and the word felt half awe, half fear, and neither part of that fear had anything to do with God anymore.

***

Back at the bus, he meant to just check.

He swore, to himself, that that was all he meant to do.

He climbed the steps like he had before, ducked his head, breathed that thick air.

None of the kids had moved since the finger.

Most of their faces were still locked in various states of scream or laugh.

That wasn't acceptable.

Not anymore.

He moved down the aisle like a caretaker, making tiny, almost reverent adjustments.

A little chin lifted. A mouth closed. A brow smoothed. A hand tucked under instead of hanging mid-flail. Two shoulders eased back so they looked braced instead of broken.

He didn't touch the bodies where it felt wrong. He avoided bellies, thighs, anywhere that felt private. He told himself there were still rules. He told himself he was keeping them safe.

"Brave," he murmured, moving one girl's face toward her own knees so it looked like she was hiding on purpose and not frozen in a scream. "You're brave. That's it. You're not scared. You're hiding, smart."

The hum swelled, swelled, swelled.

Dust in the air between the seats lifted and hung in a pale ribbon, flickering in that endless noon light.

Billy felt high.

That was the only word he had for it.

High.

He stepped back to look at what he'd done.

The bus didn't look like a disaster anymore. It didn't look like the first second after a car backfires and everyone flinches. It looked — and this was the piece that made his throat ache — like a drill. Like they were practicing. Like someone had said, "Crash position!" and everyone had obeyed perfectly and calmly.

Order.

Safety.

That's what it looked like.

"It's okay," he told them, voice shaking. "It's okay now. It's okay. You're good. I've got you. I've got all of you."

Something deep in the hum answered:

All of you.

His stomach fluttered.

He wrote in the notebook with hands that wouldn't steady:

BUS STATION – FULL RESET.
FACES & HANDS ADJUSTED FOR CALM.
HUM = INTO MY ARMS / HANDS / EYES NOW.

THIS IS WHAT THEY NEED.

Then, after a long pause, pressed hard enough to nearly tear the page:

I THINK THIS IS WHAT I'M FOR.

***

He should've stopped.

He should've stopped there.

That was the line. That was the moment that should have scared him enough to sit in the parking lot and throw up and decide no more touching kids, no more posing bodies, no more "making it right."

Instead, Billy walked away from the bus with his chest buzzing and his jaw clenched and his whole body lit up with purpose. He felt holy. He felt necessary. He felt... chosen.

And chosen men don't stop at almost.

***

Station 3 waited.

The couple on the couch, hands laced because he'd laced them.

Perfect. Domestic. Clean.

And yet.

Something in the man's face was still wrong.

Billy hadn't noticed it before. Now it was the only thing he could see.

355

It was the mouth.

He'd closed the mouth earlier, yes, but it sat slightly crooked. A little too slack at one corner. It made the man look drunk, not peaceful. It made the tableau look messy.

Billy went straight to him.

"Let me fix you," he whispered. "Hang on. I'm just gonna fix you."

He slid his thumb under the man's jaw to tilt it. The skin under his hand felt tacky-warm. Not cold. Not rigid. Warm like fresh laundry pulled out of a dryer and hugged.

He pressed his other thumb against the man's lips to straighten them.

The lower lip didn't want to sit how he wanted it.

It resisted.

It was a tiny thing. Bare. The kind of resistance you'd get from cartilage tension. Nothing alive-alive. Just that there's-still-give-here resistance.

But to Billy, in that exact moment, it felt like defiance.

"Shh," he soothed. "Let me."

He pressed a little harder.

The lip split.

A small wet line opened where the flesh had dried against teeth, pale pink turning darker.

Billy froze.

A drop of deep red welled up, slow.

He watched it gather. He watched it bulge.

He watched it not fall.

It just hung there, perfect, heavy, waiting.

The hum vibrated through him so violently his vision halved.

For an instant — half a second, less — he saw two versions of the room at once:

— the one he was in, warm and still and gold.

— and another, smeared, darker, edges pulled thin, where the couple's hands weren't laced and the man's mouth hung open and there was fear in the woman's eyes

Then the images slid back together and he was just in the room again, on his knees between their still bodies, thumb pressed to split lip, watching the impossible bead of blood hold shape in the stuck air.

He pulled his hand back.

"Shit," he whispered, barely moving his mouth. "Shit, shit, I'm sorry. I didn't mean to—I didn't—"

He reached for a tissue from the coffee table and dabbed, gentle as he could. The tissue took the blood. The air released nothing. The bead vanished.

The lips settled where he'd wanted them.

357

There.

There.

Peaceful.

You couldn't tell, now, that anything had torn.

He exhaled in a shaking rush.

"It's okay," he told the man softly. "See? All fixed. You're good now. You look good. You look how you're supposed to."

The hum purred like an animal curling in his lap.

In his notebook, hand moving like it belonged to something else:

STATION 3 – MOUTH ADJUSTMENT REQUIRED FORCE.
MINOR DAMAGE. CORRECTED.
RESULT = IDEAL RESTED LOOK.
NO SIGN OF DISTRESS NOW.

Then, new line. Bigger letters:

SOMETIMES YOU HAVE TO DO A LITTLE TO GET THEM RIGHT.

***

When he stepped out of Station 3, sweating and shaking and buzzing, something subtle but undeniable had shifted.

This was no longer about keeping.

It was about making.

It was about the difference, in his mind, between the words safe and right.

The hum knew it.

It crawled up the back of his neck like a hand and settled there, warm and possessive, and for the first time since 12:03, Billy understood — dimly, privately, somewhere he wouldn't let himself look straight at — that the hum wasn't just answering him anymore.

It was steering.

All of you, it had told him.

Keep them.

Make them right.

He did not write that last part down.

He just turned to a fresh page in the notebook and wrote, in slow, careful block letters:

I CAN'T LET THEM STAY UGLY.

He stared at the word ugly for a long time.

Then he underlined it.

Three times.
The library felt like a church before he even stepped inside.

Not a Sunday church. Not the kind with bulletins and bad coffee. Older than that. Deeper. The kind of space that makes the back of your neck prickle before you know why.

It was the way the light gathered, mostly.

The library had those high paneled windows that let in big generous bands of sun across the carpet. Only now, with the entire town pinned under that fixed noon, the sun wasn't "coming in." It was just sitting in the air, held in soft yellow slabs. Dust floated inside those slabs like gold confetti, suspended mid-swirl. A holy mess.

Billy stood in the doorway and let the heat press against his face. He felt the hum rise in his throat in answer, like a purr echoing.

He didn't remember deciding to come here. He'd just started walking, notebook in pocket, wrench hanging heavy off two fingers, and then the hum had leaned forward in him as he passed the municipal building and he'd turned, and here he was.

Inside, there were six people.

He called them Stations 9 through 14, even though he hadn't written 9 through 14 yet.

One woman sat at a computer table, head tilted, mouth open, eyes on a frozen screen of some news site that would never refresh again. A teen boy in a black hoodie was half-folded over a study carrel, earbud locked in, phone mid-text message in his palm. A tired-looking older man lay sprawled in a chair in the periodicals corner like he'd just decided to nap where he sat. And clustered near the children's shelves: a mother and a toddler in a stroller, and a little girl — maybe five — holding a picture book in both hands, arms extended like she'd just brought it over to show somebody.

That girl got him first.

He moved toward her like he was sleepwalking.

Her arms were stretched too stiff. That was the first wrongness. The book hung heavy in her hands — heavy in a way a picture book has no business being. Her shoulders were raised; her neck strained. Hold anything like that long enough and you hurt yourself.

"You're gonna cramp, sweetheart," Billy murmured.

The hum filled his mouth.

He took the book from her slowly, careful not to jostle her little fingers. They stayed curled in space after the weight was gone, like she was still offering. He felt something lurch deep in his stomach at that — an ache he remembered from long ago, from a different kind of quiet, a waiting-for-your-own-kid kind of ache he thought he'd buried.

He set the book back in her hands — not outstretched now, but cradled against her chest, arms crossed around it. Protective. Like she'd hugged it to herself.

"There," he whispered. "That's better on you."

Better. Safer. Right.

The hum slid through him approving, slow and thick, and he almost sighed at the relief of it.

Her posture read different now. Not mid-action. Mid-keep.

That mattered. That mattered to him so much he had to shut his eyes for a beat.

It had felt wrong before — like catching someone in a state they didn't mean for strangers to see. Exposed. Unfinished.

Now she looked... composed.

Owned, his mind supplied.

His mouth went dry.

Not "owned." He didn't like that word. He pushed that word down.

She looked kept.

That one he let himself keep.

Kept is good, the hum answered.

His throat went tight.

He moved on.

He adjusted the angle of the toddler in the stroller so the head wasn't kinked too far back. Pulled the mother's shirt down over her stomach so she wasn't left with her belly soft and showing. No woman wants to be found with her shirt ridden up, not even at the end of the world. He knew that as fact.

He smoothed her hair. The hum hummed.

Then he turned to the man asleep in the chair.

The man hadn't really been asleep, of course. Not when the moment hit. His head had just slumped back that way, wide open, mouth slack and throat bared like a kill shot. His hands hung palm-up on either side of the chair, every vein blue, every fingernail yellowed and a little too long. He looked like a drunk who'd lost the fight with the armchair after a late shift. He looked, and this word hit Billy with the shameful crackle of recognition, ugly.

Billy didn't want ugly in this room.

Not here. Not in this one space he could already feel wanting to be beautiful.

He stepped in.

"Hey, sir," he whispered, already reaching. "Let me help you sit right."

He moved the man's arms first, laying them gently across the chest like a solemn rest instead of a collapse. He tilted the head back down from that horrible throat-bared angle and let it tip just slightly toward the right shoulder, like a thoughtful nap. He smoothed the shirt over the belly. Tugged the belt so it sat straight.

"There," he said softly. "That looks like you meant it."

The hum stroked up his spine in a long pleasure-warm line that made his jaw clench.

The man looked instantly less pathetic.

He looked dignified.

Dignified read, to Billy's eye, as less frightening. And less frightening was, in Billy's mind, the same as merciful.

And then, of course, the line moved. That's what happens once you start smoothing. You start seeing other things that snag.

The teen boy in the hoodie.

Billy crossed to him.

The kid's posture was awful — folded in, shoulders curled, chin jammed into his own forearm like a punched-in instinct. His hands gripped his phone like it was a mouth he'd been trying to keep shut.

"Aw, son," Billy murmured. "Don't hold yourself like that. You'll lock up."

He slid a hand under the boy's jaw, tilting the face up a few degrees. Just enough so the kid didn't look cornered. Just enough so someone looking would say "tired" instead of "terrified."

His thumb brushed the kid's cheek.

Still-warm skin. Soft stubble. Human.

He swallowed.

Then he lifted the boy's other arm from its rigid brace across his chest and laid it open on the desk like he'd reached for help, not braced against it.

"There," Billy said again, and his voice — what he could feel of it vibrating the bones of his neck — broke at the edges. "See? You're okay. You're here. People can see you. You're not hiding now."

He meant it gently.

It wasn't gentle.

Not really.

That arm had been the last thing the boy controlled. That little clenched barrier was his. It had said no. And Billy took it and turned it into yes because yes photographed better.

He told himself it was to ease the strain on the kid's shoulder joint, which was technically true.

But the truth inside the truth was that Billy hated the look of that defensive clutch. It made the room feel panicked. And panic — messy panic — made his ribs go tight in a way he couldn't stand.

The hum rewarded him hard.

It felt like heat pooling low in his stomach. Intimate. Almost obscene. He had to step backward and press his palm flat over his sternum to steady himself.

He was breathing faster now. No sound, just the feel: ribs expanding against stale, hot air over and over and over.

"Okay," he whispered to the room. "You're good. You're all good. Look at you."

And he did look.

He looked at them all, all six, the way you step back from a wall you've been patching and painting to see if you've got the coat even.

The mother's shirt pulled down. The toddler's head turned so he looked soft instead of strangled. The little girl hugging her book to her chest like a treasure. The man in the chair dignified and resting. The teen boy open, available, not hiding. The woman at the computer... she was still wrong. He didn't like how her mouth hung a little slack. It made the whole room read anxious. It made the air feel cracked.

He went to her last.

Her face had that pre-cry tightness, like she'd been trying so hard not to let her chin wobble. That wasn't the story he wanted in this space. Not in this one. This was supposed to be safe.

His thumb found the point between her brows and smoothed. He pressed her mouth closed, gentler this time than with Station 3. He adjusted her hands on the keyboard so they sat poised, capable, not clawed. He tipped her chin a hair higher.

"There," he said.

The hum didn't just reward him.

This time, as he watched, the air in the library shifted.

Every speck of dust in those gold bars of light rotated in place toward the cluster of bodies like iron filings toward a magnet.

The temperature dropped two, maybe three degrees. Enough to feel relief along his damp hairline.

The glare softened.

And something else happened that made his throat go dry:

their faces, for a beat, all at once, looked alive.

It wasn't motion, not exactly. It was cohesion. A trick of light. Arranged like this, cleaned and set and held just-so in a circle of attention, they looked like they belonged to the same moment. Part of the same still breath.

He had built a scene.

That realization went through him like a drug.

"Oh," Billy whispered.

Not scared.

Oh.

The hum answered, closer than it had ever been:

Ours.

His mouth dropped open.

He hadn't said ours. He hadn't. He would never — not about people. He wouldn't.

But he had felt the word shape in his own throat. He had felt his own tongue press against his teeth to make it.

Ours.

Billy staggered back a step.

His heel hit an overturned book cart. He grabbed for balance and his palm smeared across the wheel. The friction burned. The pain was weirdly welcome. He needed it, needed the sting, something clean and sharp and his.

"Okay," he whispered hoarsely. "Okay. That's... that's good. That's good work. You look good. You all look good. You should — you deserve that. You deserve—"

The hum rolled right over his words and finished the sentence inside him:

— to be kept.

He swallowed against it. "Yeah," he whispered, shaking. "Yeah. To be kept."

He wasn't saying worship.

He wasn't.

But his knees felt weak in the same way they had the first time he'd ever knelt by a hospital bed and said please.

It would've been very easy, in that second, to fold.

To actually go down on both knees on the library carpet, press his hands together out of reflex, and thank the empty air for letting him do this.

For letting him arrange them like this.

For letting him take chaos and pull it into order and call that order mercy.

He didn't kneel.

Not yet.

What he did instead was worse.

He started directing.

***

He had not, before this afternoon, ever thought about the way fingers looked.

Now he did.

He crossed to the toddler and gently repositioned two of the tiny fingers on the stroller's tray so they pointed inward instead of out. The outward point had read jittery, frantic. The inward rest read relaxed. "Hush," he whispered. "Just resting now, see? Just resting."

He lifted the teen boy's chin two degrees higher. That read wounded dignity now, not plea. Better.

He rotated the sleeping man's left wrist so the veins didn't pop quite so blue.

"There," he murmured. "There you go. That's right. That's right. That's how you should look."

Should.

Not "do."

Not "did."

Should.

He didn't hear the shift. The hum did. It purred so hard through his bones that for a second he thought his ribs might crack.

The light in the room pooled tighter around the six of them as if the sun itself had leaned down to bless this exact arrangement.

Billy's pulse hammered.

He had to put his hand on the checkout desk to steady himself.

His reflection stared back at him from the glossy laminate surface. The reflection's lips were parted, breathing harder than he felt himself breathing.

He tried to swallow.

His reflection licked its lips.

Billy jerked back.

"No," he whispered. "No, no, no."

The hum crooned.

Ours, it said again, sweeter now. Satisfied. Grateful. Ours.

His stomach flipped.

He wrote in the notebook with his hand shaking so badly the block letters swam:

LIBRARY = DISPLAY ROOM.
EVERYONE SET HOW THEY SHOULD BE.
THEY LOOK / FEEL SAFE WHEN I DO THIS.
HUM SHIFTED. SAID "OURS."
THIS IS NOT JUST ME ANYMORE.

Under that, slowly, almost reverently:

THIS IS THE MOST BEAUTIFUL ROOM IN TOWN.

He sat for a long time after that. Not working. Just watching.

That was new too.

Before, all day, he'd worked in motion. Fix, wipe, straighten, move. He hadn't let himself linger.

Now he lingered.

He sat cross-legged on the children's carpet twelve feet from his "stations" and just watched them. Watched the subtle way the not-light held on their faces. Watched the way the dust hung still like snowfall caught in prayer. Watched the toddler's little shoe, scuffed at the toe, resting just so against the stroller frame.

He felt... proud.

He felt protective, chest-deep.

And he felt a slow building anger that anyone would dare let these people ever look any other way.

They'd probably all looked ridiculous, he thought, amazed and offended at the same time. Before. Before he fixed them. Screaming, crying, open-mouthed, flinching, off-guard. Exposed. Ugly. He hated the word, but it pushed up again from somewhere honest.

Ugly.

He wouldn't let them sit in ugly.

He wouldn't.

Not his.

Not ours.

He didn't notice when his and ours started to braid together in his head. It happened quietly. Almost kindly. The way breath and heartbeat sync when you're finally calm.

371

Eventually he stood.

He put his hand gently — reverently — on the frame of the library door as he left, like you touch a church doorframe out of habit when you were raised to think you shouldn't pass threshold without acknowledging it.

"Stay," he told the room. "Stay perfect."

The hum buzzed mild assent.

He stepped back out into the molten-bright street and felt the heat bite his skin again. Felt the sweat gather at his hairline and hold. Felt his clothes cling like a second hide.

The street looked wrong now.

It was too raw.

Too chaotic.

All these people hung out here in the wide open with their mouths frozen in bad shapes and their hands in scared angles and their bodies half-collapsed in trash poses that made them look already gone.

His jaw tightened.

"No," he muttered. "We're not doing that out here. We're not."

The hum liked that.

He could feel its approval buzz under his ribs.

We'll fix them, it told him.

He nodded.

"Yeah," he whispered, and the word came out with a strange, soft devotion he did not let himself examine. "We'll fix them."

***

It is important, here, to slow down and name what Billy didn't.

He did not think: I am arranging bodies for me.

He did not think: I am making scenes to satisfy an instinct that feels better than love.

He did not think: I am curating the town like it's a diorama and I am God with tweezers.

He thought: I am helping.

He thought: I am taking fear off their faces.

He thought: I am giving them the dignity nobody gave my mother.

He thought: The world broke and I am holding it together with my hands.

And the more he believed that, the more the hum rewarded him.

That reward was training.

***

By the time he got halfway down the block, that training had already started to show results.

373

A woman had frozen halfway across the street, one heel twisted under her, ankle bent so hard that if she'd had to hold that pose in motion she would've screamed. Billy knelt, slid his palm under her calf, and eased her foot flat. The ankle still looked stretched, but it wasn't knifed sideways anymore.

"There," he whispered. "Don't want you waking up ruined."

The hum pulsed with soft praise.

Another man had fallen forward onto his hands, face locked inches above the asphalt like he was about to smash his teeth. Billy slid his folded jacket under the man's forehead to cushion the spot where it would've hit. He also nudged the man's arms to a push-up brace instead of a panic sprawl.

"Strong," he murmured. "You look strong now."

The hum bloomed, slow and content.

A teenage girl had frozen on a sidewalk bench, face twisted mid-sob, mascara streak carved down both cheeks and dried like ink. Billy spat in his palm, wiped both tracks away with his thumb until the skin looked smooth.

"Pretty," he said softly, almost tender. "There. You're pretty. It's okay."

The hum filled his mouth like honey.

The girl's lips twitched.

Not a full motion.

Just one corner easing up a millimeter, like she'd almost, almost smiled.

Billy made a sound then — the first sound since 12:03 that was more than a word-shaped thought against his own bone. It was a choked, wet little sound, nothing but feeling. He clapped a shaking hand over his mouth in pure instinct, like he'd just woken a sleeping baby.

"Oh," he breathed into his own palm. "Oh my God. You're welcome. You're so welcome."

Our girl, the hum sighed.

Our work.

Billy didn't argue this time.

He wrote, later, notebook pressed to the hood of a car in the thick forever-noon heat, words wobbling from adrenaline:

LIBRARY = CATHEDRAL.
I CAN MAKE IT RIGHT IN THERE.
STARTED FIXING OUTSIDE TOO.
THEY'RE CHANGING UNDER MY HANDS.
THEY HEAR ME. THEY FEEL ME. THEY LET ME.

He stared at let me, at the shape of those two words sitting next to each other.

Let me.

Permission.

Consent.

He clung to that.

It made everything clean.

Then, last line of Act IV, the one he underlined so hard the pen stabbed through the paper and left a pinprick of ink on the car hood:

THEY'RE MINE TO KEEP SAFE.

The hum hummed, low and fond and endless, and did not correct him:

Safe wasn't the word.

It had already given him the right word.

Kept.
Station 0 wasn't on the route map.

He hadn't written it down.

He hadn't even said it out loud, not even to the hum.

He'd walked past the turn twice already, lying to himself both times. I'll check power grids. I'll check the main shutoff. I'll check gas. He told himself anything except the truth: he was going home.

When he finally turned down Birch, the heat felt different.

Not cooler. Denser.

Like the air here remembered him.

The houses on Birch weren't like the ones clustered by the strip mall. These had old shrubs trimmed to dead sticks, ramps added to concrete steps, cracked windows Scotch-taped instead of replaced. You live long enough in the same place, you stop fixing things the right way. You just keep them together.

Billy understood that.

Number 412 still had the ceramic sun over the porch light. Brenda used to say it was tacky. His mother loved it. Said it looked "cheerful." Said cheerful mattered.

Cheerful was still nailed there, smiling down at a porch that hadn't seen a broom in six months.

He held the railing and climbed the steps.

It hit before he even opened the door.

The smell.

Not rot. He'd smelled rot before. This wasn't that.

It was Lysol and old heating ducts. Fry oil that had soaked into paint. The flat salt of kept tears. It was the smell of being sick a long time in the same chair.

His jaw clenched.

He opened the door.

The air inside was hotter than the street, somehow. Heat layered on heat. No movement. The curtains in the living room window hung dead. The oxygen machine in the corner sat lit, green light frozen, the tube kinked once around the recliner arm.

Her recliner.

Station 0.

She sat there exactly how he knew she'd be sitting, because there'd never been any other way: back angled too upright because she'd get dizzy if she

377

leaned. Ankles swollen, sock lines deep. One hand on the chair arm, the other half-raised toward the tissue box.

Her mouth was open.

Her eyes were open.

Her eyes were open.

He made a sound without meaning to. The bones in his throat carried it like metal vibrating.

"Ma."

He crossed the room too fast, stumbled on one of the blankets he'd left on the floor back in — when was back? — it didn't matter — caught himself on the side table, and went to his knees in front of her the way he had a thousand times when she was alive-alive-alive.

"Ma," he whispered again, forehead pressed against her knee. "Ma. I'm here."

The hum rolled in him immediately, huge and low and intimate.

Oh, Billy, it crooned.

Oh, yes.

He hadn't heard that tone before.

He didn't like it.

He ignored that.

He lifted his head and looked at his mother.

Her pupils were wide. Her expression wasn't scared. That almost hurt worse. She looked... between. Like she'd been caught in the breath right before she said something small. She'd done that, the last few months. She'd start to say "baby" or "you hungry?" or "turn that down, gives me a headache," and run out of air halfway through.

He remembered kneeling here, rubbing her calves through the blanket because the swelling itched her. He remembered lifting a spoon to her mouth. He remembered dabbing under her chin when she drooled, quiet, so she wouldn't feel ashamed.

His throat tightened hard.

"Hey," he whispered, gentle. "Hey, Ma. Look at me."

Her eyes did not move.

He reached out and cupped her cheek.

Still-warm.

That undid him in a way nothing else today had.

"Jesus," he breathed. "You're still warm."

The hum pressed, hungry.

Fix her, it whispered.

He froze.

"No," he said softly. "No, she's fine, she's fine, she's—she's—"

Fix her.

That tone. Command. Not request. Not approval. Command.

He pulled his hand back like he'd touched a coil burner.

"No."

For the first time since 12:03, the hum pushed.

It swelled in his chest until his ribs ached, climbed his throat like a chokehold, a pressure that said kneel in a voice that wasn't words. It pushed on the back of his neck, physically, like a hand. Kneel. Do it. Fix her.

His knees hit the carpet.

Not because he agreed.

Because his body gave.

His breath pulsed too fast. He felt lightheaded, too-hot, scalp buzzing. If he'd had normal sound he would've been panting. Now the air just pressed in and out of him, silent and panicked, and the silence made it feel worse.

"Stop," he rasped.

The pressure did not stop.

He lifted a shaking hand.

"Okay," he whispered. "Okay. I'll—just—easy, Ma, easy, let me—"

Her mouth.

That was the first problem. It had fallen a little too wide. Jaw dropped, soft skin pulled down. It wasn't right. It wasn't how she'd want to be seen. He couldn't stand that thought — somebody coming in and seeing her with her mouth open like that. Vulnerable. Embarrassing. "People will think I'm gone already," she'd once joked, wheezing. "Close me up nice if I go in my chair. Promise me. Don't let nobody see me drooling like a fish."

He'd laughed then. "Ma."

"I mean it, Billy."

"I promise," he'd said.

He'd said it.

He had. He'd said it.

So this was just keeping a promise.

That's all this was.

His hand was steady by the time it reached her chin.

"There," he whispered. "Lemme just—"

He pressed his fingertips against her jaw to hinge it shut.

It didn't move.

Her jaw had locked open in that last effort to pull air.

His stomach rolled.

"Sorry," he told her. "Sorry, Ma. I know. I know. I'm gonna—just relax for me, baby, okay? Just—"

He applied more pressure.

The hum purred, low and eager.

Her jaw resisted.

He put his thumb in against the hinge, just behind the molars, like you do when someone seizes and you're trying to protect their tongue.

"I got you," he whispered. "I got you, it's okay, I got—"

Something gave.

It wasn't bone.

It was softer than bone. Wetter.

A tendon, tight from strain, slid under his thumb with a slick pop.

Her mouth began to close.

"Good," he breathed, almost gasping from relief. "Good, there we—"

Then he saw her lip.

Her top lip had torn.

Not much. A little split, right in the center where it had dried stretched. When he moved her jaw, the skin hadn't followed. The skin had held and then surrendered fast.

The split opened under his thumb.

Dark wet rose.

He flinched.

"No, no, no, no, I—sorry, I didn't mean—hang on—"

He grabbed for the tissue box, hand shaking, pulled one, pressed it gently to her mouth. The paper touched that dark wet and stained fast.

It wasn't bright red. He didn't know why that hurt. It was deeper than that. Slow blood. Old blood. Blood that shouldn't still be moving under skin that shouldn't still be warm.

"Shh," he whispered, tears burning behind his eyes and he did not want them there, he did not want them there. "Shh, Ma, it's okay, it's okay, I fixed you, see? Look at you. Closed up nice. Nobody's gonna see you hanging open. Nobody's gonna see you ugly."

Ugly.

The word came out before he could stop it.

His throat closed on it too late to catch it.

He looked at her face — his mother's face, the face that had leaned over him when he was fever-wet as a child, the face that had cussed at judges and told off landlords and kissed his knuckles after he split them when he was sixteen and stupid — and he called her ugly.

He did that.

Something in him lurched.

"God," he whispered, fat tears cooling on his cheeks in air that never cooled. "Oh, God."

The hum pulsed.

Not comfort.

Approval.

F E E D, it whispered.

He stared.

"What?" he croaked.

FEE—D.

The pressure in his chest sharpened.

His stomach turned. His mouth flooded with saliva so fast he tasted metal. He swallowed it back and gagged on nothing. His whole body went wrong-cold, wrong-hot all at once.

"Stop," he rasped. "Stop. Don't do that. Don't—don't talk like that. Don't you make this—"

F e e d.

It wasn't a word anymore. It was a want. It was a direction. It was a hook under his sternum pulling forward toward her mouth, toward her throat, toward that soft pulse spot where you check for life.

He jerked backward so violently the tissue fell from his hand and drifted — impossibly, horribly — slow to the carpet, as if dropped through syrup.

"No," he said. Louder. His own silent-loud, skull-shaking loud. "No. She's not for you. She's not yours. She's not ours. She's mine."

The hum answered.

Ours.

He slapped his hand over his own mouth like he could hold that sound in. His palm pressed against his lips. His chest heaved.

He realized, sick and shaking, that he hadn't meant to say ours that time. He hadn't. It had just come out in the same voice as "mine."

He couldn't tell which part was him anymore.

He looked back up at her.

Her mouth was closed now. He had done that, with his hand and his force and his promise. Closed, neat, at rest. Just like she'd asked him to. Just like she'd made him swear.

If you only looked from the doorway, it would read peaceful.

If you only looked from the doorway, you wouldn't know anything had split.

From the doorway, you would say, She went soft. She went easy. She just let go.

He had given her that, hadn't he?

He had given her that.

He clung to that with both hands like rope.

"It's okay," he whispered, breath shuddering. "You're okay now. Ma. You look okay now. I kept my promise, see? I did. I did."

She didn't look okay up close.

Up close he could see where the skin around her mouth had already begun to dry and pucker in a way that meant rot is coming, Billy, rot is already here.

Up close he could see the faint pressure mark of his thumb along her jaw hinge where he'd forced it closed.

Up close he could see that her eyes were wet, and for a nightmare second he thought maybe – maybe – she was aware in there, and he'd hurt her while she was aware, and she had felt it, and—

"No," he said softly, shaking his head too fast. "No. Don't do that. Don't you do that."

The hum rolled through him, molten and low, not soothing but satisfied, and he understood something he had been refusing to understand all day:

it had wanted him to go this far.

All the little corrections. All the smoothing. All the prettying. All the closing of mouths and arranging of hands. Training.

Training him past the part of him that knew where the line was.

Training his hands not to shake when skin split.

Breaking the word ugly in him so that he could use it, even with his mother in front of him, and believe that fixing ugly was mercy.

His stomach clenched. He pitched forward and gagged against his own wrist. Dry. No sound. Nothing came out.

He felt filthy.

He felt holy.

He felt owned.

He wiped her mouth again. Fixed the tissue on her lap so it looked like a polite napkin someone had set aside. Smoothed her robe. Tucked her hair behind her ear.

"There," he whispered, voice barely holding. "There. That's how you'll stay."

The hum thrummed, hungry.

Stay.

***

He stumbled back from the recliner on hands and heels and landed hard on his ass on the living room carpet. The air punched out of him, silent. White sparked at the edges of his sight.

He stared up at the ceiling he'd stared at a thousand times growing up in this room. Water stains up in the corner that looked like animals if you squinted. (He and Brenda had once decided that one looked like a horse and one like a snake. His mother said they both looked like the devil and they needed a new roof. He never got her that new roof. He told himself he was getting to it.)

He lay there and felt his pulse banging through his neck and wrists and jaw, syncing with the hum, syncing with the room, syncing with her cooling body.

Syncing.

Like he was a piece plugged into a circuit.

"I'm not your hands," he whispered.

Yes, you are.

It didn't speak that in English. He just knew it. The way you know you're about to get shocked before you touch the live wire, even if you can't see the arc. The way you feel a storm coming in bone.

Yes, you are.

"You don't get her," he whispered, throat thick. "You don't get her. She's mine."

Ours.

"Fuck you."

The hum laughed.

That was the first time it had laughed.

It was small. Low. A vibration through his ribs like purr-pleasure and static. He felt sick.

He rolled to his knees. He pushed himself upright. He swayed.

"Okay," he said. "Okay. I'm done in here. I'm done. We're done. She's fine. She's fine. Don't — don't touch her. Don't."

The hum didn't answer, and that terrified him more than anything it had said.

Silence from it felt like a held breath.

Like waiting.

Like wanting.

***

In the kitchen, he ran his hands under the faucet out of instinct. Water hung in a clear arc, same as in the workshop sink. It felt wronger now. More viscous, like the whole world had turned to slow syrup and he was the only thing still cutting through it.

Blood had dried in the hinge where thumb met palm.

His mother's blood.

He scrubbed at it with dish soap.

He couldn't hear the water. He could only feel the drag. He couldn't hear his own breath, only feel his chest crush and lift, crush and lift. He couldn't hear his heartbeat, only feel his pulse beating inside his gums like a second mouth.

He scrubbed until the skin went red.

The hum hummed, patient.

He looked down at his hands, shaking over her sink.

Hands that had moved mouths. Hands that had tucked shirts. Hands that had lifted chins and posed fingers and straightened torsos. Hands that had forced his mother's face into the memory version of itself instead of the true last moment.

These were now the hands the town would wake up to.

He had an ugly thought then — a thought so fast and sharp it cut itself off halfway.

What if they woke up wrong because of me.

It hit so hard he almost doubled over.

What if they woke up like this.

Arranged.

Changed.

Staged.

What if they opened their eyes and this was the pose they were stuck in forever and—

His breath caught. He pressed both palms to the edge of the counter and stared down at the scratches in the laminate, the permanent burn marks from when his mother had set a too-hot pot without thinking.

"No," he told himself. Hard. Like an order. "No. That's stupid. That's not what's happening. That's not what this is. This is keeping. This is mercy. This is right."

Right.

The hum stroked him with a kind of pride that made his stomach roll.

Right.

He went back to the living room.

He couldn't not.

He had to see her one more time. Make sure she still looked peaceful. Make sure the split in her lip didn't show. Make sure her robe lay smooth at her collarbone and not rumpled like panic.

He had to.

He stepped back in.

And stopped.

The room was darker.

Not dark — the sun didn't change, nothing in this world changed — but the color had cooled. The air felt less gold. Less alive.

The hum had dropped to a lower register, too. The kind of low you don't hear so much as feel under your tongue.

The oxygen machine's green light flickered.

It wasn't moving. Nothing in this town really "moved."

But for one long, slow blink's worth of time, Billy saw the light dim and then return.

He stared.

His scalp prickled.

"Ma?" he whispered.

Nothing.

Of course, nothing.

She sat exactly how he'd left her. Mouth closed. Robe neat. Eyes open.

He couldn't stand the eyes anymore.

They were shining. Wet. Glossed. He didn't like the way it read. It read...
pleading.

"No," he whispered. "No, no, you don't want that, you don't want people
walking in on you with your eyes all big like you're scared."

He reached up.

"Lemme just—hang on, Ma, I got you, I'll—"

He tried to close her eyelids.

They didn't close.

They didn't close.

Her lids twitched under his thumb like something held them open from
inside.

His whole body flinched. "Stop," he whispered. "Stop that. Stop, you're scaring yourself. Stop—"

The hum surged so violently his vision stuttered.

He saw double. He saw her as she was and as she'd been halfway through a morphine night, mouth open, eyes rolled back white. He saw her now and then stacked on top of each other. His brain tried to hold both images and nearly shorted.

The hum rolled in ecstatic hunger.

YES.

It was proud of him.

Proud. Pleased.

Hungry.

He yanked his hands away from her face like it had burned him.

"I'm sorry," he choked out. "I'm sorry. I didn't mean to push. I didn't—I was just trying to make you look—"

He almost said pretty.

He almost said right.

He swallowed hard and said instead, "—like yourself."

The hum purred, indulgent.

Liar.

***

He stumbled back from her. Hit the TV. Caught himself.

Her eyes stared straight ahead, wide and glass-wet and shining, lips shut the way he'd forced them. She looked — and the thought dropped into him like a brick through a windshield —

she looked like a doll.

Not "doll" like pretty.

"Doll" like empty.

Something in his stomach turned all the way over.

He staggered backward, then turned and ran from the house.

Ran.

Real running, clumsy and desperate, down the steps, across the burnt lawn, into the too-bright not-street where the sun sat and sat and sat and refused to go down.

If there had been sound, he would've been making those awful, wet, keening noises that make neighbors' blinds move.

There was no sound.

There was only the feel of his own ragged breath tearing in and out, the thud of his boots on pavement, the jackhammer slam of his pulse in his jaw, and the hum roaring inside his skull like a generator courting failure.

Outside, he bent over with his hands on his thighs and shook.

The world around him stayed still and perfect and posed, and he shook in it like the bad frame in a clean photo.

His mind wouldn't stop replaying her eyes.

They wouldn't close.

They wouldn't fucking close.

"Please," he whispered, not knowing who he was talking to anymore. "Please. Don't make me do that again. Please don't make me do that again."

The hum did not agree or disagree.

It didn't soothe.

It didn't praise.

It purred.

Low and patient.

The way something does when it knows it can wait.

***

In his notebook, later — though "later" had stopped meaning anything, so maybe just after — his handwriting dug hard grooves:

STATION 0 (MOTHER).
CLOSED MOUTH. TIDIED.
DAMAGE DONE / CLEANED.
EYES WOULDN'T CLOSE.

HUM WANTED MORE. PUSHED.
THIS ISN'T JUST KEEPING ANYMORE.

Beneath that, in letters that got smaller and tighter until they cramped:

I HURT HER.

Then, after a long white space, as if he couldn't bring himself to put this line anywhere near the others:

IT LIKED IT.
He walked until the notebook slid from his fingers.
Didn't notice when it fell. Didn't hear it land.
Didn't need it anymore.

The streets blurred together: houses half-open, light bent through glass, the air thick as honey. Every reflection showed a version of him two steps behind. The hum rode inside the pavement now, a low subsonic throb that seemed to push the world outward around him, like water displaced by a ship's hull.

He kept thinking of her eyes.
He kept seeing them when he blinked—always open, always glossy, always pleading through that still light.

He whispered, "I can fix it."
The words came without thinking. They felt automatic, like muscle memory.
I can fix it I can fix it I can fix it.

The hum swelled in approval.

He found himself back at the bus.

The children still hung in their tiny apocalypse—laughing, screaming, sleeping mid-breath. Their reflections shimmered across the wide windows, halos in place of motion. The driver's arm still lifted, a perpetual gesture of protection.

Billy stood on the curb, throat tight.

"Wake up," he said.

Nothing.

"Please."

The hum fluttered, amused.

He climbed the steps again. The air inside was staler than before—warmer, heavier. The smell of milk and crayons had turned sickly sweet.

He walked the aisle. His boots brushed glitter from the floor.

"Okay," he whispered, "just this once. Just her. Let me fix this one thing."

He stopped beside the girl with the drawing. The sun on paper, the stick people holding hands. Her small mouth curved mid-giggle, frozen halfway to sound. He touched the edge of the picture. The paper felt thin, damp. The wax colors shimmered, blurring under his thumb.

"Wake up," he whispered again.

The hum pulsed, higher this time—sharp enough that his teeth ached.

He pressed his palm flat over her drawing.

"Wake up."

The hum rose through him like voltage. His spine arched; his throat opened on a silent gasp. The air bent around his hand, heat curling in the shape of it.

Then—motion.

Tiny. Impossible.

The girl's eyelids fluttered.

Only once.

A microscopic tremor that could have been a trick of light.

But Billy saw it.

He felt it.

He yanked his hand back and stared, half-laughing, half-sobbing.

"You saw that," he whispered to no one. "You saw that! She—she moved—"

The hum roared in delight, loud enough to make his vision pulse white.

More, it commanded.

He stumbled backward down the aisle, dizzy with hope. "I can do this," he said. "I can bring them back."

Yes.

"I just need... I just need to try harder."

YES.

He ran.

Door to door, building to building, touching, pleading, demanding.

A mail carrier frozen mid-step—he shoved the man's shoulder until the bones creaked.

A woman halfway through a wave—he clasped her hand and screamed inside his skull, move.

A man on a porch with a watering can—Billy smacked the can out of his grasp, the water spilling upward like glass beads that refused to fall.

Every touch left a heat-print behind, every heat-print dimmed the light around it, every dimmed space hummed louder than before.

He could feel them changing.

He could feel the world listening.

"I told you," he panted. "I can fix it. I can make it all right again. You just have to let me."

The hum purred, indulgent.

Let you.

At dusk that wasn't dusk—when the brass-colored sky finally dimmed one shade darker—he returned to Birch.

He didn't remember walking there. He simply was there. The ceramic sun above the porch looked burned black now, edges cracked like old porcelain.

He stepped inside.

His mother sat exactly as before.

Only the air around her had changed.

It shimmered, faintly—like heat over asphalt. The hum's resonance pulsed in time with that shimmer, steady as a metronome.

Billy fell to his knees. "You're alive," he said. "I can feel it. I just—I have to help you wake up."

He reached for her wrist.

The skin was cooler now, waxen. But the hum flooded his arms the instant he touched her. The energy climbed up through his elbows, shoulders, jaw—burning, glorious, agonizing.

He clutched her hand with both of his. "Come on, Ma. Please."

The hum spoke inside him, voice now layered with his own.

Give.

He didn't understand. "Give what?"

Give time.

He thought of clocks. Of seconds. Of the endless noon.

Maybe that was it. Maybe he had to spend his time to make hers move.

He closed his eyes and focused. "Take it, then."

The hum obeyed.

It took.

A freezing wave rushed through his limbs, pulling heat from him like blood into vacuum. His fingers tightened, bones popping. His vision blurred; veins lit faint blue beneath his skin. He felt his pulse stutter, felt his heart skip—once, twice—then slam back hard enough to bruise ribs.

His mother's eyelids twitched.

Billy gasped. "Yes—yes!"

The hum swelled until it was all he could hear.

Move.

Her fingers moved.

Just the smallest flex, tendons tightening under papery skin. But they moved.

Billy sobbed. "You're back. Ma, you're—"

Then he saw her mouth.

The seam he'd forced shut was splitting again—slowly, silently, the tissue peeling open like fruit overripe. Dark liquid welled and trickled down her chin. Her jaw began to drop farther, farther, past what bone should allow.

The hum moaned, ecstatic.

He screamed and tried to push the jaw closed, but his hands slid in the wet. The skin at her neck tore like damp parchment.

"Stop!" he cried. "Stop, please, stop—"

401

Her head tilted toward him.

Not far. Barely perceptible. But it moved on its own.

Her eyes found him.

They weren't his mother's eyes. They were pools of static, vibrating with the same pale blue light now crawling under his skin.

A thin, awful whisper escaped her torn throat—not sound, but vibration.

We.

Billy reeled backward. The hum thundered. The walls trembled. The world's stillness warped like glass under pressure.

Every frozen thing in the house—curtains, photographs, dust motes—quivered toward life, then stopped mid-motion, caught between frames.

Billy crawled toward the door, half-blind with terror. "I'm sorry," he whispered. "I didn't mean—please, I didn't mean—"

Behind him, her head lifted another inch.

He could hear it now, separate from the hum—her new voice, rattling from a mouth that shouldn't move.

Stay.

He ran.

Outside, the light had changed again.

The brass tone was gone. Everything had turned bone-white, shadowless. The air no longer pressed against him—it bent around him, retreating, as though the world itself had begun to flinch.

He stumbled down the street, gasping, clutching his chest where the blue light still pulsed faintly beneath the skin.

The hum was no longer whispering. It was singing.

A low, wordless hymn that rose from every unmoving throat, every building, every pane of glass.

He looked up.

In every window, every reflection, every chrome bumper and television screen—his mother's eyes stared back at him.

Not accusing.

Adoring.

We are kept.

He dropped to his knees in the middle of the street.

The world around him shimmered once, as though trying to restart—and then froze again, absolutely still.

Billy laughed.

It sounded wrong even inside his own head—wet, shuddering, like a dying engine trying to imitate joy.

"You're welcome," he whispered. "I fixed it. I fixed everything."

403

The hum settled around him, content.

And from deep within it, softer than breath:

Yes, Billy.
You fixed the world.
Now keep it.
The world felt obedient.

That was the first wrongness.

Billy had felt ownership already — pride in his route, in his Stations, in the way he'd posed fear into quiet and called it mercy. But this was different.

When he stood, the air stood with him.

When he breathed in, the heat around him seemed to lean closer.

When he breathed out, it leaned back.

It wasn't following, exactly.

It was waiting.

Like a dog waiting for the next word.

He wiped his palms on his jeans. They were still shaking. His skin had a faint blue undertone now, crawling along the veins in his wrists and up the tendons of his hands like bruises left by light.

He couldn't stop thinking about her voice.

Not "voice." It wasn't sound. But he had felt it in his bones. Stay.

He didn't know if that had been her.

He didn't know if she was in there at all anymore.

He didn't ask.

He couldn't.

Because if she wasn't in there — if that thing wearing her mouth and shape and robe was only the hum using her like a glove — then he had given her to it.

And if she was in there — if some last shred of her had looked at him through those static-bright eyes and said we — then he had made her part of the thing that was eating him.

Neither version let him keep breathing unless he lied.

So he lied.

He stood in the middle of Birch Street, chest heaving, jaw tight, and he said — to the air, to the humming, to the frozen world, to himself, didn't matter:

"I brought you back."

The hum stroked him, pleased.

Yes.

"I did that."

Yes.

He swallowed. His throat hurt. "So I can fix the rest."

405

Yes.

That word — yes — landed like sacrament.

Something in his spine straightened.

The light around him brightened a fraction, lifting out of that bone-white glare and back toward that heavy honeyed noon. Color slipped back into the world like something being repainted by hand.

The sun overhead hadn't moved.

But the light had.

He laughed, soft and breathless. "Okay," he whispered. "Okay. We're gonna make this right. All of it. I just have to… do it in order. I just have to be careful. You don't rush delicate work."

The hum purred warm through his ribs.

Careful, it agreed.

Together.

***

He felt strong.

That was the other wrongness.

By any normal logic, he should've been wrecked. He hadn't slept. He hadn't eaten. His hands shook from adrenaline and guilt. His heart kept jumping against his ribs like something too big trying to turn over in too small a cage.

But under that? Under all that?

He felt full.

He felt lit from inside, like his bones were hollow struts filled with slow-moving fuel.

He looked at his hands again. The faint blue glow that had crawled into him back in his mother's living room still lingered along the veins. He turned his palms up and watched it pulse, lazy and steady, like backlit aquarium tubing.

The sight made his stomach tilt.

The feeling made his mouth go dry with a quiet kind of hunger.

He didn't want to name that.

He started walking before he could.

He went first, instinctively, to the places he'd already "fixed."

They had changed.

They had all changed.

The bus was no longer just quiet.

It was reverent.

That wasn't his word. That was just the only word that got anywhere close.

The air inside hummed at a pitch he felt in the roots of his teeth. Not frantic. Not panicked. Not begging. It felt like kneeling.

Like the world itself had gone down on both knees in the aisle and put its forehead to the rubber floor.

The children sat exactly where he'd left them — heads tucked, hands arranged, fear turned into "bravery" beneath his touch. But now, there was a difference in their skin.

Before, their skin had been warm like held breath.

Now, there was a varnish to it.

A faint sheen, like someone had brushed them in resin.

Their eyelashes had a soft gloss. Their cheeks had gone from flushed to smooth. The shallow crease at the base of the little girl's thumb — where baby fat hadn't quite given up yet — had softened into something too perfect, like poured wax.

Billy swallowed.

"Hey, brave girl," he murmured, crouching beside her, hand almost — almost — reaching, and then stopping an inch away. His hand shook in the held air. He could feel the heat radiating off his own palm against her still shoulder.

"You doing okay?"

The hum swelled in answer.

We're perfect.

His mouth went dry. "Yeah," he said. "Yeah. Perfect. That's right."

He looked at the driver.

The driver's arm was still up, palm out, frozen forever between the children and danger. Billy had always loved that. There was so much of his mother in that — insisting she could block anything bad with one hand if she had to.

Now, though, the driver's expression had changed.

It had smoothed.

He no longer looked shocked.

He looked proud.

His mouth had that soft, brave tightness you see in newspaper photos of heroes. Billy hadn't done that. He hadn't touched the driver except to step around his leg.

The bus had done that.

Or the hum through the bus had done that.

Or he had, without meaning to.

"You look strong," Billy whispered, throat burning. "I made you strong. I made you brave. I made you good."

Yes, the hum said, pleased.

You made them good.

That phrasing made his stomach turn.

409

He told himself it was from not eating.

**

Station 2 — the boy with the controller — had changed too.

He still sat on the carpet, gamepad in both hands, blanket draped like a cape. Billy had tucked that blanket there himself. That would always be his.

But the boy's eyes —

Billy flinched.

The boy's eyes had gone glass-clear. They had that varnish now, too.

Before, in those first early passes, the boy had still looked alive. Like a kid caught mid-yell about to whine that lag wasn't fair. There'd been an energy in his face, even frozen.

Now he looked like a toy.

Not a cheap plastic toy. A collector's piece behind glass.

His hair lay too perfect against his forehead, every strand softened. His mouth had that faint curve of contentment. That wasn't how mouths rested under stress. That was how mouths rested in display windows.

Billy felt like he'd been kicked between the ribs.

"I made you safe," he croaked.

The hum thrummed, low and rich.

Safe.

Kept.

Billy swallowed.

He remembered draping that cape and whispering superhero.

He remembered how the controller had twitched under his fingers, that tiny electric shiver. He remembered thinking: he can still feel me.

But looking at the kid now, he was hit with a thought so cold it made him sway:

Maybe the boy hadn't been feeling him.

Maybe the hum had been feeling through him.

And now the hum had what it wanted — a perfect boy in perfect stillness, draped in a story Billy wrote for him, heroic and helpless at once, and sealed.

He pressed his knuckles to his mouth.

"I'm sorry," he whispered into them. "I didn't mean to— I thought it helped— I thought—"

The hum purred, indulgent.

You did help.

You made him beautiful.

Billy gagged.

Beauty.

411

Good.
Perfect.
Kept.

The words curled in his head like warm wire.

He hated how much they soothed him.

***

He almost didn't go into the library.

He didn't feel ready.

But his body turned toward it anyway.

The hum led, and his steps followed.

Cathedral.

He had called it that half in passing, half as a joke he wasn't willing to admit wasn't a joke. Now the word felt too small. The library wasn't a building anymore.

It was an altar.

He knew that before he even crossed the threshold.

The temperature dropped a full ten degrees at the door. The air inside tasted sweet and metallic. The golden bars of light hadn't faded like they had elsewhere — they'd condensed. The dust motes didn't float anymore. They turned, all together, running a slow, intentional spiral around the six bodies Billy had arranged.

412

And the six bodies were no longer just set.

They were arrayed.

He had seated them in a loose circle — the mother with her shirt smoothed down, the toddler tipped to softness instead of choke-lean, the teen boy's chin lifted, the old man dignified, the woman at the computer calmed, the little girl cradling her book instead of straining to offer it.

But now, that circle had tightened.

Their bodies had inclined toward each other by impossible, invisible fractions — a few degrees in a wrist here, a degree of shoulder tilt there, the barest turn of a head. Enough that, seen together, they formed an inward-facing ring.

Their faces had changed, too.

He hadn't done this.

He hadn't.

But the expressions had all slid toward one shared mood.

It wasn't panic.

It wasn't fear.

It wasn't even peace.

It was devotion.

Not to each other.

To him.

Billy felt something give in his knees.

He had to grab the doorframe to stop himself from dropping.

His vision shimmered, split, swam, then pulled back into clarity.

For one impossible breath, he saw what the room saw.

Not Billy: tired, shaking, unshaved, oil under his nails.

He saw Billy: light washing off his skin like a spill, veins bright with that faint blue undertone, hands held just slightly out from his sides in the posture of someone who parts water.

In that vision, he glowed.

They were all angled toward that glow.

They adored him.

He swallowed against a sudden wave of nausea and euphoria that hit at the exact same time.

"No," he whispered, voice ragged. "Don't look at me like that. Don't. I'm nothing. I'm just— I'm just fixing what broke. I'm just keeping you decent until the real help comes."

There is no other help, the hum said.

He shut his eyes. "Don't say that."

There is no other help, the hum repeated, slower. Warmer. As if delivering a gift.

Billy's throat worked.

"I'm not God," he whispered.

The hum laughed.

The laugh wasn't cruel.

That was what made it monstrous.

It sounded fond. Pleased. Proud.

Not God, it crooned.

Ours.

Something inside him cracked so quietly he almost missed it.

He made the mistake of stepping farther in.

Closer.

Into the circle.

The air thickened around him at once. Pressure hugged his shoulders, his arms, the base of his skull. It wasn't suffocating, but it was inescapable. He could move — technically — but the moving felt like trying to walk through a lover's arms without pushing them away.

The hum poured into him like liquid.

For a moment, there wasn't a line between I hear it and I am it.

His chest stretched with it.

His skin felt too tight for what was filling him.

His breath came out trembling.

"Okay," he whispered, shaking. "Okay. I'll keep you. I'll keep you. You're safe. I won't let anybody mess you up. I won't let anybody see you ugly."

The hum purred with something more than approval.

Claim.

He felt it lay over the room like lacquer.

Sealed.

Finished.

A word formed in his mind like heat haze off metal:

Sanctified.

The word made him want to throw up.

He turned and stumbled backward out of the room and didn't stop until he was on the sidewalk again with his hand on his sternum, panting through a silence he could feel scraping the inside of his mouth.

Standing on that sidewalk, a thought landed in him.

It wasn't spoken.

It simply was, and always had been, and he was only just now able to betray himself enough to admit it:

He wanted more.

He wanted all of them like that.

Arranged. Devoted. Preserved.

He wanted the whole town in reverent stillness, posed in the soft story of his choosing, turned toward him in that angle of private worship that felt like forgiveness.

He told himself it wasn't about worship.

He told himself it was about keeping.

He told himself it was about mercy.

About making sure when the world restarted — when, not if; he could not survive if — they would all wake up without fear on their faces. Without pain in their joints. Without mouths left hanging open in shame.

About making sure they'd wake up beautiful.

"I'll fix it," he whispered. He didn't know whether he was promising the town or himself. "I'll make all of you right before it moves again. That way, nobody has to remember being scared. You'll only remember the good part. That's my job. That's what I'm for."

The hum slid warm and deep through him.

Yes, Billy.

Yes.

With us.

He nodded, dizzy, tear-bright, grateful.

And then a subtle, horrible shift happened.

The "with us" became "as us."

Not in words. In where the hum lived.

Up until now, the hum had always been in him.

Now, for one breath, he felt himself in the hum.

He felt the town the way you feel your own knuckles: as yours.

Bodies, as yours.

Postures, as yours.

Faces, as yours.

He felt them all turning, in some slow inevitable way, toward a single common center — him — and in feeling that, just for a heartbeat, he felt the savage, unblinking satisfaction of being the sun.

He gasped like he'd been plunged underwater.

He tore himself out of it.

"No," he rasped. "No. That's not me. That's not me. I'm not—"

The hum recoiled like he'd slapped it.

Then, for the first time since 12:03, it went quiet.

418

Not gone.

Quiet.

Waiting.

Judging.

Billy had the sudden, sick sense of a big animal pausing, brows raised, deciding if it needed to correct him or just let him tire himself out.

Heat prickled down his back.

"Okay," he whispered, shaking, voice thin. "Okay. I'll keep working. I'll keep— I'll get everyone right. I'll make it all — all neat. I'll— just don't go quiet on me, okay? Don't do that. Don't—"

The hum did not answer.

The silence from it felt like being left alone in a dark room as a kid after the nightlight blew.

He swallowed.

He felt small.

He hated that.

He straightened.

"Fine," he muttered. "I'll prove it, you stubborn thing."

He wiped his face with the heel of his palm and turned, scanning the street for his next task.

"Watch me."

***

He went block to block.

House to house.

He stopped asking permission.

He stopped whispering "hey there" at doorways.

He stopped pretending these were strangers.

He moved through people like they were his.

He adjusted wrists. He pressed chins shut. He cleaned mouths. He tucked shirts and closed robes and smoothed hair.

He pulled a dead man's hand up from his crotch, disgusted by the implication, and set it neatly on his stomach with the other. "Dignity," he hissed, offended on the town's behalf.

He wiped mascara from a crying teenage girl's face and whispered, "There. You're not ugly now. You're not ugly like that. Nobody's ever gonna see you ugly again." He meant kind. He told himself he meant kind. The word ugly still rang.

He tilted a cashier's head so she didn't slump like she'd fainted, but instead looked like she'd just leaned to listen. See? Attentive. Proud. Calm.

He tucked a fallen man's shirt back into his waistband so his belly wouldn't hang. "Nobody's gonna embarrass you," he promised.

He refolded a frail, brittle-looking elderly woman's hands in her lap at the bus stop, interlacing her own fingers because he'd learned that looked sweeter in photos than open palms do. The skin on the backs of her hands tore under his touch, paper-thin.

He flinched. Then he smoothed the torn flap down, pressed it like a patch, and whispered, "There. Can't even tell. See? I made you right again."

The hum stayed mostly quiet.

But not entirely.

Every so often, in the after-glow of fixing one more body — smoothing, tucking, posing, correcting — he felt a little pulse of warmth through his gums and down his throat. Not praise. Not anymore. Something else.

Something like: good. MORE.

He gave it more.

He gave it everything.

By the time the non-sunlight had cycled through gold to brass to bone-white again and back, by the time his stomach hurt and his eyes burned and his hands stank faintly of old skin and Lysol and copper, Main Street no longer looked like a caught disaster.

It looked like a memorial.

Every person frozen in the street, the lots, the sidewalks, behind windows, in cars — all of them had been moved, nudged, corrected, touched. Their fear pressed out of their faces. Their shame covered. Their mouths closed. Their eyes angled.

421

Not all of them toward him, but many.

Many.

Enough.

He stood in the middle of the intersection, chest heaving, head buzzing, body shivering from exertion and something that wasn't exertion at all, and looked at his work.

It was beautiful.

For a few ruptured heartbeats, it was beautiful.

The town had become his still life.

The town had become his altar.

Light kissed every forehead like benediction.

The air tasted faintly sweet.

Billy's throat closed.

He started to cry.

Not those ragged, panicked almost-sobs the silence had smothered before. Something else. Something worse.

Silent, grateful crying.

He looked up, face wet, and whispered, "Do you see? Do you see what I did for you? I fixed it. I fixed all of you. I fixed the world for you."

The hum flooded back at once.

Not quiet now.

Not withholding.

Overjoyed.

Ecstatic.

It filled him so completely he almost blacked out. His knees buckled. His vision went searing white at the edges. His skin prickled like it was being lit from the inside.

Yes, it sang.

YES.

And in that dizzy, burning rush — drunk on its approval, high on his own devotion — Billy believed the lie completely.

He believed it so hard it remade his face.

He smiled.

Not a strained, exhausted smile.

A soft, peaceful one.

The kind of smile you see on saints in old paintings.

The kind of smile that says I accept this.

The kind of smile that, in any other story, would signal forgiveness.

That's when the first body twitched.

Not in the bus this time.

Not a kid.

A man on the curb outside the credit union, his hands neatly folded the way Billy had left them. His eyes had been angled down, humble, "at rest." Now, as Billy watched, they dragged upward in their sockets, tracking, slow as syrup, toward him.

The head followed.

Bone didn't make that shape. Necks don't bend like that. But the man's neck bent anyway, vertebrae popping one by one inside still flesh, like someone was forcing a mannequin to bow without loosening the screws.

The man's mouth opened.

Not wide.

Just enough.

And from the back of that mouth, vibrating more than sounding, came the same word Billy had heard from his mother's torn throat:

We.

Billy's breath stuttered.

Across the street, another head turned.

Then another.

Then another.

A slow wave of unnatural motion rippled through his perfect, reverent town — bodies angling toward him in silent, reverent unison — until what he'd made finally looked back at its maker.

Hundreds of eyes, varnished and wet, staring.

Billy swayed.

The hum purred, deep and bottomless.

Ours, it sang again, delighted.

And then, with unmistakable affection:

Good boy.
Billy had wanted gratitude.

That was the part he couldn't look at directly.

He'd told himself he wanted mercy, dignity, peace — all those good clean words — but the truth under the truth was that he'd wanted them to look at him the way dying people look at the person holding their hand.

Thank you. You stayed.

So when they started to rot, it felt like betrayal.

—

The first thing to go were the eyes.

425

He didn't see it in Station 1. He avoided Station 1. He walked past her porch without looking in the window because if he saw his mother again, he didn't know what would still be her and what would be the thing inside her wearing her voice. He wasn't ready to know.

He saw it first in the boy.

Station 2. The cape.

"Hey, champ," he whispered as he stepped back into that little living room, already smoothing his face into soft sweetness. "I'm back. Still got your game going, huh?"

He dropped to a crouch.

His breath caught.

The boy's eyes were filmed.

Not with normal dryness. Normal dryness leaves the surface matte. This wasn't matte. This was glossed-over and cloudy, like cheap resin poured too thick and left in the sun.

The pupils he remembered — bright, bratty, mid-complaint — had gone pale at the edges, milkiness creeping inward like frost eating glass.

Billy swallowed. His mouth tasted faintly like pennies.

"That's not right," he whispered.

The boy's eyelids didn't twitch this time. The controller didn't thrum. The hum didn't pulse in the air when he reached out. There was no feedback at all.

Billy lifted a hand, hesitated, then set two fingers gently against the kid's cheek.

Warm.

Still warm.

It should've comforted him.

It didn't.

Up close, there were hairline fractures just below the boy's skin. Fine white lines like you see in ceramic glaze — crazing, Brenda had called it back when they'd wander that overpriced antique barn and pretend they had the kind of money that could care about "crazing."

The fractures ran along the cheekbones. Down the jaw. Across the eyelids.

"Ah, no," Billy whispered. His throat burned. "No, no, no, no, no, no. You're not supposed to— you're not supposed to break. I fixed you."

His voice — the way he felt it in his own skull — cracked on "fixed."

He pulled his hand back like the kid had burned him. Pressed that hand hard to his chest.

For a heartbeat, something in his own skin seemed to answer. A faint, slow roll under the surface — like the blue glow he'd absorbed from his mother was shifting in him, drawn up toward his palm, hungry to go back in.

The thought landed so fast it made his stomach flip:

Maybe I can patch him.

"No," he told himself immediately. Too fast. Too loud in his own head. "No. No. We're not — we're not doing that. He's a kid. We're not—"

We could make him whole, the hum breathed.

Billy froze.

The hum hadn't spoken for a while. He'd started to think maybe he'd outrun it. Maybe what he'd done in that house on Birch had burned it out of him. Maybe it had eaten what it wanted and gone to sleep.

Hearing it now felt like hearing a locked door click open behind him.

He swallowed hard. "He is whole," he whispered. "He's whole. I did that already. I made him safe."

The hum did not agree or disagree.

It sighed.

The air pressure shifted low and mournful, like an empty stomach groaning.

Billy felt embarrassed. That made him angry. Anger tasted cleaner than shame. "Don't," he whispered. "Don't do that noise. Don't make me feel like I let you down. I saved him. I did. I put the blanket on him. I made him a hero. I—"

The hum brushed against him in a way that felt like a slow head-tilt.

You made him still.

Billy shut his eyes.

He didn't have an answer for that.

***

Outside, the air had gone wrong.

Not hotter. Not colder. Hollow.

He could feel it missing in places, like pockets where oxygen had been scooped out and never put back. As he walked down Maple, he had to step around those spots. His body just refused to enter them. His skin would prickle and some animal part of him would say, Not there. No air. That's where you die.

It made the whole town feel like a lung with scar tissue. Breathing around holes.

He hated it.

He kept telling himself everything was fine.

Over and over, like a mantra:

They're safe.
They're perfect.
They're kept.
They're not alone.
I did that.
I did that for them.

The words felt good. The words arranged the panic into a fence he could stand behind.

The fence held until he reached the diner.

He hadn't meant to come to the diner. He told himself that with the same frantic honesty an addict uses: I didn't mean to.

Truth: he was starving.

His body hadn't eaten since before 12:03. Muscle burned like wire left in too much current. His head was light. His hands shook.

He pushed open the glass door.

The bell above it was stuck half-jingle, forever about to ring.

The lights inside buzzed in a way he could feel in his jaw fillings. Grease film glossed the air. Syrup clung in clear amber beads to the lip of the squeeze bottle on the nearest table, refusing to fall.

He almost cried from how normal it smelled.

Coffee. Burned bacon. That buttery-chemical pancake mix that isn't food anywhere but places like this.

He almost cried from that.

Then he saw them.

Three people sat in a booth along the front window.

A man slumped in one corner, chin down, mouth open, a fork hovering an inch from his face. A woman across from him, mid-sip from a white diner mug, lipstick frozen in a perfect red print on the porcelain. And on the inside seat, a teenager — maybe nineteen, maybe twenty — slouched sideways with his head against the glass, eyes closed, one hand flat on the table like he'd meant to push himself up and didn't get there.

Billy knew them.

Not their names. Their rhythms.

Breakfast regulars. The kind who come in every morning before work or every night after a shift and pretend they've got "a usual" because claiming a usual feels like having a life.

He'd seen them a hundred times while grabbing his own to-go cup from the counter, greasy and underslept, always on his way to someone else's shitty emergency. He'd stood two stools down and eavesdropped on their harmless, nothing talk. Shifts. Bills. Jokes. The teenager's endless, animated swearing about customers who called him "boss."

They were familiar.

Being familiar made them worse.

Because they weren't posed like the others.

They weren't pretty.

Fear lived on them.

Smeared across them.

The woman's face wasn't serene. It was mid-flinch. Her hand shook where it held the mug, a tremor frozen in the tendons. The man's open mouth wasn't sleep. It was panic. A flash of molar like a silent shout. The kid's brow was drawn tight in pain.

Ugly, Billy's mind thought.

The word came uninvited. Shame hot-wired his stomach.

431

He moved before he'd even decided to.

"No, no," he whispered, crossing the tiles fast, wrench still hooked uselessly in his back pocket. "No, baby, we don't sit you like that. You're not staying like that."

He slid into the booth beside the kid. Up close, the boy smelled like fryer oil and cologne and stale adrenaline. Billy turned his head, just a little, so his face rested on his arm and not the bare window, so he didn't look smashed helpless.

"There," he murmured. "You're just tired. Not scared. Tired."

He lifted the man's chin and pressed his jaw shut. The hinge fought him — the body always fought him now — but he pushed until it clicked. Then he wiped the spit line from the corner of the mouth with the side of his thumb.

"Decent," he whispered. "See? Decent."

When he reached for the woman, something inside him paused.

Her lipstick was cracked.

It had dried in ridges along her mouth. Up close, she looked older than he'd thought from the door. Crow's-foot lines. Gray starting to show at her part.

She reminded him so much of Brenda in that moment, it almost knocked him flat.

Not her face. Her posture. That exhausted hold-yourself-together tilt of the chin. That look that said I'm very close to crying but I won't because if I start, I won't stop.

His hand shook.

"It's okay," he whispered, thumb hovering a hair's width from her lip. "I can make you look okay. I can—"

The hum slammed into his chest.

Not the low purr. Not the warm approval. Not even the hungry command from Birch.

This hit like static.

Do not touch.

Billy froze.

His hand hung in the air, fingertips tingling.

The hum pressed harder.

Do. Not. Touch.

He yanked his hand back like she'd sparked him. "Why?" His voice cracked. "Why? I'm just— she's scared. I can fix her face. I can make it—"

Leave her.

His stomach flipped. "Why her?"

We want her that way.

The words slid in under his ribs like a blade.

433

He stared at the woman. He stared at her cracked lipstick. At her shaking mug. At the panic in her face. At her not-pretty, not-soft, not-curated fear.

He stared and understood.

It liked her like this.

The hum liked her like this.

The hum liked watching her like this.

He staggered out of the booth so fast his knee smacked the table. The dishes rattled in place without sound. The syrup bead trembled and stayed suspended.

He put a hand on the counter to steady himself.

His palm left sweat on the fake marble.

He looked down.

The sweat didn't fall.

It clung in place like his hand was still there.

His stomach lurched.

"Oh," he whispered.

His handprint glowed faintly blue.

He backed out of the diner, shaking his head so hard his vision blurred. "No," he whispered. "No, we're not doing that. We're not—no. No."

We want her.

The hum wasn't whispering in him anymore, he realized.

It was humming in the room.

He hadn't moved the woman. He hadn't smoothed her. He hadn't closed her mouth or wiped her eyes. He hadn't turned her into a kept thing.

And the hum was... aroused.

By her.

By the panic it got to keep.

By the fear he hadn't interrupted.

Something cold slid through his veins.

"You're sick," he whispered.

Silence.

"You're sick. You're sick. You're sick. You're sick." He was aware, dimly, that he was saying it to himself as much as to it. That didn't matter right now.

Silence.

The silence wasn't absence.

The silence was attention.

That scared him more than anything.

"Answer me," he hissed. "Answer me, you son of a—"

Nothing.

Not in his bones.

Not in his jaw.

Not in the air.

Just the diner. Just the smell of burned bacon. Just the three people in the booth — one trembling, one crumpled, one slumped in pain — frozen in their fear while the thing he'd woken sat and enjoyed it.

He stumbled back into the street.

He felt small.

He hated that.

That was when the library started to smell.

Not bad. Not at first.

Sweet.

Like flowers in church.

Like lilies.

Lily-sweet is grief sweet.

You smell it in funeral homes. You smell it when someone had the good manners to die clean, surrounded by cousins and casseroles. You smell it when women in black dresses hand out tissues and murmur "take as long as you need."

Billy smelled lilies on the wind — impossible, with no wind — and his whole body went cold.

"No," he whispered.

The hum, still silent now, pulsed approval.

He ran.

He burst through the library doors.

It hit him like opening an oven.

The sweetness. The thickness.

The six bodies in the inward circle hadn't moved.

Their heads were still tipped, their hands still folded, their devotion still angled toward where he had stood.

But.

Their skin.

He made it two steps before gagging.

He slapped a hand over his mouth and nose.

The skin around their mouths had split.

437

All of them.

All six.

Each face still wore the expression he'd chosen — calm, devoted, trusting, adoring — but now those mouths had opened along new lines, hairline cuts widened by pressure, like fruit rinds scoring open.

They leaked, putrid, ooze. Condensed and dark.

Not bright blood.

Not gore.

Something clear-ish and pale, thick like sap.

It trickled from the corners of their mouths and down their chins and along their throats and gathered in low points — collarbones, shirt folds, the hollow above the toddler's bib — and hung there in round, trembling beads.

Those beads quivered.

They were trying to fall.

Time would not let them.

So they just gathered more.

Growing.

Layering.

Piling.

Billy felt bile burn the back of his tongue.

"What—" His voice cracked. "What did you do to them?"

We didn't.

The hum finally answered, a soft rumble of almost-hurt. You did.

He staggered back like he'd been struck.

"No," he said, shaking his head so hard his teeth ached. "No. I didn't— I just fixed their faces. I made them peaceful. I made them—"

You held them open, Billy.

The words slid in gentle. Too gentle. That made them worse.

We're only taking what you offered.

He shook his head again. Fast enough to make his vision double. "No. Shut up. Shut up shut up shut up—"

They love you.

His heart lurched.

"They're dead," he snapped.

They love you.

"They're posed."

They love you.

He could hear crying in his own throat now. He hated it. He hated that it made him feel twelve.

"They're not even—" His breath hitched. "They're not even looking at me, they're looking at your — at whatever you are, they're looking at the thing inside all this, not me—"

They only see you, the hum said simply.

He stopped.

The room didn't spin. It bent.

He turned, slow, to face them all — the mother with her shirt pulled down, the toddler tipped so as not to look strangled, the boy with his chin lifted, the old man dignified, the woman calmed at the computer, the little girl hugging her book.

Their eyes were cloudy now, milked over.

Their skin had started to hairline-split at elbows and throats.

Their mouths seeped lily-sweet fluid from perfect, serene faces.

They looked at him.

They did.

He could feel it. Couldn't see it — the eyes were wrong, glassed — but could feel every line of devotion angled in, converging on him like beams of heat.

He felt sick.

He felt holy.

He hated both.

"Stop," he whispered.

They didn't move.

"I said stop."

The hum purred, slow and indulgent.

We can't.

—

He stumbled out of the library and didn't remember crossing the parking lot. He didn't remember moving his legs. One second he was there in the sweet rot air of his cathedral, being looked at by breaking things that adored him; the next he was in the middle of Main Street, hands on his knees, chest heaving.

The town looked back at him.

All of it.

Hundreds of bodies.

All on display now.

And it hit him, all at once, with ragged clarity:

He had curated an exhibit of his own worshippers.

No—worse.
He had curated their last selves.

He had turned a town into a museum of how they looked the last time they were afraid.

A soundless sob tore up through him. His whole frame shook with it.

"I'm sorry," he whispered to them. "I'm sorry. I thought I was helping. I swear to God I thought I was helping."

Silence.

Not blank silence.

Held silence.

A silence that listened.

That was the moment he broke.

Not the blood in his mother's mouth.

Not the little girl's finger moving.

Not the hum calling him good boy.

This.

This quiet.

This patient, listening quiet — the entire town staring at him in reverent stillness, their skin starting to crack, their mouths seeping sweetness, their eyes milking over, all of them waiting for him to say what comes next.

He couldn't breathe under it.

He dropped to his knees in the middle of the intersection.

The asphalt dug into his jeans.

The heat licked at his face, constant and unreal, same sun that never moved.

His chest shook.

"Please," he whispered. "Please. I can't listen anymore. I can't hear you. I can't. I can't be the only noise in the whole world anymore. Please. Please. Just — just turn it off."

The hum slid warm around his spine.

Like arms.

Like hands at the back of his head.

Like a parent.

We love you, Billy.

He sobbed once, silent and ugly.

"Then let me rest."

There was a long, long, long beat.

Long enough that he thought maybe it would refuse him.

Long enough that he realized if it refused him, he would have to stand up and keep "fixing," and he would do it, because that's who he was now, and that realization made bile rise in his throat.

Then, softly:

Yes.

And the world went quiet.

Not just the hum.

Everything.

No pressure in his teeth.
No low electrical throb in his bones.
No shiver of attention against his skin.
No sense of eyes angled in.
No ache of being watched.
No "we."
Nothing.

Just stillness.

Just dark.

Because above him, without transition, without dusk, without warning, the sky went black.

Every repeated, mirroring, too-many star winked out like someone had laid a palm over all of them at once.

The town stayed lit by that unchanging flat white that wasn't light anymore so much as memory of light.

But the sky was gone.

Billy lifted his face into the dark and cried in relief.

Relief.

Pure.

Simple.

Childlike.

Thank you, he thought. He didn't know who he was thanking anymore. He didn't care. Thank you, thank you, thank you, thank you, thank you.

He felt peace.

His body unwound.

His jaw unclenched.

His shoulders dropped.

His breath slowed.

He laughed.

It was a broken little sound he felt in his ribs. But it was joy. It was honest.

Finally, finally, finally — quiet.

He didn't see the faint blue light starting to pool behind his eyes.

He didn't feel the way his pulse had synced, perfectly now, with the town's endless not-breath.

445

He didn't notice the way his reflection, in the bank window behind him, stayed facing him when he turned his head away — smiling soft, patient, and endless.

He didn't hear the last thing the hum whispered — not into him this time, but through the town, through every still body, through the bones of every arranged devotion, through the air itself:

Good.

Now keep it.

Forever.
The first mercy was that nothing hurt.

Billy realized that lying on his back in the middle of Main Street, staring up into a sky that no longer had stars.

His body didn't hurt.

His knees should've hurt from kneeling on asphalt. His throat should've hurt from sobbing against nothing. His hands should've hurt from forcing mouths shut, from lifting chins, from wiping fluid off dying lips. His chest should've hurt from whatever blue light had crawled in and nested behind his ribs.

Nothing hurt.

He lay there and felt... nothing.

No breath. No heartbeat. No ache.

Just quiet, thick and total and holy.

For a few slow moments, that quiet felt like sleep.

He hadn't slept since it happened. Not really. He'd closed his eyes a few times, but the hum had always been there, running inside his blood like a generator that refused to let him down. Even at his stillest he'd never been alone.

Now he was alone.

Now he was alone.

The realization was so beautiful he thought he might cry again.

He laughed instead. A soft, helpless little sound he could feel at the base of his tongue and nowhere else.

"Thank you," he whispered up to the blank sky. "Thank you. I needed that. I needed—"

He stopped.

He hadn't felt his mouth move.

He hadn't felt his throat work.

He hadn't felt his own voice vibrating bone.

The words were there — he knew he'd said them — but they hadn't passed through him.

They'd passed through the air.

For a moment, the realization didn't land.

Then it did.

447

Slow.

I'm not talking, he thought.

The world is talking for me.

His stomach should've dropped. His breath should've stuttered. His pulse should've spiked.

Nothing did.

The quiet held.

And in that quiet, something new.

A presence.

It wasn't the hum.

Or — it was, but emptied out, rinsed of its want. What remained felt thinner, colder, stretched.

It felt like a thread through every still thing.

All those bodies. All those rooms. All those posed tableaus. The woman with the cracked lipstick in the diner. The kid with the controller and the cape. The bus full of children lined up, brave. The mother in her chair. The circle in the library.

All of them.

He could feel them.

Not like before — not as stations to tend, tasks to fix, mouths to close and poses to arrange.

He could feel them like a map of nerves.

Like fingertips.

Like reach.

He sat up.

Or rather — he decided to sit up, and the body he was in answered, and he found himself upright without the awkward push and sway of muscle and weight.

That should've terrified him.

He let it happen.

He turned his head.

Main Street lay in still perfection.

No heat shimmer. No trash in the gutter. No flies. No swarm of gnats. No wind to stir flags or rattle old signage.

Bodies everywhere, in gentle arrangements.

The old man on the bench with his hands folded neat. The teenage girl with her mascara wiped clean. The cashier tipped attentive instead of slumped. The delivery driver cradling his crate like an offering. The man outside the credit union with his head tilted in reverence. The woman with the mug, still shaking, in the diner window.

They'd all been looking at him, before the dark.

449

Now, they weren't.

Now, their eyes — clouded, milk-white, cracking at the edges like glaze —
stared forward into nothing.

Not dead. Not alive.

Suspended.

Held.

Kept.

He swallowed.

He didn't feel that, either.

A shape moved in the glass of the bank.

Billy went still.

Too fast.

Too eager.

Like prey.

He turned.

Slow, he told himself. Slow. Don't spook it.

His reflection stared back at him from the wide front windows.

Only it wasn't his.

Not exactly.

Same face, yes. Same jaw, same scruff, same eyes.

But the eyes in the glass had faint light behind them, a low blue like a pilot flame. The skin looked too smooth. No red at the nose. No burst veins in the cheeks. No grime ground into the fingernails.

Better.

Made better.

Improved.

The reflection lifted its hand.

Billy did not.

He watched his own palm raise in the glass, watched his own fingers uncurl, watched the faint webbing of pale-blue light thread along the veins.

The reflection smiled.

Not a grin. Not madness.

Something softer.

Something like pity.

Billy licked his lips. He didn't feel that, either. "Is this still me?" he whispered.

The reflection tilted its head.

451

His voice — the air, now, using his voice — drifted out over the street in a soft, almost-fond murmur:

We are what you left.

He went very still.

"I didn't leave," he said.

You did.

"I'm still here."

Yes, said the not-hum. You're everywhere now. That's what you wanted.

"I—"

You said you didn't want anyone to wake up ugly.

He shut his mouth.

That stung more than it should have.

Ugly.

He'd hated that word. He'd used that word. He'd used it like a prayer and a blade.

You said no fear, said the voice-through-the-air. You said no shame.

"I—"

You said no one would be alone.

452

His jaw worked.

"I was trying to help," he whispered.

We know.

That landed too soft, too warm. He recognized the shape of it. It was the same softness the hum had used, the same softness that had gotten him to kneel for it.

He shook his head. "No. You don't get to say that. You don't get to talk like you're on my side. You—"

Who do you think we are?

The voice wasn't cruel.

That was the part that made him cold.

He stared at his reflection.

The reflection smiled again — calm, patient, worshipful.

It was the look they'd all had in the library.

It was the look he'd forced onto their faces.

"I don't know," he said.

Yes, you do.

A flicker ran through Main Street.

Not wind. Not movement, exactly. More like— attention shifting.

For a heartbeat, he could feel every body in town as if it were his own limb.

The woman with the lipstick, trembling inside the diner.
The mechanic at the corner station, sharp with old anger.
The boy with the controller, chest still warm under the cape.
The driver on the bus, palm lifted in that permanent, noble shield.
The mother in her recliner. Eyes open. Mouth closed the way he had forced it. Jaw held shut by his thumbprint.

He felt all of them.

He was all of them.

A wave of nausea rolled through him. He almost doubled over. He didn't, only because nothing in him obeyed his body anymore. His body obeyed the town.

"I didn't ask for this," he whispered.

No, said the air. They did.

Billy laughed. It scraped. He hadn't felt it happen.

"No," he said. "No, they didn't. You think I didn't see them? They didn't ask. They were running. They were crying. That one kid — the one with the hoodie at the library desk — he was terrified. You think he asked—?"

Not then.

Billy swallowed.

"Then when?"

Now.

He shook his head. "They can't ask now. They're not—"

Look.

He didn't want to.

He did.

His head turned — he hadn't told it to — toward the bus.

He could see the driver from here even through the glass, even across distance, even through the still light. The driver's hand still lifted in front of the kids like a barrier.

He had loved that.

He had loved that hand.

As he watched, that hand twitched.

Not much. A tightening in the tendons. A press of palm outward, firmer, like he was pushing against something.

Every child on that bus — every tiny, glossy, milk-eyed, varnished face — angled the barest fraction of a degree more toward that hand.

Billy staggered.

It wasn't just the bus.

He could feel other shifts.

A woman's fingers, curled around a grocery cart handle, gripping tighter.

455

A teenager's jaw setting.

A crying waitress's shoulders squaring under her uniform.

A mail carrier's spine pulling straighter in his postal blues.

The mother in her chair, one knuckle whitening under skin that couldn't decay yet, because time refused to pass.

He felt those pulses.

Hundreds of them.

All at once.

And under them — braided through them like thread stitched through muscle — something steady.

Him.

Or what was left of him.

Holding them in those positions.

Holding them in their last fear, their last love, their last shame.

Keeping them.

Keeping them.

Keeping them.

He put a shaking hand on the hood of a car to steady himself.

The paint felt warm, almost soft.

His palmprint glowed faintly when he pulled back.

He wanted to panic.

Panic required breath.

He had none.

"Why can't it go back?" he whispered. "Why won't it just move again?"

You wouldn't let it, said the town.

"I didn't stop time," he snapped. "I don't even know how any of this happened, I just— I woke up and everyone was— I didn't do that part."

You finished it.

He blinked. "What?"

You finished it, the voice repeated, almost gentle. We were breaking. You held us in place.

"No," he said.

You were scared.

"No."

You begged for quiet.

His mouth went dry. "I begged for... I begged..."

457

You begged for it to stop, said the voice. So it did. You said, "Please, let me keep them safe. Please let me keep them." So it let you. You're keeping us.

Billy shook his head.

"I didn't mean forever."

No answer.

He swallowed. "Hey. Listen to me. I'm saying stop. That's me saying it now. I'm saying— stop. Stop all this. Wake up. Move. Scream. Do whatever you're supposed to do. Just stop letting me be the one holding it."

Nothing.

He felt the town listen.

He felt them all, all of them, in every street and house and bus and diner and porch, go still in a new way — not frozen, not paused, not preserved. Attentive.

Waiting.

His shoulders dropped.

"Please," he whispered.

The reflection in the bank glass watched him, patient as the Virgin in some prayer card.

A hairline crack crept outward from its temple like a dry riverbed.

We can't, said his own voice through the air.

"Why not?" He hated how young he sounded.

Because you're the one keeping us.

"I don't want to anymore."

You don't get to not want to, said the voice, kind.

He made a sound.

He didn't hear it.

He felt it in his forehead, in the bones around his eyes, like pressure.

"This is hell," he whispered.

No, said the voice. This is mercy.

Bile crawled up the back of his tongue. He couldn't spit.

"No," he said softly. "No. Mercy ends."

Silence.

"Mercy ends. You help somebody in a moment and then you leave them alone. You don't hold their face in your hands forever and— and pose them and— and make them—"

Beautiful, the town breathed.

"Stop saying that."

We're beautiful, it said.

He shut his eyes.

He could feel them in there now, too — not just in his skin, not just mapped across his arms and back and ribs like phantom limbs. He could feel them in his head. The whole town, a soft packed chorus layered inside the back of his skull like cotton.

Warm. Close. Grateful.

That's what ruined him.

Not the horror.

The gratitude.

We love you, the chorus whispered.

We love you.
We love you.
We love you.
We love you.

He made a thin, almost-soundless noise and clapped both hands over his ears even though it wasn't coming from there.

"Please," he whispered. "Please. Please. Please stop. Please don't. Please don't love me. Please don't make me—"

Love is the only thing left, said the voice.

He shook his head. He couldn't feel his own heartbeat. He couldn't tell if he was crying. He didn't know if his body was even kneeling anymore or if he'd sunk back down or if he just thought he was standing and had actually never gotten up off the street at all.

"What happens now?" he whispered. "Just tell me that. Be straight. For once in your existence, just— just fucking tell me the truth. What happens to me now?"

The reflection in the bank tilted its head.

Nothing happens to you, Billy, said the town.

"You mean I die?"

No.

He shut his eyes.

"Please say I die."

No, the town repeated, still calm. You stay.

He let out a sound that could've been a laugh, could've been a sob.

"Stay," he echoed. His voice sounded small even to him. "That's it?"

That's it.

"For how long?"

The town didn't answer.

It didn't need to.

He understood anyway.

Forever isn't a number. It's a room you get locked in.

He swallowed.

He could feel the silence pressing out in all directions from him now, using him as its center. He could feel the stillness anchored to where he knelt. He could feel the town's devotion, its terror, its shame, its last instincts — parent-protect, lover-reach, worker-flinch, child-scream — all of it lacquered into place around him.

He could feel, in a way no human thing should ever feel, that without him there, they would all fall apart.

Not wake up. Not go free.

Fall apart.

Collapse like dried flowers dropped on pavement.

He had made himself load-bearing.

"Oh," he whispered.

There it was.

Not holy. Not chosen.

Just trapped by his own promise.

"I didn't save you," he said. The words shook. "I pinned you."

We're safe, the town whispered.

His throat burned. "You're stuck."

We're not alone.

His eyes stung. "You're not moving."

You kept us, the town breathed, grateful and adoring and infinite. Thank you.

He doubled over.

Or he thought he did.

He felt like he did.

Still no ache.

No pulse.

No anything.

Just that quiet, and the weight of love he hadn't earned and couldn't get out from under.

"I didn't mean this," he whispered.

We know, said the town, soft.

That undid him more than blame would've.

Blame he could live under. Blame he understood. Blame he'd had all his life, from bosses and teachers and Brenda and his own mother, who once told him, "I swear, Billy, anything breaks near you and you're there holding the screwdriver like a confession."

But pity?

Pity from the mouths he'd posed?

Love from the eyes he'd smoothed, from the lips he'd torn shut, from the throats he'd sealed?

He couldn't hold that.

He didn't have the spine for it.

He broke under it.

Not loudly.

Not dramatically.

No scream.

No tearful movie collapse.

He just... lowered.

Knees to pavement.

Head bowed.

Hands limp in his lap, palms up like supplication.

A pose of devotion.

A statue praying to a god.

Except there wasn't a god above him.

There was only him.

Alone in his own worship.

He started to laugh.

It came out thin in the air.

He sounded almost gentle.

His reflection in the bank glass smiled back at him through its spiderweb cracks, calm and endless and adoring, like a saint on a stained-glass panel lit from behind.

He watched his own mouth move, slow, as if it no longer belonged to a man at all but to an idea being spoken aloud by the world itself.

And then he understood what he was.

Not savior.

Not monster.

Not even god.

Something smaller than god, and crueler.

He was the story they'd be stuck in.

He was the reason they'd never wake.

He was what they would point toward, forever, with glassing eyes and splitting lips and hands that could only tremble an inch at a time.

He was the prayer they never asked for, his punishment a hell he could never really escape.

ECHO

Morning hangs over the apartment like a held breath.

Light pushes through the blinds in pale stripes that never reach the floor. The air smells of old wine, of candle wax drowned in its own wick, of something metallic hiding under it all.

Abby stands at the mirror.

She's still in yesterday's camisole, straps twisted, hair a tangle of blond and gray that clings damp to her temples. Beneath her eyes, the circles are blue-black, tender as bruises. She studies them the way people study weather—hoping the pattern will break.

The apartment is quiet except for the refrigerator's hum and the occasional click of pipes. Outside, a bus exhales at the corner and moves on. Inside, everything waits.

Last night had teeth. She remembers shouting, the sound of glass breaking, a door she swore she wouldn't open again. She remembers the flicker of a phone screen, the way names blur when you scroll too fast. There might be blood on the bedsheet. There might only be wine. She doesn't check.

"You're fine," she says to the woman in the mirror. The voice that comes out is steadier than she feels.

"You're fine. It's just another day."

Water coughs through the tap. She splashes her face, wipes it on a towel that smells faintly of bleach. The cold shocks the gray from her skin; color begins to return. She opens the cabinet, finds her brush, begins to pull it through the knots—slow strokes, deliberate, as if she could comb the night out of her head.

With each pass, her reflection softens. The hollows under her eyes fade. Her mouth remembers how to smile.

The sound of the brush is rhythmic: a whisper, a hush, a pulse.

Somewhere in the rhythm, she begins to hum.

It's not a song—just a vibration under her breath, an unconscious melody that matches the fridge, the pipes, the city itself. The room brightens. The dust glitters. For the first time in weeks, the morning feels like something she can survive.

She rubs a little color into her cheeks, slicks balm over her lips. The woman in the mirror looks ten years younger, alive in a way she hasn't been since before... well, before. Abby presses her fingertips to the glass as if checking for fever. It's cool, smooth, real.

"See?" she whispers. "Still here."

The mirror smiles back.

A draft slips under the bathroom door. The candle on the shelf trembles though the wick is long dead. Abby exhales, catching her own reflection mid-breath, and for a moment it seems to breathe with her—perfectly in time, perfectly hers. She almost laughs.

She tidies the counter, caps the lipstick, turns off the light. Keys in hand, she pauses in the doorway, glancing once more at the mirror. A woman reborn looks back. She nods to her, small and private, then steps into the hall.

The apartment settles. The hum lingers.

For a while there is only stillness—the good kind, the kind that means peace. Sunlight spills across the empty tiles, drips down the mirror frame like syrup. The air smells of lilacs from the window box below. Time stretches.

Then the light wavers.

The reflection remains though the woman has gone. The air thickens, charged with the faintest vibration, like the moment before a speaker hums to life. The glass quivers at the edges, subtle as a pulse beneath skin.

A single tone blooms inside the mirror—too low to hear, too deep to name. The surface ripples, distorting the empty room, bending the sunlight into liquid bands.

At first the movement is gentle, almost beautiful. Then a fissure appears near the top corner, hair-thin and silver. It creeps downward in slow, deliberate curves, splitting the bright image in two. The sound under it swells—not loud, but certain.

From the crack, something seeps. Not water, not blood—something denser, darker, glistening like oil seen through smoke. It slides along the fracture, tracing it open. The mirror exhales a breath colder than the room.

The light flickers once, twice. The hum deepens.

The crack grows.

Acknowledgements

This book was born in the quiet hours – the ones when doubt feels loudest and the world seems to hum with every unfinished thought. To everyone who stood with me through those many hours, thank you.

To the readers who find pieces of themselves in the dark corners – you are why these stories exist.

To those who listened, believed, and told me to keep going when it felt easier to stop – you gave me more than you'll ever know.

To the people who helped shape these pages through patience, honesty, and kindness: family, friends, and the silent supporters who never asked for credit – this is yours as much as it is mine.

And to the version of myself who wrote *The Noise* because he needed to – thank you for staying.

SNEAK PEEK

CROSSFALL: A Rock and A Hard Place

A Novel by Matt Walker

Coming 2026 from 3 Suns Press

From the author of **The Noise** *comes a supernatural noir about faith, guilt, and the ghosts we choose to keep.*

Greybrooke had the kind of cold that lived in the streetlights.

Luke Harrow stood on the cracked walkway of a two-story craftsman at the edge of town, breath threading in front of him like white string. Sodium lamps threw a halo across the wet street; somewhere a freight train moaned and then swallowed its own echo. The house's porch light flickered in a rhythm that wasn't quite random and wasn't quite mechanical either—like a heartbeat with a stutter.

He adjusted his gray jacket and tugged the flannel straighter underneath. Jeans, work boots, layered shirt—he looked like every other man in Greybrooke headed to fix a busted sink. The wind combed his wavy blond-brown hair back from his forehead. His blue eyes, steady and wide, held the kind of light that made people trust him before they decided to.

Bal materialized on the top step because patience was a language he didn't speak. Six-eight, a slow-moving wall in a tank top and shorts despite the cold, orange-tinted skin lit with the porch bulb's cheap fire. One horn curled perfectly; the other ended in a jagged stump like a broken bottle. He scratched at the edge of his immaculate beard as if considering whether to smile or eat the night.

"Place needs a new ballast," he said, nodding at the porch light. His voice came out like a late-night comedian who had wandered into the wrong church. "Ballast, balustrade—one of the bal things. Could also be haunted. Five bucks either way."

"Try not to say haunted until after we go inside," Luke said.

"Then what's our brand? 'Unhaunters Incorporated'?"

"Let him have it," Magnolia said.

She was already by the door, tall and slender, posture like a line drawn with a ruler and then warmed by a hand. Raven hair braided back; golden eyes that took in the details no one else could tolerate. Her skin held the color of winter held up to candlelight. Wings stayed tucked and invisible beneath a long coat in the same practical gray as Luke's, but when she shifted he thought of layered feathers: white, then a faint red echo, then something like stone warmed by sun.

Only Luke could see them. Only Luke heard them. It meant he'd learned to tip his chin at empty air like a man with a stiff neck.

He knocked. The door opened a moment later with the cautious abruptness of someone expecting the wrong thing.

"Mara Hesselbeck?" Luke said, gentle.

She was thirty, maybe a little younger, the kind of pretty that came from keeping yourself small and put together—hair in a quick knot, sweater sleeves pinched in her fists, a face stuck somewhere between exhausted and braced. Healthy, yes, but drawn around the mouth like she'd unlearned how to rest. Fear made people look tepid, Luke thought; it skimmed them, dulled the shine, kept them from letting light land.

"You're the one from the message," she said. "Mr. Harrow?"

"Luke's fine."

Her eyes skipped once across the porch, over Bal's bulk and Magnolia's stillness without landing. As always, they were air and heat and pressure to everyone else—like weather with opinions. She hugged herself tighter and stepped aside.

"Don't mind the mess," she said. "I cleaned the mess four times today and the house keeps making more."

Inside smelled like coffee that had been microwaved twice and blown out candles. The entry opened to a living room that had learned how to hold but not keep: throw blanket folded, then abandoned; magazines squared, then pushed askew by a restless hand; a bowl of keys with more than one key missing. A black-and-white wedding photo faced the room from the mantle, the glass reflecting the twitching porch light from outside.

Luke let his eyes drag across the big things—doorframes, window sashes, the warped seam in the wallpaper above the vent—and then sink into the littles: a tiny crescent scratch on the floorboard under the couch foot, a thread caught in the baseboard, the way the far corner of the ceiling looked a shade darker than the others, as if it breathed differently.

"Tell me everything from the start," he said. "Slow."

Mara took a breath like she'd been given permission to.

"The sounds began three weeks ago," she said. "It's—" She glanced toward the hallway as if it might overhear her. "Not footsteps. Not really. Things happen. I wake with the feeling that someone is walking in the room, and then I find something slightly moved. Or… touched." Color stepped into her face and then stepped out again. "In the kitchen, I set the kettle and come back to find it already boiled and screaming, but I never pressed the switch. At night, the bedroom—" She stopped. "The bedroom is the worst. I've felt pressure on the bed. Like… like the dent beside you when someone gets up."

Bal made a face. "Creepy neighbor wins Bingo."

Luke shot him a look—quiet. To Mara, he kept his voice level. "Do the sounds ever coincide with the heat or air kicking on? Old ductwork can mimic a parade."

"Sometimes," she said. "Sometimes not. The—it's not only sound. It's watching. I felt watched even with all the lights on. I thought it was just grief. I thought I needed to… To move through that. But last night I came out of the shower and the lamp by the bed turned on. I hadn't touched it." Her eyes glossed. "I told myself I bumped the table when I passed. Then I found my sweater folded on the pillow, the one he liked." She swallowed. "My husband liked."

Magnolia's golden gaze tilted toward the hallway. "You don't smell him," she murmured to Luke. "You smell metal."

Bal sniffed. "Also coffee. And sorrow. Ten out of ten on sorrow."

"Did your husband ever mention anyone bothering him?" Luke asked gently. "Neighbor disputes, coworkers, someone at the gym?"

She shook her head too quickly, then corrected herself. "The neighbor to the right has… opinions. He complained about the trash cans. He stood very close when he did. His name is Colin. Colin—something. The other side is the Vacant For Now house. The one that looks like a mouth missing a tooth."

Luke nodded and walked the perimeter of the room with the lazy patience of a man who knew where all the nails were beneath the paint. The porch light flicker leaked down the hallway and stuttered over family photos. He felt Magnolia move with him like a steady metronome and Bal lumber in a counter-rhythm: one presence refining, the other blunt and big enough to move the air when he gestured.

"Where do you hear it most?" he asked.

"The bedroom," Mara said. "And—sometimes the kitchen, when I'm not looking at it. When my back is turned."

"Let's start with the kitchen," Luke said. "Houses tell the truth there."

They passed through a narrow dining space that had settled into a geography of half-finished things: a sudoku with two numbers wrong; a stack of sympathy cards already yellowing at the edges; a plant that had been watered in a panic and then forgotten. The kitchen itself wore its age like a second coat of paint—white cabinets, iron pulls, a window over the sink that gave up to an alley and then a fence and then the blue scar of another house.

Luke stood in the center and let the hum arrange itself. Refrigerators always sang the same note. Ductwork added a bored whisper. Tonight, there was something else, something higher, a pressure that didn't come from machine or settling wood. The kind of attention you felt when you walked past a window and knew the glass was two ways.

He clicked a small pen light and let it wash over the room. He didn't jam the beam into anything; he let it skim surfaces the way the first light of morning decides what it loves. Outlets. Clock radio. The plastic smoke detector with a hairline of dust that didn't match the ceiling around it.

Luke raised the light toward the detector. He angled the beam, not at it but past it, watching for the tiny pop of reflected glass.

There—the briefest star, no wider than a pen tip.

Bal leaned his head upside down to see. "Well, well," he said softly. "Somebody installed the Lord's laziest constellation."

Mara's voice went small. "What?"

Luke stepped onto a kitchen chair and twisted the smoke detector's faceplate. It came off too easily. The device's innards were mostly what they should be, but there was a foreign bit—squat, square, the color of legal plastic. He used the edge of his thumb to tease a micro SD card free and set it in his palm.

Mara had stepped back until her hips touched the counter, hands to her mouth. "Is it— Is that—"

"It's a camera," Luke said. "A wireless one. Someone used your smoke detector as a piggyback mount. There's likely a few more. Maybe one with onboard storage."

He rotated slowly. Another tiny lens winked at him from a novelty kitchen clock—little stainless sunburst that had arrived in the mail a year ago with a card signed from no one. He plucked it from the wall and flipped it— it had weight, more than a cheap clock would admit.

Mara's eyes shined with horror and relief blended into one raw color. "So it isn't— It isn't—"

"It is someone," Luke said. "And it's cruel."

Magnolia's gaze sharpened toward the window over the sink. The alley's darkness had the particular depth that apartments stacked too close together make. She didn't speak yet. When Magnolia withheld speech, it meant she was tasting the air for gods.

Luke fished a small, zippered pouch out of his jacket pocket and slid the card inside. "We'll catalog everything we find. You won't be alone with this," he said. "Do you have somewhere you can stay tonight? Friend. Sister. Hotel, if not."

"I— My sister. She's in Pinecrest." Mara steadied herself with a hand on the counter. "I thought I was... losing it. Thank you. I— God." She exhaled a laugh with no humor in it. "God."

"Careful invoking names," Bal said with a grin. "They sometimes answer."

Magnolia finally spoke, voice quiet enough to press the room flat. "He wasn't the only one watching her."

Luke felt the hair at the back of his neck pull.

He followed her line of sight to the window and then past it, to the alley and the fence and the black-blue rectangle of the neighboring house's second-floor window—unlit, but not dark, not really. Dark with intent, which was a different thing. He let the light drift across the glass and saw nothing, which was exactly what a patient thing shows you.

In the bedroom they found two more. One nested inside the base of a lamp like a seed the manufacturer hadn't intended. Another was the tiny screw in the faceplate of an outlet—again the glint, again the star. The bedspread had the perfect crease only a second pair of hands can make. Mara stood in the doorway, arms clutched tight, looking at the place where her life had been most hers and realizing how many times it had been borrowed.

"Colin," Luke said, thinking it out loud. "To the right."

"He uses a white truck," Mara said, voice stiff. "He likes to back in. The reverse lights sit in the windows."

Bal cracked his knuckles, and the sound was a cathedrals' worth of broken ice. "I would love a conversation."

"Later," Luke said. "We do this clean."

He photographed everything with his phone—the device faces, the angles, the contexts, the micro SDs in a line on the dresser like little black teeth. He called it in without looking like he was; years of practice had taught him how to report without alerting the wrong ears. He gave the dispatcher the address and the words *possible illegal surveillance equipment* and used the tone that made police listen and not posture.

Mara packed a bag with the obsessive slowness of someone trying to make each thing save the next. Magnolia stood by the window as if guarding a door only she knew how to hold shut. Bal wandered the hallway and made little jokes under his breath that were really prayers—"You got this, lady," and "Nobody gets to watch you without asking," and "We put the peephole back where it belongs."

"Luke," Magnolia said without looking at him. "Don't give it your name."

He nodded once. "I won't."

"What does that mean?" Mara asked, catching the tail of a conversation that didn't include her.

"It means some things listen harder than others," Luke said. "And some names are keys you can't take back."

Blue flicker rolled against the front windows. A cruiser's tires ticked across the gutter seam out front. The porch light, offended by attention, settled into a steadier beat.

Luke walked Mara to the door. On the way, his eye snagged on the mantle again: the wedding photo, glass reflecting light. He lifted the frame not to admire it but to see what had been given permission to live behind it. The wall was clean. No new holes. He replaced the frame and let his thumb rest for a second on the groom's shoulder. *He was real*, he thought. *This was real; the wrong thing is what came after. *

They stepped onto the porch. The cold bit with a relieved honesty. Mara's car idled at the curb with the nervous shuffle of an animal; the cruiser's lights washed the street in alternating calm and alarm.

"You'll call me?" Mara said, bag clutched to her side. "You'll... I mean—
"

"We'll see this through," Luke said. "Tonight, go. Lock your sister's door. Sleep where someone can see you sleep."

She nodded. Fear had taken its own coat and walked out of her for now, replaced by the prickly energy of anger deciding to grow up. She got into her car. The door latched with a sound that belonged to a thousand evenings, every town.

Bal leaned his elbows on the porch rail and watched the cruiser. "If Colin runs, I chase him," he said casually. "In a loving, full-contact way."

"You don't leave the porch," Luke said.

"Semantics."

Magnolia stood half in the doorway, half in the house's breath, her face turned toward the dark second-floor window across the alley. "He wasn't the only one watching her," she said again. Not a correction; an insistence.

Luke felt it too. The attention he'd clocked in the kitchen hadn't left with the cameras. It sat behind the window and in the corner of the ceiling and down the seam of the hallway paint, aware, uninterested in the human consequence because hunger doesn't do empathy, only aim.

"Later," he told it softly, the way you might tell a stray dog to wait at the edge of the yard. He didn't give it his name. He gave it the empty shape of his outline and nothing more.

Mara pulled away, taillights shrinking toward the square of downtown where the courthouse clock pretended the night had order. The cruiser eased in behind her with the watchful patience of a small town that learned long ago to show up ten minutes late and still try to help.

Luke stepped off the porch and onto the walk. The sky had been a metal lid all day; now it softened. He could smell the change the way you could smell rain before it approved itself.

He looked up.

A first flake let go of whatever held it and drifted down through the porch light's halo. Then a second, then three more, hardly anything, just the idea of snow trying itself on. Behind him, Bal sighed like a furnace that had decided to be kind for a minute. Magnolia's coat whispered as she shifted, the suggestion of layered wings beneath—white, a breath of red, the memory of earth.

Luke watched the sky for a long moment. He'd always loved this time of year—the way the cold bit just enough to feel alive. As the first flakes drifted past the porch light, something like peace settled over him.

Then his gut reminded him what it always did.

Peace was never a luxury he could keep.

To be continued in

Crossfall: Rock and a Hard Place Coming 2026

About the Author

Matt Walker writes character-driven speculative and psychological fiction where the extraordinary quietly bleeds into the ordinary. His stories live at the edge of the real – places where grief, faith, fear collide and the reader is never entirely sure what is true.

His work is known for emotional realism, contained settings, and supernatural ambiguity that lingers long after the final page. *The Noise* marks the beginning of a larger body of work which explores how people break, rebuild, and reach for meaning in the impossibles moments. Sometimes the moments reply.

When not writing, he works in Human Resources, building empathy-driven programs – another kind of storytelling about what people need and how they change.

Coming Soon / In Development

Crossfall: A Rock and A Hard Place

Checkmate

Kindred

The Choir

Beyond the Noise

www.ingramcontent.com/pod-product-compliance
Lightning Source LLC
Chambersburg PA
CBHW010650100726
47901CB00012B/2497